Blood Legacy:
The Story of Ryan

Top Cow Productions Inc.
&
image comics

Also available from Top Cow Productions & Image Comics:

CYBERFORCE: ASSAULT WITH A DEADLY WOMAN (ISBN: 1-887279-04-0)
CYBERFORCE: TIN MEN OF WAR (ISBN: 1-58240-190-X)
THE DARKNESS DELUXE COLLECTED EDITION (ISBN: 1-58240-032-6)
THE DARKNESS: SPEAR OF DESTINY (ISBN: 1-58240-147-0)
THE DARKNESS: HEART OF DARKNESS (ISBN: 1-58240-205-1)
DELICATE CREATURES (ISBN: 1-58240-225-6)
KIN: DESCENT OF MAN (ISBN: 1-58240-224-8)
MAGDALENA: BLOOD DIVINE (ISBN: 1-58240-215-9)
MEDIEVAL SPAWN/WITCHBLADE (ISBN: 1-887279-44-X)
MICHAEL TURNER'S FATHOM: HARD COVER (ISBN: 1-58240-158-6)
MICHAEL TURNER'S FATHOM: HARD COVER L.E. (ISBN: 1-58240-159-4)
MICHAEL TURNER'S FATHOM: PAPERBACK (ISBN: 1-58240-210-8)
RISING STARS: BORN IN FIRE (ISBN: 1-58240-172-1)
RISING STARS: POWER (ISBN: 1-58240-226-4)
TOMB RAIDER: SAGA OF THE MEDUSA MASK (ISBN: 1-58240-164-0)
TOMB RAIDER: MYSTIC ARTIFACTS (ISBN: 1-58240-202-7)
WITCHBLADE: ORIGINS (ISBN: 1-887279-65-2)
WITCHBLADE: REVELATIONS (ISBN: 1-58240-161-6)
WITCHBLADE: PREVAILING (ISBN: 1-58240-175-6)
WITCHBLADE: DISTINCTIONS (ISBN: 1-58240-199-3)
WITCHBLADE/DARKNESS: FAMILY TIES (ISBN: 1-58240-030-X)

To order by telephone call
1-888-TOPCOW1 *(1-888-867-2691)*
or go to a comics shop near you.

To find the comics shop nearest you call
1-888-COMICBOOK *(1-888-266-4226)*

visit us on the web at
www.topcow.com

ISBN: 1-58240-248-5

Published by Image Comics®
BLOOD LEGACY: THE STORY OF RYAN, Vol. 1, 2002. FIRST PRINTING.
Office of Publication: 1071 North Batavia Street Suite A Orange, California 92867.
BLOOD LEGACY™ it's logo, all related characters and their likenesses are ™ & ©
2002 Kerri Hawkins and Top Cow Productions Inc.
ALL RIGHTS RESERVED. The entire contents of this book are © 2002 Top Cow
Productions Inc. Any similarities to persons living or dead is purely coincidental. With
the exception of artwork used for review purposes, none of the contents of this book
may be reprinted in any form without the express written consent of Kerri Hawkins,
Marc Silvestri or Top Cow Productions Inc.

What did you think of this book? We love to hear from our readers.
Please email us at: **bloodlegacy@topcow.com.**
or, write to us at: Blood Legacy c/o Top Cow Productions Inc., 10390 Santa Monica Blvd., Suite 110 Los Angeles, CA. 90025

for this edition
Collected Editions Editor / Art Director—Peter Steigerwald
Managing Editor—Renae Geerlings
Editor In Chief—David Wohl
Book and Cover Design—Jason Medley

for Top Cow Productions Inc.
Marc Silvestri—chief executive officer
Matt Hawkins—president / chief operating officer
David Wohl—president of creative affairs / editor in chief
Peter Steigerwald—vp of publishing and design / art director
Renae Geerlings—managing editor
Chris Carlisle—director of creative affairs
Frank Mastromauro—director of sales and marketing
Alvin Coats—special projects coordinator

for Image Comics
Jim Valentino—publisher; Brent Braun—director of production

BLOOD

LEGACY
THE STORY OF RYAN

by KERRI HAWKINS

CHAPTER

THE LAST BODY FELL TO THE GROUND WITH A THUD AS the woman leaned down to turn the gas lever in the fireplace.

The woman stood upright, a lithe and graceful movement considering the severity of her injuries. She glanced around the room, counting a total of 18 bodies, their limbs in various states of contortion, their injuries all more devastating than her own.

She perused the damage in the sudden silence, catching sight of herself in the far mirror. She moved closer, examining the damage to her face with a passive expression. Her hair was so matted with blood it was difficult to discern its true color. Her clothing was so bloodied it appeared a damp black in the dim lighting.

She turned from the mirror, disinterested. Her gaze again swept around the penthouse, searching for any signs of remaining life. The marble steps were stained with blood. The sprawled bodies were grotesquely positioned. The contorted limbs made no movement. Shards of glass impaled chests that no longer rose and fell.

The hiss of the gas seemed loud to her, although in reality it was barely discernible. She could hear the sounds of sirens far off in the distance. She moved to the sliding glass door, then on to the balcony. She stared downward at the black street 24 stories below. She could smell the gas now, seeping into the night air.

She re-entered the penthouse and glanced around, searching for her bag. She saw it on the far side of the room, clutched in the arms of a young man whose head had been removed, none too neatly. She retrieved the bag, showing little compassion for the recently deceased. She removed a small brick of what appeared to be white clay, then gently set it on the table in the center of the room.

The sirens were closer, and the woman returned to the balcony. The smell of gas was powerful now, nearly overwhelming. She removed a bloody but intact case from her shirt pocket. She snapped the case open and removed a small cigar that she lit with practiced ease. With a flick of her wrist, she sent the matchstick flying off the balcony, the flame flickering out as it fell. With startling visual acuity, she tracked the match until it hit the ground, 24 stories below.

The woman puffed on the cigar contentedly a moment, her demeanor in stark contrast to her grievous injuries and the bloody scene behind her. The sirens were only a block away. She removed the cigar from her mouth, gazing at the red tip thoughtfully. With a surprisingly supple move, she stepped up onto the railing of the balcony, balancing effortlessly on the slippery surface. With no regret or hesitation, she flicked the remainder of the cigar into the room behind her, then stepped off the railing into the darkness as the world behind her exploded.

CHAPTER 2

Dr. Susan Ryerson gazed through the microscope, searching for the telltale signs of metastasizing in the biopsy. There were none, and she stepped back to make a notation of this in her records. She leaned forward to make another observation when the phone rang. She reached over, pressed the "speaker" button, then returned to her microscope. She brushed her red hair out of her eyes, peering into the eyepiece.

"Hello?" came the uncertain voice over the phone.

"Oh, hello," Susan said belatedly, realizing she hadn't even greeted the other person. Her distraction was evident to the person on the other end of the line.

"Hey doc, if you're busy...."

Susan stood upright, again brushing her red hair out of her blue eyes. "No, Mason, that's okay. What do you need?"

Mason was still hesitant. "I've got something you should see in the basement, might help your resea-"

"Okay," Susan said, hurriedly cutting him off. She was uncomfortable discussing this with him over the phone. "I'll be down in a few moments."

Susan removed her lab coat, smoothing her stylish suit. She was small and slender, but carried herself with self-confidence. Although a mere 34 years old, Susan Ryerson was a well-renowned researcher and full medical doctor.

Renowned or not, Susan thought to herself, the scientific community would not look kindly on her use of human bodies unethically (and illegally) obtained from the county morgue. Susan attempted to rationalize the breach in ethics by telling herself the ends justified the means. She only used bodies that no one claimed and would be unceremoniously disposed of, anyway. The way she saw it, this was a final chance for these people to contribute something with their lives, even if it was only through their deaths.

Susan exited her private lab and used her security code to access the elevator. She stepped into the waiting elevator and leaned against the wall as the car dropped smoothly into the basement. The facility she worked for was a contradiction of sorts. It possessed one of the finest trauma centers in the United States, yet doubled as the county morgue. It fostered some of the most advanced medical research in the world, yet it routinely resembled a war zone. The hospital lost a fortune to patients with no insurance, yet made a fortune through the research and development wing. Patents and contributions were the big moneymakers in this hospital, not patients.

Susan Ryerson possessed four such moneymaking patents. She had discovered a unique drug delivery system, a method of stabilizing glutamine in solution, and two anti-obesity drugs. She saw little of the monetary returns from her million-dollar patents, since her research had been completed under contract with the hospital, but she lived comfortably and was given free reign in her research. It was the latter that gave her impetus to continue.

The doors to the elevator opened and the smell of formaldehyde struck Susan full force, causing her to wrinkle her nose. She moved down the dimly lit hallway into a brightly-lit office. It was empty. A scribbled note on the chalkboard said simply "IN AUTOPSY."

Susan retraced her steps down the hallway and passed the elevator. She pushed through another set of double doors and the air was noticeably cooler. She lifted the latch on the heavy metal door to the meat locker.

"Meat locker" was not actually the appropriate name for this room. But in typical morgue humor, it was an apt description. Unlike the neatly aligned cubicles seen in film and on television, this room reflected a more accurate reality.

Hundreds of bodies were piled on gurneys and on shelves against the wall. Sometimes three deep, the bodies were enclosed in large, see-through plastic bags. Because of its dual role as hospital morgue and county morgue, most of the people here had died violent deaths, a fact evident by the twisted and contorted limbs pressed against the plastic. Gaping mouths were open in endless silent screams, or perhaps in endless silent snores.

Susan had the odd thought that even the recently dead looked nothing like the living. As she glanced around at the bodies, she thought how fine the line was between life and death. Death was the demon she chased in her research, yet no one had come up with an apt description of what exactly it was that separated these bodies from her.

Susan snorted quietly at her own mental ramblings. She could see herself at the next medical board meeting discussing her new definition of clinical death:

"It's a lot like obscenity, gentlemen. I can't define it, but I know it when I see it."

The formaldehyde smell was stronger in here and Susan couldn't help but make the connection to her high school science course; these people in their ziploc bags reminded her of giant fetal pigs.

She moved further into the room. To the right were the "crispy critters," people who had burned to death and who would now literally break into pieces if touched. They had their own unique stench that not even the formaldehyde could completely disguise. They were not of much use to her.

To the left, against the wall, was a set of what appeared to be bookshelves, or perhaps mail cubicles. But upon closer inspection their true purpose was revealed. The soles of tiny little feet could be seen sticking out of the end of the cubicles. Tiny little feet with tiny little toes with tiny little tags on them. This was the only part of the morgue that bothered Susan. It didn't have a nickname; it was just where they kept the dead babies. She could not use any of the dead infants; it was one breach of ethics she could not force herself to commit.

She moved through another set of doors into a brightly-lit room. The air was warmer in here, and a little more putrid. The bodies had to warm up a little before they could cut on them.

A slender black man leaning over a corpse looked up. His face broke into a sunny smile. "Hey, it's my favorite doctor. You sounded kind of busy on the phone. You working on something good?"

Susan moved closer to see what he was doing. "No, not really. I'm more in a fact-gathering mode right now."

Mason set down his instrument and removed one bloody glove. "Oh, then I don't know if you'll be interested in what I have for you."

Susan glanced down at the body on the table, unwilling to leap immediately into their mutual indiscretion. "What are you working on?"

Mason picked up a clipboard. "Hit-and-run. Twenty year-old male. They're trying to match injuries to mechanism, that sort of thing."

Susan nodded. Mason was a recognized forensics expert as well as coroner. He replaced his bloody glove and pointed to another nearby gurney. "I think I've got another slasher victim. Thirty year-old female. Same type of injuries, same type of death. They need to put that guy away. It's not good when my business is booming."

Mason continued his casual conversation as he cut on the body in front of him. Susan watched with only mild interest, glancing around the room. This room always seemed to have a fungal quality to it, although it was spotless. Spotless, she thought, wrinkling her nose slightly. The place may have been sterile, but it would never be clean.

Mason stopped in the middle of what he was doing. "Hey, I'm sure you've seen more than a few of these. Let me show you what I've got so you can get back to your work. Come over here and take a look at this."

Mason was already moving across the room and Susan had to walk around the table to follow him. He pulled the sheet back from a gurney against the wall.

"How old do you think she is?"

Susan stared at the profile of a woman, an incredibly beautiful woman. Shoulder length golden hair surrounded perfect features. Long dark eyelashes rested against high cheekbones above a full, sensual mouth. It was the profile of a sleeping angel.

Susan moved closer and the illusion of sleep was immediately shattered. The right side of the woman's face was crushed inward, and dried blood was splattered down the right side of her body. The remnant of clothing that was left appeared black, but was actually encrusted with dried blood.

Susan took a step back so she could not see the damaged side of the face. She examined the woman's features and could see why Mason was in a quandary. The woman could be anywhere from twenty to forty.

"Who is she?"

Mason glanced down at the clipboard. "That's why I called you. She's a Jane Doe. Apparently was involved in one hell of a fight. I'll be damned if I can determine her age, though."

Susan understood his indecision. The woman had an ageless quality about her; perhaps twenty to forty was too narrow a range.

"Take a look at this."

Mason pulled the sheets upward from the bottom of the gurney. Susan moved to look and let out a small gasp.

The woman's legs had numerous compound fractures with bone protruding in several places, most noticeably where the right femur had broken through the side of the thigh.

Susan looked closer, something did not seem quite right, beyond the obvious fact that the woman's bones should not be protruding from her body. She glanced up at the length of the torso.

Mason nodded, following her train of thought. "She's about six inches shorter than she should be. Her legs are telescoped." He glanced at the clipboard again. "She appears to have jumped from some unbelievable height. They thought she was involved in that terrorist bombing downtown, but they found her several blocks away. There was no evidence she was dragged or carried." He paused, looking down at the body, "And it's not likely she walked." He cocked his head to one side, examining the damaged legs. "Whatever she jumped from, it looks like she landed on her feet."

Susan glanced at the length of the torso. "She was tall, then."

"I would guess around six feet. She's also a good 25 inches across the shoulders. Between that and the quality of muscle she carries, I would guess she had the body of a world class athlete."

"Have you done any work on her yet?"

Mason shook his head. "No, she really doesn't have any priority. She's been here for some time now, case remains open, ruled as a homicide. But I was given instructions to go ahead with the autopsy, then dispose of the body. I've been keeping her in the icebox. Don't really know why," he said self-consciously, "I just felt like doing so."

The "icebox" was a neat row of refrigeration units in another room. It was a step above the meat locker, and closer to the television/film version of body containers. It was where they put bodies needing identification by next of kin. They sure as hell didn't want the next of kin walking into the meat locker.

"Jane Does" were rarely put in the icebox, but strangely, Susan understood Mason's compulsion to do so. She felt an odd sadness as Mason pulled the sheet back over the woman's body.

"I thought maybe you could give her one more chance to make a difference, since they'll probably never find out who she was."

Susan felt suddenly grateful to Mason, that he had reframed her ethical struggle in such a way. She nodded thankfully to him. "Yes, I think I can use her. I'll make arrangements to have the body moved upstairs after hours."

Susan opened the door to her house, carefully eyeing the walkway behind her. She lived in a low-crime area and the walkway was well lit, but one could never be too careful at 5 o'clock in the morning. She had stayed at the lab far later than she realized.

She pulled the tasseled cord to a lamp and soft light fell on beautiful antique furniture. She set her paperwork down on a smooth, mahogany desktop. The room, a study in luxurious grace, was also in meticulous order.

Mr. Earl, her gray, short-hair cat, leaped up onto the cushioned seat. She picked him up and scratched the back of his head. She set him back down and he trotted into the kitchen behind her, knowing he would be fed. Mr. Earl was one of two allowances of disorder in her very ordered and elegant world.

Susan boiled a cup of Earl Grey tea, her favorite, then settled in her chair near the bay window where she could watch the sunrise. Mr. Earl leaped up into the chair and settled in her lap next to the steaming cup of his namesake. She stroked the back of his neck as she sipped her tea.

For some reason her mind kept returning to the golden-haired woman in the morgue. Perhaps it was simply because her research that night had been mundane, but Susan found her thoughts returning to the dead woman with unusual frequency. Certainly the woman's injuries were notable, but Susan did not generally dwell on any of her research subjects, and technically the woman wasn't even her subject, yet.

Susan finished her tea and rinsed the cup out in the sink, setting it to dry in its rack. She let Mr. Earl out, then turned as she heard the sound of little padded feet across her wood floor. Her five year-old, Jason, stood in the doorway, his red hair tousled and his eyes still sleepy.

Susan held out her arms and he ran into them, his little padded feet slipping and sliding on the floor. She picked him up, hugging him tightly.

"Did you sleep well, munchkin?"

He tried to appear petulant, but his effort was comical. "No, I was waiting for you to come home."

"Now don't you act that way," said the large, genial woman in the doorway. She moved into the kitchen, patting Susan on the shoulder. "Your mommy works very hard."

Susan smiled at the older woman, grateful for her support. "I'm sorry, Neda. I should have called-"

Neda gently cut her off. "I know how you are when you work. I slept in the spare bedroom. And little bossy boy here," she said, affectionately ruffling Jason's tousled hair, "Was asleep at 8 o'clock." She held out her arms for the boy, addressing Susan. "You're very tired. Why don't you go to bed and I'll get Jason breakfast and get him to school."

Susan hugged her son tightly, then gratefully handed him over to the woman. "You're a godsend, Neda. I'll set the alarm so I can pick him up."

CHAPTER 3

Susan took a few days respite from work to spend with Jason, then returned to the lab. It was one of the benefits of being a prime producer for the hospital; she could name her own hours.

She donned her lab coat, making a mental note to call Mason in a few hours and make arrangements to get the body. She hoped he still had it in the icebox. She settled down to review her notes.

Mason pulled his latex gloves from his fingers with a snap. He pulled hard on the fingers of the gloves, then released them. They shot across the room like a rubber band, bounced against the wall, then slid down the wall into the waste receptacle.

"Two points."

He meandered down the dimly lit hallway to his office. He turned on the small lamp on his desk, then killed the overhead flourescents.

"That's more like it. A little ambiance."

He stretched out on the worn couch next to his desk. A short nap wouldn't hurt anything; he didn't have any pressing cases right now and it had been slow the night before. He pulled a tattered pillow to his chest.

He was just beginning to relax and drift off to sleep when suddenly he was jerked rudely awake. Something was not quite right. He listened intently, but it wasn't really a sound that he was listening for.

Mason sat up. If it wasn't a sound he was listening for, then what the hell was it? That didn't make any sense. He started to settle back in the couch, rearranging the pillow.

He sat back up. What the hell was that smell?

Mason was so used to the odors associated with the morgue he could no longer smell the formaldehyde. But that wasn't formaldehyde he was smelling now.

"Shit."

He tossed the pillow to the floor. His bet was those computers had gone off-line again, and that was bad news.

He walked down the hallway, turning right at the elevators. Ever since they had changed the refrigeration units from manual to computerized, they had been nothing but trouble. It had been a simple thing for him to check the temperature gauge every few hours and adjust the thermostat accordingly, but no, they decided they could save pennies, hell, even nickels a month in energy bills if a computer did it for him.

He pushed through the door of the control room. The first time this baby had gone down, the icebox had pretty much melted. Next-of-kin identification had not been pleasant that week.

Mason examined the controls thoughtfully. Everything appeared to be functioning properly. All temperature levels read normal. All computers seemed to be on-line.

His puzzlement growing, Mason pushed through the doors to the icebox and caught his breath. The smell was definitely coming from in here. He flipped the switch to his right, but nothing happened.

Oh, that's right, he thought sarcastically, another energy saving device. The lights are controlled by computer, another cost efficient and totally impractical idea. Just what young aspiring trainees needed, the lights in the morgue going off and on, apparently on their own.

Mason stood for a moment while his eyes adjusted to the dim light. He scanned down the row of units. He was ready to turn away when out of the corner of his eye he saw what he was looking for.

Another drop of water landed on the floor.

Mason walked over and bent down to the puddle on the floor. He glanced up to the units where the condensation was coming from. He touched the lower unit and it was warm to the touch. He slid his hand up the metal surface as he stood. This unit was nearly hot. In fact, it appeared this unit was the one malfunctioning and radiating heat outward to the adjacent units.

Mason lifted the handle on the middle unit and pulled the drawer outward. He felt a pang when he saw the golden hair; he was hoping it had not been her unit, but apparently it was. He would have to let Susan know her research subject probably wouldn't keep much longer. He leaned forward, though, puzzled. He was surprised the stench had not overwhelmed him. It appeared the smell was coming from the adjacent units.

Mason was just about to shut the drawer when he stopped and pulled it out a little further. Something seemed strange about the body he had put in here days ago. He pushed the plastic closer to the face so he could get a better look, but the plastic was still blurry. He reached in with both hands and unzipped the top portion of the bag so the woman's face was exposed.

He stared at the face, trying to figure out what was bothering him. He was surprised at the lack of stench when he opened the bag. He shrugged his shoulders; so this body was not decomposing as rapidly as the others were. Hell, she looked better now than she had three days ago.

Mason stopped. Maybe that was what was bothering him. Maybe she did look better than she had three days ago.

Mason shook his head. Or maybe he had just mentally exaggerated her injuries. He didn't know why he was so infatuated with this particular body; he was beginning to worry about himself. If he started having necrophilic fantasies, he was definitely going to find another job.

"Okay Mason. Enough of this. Time to go find out what's wrong with those computers."

He reached down and began to zip the bag. The zipper caught and he briefly struggled with it.

And then Mason's heart stopped.

The woman's face was framed between his suddenly nerveless fingers. The side that was crushed inward had left the orbit intact, as well as, presumably, the eyeball itself. This presumption was proved suddenly and emphatically correct.

Because the eyeball was looking at him.

Susan poured herself the first cup of coffee from her freshly brewed pot. She laced it with a touch of honey and a touch of cream, and was just preparing to savor her first sip when the phone rang. She pressed "speaker" and mumbled a hello.

"Uh, Dr. Ryerson?" came Mason's uncertain voice.

Susan stretched her neck from side-to-side, still trying to wake up. "Yes Mason?"

"Uh, doctor, do you think you could come down here and check something out?"

Susan tried to press her chin to her chest to get the rest of the kinks out. "I was going to come down later anyway. Can it wait?"

"Ummm," he said uncertainly, "I really don't think so. I really wish you'd come down here now."

Susan stood upright, finally sensing the agitation in his voice. "Is everything all right? What's wrong?"

For once it was Mason who did not wish to disclose over the phone. "I really think you should come down here."

Susan stepped off the elevator to find Mason waiting for her in the hallway. He seemed shaken. Susan touched his elbow, intending to guide him down the hallway, but he stopped, almost afraid to continue.

Susan looked at him curiously. "Mason, what's wrong with you? Why are you acting like this?"

Mason was not sure where to begin. "Doc, I thought the refrigeration units went off-line so I went to check them." He stopped, trying to steady his voice. "The units were warm like something was heating them up. I opened her drawer and unzipped her bag, and she opened her eye and looked at me."

Susan was confused. "What are you talking about? Who is 'she'?"

"The woman with the gold hair. The one who jumped out the window."

Susan felt a slight misgiving but dismissed the feeling. She knew immediately whom he was talking about.

"Look, Mason. You and I both looked at her injuries. There was no way she was alive." She searched for a plausible explanation. "You of all people know how bodies settle. Isn't it possible you jostled her and her eyelids rolled back?"

Mason relaxed only a little. "Yeah," he said doubtfully, "I guess that's possible." He didn't know why he didn't reach that conclusion himself, and why it didn't seem to appease him.

Susan nodded. "Why don't we go in here and you can show me what happened. Okay?"

Mason nodded, but was not enthusiastic about re-entering the icebox. "Okay," he said doubtfully, "That sounds like a good idea."

Susan took three steps, then stifled a gag. "Well, something is definitely wrong with the icebox."

She followed him into the control room and he fiddled with the computer a moment until the lights in the adjacent room came on. She followed him into the icebox.

One of the drawers was left partially open and upon approach, Susan saw the body of the woman she had seen previously. The bag was unzipped to just below her chin, but other than that she looked exactly the same. Both eyes were closed.

Susan reached down and unzipped the bag a little more. She felt a little foolish, but she poked the woman in the chest. Cold and hard. She stepped back and indicated that Mason should do the same. He was starting to feel foolish as well, and more so when he leaned over and poked the corpse. Cold and hard. The woman was obviously dead.

He stepped back. "Look, doc. I'm really sorry. Maybe I've just been working too hard, or maybe I had a bad dream or something. I've never had a hallucination like that before."

Susan grasped his shoulder. "And I've never known you to do anything but laugh down here, and sometimes I think you do it to cover up the things that bother you. You know it's okay. Even coroners sometimes get the creeps."

Mason let out a huge sigh of relief. "Maybe you're right. I think this one bothered me a little more than most." He reached down and started to re-zip the bag.

"Hold on just a minute."

Mason stopped. Susan was looking at the woman's face strangely. "Did you clean her up?"

Mason shook his head. "No, I usually let morticians do that. I figured it wouldn't get done in this case."

Susan shook her head as if to clear it and went to zip the bag. She stopped again, examining the face more closely. "You know," she said uncertainly, "I would swear there was a lot more damage to the right side of her face."

Mason did not agree or disagree.

She shook her head in disgust. "Now I'm being foolish. It's probably just more of the body settling." She reached for the zipper for a third time, and for the third time she stopped.

"You know," she said, then trailed off. She glanced up at Mason. She reached down and began to unzip the bag the rest of the way. She peeled the plastic back so she could get a good look at the damaged legs.

Mason looked down at the legs. They appeared much the same to him.

They did not to Susan. She shook her head in confusion. "Didn't she have a compound fracture of the right femur?"

Mason glanced down at the right leg. There were several compound fractures, but none of the right femur. He was confused as well. "I thought there was a fracture at the femur."

Susan stared at the leg a long moment, then snatched at the zipper. "This is ridiculous. You've been working too long and I'm still half asleep." She zipped the bag up in one fluid movement until it snagged near the chin. She pushed the zipper away from her.

"That's fine. Let's see if we can get refrigeration back on-line." She started to walk away and stopped when Mason didn't move. She walked back over to him, leaning across the body to grab his shoulders. She looked into his eyes.

"Mason, this is crazy."

"Aaaahhh."

The sigh was deep and heartfelt and very loud in the silence.

And it didn't come from Mason.

Both Mason and Susan looked down at the body between them.

The body coughed.

Susan wasn't sure if she had taken eight quick steps back or simply covered the whole distance in one huge leap. Mason had covered a similar distance in the opposite direction and now stared at Susan across that chasm with wide eyes.

Susan was in a fundamental, accelerated decision process. Should she react as she wanted to, which was to scream and run like hell? Or should she react as she was trained to, like a doctor?

She reacted like a doctor.

"Let's get this woman to ER," she said, trying to keep her tone even, "NOW!"

The gurney smashed through the double doors with Susan leading it from the side and Mason pushing it from behind. A young intern was running along side, trying to keep up.

"Who's the doctor on duty?" Susan barked at him.

He tried desperately to get a quick look at the status board as they rolled past. "I think Dr. Goldstein and a first-year resident."

Susan inwardly sighed. She and David Goldstein did not get along. He was jealous of both her work and the privileges that came with it. He had not been as successful a researcher as she had, which was why he was still working ER. If she could have chosen anyone not to be there, it would have been him.

The no-nonsense nurse from the front desk caught up with them, and Susan turned to her. "Norma, find Dr. Goldstein and get him in here. Then join us in trauma, stat."

The nurse nodded, trying to get a look at the patient on the gurney. She hadn't seen anyone come in. She was quite certain she could find Dr. Goldstein down the hall by the coffee machine and/or with Nurse Fields.

Mason hit the automatic release and another set of doors opened in front of them. The young intern was joined by the first year-resident, and Susan motioned for them to take their positions.

"Mason, take the feet. I've got the head. You-"

"Baxter. Carol Baxter," the resident said helpfully.

"Yeah, Baxter, you go there. On my mark, one, two..."

On three they lifted the patient in a practiced motion and slid her onto the table. Both Baxter and the intern had puzzled looks on their faces. This body did not feel quite right.

"You-" Susan pointed at the intern.

"Louis."

"Louis, get me 5 milligrams of epinephrine, 1 milligram of atropine, and 100 milligrams of lidocaine." Susan pulled the sheet back from the body. "Baxter, set up an IV push. Mason, drag the EKG over here. I'm not getting any pulse."

Susan became aware of the fact that Baxter and Louis were just standing there, stunned looks on their faces.

"What are you two staring at? I need that IV push now!"

Baxter started to move, then stopped. She did not want to risk Susan's wrath, but she felt she had to say something.

"Uh, Dr. Ryerson," she began uncertainly, "This person is dead."

Susan felt her temper flare. Just because she was in R & D these days didn't mean she had forgotten everything she knew. "Do you think I don't know what a dead person looks like?" she demanded. "When you've been a doctor as long as I have, you can begin questioning my decisions! Until then, just do as I say!"

The scathing reply had the desired effect: both assistants sprang into action, following her orders out of blind obedience more than anything else. Mason dragged the EKG over and Susan quickly attached the electrodes, eyeing the heart monitor. She had a flatline.

"Clear!"

Baxter was having a difficult time inserting the IV into the cold, hard flesh. At the doctor's command, she jammed it beneath the skin and took a step back.

The body jumped off the table in a mockery of life. Susan glanced at the monitor.

Flatline.

Susan motioned to Baxter and Louis. "Start CPR. See if you can get some kind of pulse." She began struggling with the intubation tube; the esophagus was generally much more yielding.

"Doctor, what are you doing?"

Norma came through the door, wearing newly donned sterile clothing. She stared at the corpse on the table.

Susan ignored her for the moment. "Louis. Give me those syringes." She, too, had difficulty injecting the drugs and ended up jamming the needle to puncture the skin before she could depress the stopper. She turned to Norma.

"I think we have a case of deep comatose, possible hypothermia. All life signs have slowed to imperceptible levels. The patient is in a deep state of unconscious."

Norma looked at the body on the table. "Doctor, the patient is dead," she said matter-of-factly. She looked at the heart monitor, then at the respirator. "She has no life signs."

The room suddenly grew quiet. Baxter and Louis both stopped what they were doing and watched Susan with trepidation. It was both eerie and embarrassing to watch such a distinguished member of the faculty lose it like this.

Susan felt a hot flush on her neck. It seemed that nothing she was doing was getting a response from the victim. She adjusted the tubing on the respirator and forced another injection. A different nurse appeared to offer assistance.

"Monitor her vitals," Susan barked at her. The nurse stepped back, and with some confusion began to write zeros on the medical record. She did not want to look at the corpse on the table.

Mason was standing back, watching the respirator. He kept having to remind himself to breathe as he willed the bag to rise and fall. He, too, was growing increasingly frustrated and more than a little embarrassed.

Susan looked up from the body. She was debating whether to attempt another defibrillation. Emergency medical care had generally already ended at this point and it was simply a matter of pronouncing death. She felt a wave of doubt wash over her as she stepped back from the table.

"Any suggestions?"

The question was directed at those present in the room, but it was Dr. Goldstein coming through the door who answered it.

"Yeah, how about burying that thing?"

Susan looked over at him. "Goldstein, I'm glad you're here," she said, trying to sound convincing, "We've got a patient in a pronounced vegetative state-"

"Nurse," Goldstein interrupted, "What do you show for pulse?"

The nurse looked down at her clipboard, although that was unnecessary. "Zero."

"Respirations?"

"Umm, zero."

"Blood pressure?"

"None."

Goldstein peeled off the gloves he had just pulled on. "There you have it. I hope that's not why you called me in here, Susan."

Susan felt stubbornness war with her doubt, and the sarcasm in his voice increased that stubbornness. "David, we've seen several signs of life. I heard her cough in the morgue-"

Goldstein was incredulous. "You brought her up from the morgue? Have you lost your mind, Susan?"

Susan started to say something to defend herself, then snapped her jaw shut. Goldstein continued his sarcastic tirade. "Now, I know how precious your research is to you, but this is real-world, Susan. This person is dead, and none of your patented procedures are going to bring her back."

The silence was suddenly very loud in the room. Susan glanced down at the mangled corpse, the hot flush now traveling from the back of her neck to her cheeks. She wondered if her face was as red as her hair. She tried to salvage whatever dignity she could from the situation.

"Mason," she said calmly, her voice betraying only the faintest quiver. "Perhaps it was just the body settling as we discussed. Better to err on the side of caution. Would you please continue with the original arrangements for this body?"

Mason nodded, embarrassed for himself but even more so for the doctor. He felt terrible at the humiliation he had caused her. "I'll get on it right away, Dr. Ryerson."

Susan nodded to the intern, the resident, and to the two nurses. "Thank you for your assistance. I'm sorry if I caused you any inconvenience."

She brushed by David Goldstein without another word.

Susan slowly pulled her lab coat back on. What in god's name had gotten into her? She was normally so calm, so logical, so rational. Yet she had just dragged a body out of the morgue and attempted to bring it back to life, a la Frankenstein. And to make matters worse, David Goldstein had been there to witness her folly. She was certain to hear about this at the next staff meeting.

Her thoughts were interrupted by a banging on the lab door. She had been so engrossed in self-reproach she had not heard the elevator. She looked out the window and was shocked to see Mason peering back at her, the gurney in front of him. She quickly opened the door, pulling both he and the body inside.

"Mason, what are you doing?" she exclaimed, "Have you lost your mind?"

Mason was apologetic but unrelenting. "I'm sorry, doc. I think something's going on here. I think you should hook this lady up to some of your equipment."

Susan was exasperated. She had already suffered enough humiliation for one day. She did not want to be seen smuggling bodies into her lab in broad daylight. In fact, she corrected herself, she did not want to be seen smuggling bodies into her lab at any time of day.

"Mason, " she began, trying to sound calm and convincing, "This woman is dead. She's been dead for quite some time now. There's nothing we can do for her."

Mason's jaw was stubborn. "Then it won't hurt to hook her up to some equipment."

Susan started to argue, then relented. Nothing she was going to say was going to sway him. "Okay, we'll hook her up to an EKG one more time to see if we get anything. If not, we call it quits and I put her back on ice." She glanced over her shoulder. "But bring her in here, for god's sake. I can't believe you brought her up here."

Mason pushed the gurney into the next room and Susan pulled the door closed behind her. She used this room to conduct experiments on the effects of sleep deprivation on the immune system, and it was full of monitoring equipment for that purpose.

Susan pulled the sheet down from the woman's torso and placed the pads from the EKG on the corpse's chest, feeling mildly foolish as she did so. She flipped the switch to the monitor, and the display immediately settled into a flatline. She gazed at the screen for a few moments, then at Mason.

"How long are we going to wait until this convinces you?"

Mason glanced down at the hard, cold flesh, then at the glowing screen with the thin blue line running across it. He himself was starting to lose conviction. Perhaps he was just trying to make up for the damage he had caused in the emergency room. Perhaps he just didn't want to accept the death of this beautiful woman. Perhaps he should just let things go.

The single beep was very loud in the quiet of the room. Both pair of eyes turned to the monitor to watch the single jagged peak travel across the screen before it returned to flatline.

"That's probably a malfunction," Susan offered uncertainly in the silence.

"It's not," Mason said, his conviction returning. He glanced over at the edge of the gurney. "Look at that."

The bag of blood from the emergency room was still hanging from its hook. They had turned the stopvalve when all attempts to revive the woman had failed. The blood trapped in the tube remained. As both of them watched, the blood level in the tubing slowly dropped until it disappeared. Susan reached up and turned the stopvalve. The blood from the bag began to snake downward through the curving tube. The IV that had been so haphazardly inserted held and the blood disappeared into the woman's arm.

"The blood should be pooling underneath the skin." Susan said hesitantly, finding no signs that it was doing so. She glanced up at the bag, which was now a third gone. "Or not going in at all."

Another beep broke the silence and another jagged peak swept across the EKG screen. Susan stared at the screen, then down at the body in front of her. She was baffled by what was going on, but knew she was not taking this body back to ER. She turned to Mason. "Do you think you could 'acquire' some more blood? Most of the samples I have up here are not sterile."

Mason nodded. "Sure doc, I can 'acquire' anything you need." He took one last look at the body, then quickly disappeared.

Susan turned back to the body, which still looked like a cold, dead corpse. She tried to come up with a plausible explanation. She knew of cases where people had fallen into ponds or lakes and were trapped beneath the ice for several hours. Their vital signs slowed to nothing, including brain activity. Perhaps this woman was in a similar state, although it hardly seemed possible. If the woman were capable of being revived, she most certainly would sustain severe brain damage.

Mason returned in a frighteningly quick time considering the illegal activity he was engaged in. He carried four bags of thick, red blood. While Susan prepared to replace the original bag, which was now almost empty, Mason watched the blue flatline move across the screen. "Why don't you hook her up to the EEG?"

Susan glanced over her shoulder. "What?"

Mason motioned to the EEG. "Hook her up, see if you can get any brain activity."

Susan was still skeptical, still not quite accepting what was in front of them. "Well, the brain requires oxygen to function. If you don't have a pulse, and you don't have respirations, you're probably not going to get any brain activity."

Mason returned to his earlier argument. "What have you got to lose?"

Susan glanced over at the EEG. Mason was right. What did they have to lose? They had already stolen a body, four bags of blood, and jumped to some wild conclusions on what was probably a malfunctioning EKG. She sighed, then moved to the EEG. She attached the electrodes to the woman's temples, then stepped back.

Mason was standing ready and he flipped the switch on the monitor, causing the screen to spring to life. He stepped back in satisfaction.

"Would you look at that."

An even, sinusoidal pattern began snaking across the phosphorous screen.

Surprise was evident on Susan's face. She still sought a logical answer, although the logical answer was becoming less and less plausible.

"This machine could be malfunctioning, too."

She moved to study the readout. "But I don't think so. This pattern is entirely too regular, but not one I've seen before." Her voice trailed off as she touched the peaks on the screen. "These look like alpha waves, but far more exaggerated than normal." She stepped back, a thoughtful look on her face. "It's almost like a sleep disorder."

Mason glanced over at the body. Now his doubt was evident. "You're telling me she's just asleep?"

The pattern on the screen changed dramatically and the regular wave began arcing up and down the grid in an erratic pattern. Susan stared at the screen in dawning recognition.

"No, I'm telling you she's dreaming."

CHAPTER 4

THE PRIEST WATCHED THE SMALL BOY AND HIS GROIN stirred beneath his rough cassock.

A useless stirring it was, he knew, for he could have anything in this village except the boy.

The priest picked some food from his teeth with a twig and shifted his position slightly so he could watch the boy's father. The blacksmith was as dark as the child was fair, and as hairy as the boy was smooth.

The boy's mother came into view, carrying a basket of bread. The priest wondered if the bread was fresh and contemplated taking his tribute. His belly was full, however, so he turned his attention back to the boy.

Tall for his age, he was, slender and well formed. He helped his mother with the basket and the two walked around the thatched hut out of the priest's view.

The priest threw the twig to the ground. Now that his one appetite was sated, it was time to sate the other.

The blacksmith watched his wife and son as he pounded the metal on the anvil in front of him. He wondered if the boy had taken his swim in the creek as required. His wife would see to that, he was sure.

The blacksmith, or "Hans" as he was known to the others, watched the priest slink away. He knew that some young girl in the village would likely lose her maidenhead, but such was life. It was the priest's privilege as a man of God to act as he would. It was not up to men like him to judge the priesthood, nor question God's way.

Hans glanced over at Will's hut. The door was tightly closed and no smoke rose from the roof's opening. Will's wife and child had been run from the village. They had shown signs of the "death" and the others in the small town had feared the spread of the disease.

Hans continued his rhythmic hammering. It was of no consequence to him; he had no pity for the woman or child. God's judgment was swift. He had nearly lost his own wife one time before and had wondered what sin she had committed to become so ill. She had lived, so God had obviously forgiven her.

Hans again glanced after his wife and son. The boy, on the other hand, had never been sick a day in his life. He must have been truly blessed by God.

The thought, for some reason, made Hans uneasy. Perhaps it was because he lived in a world where good things were often looked on with trepidation because they were forerunners to disaster.

Perhaps it was because he believed as strongly in the evil spirits of the forest as he did in the God in the heavens. Or perhaps it was because he was simply afraid of anything he didn't understand.

The boy set the basket down at his mother's feet. A woman of few words, she merely grunted at him. He set back on his haunches and glanced over his shoulder. The priest had disappeared.

The boy turned his attention back to his mother. He didn't like the priest. Didn't like the way he looked at him.

"Give me."

His mother motioned to the rock near his foot and he picked it up and gave it to her. She seemed surprised at the weight of it as she began to crush the grain. She glanced at her fair-haired son.

He was strong, strong for his size and tall for his age. She could not help but feel a little proud. It was common for women in the village to have many children; in fact it was wise as most of them died as infants. If they did not die as infants there was any number of misfortunes that could befall them. Why, young John the other day had done no more than tripped on a root. But he had broken the bone and bled out, and he died before the sun went down.

She glanced at her young son again. Perhaps he had gotten her luck. She did not know how many seasons she had been alive; she could not count and had no grasp of numbers beyond one or two. She could not know she was nearing twenty-eight years. She only knew she was one of the oldest women in the village, and had lived a very long life.

The boy was her only child. She glanced down at the few loaves of bread in her basket, comparing them to the seasons the boy had been alive. He had perhaps one more season than loaves of bread. It was hard to remember. He would be a man before too long.

"You take your water today?"

The boy glanced down at the creek. He had doused himself early this morning, as he did every day. He nodded to his mother and she continued grinding her grain.

The boy had the sudden urge to ask why he was supposed to go into the water every day, year-round. But he knew there were questions he was not allowed to ask; if God wanted him to know, he would know.

But still he pondered why he had to go into the water when no one else in the village did. In fact, everyone seemed to avoid water and only on the hottest days would they join him.

He would often overhear the other villagers talk about him, wondering aloud why his mother was required to baptize him so often. He would hear their furtive whispers, wondering why he was not allowed to take his clothes off as were the other children.

But his parents maintained their stoic silence. As long as the gold continued to come, they would continue their strange practices with their son. And truly, even if the gold stopped, their fear would give them cause to continue.

The boy wandered back toward the village. Will's son was gone, so he could not play with him. Bertha's daughter was older, almost a woman, and she probably would not play with him either.

He thought he would look for Bertha's daughter anyway. He knew she was often with the chickens and set out towards the barn. He was halfway there when he heard a scream.

He paused looking back at his father. His father also paused, hammer in mid-air, then went back to his pounding as if nothing had happened.

The boy hesitated, uncertain, then continued on towards the barn. He stood on a wooden bench so he could see over the window ledge into the stalls.

The priest was there, and he was on top of Bertha's daughter. He had hiked his cassock up around his waist and had pulled the girl's shift up to her chin.

The boy knew what the priest was doing. He had seen the animals do it, indeed, had even seen his parents do it in their one-room hut. They had awakened him with their pounding and grunting and he had watched curiously as they performed the act less than three feet from him on their shared mat. He had quickly lost interest and turned his attention to the bugs crawling through the woven mattress.

But the boy was curious now. He knew that men had an organ much different from women's, indeed much different from even a boy's. He didn't see how the priest could fit such a thing into Bertha's daughter.

That seemed to be part of the problem as the sweating priest cursed. He could not seem to accomplish what he wished to, and the squirming girl was not helping matters.

The boy cocked his head to one side. He had seen the priest's organ; the priest had shown it to him. But when the boy just stood there with his unblinking, gray-eyed gaze, the priest had shown a flash of fear and quickly left.

With a shout of triumph the priest accomplished his goal and pierced the girl. Bertha's daughter screamed which startled the boy and he fell backward off the bench. He brushed himself off and ran back towards his father. He did not want to hear the grunting priest any longer.

The boy settled down at his father's side, taking comfort in the steady clink of the hammer that drowned out the screams.

CHAPTER 5

Susan walked down the hallway of the hospital, quickly detouring on sight of David Goldstein rounding a corner in front of her. She darted into the gift shop, showing a sudden interest in the magazines. She picked one up and hurriedly thumbed through it, glancing over the cover to see when Goldstein and his colleague had passed. When the hallway was clear, she set the magazine down, embarrassed to realize she had taken a sudden interest in "Teen" magazine. She nodded at the proprietor of the store, who was gazing at her with some disapproval.

Susan quickly entered the elevator, sliding her security card through the reader. She leaned against the wall, breathing a sigh of relief as the elevator began to move smoothly upward. Her relationship with David Goldstein had only grown worse over the years, and it had started out as a disaster.

David Goldstein was already a full doctor at the time Susan began completing her residency. When she first arrived at the hospital, a few of the nurses approached her and warned her of Goldstein's wandering hands and inappropriate comments. It hadn't taken very long for him to target Susan as his next conquest. Susan quickly tired of the constant innuendo and intimate touching, so she confronted him. When that had no effect, she filed a complaint against Goldstein for sexual harassment.

Little was done regarding the complaint, but the behavior did stop. Goldstein treated her like a pariah from that point on, but that was fine with

Susan. The nurses were also secretly pleased, and Susan became an underground heroine to them.

After that incident, Goldstein ignored her for years. Susan successfully completed her residency and began her research in her spare time. Possessing far more ingenuity and dedication than David Goldstein, it wasn't long before she passed him in the hospital's hierarchy. When the first patent came in, it established Susan as a significant contributor to the hospital's coffers, and more than David Goldstein's equal.

Susan glanced upward, not really seeing the digital numbers illuminate as the elevator passed each floor. Her exalted position in the hospital, however, had not stopped Goldstein from attempting to take advantage of her several years later, probably at the worst time of her life.

She was 28 and heady with the success of her research. She had taken only a few months off to give birth to her son, then returned to the excitement of the lab. Her husband, Brent, was an angel, willing to care for their infant while Susan worked long hours. Susan was extremely happy, wondering how life could get any better.

And then she received the news that made her wonder how life could get any worse. Brent had been killed in a plane crash. The airline pilot, a 20-year veteran, had forgotten to de-ice the wings upon take-off. The plane never made it off the ground, and the ruptured fuel tanks ensured that no one survived. Susan's grim consolation was the fact that Brent had changed his mind at the last minute and decided not to take their son. Beyond that, she was completely devastated.

It was in this setting that David Goldstein again attempted to initiate a relationship with Susan. At first his warmth touched Susan, but once she realized it was feigned, she attempted to withdraw from him. Goldstein would have none of it, however, and pressed his attentions until he ended up nearly raping her in a service elevator. But the attempt was not to succeed because Susan's grief and devastation coalesced into a fury that both stunned and overwhelmed Goldstein. After kneeing him in the groin and delivering a solid right cross, she beat him nearly senseless with her handbag. He never touched her again.

The doors opened in front of her, causing Susan to start. She had almost forgotten where she was. She stepped out into the hallway. Few people had access to the research and development wing, and no one had security clearance to her lab. It was one of her demands of work conditions, allegedly to guard against industrial espionage.

In reality, Susan just didn't want to be bothered. She stepped off the elevator onto her floor, feeling the familiar comfort of her "office." The only place she felt more comfortable was with her son, regardless of location.

She peered into the darkened lab as she slid her security card through the reader. The door opened with a barely audible click, and the motion detectors turned the lights on. She waited until the door whispered closed behind her, then went into her inner sanctum. She peered through the window of the observation booth into the sterile room beyond.

The woman was exactly as she had left her. She appeared to be a corpse hooked up to some monitors. Susan glanced over at the readouts which displayed the woman's vital signs for the last 12 hours. Respirations, none. Blood pressure, none. Pulse, five.

Susan glanced at the readout closer. Per hour. Five beats per hour.

She turned back to the woman who lay unmoving in the bed. At first, Susan had stayed with the woman for 24 hours, expecting some dramatic change in her condition. But when nothing changed, Susan finally determined there was no sense in her standing by. She felt some guilt, as if she were abandoning a patient, but then was angry at herself for feeling that way. She wasn't even certain this woman was alive, and she couldn't describe any more bizarre circumstances.

The body had seemed to "draw" blood even though the IVs ran on gravity feed. That would have been strange in and of itself, but the body had "drawn" a total of 19 liters. The average human body held only nine. Susan was not certain where all the blood was going, but knew that Mason was becoming concerned after his fourth trip to the blood bank. She herself was concerned, wondering if she was not on the verge of creating the human tick.

Susan was also uncertain what she was going to do if the woman showed any additional signs of life. She had convinced herself the woman was dead and that she was just continuing treatment for experimental purposes.

Susan glanced over at the EEG readout. That was the one thing that had remained constant, the inordinate amount of brain activity. Susan had even placed the electrodes on herself to test the machine. The readout quickly stabilized into one of normal brainwaves. When she replaced the electrodes on the woman, the pattern quickly arced back into the strange but symmetrical patterns of before.

Susan donned a sterile gown, then hit the release to the door. She entered the antiseptic room and moved the full-body scan, portable MRI into place. It was quite an expensive test and Susan wasn't quite sure how she was going to justify it to accounting.

She didn't care. She exited the room and re-entered the control booth. She adjusted a few controls on the panel in front of her, then turned to watch as the blue beam slowly traveled the length of the prone body. Susan turned expectantly to the floor-to-ceiling screen on the wall next to the glass window. The screen flashed a few times then sprang to life with the full-size picture of the internal organs and skeletal structure.

Susan stared at the image for a moment, a look of puzzlement on her features. She stood up and took a step towards the image, her puzzlement turning to confusion, then concern. She was not one to talk to herself, nor was she one to use profanity, but she now did both under her breath.

"What the hell?"

Susan stared at the image, trying to figure out what was wrong. But what was "wrong" was subtle, and though she immediately recognized something was amiss, it was hard to put her finger on what exactly that was.

She cocked her head to one side, as if by looking at the internal structure from another angle she could better understand it. She turned her head to the other side, but the body was no more comprehensible.

"Where the heck is the stomach?" she murmured aloud.

She reached over and hit the print button to burn a hard copy of the readout. The full-size copy began spooling from the machine and she caught it before it touched the floor. She laid it out on the table, staring at the picture in confusion. She was unable to draw even obvious conclusions.

She glanced through the window at the prone body, then reached over to the keyboard on her computer. She typed in a few commands to load the voice activation unit, then adjusted the microphone. As she began speaking, the computer began diligently recording her words, the letters spilling across the screen.

"The heart appears to be suffering from some type of pulmonary edema," she said, her attention returning to the printout. She circled the large organ in the center of the chest. "Although pulmonary edema is an understatement. I've seen cases of pericarditis, but I've never seen anything like this."

Susan paused, cocking her head to one side. She leaned closer to look at the heart. "Actually it doesn't appear to be edema, either. It doesn't show up as fluid at all. The tissue there is contiguous with the heart muscle." Susan stopped, disbelief evident in her own voice. "It appears the heart is three times its normal size."

The computer dispassionately recorded her words, stopping when she stopped. The words began to spill across the screen as she resumed. "Perhaps this is a birth defect of some kind, or some sort of deformity. Not severe enough to cause death but perhaps something that could be adapted to over time." Susan stopped again, unable to believe her own words. A birth defect. As if anyone could live with a heart three times its normal size. She peered over the image. And she still couldn't find the stomach. Perhaps it had shrunk during the woman's comatose state.

Susan resumed her discourse. "The liver appears slightly larger than normal and the lungs appear about half-size for an adult of her size." She eyed the veins and arteries that snaked throughout the image. "It appears the subject has an extremely well-developed circulatory system. The capillarization of the muscles is extraordinary."

Susan stopped, suddenly noticing one very prominent artery. She had to look twice before she could articulate what she was seeing. Even then, her assessment deviated from her former professional monologue. "Well, I haven't actively practiced medicine in a few years," she murmured to herself, "But I remember enough to know the esophagus is not connected to the aortic valve."

Susan pushed away from the table, suddenly angry. The most logical explanation was that someone had gone in and "operated" on this corpse to make it look like a radically altered anatomy. The body in the image was impossible. Someone had created a rather elaborate scheme to make her believe this person was still alive, and she had a pretty good idea whom that someone might be.

Her mind began racing. She suddenly realized Mason would have to be in on it as well. It would have been fairly easy for he and David Goldstein to rig this entire episode, first to make her look foolish in ER, then...

Susan felt a coldness in the pit of her stomach. Then they would catch her up here, running all sorts of "Dr. Frankenstein" experiments on an obviously dead corpse. Her indiscretion involving the "borrowed" bodies would come to light, her reputation as a researcher would be ruined.

Her paranoia began to snowball. She looked to the EEG. It would be simple enough for someone to rig the machine, and the heart monitor as well. She began to cast her gaze wildly around the cubicle, searching for a camera or recorder. They could be watching her right now, documenting her actions. Her paranoid gaze settled on the computer screen, and her last words blinked at her incriminatingly.

This whole thing was a matter of manipulating Susan into believing what she wanted to believe. Mason had played her so easily, pretending to be dumb. He and Goldstein had known Susan would begin twisting the evidence in the direction of her research.

Susan leaped to her feet and rushed into the sterile room. If she could just get rid of the body before they had an opportunity to spring their trap. She could get rid of all the evidence, then play dumb when they tried to catch her in the act. If she could just get rid of this body...

She gathered the sheets, trying to wrap the body completely so that no part of it showed. But her hands were shaking so badly she nearly knocked the body to the floor, and in her struggle to catch the corpse, lost the sheet completely. The lower half of the woman's body was now exposed.

She struggled against the weight of the woman and finally succeeding in shoving the body back onto the bed. She reached down to pick up the sheet and her eyes caught sight of the woman's legs. She stopped.

For a long moment, she didn't move. She slowly stood upright, the sheet forgotten as it slipped from her nerveless fingers. She reached out, hesitantly touching the body.

The woman's legs were intact. There were no compound fractures, no broken skin, only mild bruising where before there had been horrendous injuries.

Susan gazed at the legs. She had been so caught up in looking at the internal organs on the MRI printout she had missed the obvious. She felt a cold chill whisper down her spine, but it was a very different chill than she had experienced a moment before. This was a much more primitive fear. Thoughts of a conspiracy slipped away.

Susan slowly began backing away from the body. It was still slightly askew in the bed, but she was not going to right it. Nor was she going to turn her back on it before she left the room. She felt for the doorknob behind her, then slid through the crack she opened.

Susan slammed the door, locking it. She peered through the window, not exactly certain what she expected to see.

The body just laid there. The woman appeared to be sleeping. Not completely comfortably, but sleeping nonetheless.

Susan forced herself to take several deep breaths. "Get a hold of yourself, girl. Remember, you're a scientist."

As if in support, the computer printed out the reassurance. Susan thought about turning the voice activation off, but she needed the company at the moment, even if it was self-generated.

"Okay," she said aloud, now addressing the computer as if it were another person. "We've got something new, now." She tried to return to her professional voice. "Not only does this woman possess an extraordinary anatomy, she appears to be healing at an accelerated rate."

She glanced down at the MRI printout in front of her, and her professionalism fled. "Well that was the understatement of the year, Dr. Ryerson."

She began to think aloud again. She tried to regroup, putting her research voice on. "This could be some type of chromosomal defect, or perhaps some type of genetic engineering," she paused, "But if so it's way beyond anything I've even heard about."

The EEG sprang into action behind her, and she jumped, startled. She felt foolish as she pushed her heart back down into her chest where it belonged. She glanced at the monitor, then turned to look through the glass window. Even from where she was standing she could see the twitching of the intact eyelid, could see the rapid eye movement indicating a dream state.

Susan's fascination overcame her fear as she stared at the prone body. Half the woman's face was gone. Her skin had the pallor of death. And yet she was obviously dreaming. What in god's name could be in that woman's head, to generate such activity?

CHAPTER 6

The boy still remembered the first time he saw the Man. It had been shortly after Bertha's daughter had died in childbirth. She had been small and the baby had been large. Neither had survived.

The boy was standing in the middle of the dirt road that split their small village. He was playing with some of the other boys, boys who were larger than him but never quite as strong or as fast.

They all heard the sound of hooves off in the distance and the boy looked to the west at the cloud of approaching dust. It was rare that horses came to their village; it usually meant that tribute was due.

The other boys scattered but the fair-haired one stood in the street. He was more curious than afraid. He saw what seemed to be a great number of horses; he could not count so in his mind it was simply more than two.

The horses stopped at the edge of the village, snorting and rearing, their riders trying to control them. The men atop their backs were dressed in finery, leather jerkins, steel mesh, brightly colored crests. The boy watched curiously as they gathered and wheeled about.

The horses parted as if on command and a man on a huge black horse rode through the gap to the edge of the clearing.

The boy's heart stopped. The man was looking directly at him with piercing black eyes. He seemed almost as if he had been looking for him. He studied him intently, his gaze traveling from the top of the boy's fair head to the bottom of his dusty feet.

The boy stood as if mesmerized. Indeed, if the man's troupe had decided to run him down he would have been unable to move. But instead the man wheeled his horse around with a shout and the troupe moved to follow him. As quickly as the contact had been initiated it was broken, and the band galloped to the southwest. The boy stood in the street, feeling an inexplicable loss.

It did not take long for word to travel through the small village that the band was encamped a short distance from their rough huts. There was much speculation on the identity of the visitors and whether this was a good or bad omen. It was evident that his lordship, whoever he might be, was very wealthy and powerful. Some even speculated that it might be the King, or at least a relative. Few, however, were exactly sure who the King might be and none would recognize him if they saw him. Lacking pictures or even the most rudimentary artwork, if a man didn't know another face-to-face, he didn't know him.

Hans' wife watched her son with a certain amount of anxiety. She had seen his lordship eye the boy. Her son possessed a remarkable beauty and it was only by the grace of his unknown benefactor that he remained untouched by the lecherous world that surrounded him. The priest was afraid to touch him but someone as powerful as the stranger might not know of his protector, or care.

The boy was preoccupied, stirring his watery soup with his finger. He could not seem to get the man out of his thoughts. The man had looked at him strangely, almost as if he had known him. And the man had looked at him in a way like the priest looked at him, but somehow differently.

The sun was going down and soon blackness would blanket the land. It was a moonless night, and save for a few lamps and still-burning embers, the blackness would be complete.

The boy settled onto the rough-hewn mat he shared with his parents. He heard his father's rough grunts a few feet away as the evening ritual began. The slap of flesh would keep the boy awake, but tonight he was not going to sleep anyway.

Hans finished quickly and soon his snores filled the small hut. The boy waited until he was sure he could hear his mother's rhythmic breathing, and then he rolled off the mat.

He pulled the cover back into place in the doorway, and set off toward the glow of the firelight in the distance.

No other person from the village would dare roam about at night like the boy did. They were terrified of the various creatures that lurked in the surrounding forest. Many stories of demonic creatures, half-man, half-wolf, circulated through the village. The villagers knew the stories were true; they were in the Bible weren't they?

The boy paid no mind to the stories. He knew they were true, but he was willing to take the chance. He picked his way through the underbrush with care.

He climbed a tree where he could overlook the clearing where the troupe was encamped. He had chosen a lucky spot because an elaborate tent was pitched within his view; he was sure it belonged to the man.

He clung to the branch, watching the few men still awake mill about the camp. He did not have to wait very long. Almost as if on cue, the flap of the elaborate tent was pushed aside and the man stepped out.

A serf rushed up to the man but he waved him off. The serf quickly disappeared into the shadows. The boy took the opportunity to study the man. He was tall, nearly taller than the head of a horse, and he had none of the fat the boy had seen on other feudal lords. His hair was black, as dark as his eyes, with no gray to betray his age.

The man turned and looked directly into the boy's eyes. The boy was so startled he nearly fell backward out of the tree. The man had to be further than the distance the boy could throw a stone, and the boy could throw far. He regained his balance and again locked eyes with the man.

Another man approached his lordship and their words drifted to the boy's location.

"Is something wrong, my lord? Is there something you need?"

The younger man peered out into the blackness, seeing nothing. The man spoke, and his voice was smooth, smooth like the stones at the bottom of the river that had been worn by water and time.

"Nothing you can provide me."

The reply seemed to anger the young man and he stalked off. The man watched his departure mildly, then turned his attention back to the boy.

Or at least it seemed that way to the boy. But he realized there was no way the man could see into the blackness, no way he could see across the clearing to his hiding place. Still, the boy's heart was beating so loudly it seemed the man could hear it.

The boy quickly climbed down the tree. He began to make his way back through the forest, more hastily than he had come. No sense in staying out here all night.

The boy was about half the way home when he stopped, feeling as if something was behind him. His senses strained the blackness around him, but he heard nothing. He shrugged and started on his way once more.

He again stopped, whirling around as if to catch whatever was stalking him. And that was what he felt, as if someone, or something, was in the darkness behind him. There was nothing but silence.

The boy began to trot, and then to run. Whatever was behind him seemed maddeningly close yet unidentifiable.

The boy had feared few things in his life. He had always been faster or stronger than most things that threatened him. But he was very afraid right now, and he began to crash through the underbrush, his breath coming loud and harsh and his heart pounding in his chest.

Whatever was behind him was not only keeping pace but was catching him. He could not see it but knew it was too large for a wolf and too fast for a bear. He began to dodge side-to-side in a futile attempt at evasion.

He was tackled from behind and went face first into the warm, dark earth. He could taste the rich soil in his mouth as he was grabbed roughly from behind and lifted off his feet. He was imprisoned in a grip as strong as a vice and waited to be torn limb from limb.

He did not have long to wait. He felt a piercing pain, then felt his insides turn to liquid. He saw an extraordinary redness behind his eyelids, then all went black.

CHAPTER 7

Susan tapped the blood from the syringe onto the glass slide, then tapped a cover slip into place. She held the syringe up to the light, noting the bend in the needle. She had finally gotten up the courage to re-enter the room, and had discovered the skin of the woman was not any easier to pierce.

She slid the sample beneath the electron microscope and brought the image into focus. She furrowed her brow, staring into the eyepiece.

She sat upright, tiredly rubbing her eyes. She glanced over at her computer screen. Her conversation with the machine had become more and more informal. "Well, I'm beginning to sound like a broken record, but I've never seen anything like this before." She leaned down to peer into the microscope again. "They look like leukocytes. But they're entirely too large and entirely too many. If they are white blood cells, then her T-cell count is in the hundreds of thousands. The red blood cells don't appear to be normal, either." Susan sat upright, the faintest sign of delirium in her voice. "This is not possible. Her blood is pathological. It's not infected by a virus, it doesn't appear to be antibodies, it's not anything."

Susan's vocabulary was beginning to fail her due to her exhaustion. But her fatigue was also making her extremely creative. She reached over to open a drawer and removed a test-tube from a tray. She withdrew a sample from the test-tube with a pipette, then tapped the pipette on the slide.

"I'm now introducing a fairly virulent strain of streptococcus, in vitro."

Susan said as she peered through the microscope. She pushed away from the table and flipped a switch. The image from the microscope projected up onto the screen.

Susan watched as the "leukocytes" violently attacked the phage. Within seconds, the virus was destroyed and no trace was left on the screen. The corpuscle-like creatures settled into smug inertness.

"Okay," Susan said, the delirium even more evident in her voice, "That wasn't what I expected."

She was starting to feel even more creative. She glanced over at a row of test tubes that were labeled with biohazard stickers. There were locked tight and would require her security card to release them. She pulled the card from the chain around her neck and ran it through the reader.

"Okay," she said, returning to the microscope, "I am now introducing cancerous cells to the blood sample, again in vitro." She pushed away from the desk and turned to gaze at the screen. This reaction didn't take much longer than the streptococcus. She watched as the white blood cells demolished the cancerous invader. She could not think of a thing to say.

Susan suddenly realized how exhausted she was. She had just witnessed the unimaginable, and could not articulate her observations. She had not slept in over 36 hours, and had not been home in three days. She was faced with the penultimate find of her medical career, and could not find a voice to record it.

She turned in her chair to stare at the woman through the glass. The woman's face was different and it took Susan a minute to realize she was healing, literally before her eyes.

The beeping to her right attracted Susan's attention and she glanced tiredly over at the EEG that began to chatter. She looked through the window and for once was jealous of the rapid eye movement she saw.

The boy was found the next morning, lying pale and unconscious in front of his hut. His mother's screams rent the air as his father gazed down in horror at his son's body. Hans was not certain at first if the boy was even alive, but the shallow rise and fall of his chest indicated he was. Hans' second fear was that the boy was ill and the illness would befall him. It was only a greater fear that forced him to pick up the child: the knowledge of what would happen to him if the boy died.

Hans carried the limp body into the hut and laid him on the rough mat. He backed out of the hut, leaving his wife to tend the child.

The boy lie unmoving while the sun traveled across the sky and the sliver of a moon appeared. Word came that the band had moved on. Hans returned fearfully to find the boy's condition unchanged. He was relieved to find his wife still healthy and reluctantly stayed the night in the hut.

The sun traveled across the sky thrice more before the boy opened his eyes. It was another fortnight before he was strong enough to rise.

He could remember little of his ordeal, other than he had been attacked from behind by some beast. He had little recollection of events prior to the attack, and none of those that occurred after. He did not know how he had gotten back to his village, nor how he had survived the assault.

He had many questions but did not speak them. He did not know why a wild animal would attack him and cause little more than bruising. He did not know where his weakness had come from when he was obviously uninjured.

His mother commented it seemed almost as if he had been poisoned. This seemed a strange explanation to him, but it would at least explain the odd, metallic taste in his mouth upon awakening.

Susan paid the cabby and stepped out onto the curb. She had been afraid to drive, so great had been her exhaustion. She could not remember what day it was, and had been surprised it was dark outside when she left the hospital.

Dark or not, it did not stop Jason from tearing out the front door to come scrambling down the front walk. Even as tired as she was, she picked him up as he ran into her arms. She held him tightly, raining kisses on his freckled face.

"I'm sorry, munchkin. I didn't mean to be gone so long. I missed you so much!"

Jason held her cheeks in his little hands, then pressed them together. She obligingly made fish-lips for him and he dissolved into laughter, scrambling to be free. She set him down and he ran back up the walk, calling over his shoulder.

"Neda says you must be working very hard," he said, obviously parroting his nanny's words. He stopped at the edge of the porch, his little body barely able to contain his energy as his words spilled out. "She says that maybe you will cure cancer and help lots of people." His eyes grew bright, "And," he said, "You'll make lots of money and buy good little boys candy!"

Neda came out the screen door. "You hush, little monster. Your mommy will buy you lima beans if you don't quiet down. You're going to wake the dead."

Jason screeched in mock terror at the threat of the vegetable sanctions, then ran into the house laughing. Neda turned to Susan, her expression changing to one of concern. "Are you all right, dear?"

Susan's expression was sober. The comment about cancer brought work flooding back to her. Whatever peace Jason had brought her fled as his words hit an unintended mark.

Susan shook her head. "No, no, Neda, I'm fine." She started up the walkway once more. "I'm just exhausted."

Neda was not completely satisfied with Susan's response, but helped her young mistress into the house. She clucked over her, telling her she should get straight to bed, but Susan would have none of it. She went up to Jason's room.

Jason's room was a complete contrast to the rest of the house. He was an angel when it came to caring for her antiques, her hardwood floors, her china dishes and Persian rugs. But the trade-off was that his room was completely his domain. He took full advantage of this deal and decorated it in the glorious standards of a 5 year-old.

Susan removed her coat and laid it across his chair, on top of the pile of stuffed animals that were sitting there. Jason ran over and removed the coat. "They can't breathe, mom!" He carefully laid the coat across the back of the chair.

"Sorry, kiddo. But I know CPR if things go bad."

This made Jason dissolve into giggles. "Yeah, I know. But I know B-U-T."

Susan laid down on his bed. "Okay, I give, what's B-U-T?"

"It's butt, mom! Don't you know how to spell?"

She could not help but laugh at his exuberance. "I think there's another 'T' in there, pal, if you're using it in the sense I think you're using it." She pulled his Star Wars comforter over her. "But I'm glad to see you've been reading again."

He pulled a Dr. Seuss book from the shelf. "Want me to read this to you mom?"

Susan nodded, making room for him in the twin bed. He began reading aloud to her, deeply concentrating on his pronunciation.

Neda stopped in the doorway, a tray with a bowl of steaming soup in her hands. She smiled at the picture of the two. The young doctor was already asleep, wrapped around the little boy who was so diligently reading to her of green eggs and ham. Neda would not disturb the two, and she slowly pulled the door closed behind her.

CHAPTER 8

Susan slept nearly sixteen hours. Jason was at school when she awakened, and she was saddened by the fact he would come home to find her gone again. But the thought of the woman patiently sleeping in her laboratory made her anxious, and she could not delay her return.

She made it into the lab without incident and quickly returned to the printout of the MRI. Now that her head was a little clearer, she tried to make sense of the internal anatomy. Familiar landmarks were missing; other organs were much smaller or much larger than normal. She glanced over at her computer, not really surprised to see she had failed to turn the voice activation off. Her last, delirious words blinked at her from the screen. She turned back to the printout and began anew.

"The musculature of the patient seems fairly normal, at least for an extremely well-developed athlete. The quadriceps and gastrocnemius muscles show minor tears, possibly where the bone was protruding through earlier."

Susan paused. If she had to actually stop and think about what she was saying, she wouldn't say it. What she had accepted so blithely in her delirium was starting to sink in. She continued her assessment, trying to refrain from making subjective observations.

"The skeletal system also appears fairly normal. There are what appear to be hairline fractures to the femur and the right tibia. These fractures are in the approximate locations of the compound fractions observed less than a week ago."

Susan paused. Don't think too much, she warned herself. She glanced over at the computer screen, then continued.

"The patient appears to be suffering from some type of genetic abnormality, or perhaps a state of advanced pathology. The heart is enlarged to nearly three times normal size. The lungs are shrunken, as are the liver and the pancreas. I am unable to locate the stomach or the spleen. The entire body is covered with extreme capillarization. The network of veins and arteries is extensive." Susan let her eyes travel down the picture. "Sexually, the woman appears normal externally; however, there are no apparent reproductive organs internally. No uterus, cervix, fallopian tubes, or ovaries can be seen."

Susan glanced through the glass window. "The epidermal layer is now intact, with the exception of the right cheek which is rapidly healing. The EEG machine continues to record extraordinary brain activity."

She turned her attention back to the picture on the screen in front of her. "The brain appears to be normal-sized, but the ganglia and associated nerves are-"

Susan stopped. Are what? Too numerous to mention? Too long? Too damned developed?

The phone rang, startling Susan. She suppressed her irritation, brushing at her lab coat self-consciously. She didn't know why she was jumping around like a scared rabbit. Even so, she stared at the phone a long moment before reaching over to press "speaker."

"Dr. Ryerson," she answered guardedly.

"Yeah, Dr. Ryerson," came the breezy voice over the intercom, "This is Patty, down at the lab?"

Susan didn't know if she was supposed to know "Patty" or not. "Yes?" she answered.

"Yeah, doc, I've got the blood panel results from that sample you sent down the other day."

Susan's thoughts raced. She forgot she had sent a test-tube down for a blood workup. It had been one of her first acts upon bringing the body upstairs, and she never would have done so after her examination. But her motivation at the time was to determine why a "dead" body was drawing blood, hoping to eliminate the possibility that it was indeed assimilating it.

"Yes?" Susan answered even more cautiously.

"Well, I know you're going to be disappointed, but I think you've confused your samples."

"What do you mean by that?" Susan asked.

"Well," the breezy voice went on with some authority, "You've got it marked as human but it has to be contaminated with some animal blood."

Susan tried to sound noncommittal. "Oh really? Why is that?"

It was obvious by the pause and rustle of papers that Patty began to read off a chart. "Well, some blood levels are normal. Plasma is about right. Blood creatine levels are really high. Hemoglobin is a little low."

Susan nodded, then felt foolish because she realized "Patty" couldn't see her. "Go on."

"Well, this is the bad news. We found L-gulonolactone oxidase in that blood sample."

Susan tried to hide her impatience. She worked extensively with blood panels in the field of immunology, but that didn't mean that she had every flipping, obscure enzyme memorized. "And this is a bad thing...?" she asked.

Patty snorted on the other end of the line. "Well, no, it wouldn't be a bad thing, doc. But it's just not found in human beings." She snickered some more, then regained some composure, adding, "Unfortunately for us."

Susan leaned a little closer to the phone. "Why unfortunate for us?"

Patty was happy to share her knowledge, and Susan wondered if she was reading out of a textbook. "Well, L-gulonolactone is an enzyme found in all animals, with a handful of exceptions, human beings and guinea pigs being two of the exceptions. That's too bad, because this enzyme is required to convert glucose to vitamin C, so...."

Susan finished the thought for her. "So any animal that has this enzyme is capable of producing vitamin C."

"That's right," Patty said smugly, "Vitamin C from their livers, not from a jar."

Susan's thoughts raced furiously. She would have been familiar with this enzyme had it been found in humans because Vitamin C was central to immunology. Vitamin C, once thought of as simply a cure for scurvy, was now known to maintain the body in homeostasis when faced with disease, infection, cancer, and other stresses on the immune system.

In other words, vitamin C was turning out to be one of the penultimate players in preventing the disintegration of the body.

Susan stared at the woman through the glass, the woman who was healing before her eyes. Patty's voice droned on over the speaker.

"And something else we found. Do you think you might have mixed this up with a rat or something?"

Susan tried to focus on what the other woman was saying. "Why would you think that?"

"Well, this isn't as weird as the enzyme, but it's still kind of strange. If this were a human, I'd say he or she built up a resistance to some interesting diseases, judging by the antibodies in the blood."

Susan felt a chill go down her spine. "What kind of antibodies?"

"Well," came the voice over the intercom, "Bubonic plague for starters."

CHAPTER 9

HANS WATCHED HIS BOY WORK THE METAL WITH A CLOSE eye. His vigilance was unnecessary, however, because the boy's skill was already as great as his own.

His son had grown taller and although still slender, was as strong as any man in the village. Where many had sickened and died, the boy had never been sick a day in his life.

Except for that one time, Hans thought, mentally making the sign of the cross. And the time just like it when the boy was an infant. Both times he had been pale and weak, near death for days with no cause in sight. But then he recovered and seemed stronger than ever.

The steady clink brought Hans out of his reverie. He grunted at the boy and walked around the side of the hut.

A figure out of the corner of his eye caught the boy's attention. It was the fat priest, come to stare at him again. If anything, the last few seasons had seen the priest grow fatter, and more insolent.

There was the sheen of grease on the priest's chin and the boy wondered what hearth he had just pillaged. Although no one else in the village thought to question the priest's actions, secretly the boy harbored a great resentment against him. He did not think much of this god who would give power to such a man as the priest.

The priest watched the handsome young man at work, wishing the boy would wear less clothing.

"Hail, lad."

The boy barely paused in his work. "Hail, priest," he muttered.

The priest put his hand on the boy's arm. "I said 'hail,' boy."

The boy stopped his pounding, gripping the handle of the hammer tightly in his hand. The priest did not move his hand from the boy's arm. "I would think you would have more respect for the Church, lad."

The boy stared at the hand gripping his arm, and the priest slowly removed it, taking a step backward. The boy stared at the priest for a long moment, then went back to his rhythmic clinking as if nothing had happened.

Angered, the priest waddled off under the worried gaze of the boy's mother.

The priest went to salve his wounded pride with a skin of wine. He was joined by two of his associates; rough, brutal men, filthy in both mind and body. They didn't care for the priest any more than they cared for anyone else, or indeed, even each other. But they hovered about him on the occasion when it would serve their interests. He had wine on this evening, which was one of their interests.

The three men sprawled on the rough benches, becoming drunker as the evening progressed. They spoke loudly of foul things, each trying to outdo one another in their crude fashion. The priest was actually winning this rude contest when he spotted a young girl scurrying across the street to her hut. He sat forward; she was at least six seasons, old enough.

"You there!"

The girl stopped fearfully, torn between the doorway to her hut that was so close, and the commanding tone of the priest.

"Come here!"

The girl looked longingly at her mother who stood anxiously in the doorway. Her father appeared and pushed the woman back inside. He looked sternly at the girl and waved her on to the priest. He disappeared into the hut, pulling the cover closed behind him.

"Girl, I said come here!"

The child felt fear and despair as she reluctantly obeyed the priest.

The two men with the priest leered at the little girl. This was the best part of befriending the priest. The one missing the better part of his teeth grinned widely as he felt the hardness between his legs.

The little girl watched the man grope himself and turned to flee. The priest reached out to grab her, catching only her shift which ripped loose in his hand. He laughed loudly as the now-naked girl ran for the barn.

The three drunken men chased her, laughing merrily. "First one to her gets to break her!" shouted the drunker of the two men.

It was surely a measure of the men's drunkenness that the fat priest nearly caught her first. But it was the toothless one who grabbed the little girl's ankle, tripping her up as she entered the barn. He fell upon her, his weight easily pinning her. His foul breath filled the girl's nostrils as he struggled with the rope at his waist. He pulled his organ free and with a shout of victory, grabbed the girl's shoulders and thrust forward.

It was an act he would never complete as his face exploded into blood and bone fragments. He went backward off the girl as she screamed, his neck at an odd angle. He was dead before he touched the ground, his spine snapped just below the base of his skull.

The boy moved from the shadows, holding the now-bloodied garden spade in his hand. The second man was stunned. This boy, who could not be more than 13 seasons, had nearly decapitated his friend with little more than a farming tool.

The boy turned towards the priest, who was standing there with his now-flaccid member in his hand. The sight and smell of the dead man's blood excited and enraged the boy. He knew he could probably kill the other two men with few repercussions, but the priest he could not touch.

It did not matter to him as he thrust the metal tool straight through the priest's heart. The priest's shocked expression was almost comical as he collapsed to the ground, dead.

The little girl fled screaming from the barn and the other man stared at the boy in horror. "You've killed a man of god," he said, backing away from him, "You're damned forever!" He himself ran screaming from the barn, terrified of the abomination behind him.

The boy knew he should go after the man. Whatever protection had been afforded him up until this time surely had run out. But he was suddenly tired, drained by the rush the killing had given him. He dropped his weapon and stumbled out into the cool night air, collapsing in the wet grass.

They came for him the next morning, the clergy and the soldiers from the next town. He was bound and placed on the back of an ass, and did not get the chance to say farewell to his mother who stood in the doorway as he was taken away. She knew she would never see her son again.

The men treated him roughly and he was hungry and thirsty by the time he reached the town by midday. He had never been to this town, or indeed, any town. He had never been anywhere outside his own village and it was surprising to see the number of strange faces. There was a growing crowd as his hands and feet were placed in the stocks.

He glanced to his left. A man was pinned there, alive but with his head hanging down and his swollen tongue protruding from his mouth. His stench was nearly unbearable as both his hands and feet were rotting off. The boy turned to his right where another young man, perhaps a few seasons older than himself, was confined. He had not been there as long but the skin on his face was beginning to crack and peel from the constant exposure.

The boy turned his attention to the crowd. They looked at him with a kind of malicious glee, hoping his sentence would be carried out immediately. When it was not to be, they expressed their disappointment by throwing rocks and whatever objects they could find at the three prisoners. One young man even defecated in the street then picked up his own excrement and threw it at the stockade.

The boy was glad it hit the prisoner to his right and not him, but he was left with the stench of the feces and the rotting vegetables as the crowd tired and left the three in their misery.

The boy did not want to talk to either of his companions. The man to his left occasionally shouted out in delirium, but beyond that it was largely quiet in the town square. The boy began to cramp in the awkward position and tried to shift his weight, but it was no good. The cuts and scratches he had received from the thrown objects began to itch as the blood mingled with his sweat.

Finally the unrelenting heat began to diminish as the shadows lengthened. The older boy to his right began to fidget in fear and he wondered what could be worse than what they had already endured.

He quickly found out as a group of leering men stumbled over to their location.

"Are you sure we can't have the pretty one? I'm sure he wouldn't mind too much."

Another man punched the first good-naturedly, but with warning. "No, can't touch that one. He's a priest-killer anyway. You don't want to bugger the damned."

The man moved behind the boy and smacked him on his rear. "I don't know, might be worth it."

The other man laughed uneasily and pulled him away from the boy. "Stop foolin', Tom, we got this one here."

The boy could not see what the men were doing behind him but he quickly pieced it together by the squeals of the boy next to him. The men, four or five at least, began to rape the older boy. They took turns and it was apparent from the different voices that others came and went. The boy next to him was slammed forward and back in his stocks as the men took him from behind.

The younger boy swallowed hard, feeling his backside cringe although he was not being touched. Although sympathy was deemed of little worth, he could not help but feel it for the other boy.

"Hey Nell! Too bad you don't have a tool, you could come over here and give us a hand, so to speak."

The men all laughed raucously at the joke and a female joined in. "I got the only tool I need right here."

The boy tried to look over his shoulder. The woman was just barely in his field of vision and was moving out of it as she came toward them. But not before he saw she held a broom in her hand.

The men laughed even louder at her crudeness. "Then by all means, m'lady, join us!"

There was a chorus of agreement. The boy could not see what was going on but knew the woman had indeed joined them when the older boy's squeals turned to screams and the laughter of the men increased.

The sound of hooves drowned out the laughter and a sharp crack of a whip elicited cries of pain from some of the men. The band scattered, angry and frightened.

The boy had no idea what was going on. A band of horses circled the stockade, creating a cloud of dust. The town lawman came stumbling out of the nearby pub with the local clergy in tow. "What's your business here!" he demanded.

The leader, an older, elegantly dressed man replied. "Release this boy immediately."

The clergyman began to protest but the man cut him short, throwing down a piece of parchment. "It has been approved by his Grace, as you can see by the seal. His Grace does not appreciate his orders being questioned or disobeyed."

The local priest glanced at the parchment and although he could barely read, it was indeed his Grace's seal. The elegant man looked down at him disdainfully. "Release him. Now!"

The lawman scrambled to obey, fearing both the specter of his Grace's wrath and the more immediate threat of the band of well-armed men. The boy felt the stock loosened and tried to stand upright. He nearly fell because he could not feel his legs. One of the soldiers who had dismounted caught him, holding him upright until he regained feeling in his legs.

The boy was confused and looked upward to his savior, but the man on the horse had no compassion in his gaze. "Were you touched?"

The boy shook his head and the man seemed satisfied. He turned his attention to the lawman. "Give the boy a horse so he can return to his village."

A horse was quickly brought out. The boy looked at the animal with misgivings. He had never been on a horse before. The band of soldiers moved to the edge of the town, with the exception of the man in charge.

Events were happening so quickly that the boy had a hard time grasping the fact that he was leaving. He glanced over to the stocks where he had so recently been confined. The older boy, still confined, had blood dripping from his mouth. He walked over to him.

The older boy looked up at him, dazed. There was little room for compassion in this harsh world, but the older boy would make one request of this one whom was so obviously blessed. He swallowed hard and sought to wet his tongue so he could speak. He finally croaked out the words.

"Please kill me."

The boy looked down at the young man who was only slightly older than him. He clenched his jaw and felt a despair settle over him.

The man in charge nudged his horse and it moved next to the boy. He drew his long sword out of its sheath and offered it hilt first to the boy. There was harsh amusement in his eyes.

The boy took the sword; it was heavy, but not too heavy. He glanced down at the youth in the stockade, took a deep breath and hefted the sword over his head. With one swift motion he sliced downward. The sword flashed through the air and cut the youth's head off.

The boy stared at the blood on the sword, feeling lightheaded. He walked to the woman still holding the broomstick in her hand. He raised the sword and she cringed backward. But he only grabbed the cloth of her rough dress and wiped the sword clean.

He walked back to the man and handed him his sword, hilt first. The man looked down at him with an indecipherable expression, but the boy sensed his actions had been unexpected, and had met with approval.

He struggled to pull himself on the horse and the man slapped the horse's rump before he was completely settled. The horse bolted for the edge of town and the man watched him until he was completely out of sight. Then, without a glance at the townspeople, the man rejoined his band and they rode off in the opposite direction.

Hans was surprised to see his son. He was pleased because the boy could return to work. The horse, also, was a welcome addition.

There was much gossip about the village at his return. It was whispered that he may have escaped punishment on earth, but would surely face punishment in the hereafter. The boy did not care. He did not share his story with anyone, not even his mother. She did not ask.

Few in the village would have anything to do with the boy, but again, he did not care. He was more than willing to spend his time alone. Only the small girl would approach him, and only she was allowed to intrude on his thoughts. She did not smile or speak, but she would bring him water when he was thirsty, and fix him food.

CHAPTER 10

Susan examined the markers in the blood panel in front of her. After ensuring the blood sample from the lab downstairs would be destroyed, she obtained a new sample from her patient. She confirmed the presence of both the enzyme and the antibodies, and made several interesting discoveries herself.

The woman had no detectable levels of testosterone or estrogen. Her GH, or growth hormone, levels were off the record. She had glutathione present in unbelievable levels, and blood creatine present in staggering amounts. Any one of these things would have been strange, but together they began to form an astounding picture.

Susan had no explanation for the woman's accelerated healing, but if she wanted to create a person with such an ability, an abundance of easily obtainable, self-generated vitamin C would definitely be the starting point. Vitamin C aided in the production of collagen, a type of biological "glue" that held everything in the body together. That could begin to explain the repair of the skin. Glutathione was another antioxidant with disease-fighting properties similar to those of vitamin C.

Growth hormone and creatine were more involved with strength than with healing, although theoretically they would aid in that as well. Under normal circumstances, the purpose of growth hormone was pretty straightforward: it made children grow. In adults, it was regenerated primarily in sleep and was responsible for muscle hypertrophy, or an increase in muscle size. Susan had heard of bodybuilders and athletes using GH to build muscle or enhance performance, sometimes with horrible side effects. But she had never seen anyone with the levels this woman had. Creatine had a similar strength-enhancing function. It was crucial in converting ADP to ATP, an energy conversion process responsible for all muscle contraction.

In short, the woman was a pharmacological wonder and had a blood profile the most expensive steroids in the world couldn't buy.

Susan could see the body out of the corner of her eye. She glanced up, staring at the patient through the window. Nothing about the patient seemed different, so she glanced back down at the work in front of her. Something was nagging at her, however, and she peered through the window at the still body. She stared for a long moment, unable to discern what was attracting her attention.

And then her heart stopped.

The sheet covering the woman's chest very slowly rose then settled once more. Susan wasn't certain of what she had just seen and held her own breath until she saw the sheet begin to rise again. She glanced over at the monitors. They had started registering respirations a few moments ago.

Susan very slowly stood up. She was frightened, but not certain why. Wasn't this what she was waiting for? Wasn't this what she had been working towards? Isn't this what she should have expected?

She stared through the window. "Waiting" was one thing; actually getting what you were waiting for was quite another. She took a deep breath, trying to calm her irrational fears.

Almost like a child daring herself, Susan moved to the door. She hesitated only a brief moment, then unlocked it and stepped into the room beyond.

The quiet in the room was eerie. Susan had been alone in the control booth, but it had been filled with the hum of the monitors, the various beeps of the computer, and her own noise of movement.

But this room was tomb-like in its silence. The only sound was the scrape of the sheet against itself as the woman's chest slowly rose, then fell. The utter stillness seemed to magnify this only motion in the room.

Susan tried to be clinical about this observation. The woman's respirations were shallow and far apart, but she did appear to be breathing regularly.

Susan took a step forward, then stopped. She took a deep breath herself, her exhalation loud in the silence. She braced herself to take another step.

The shrill, steady beep came forth so loud in the silence that she stifled a scream. She clutched her hand to her chest, then turned in panic as EKG chattered to life behind her. The display went from flatline to a pattern of steady, jagged peaks.

Susan froze. The woman's heartbeat was fast and erratic and seemed to boom in the stillness of the room. Strangely, the heartbeat was out of sync with the EKG, and it took Susan a moment to realize it was her own heartbeat she was hearing, not that of the sleeping woman. She took a deep breath, calming herself and the heartbeat receded. The only sound in the room was the slow, steady beep of the EKG.

The woman did not move, but her eyes twitched. Susan's heart rate jumped back up and she had the terrifying impression the woman was going to open her eyes. But instead, the eyes began their rhythmic pulsing that signified the woman was dreaming.

The boy was working with his father at the anvil. His mother and the small girl were out in the fields. He glanced up occasionally in their direction, but he could not see them because they were too far.

A cloud of dust attracted his attention. It seemed to be heading in the direction of his mother and the girl. He watched with concern and finally removed the blacksmith's apron he was wearing. He began trotting, then running in that direction.

He crested the hill in time to see the band of horses circling the two women. The boy's mother clutched the girl to her breast. Both women were terrified and the boy felt his anger burn. The men weren't hurting them but their laughter infuriated him.

He ran into the path of one of the horses and it reared, throwing its rider to the ground. The boy kicked the man in the head and continued running towards his mother. With a great leap he tackled another man off his horse. He took the man's sword and stood holding it awkwardly.

A handsome young man raised his hand and the men came to a halt.

"Look, the whelp wants to fight."

It took the boy a moment to recognize the man. It had been many years before when he had been hiding in a tree. This man had been waved away by another, and he had stalked away in anger. The boy wondered why he had returned.

"Teach him a lesson, Derek."

Derek dismounted from his horse and unsheathed his sword. "Come and play with me, boy."

It was clear Derek did not take the boy seriously as he held his sword loosely in his hand. The boy sprang forward with surprising speed, and although untrained, struck with surprising force. Derek barely brought his sword up to parry and was unprepared for the boy's counter. A trickle of blood appeared on his arm.

Derek was furious. "You little bastard."

He sprang forward and the boy countered his attack. Derek was once more surprised by the boy's strength, and growing angrier each passing moment. His men were beginning to laugh at him, taunting.

Derek sprang forward with a feint that the boy went for. Realizing he had overcommitted, the boy struggled to block the next blow that glanced off his sword and nicked his collarbone. Infuriated by the pain, the boy struck out, this time slicing Derek's other arm.

The men laughed heartily at this slight, and Derek went into a mad rage. He delivered a flurry of blows that the boy struggled to counter, moving backward. He tripped over a root and went down, losing his grip on the sword. Derek smashed the sword from his hand and the boy raised his arms in front of his face in a vain attempt to block the oncoming blow.

The sword came flashing down but instead of meeting flesh it met cold steel. The boy glanced up, his eyes adjusting as the horse moved and its shadow covered him.

The Man was seated on the horse, and there was a cold fury in his eyes. But the fury was not directed at him, it was directed at Derek.

Derek dropped his sword and fell to his knees. "Forgive me, my lord. I wasn't going to hurt the boy."

The boy took that instant to scramble to his feet, away from the hooves of the horse. The Man turned the sword on him, placing the tip just beneath his chin and forcing him to look up.

The boy stared up at the man and the man carefully examined him. His eyes were drawn to the trickle of blood on the boy's shoulder and there was a flicker of something in his black eyes.

The boy pushed the sword away from his chin. "I will not yield to you," he said defiantly.

The man sheathed his sword, amusement in his voice. "You already have."

Nearly faster than the boy could see, the man reached down and grasped his loose cotton shirt. With one hand he lifted the boy off the ground and placed him in front of him on the horse.

Derek was still on the ground on his knees so the man spoke to his second-in-command. "Make sure the woman and the girl receive safe passage to their village."

Without another word, he whirled his horse around and kicked it into a sprint.

The boy was forced to cling to the man, otherwise he was going to get a much closer look of the ground racing by beneath him. The horse covered the distance to the forest quickly and they raced through the trees at what seemed a dangerous speed. But the man controlled his horse effortlessly and finally brought the panting beast to a halt in a small clearing. The boy struggled and the man dropped him to the ground with a thud. He dismounted his horse and tied the reins to a nearby branch.

The boy sprang to his feet, eyeing the man suspiciously. But the man walked away from him and settled on a boulder, his long limbs crossed in front of him. "Come here," he commanded.

The boy squared his shoulders as if to resist but for some reason, the man's voice was compelling. He hesitated, then reluctantly moved within arms reach of the seated man.

The man grasped his shoulders, squeezing them. He examined the boy closely and the boy was uncomfortable under the intense scrutiny. The man's eye was again caught by the bloodstain on the boy's shirt, which he seemed fascinated by. The boy pulled away from him.

"You are well-formed. I am pleased."

The man's voice was deep and had a mesmerizing quality to it. But the boy had no idea what the words meant and wondered if he was about to be sold into slavery.

The man abruptly stood as if in some great internal struggle. "If only you weren't so young."

The boy stood there, feeling a strange sense of failure at his youth. He had no idea why he might want to please this man, nor why his youth should be the source of displeasure.

The man paced about, then returned to his boulder. "Come here," he commanded once more.

The boy obeyed the command but this time the man turned him bodily about and pulled him to the rock in front of him.

The boy sat stiffly, his back pressed against the man's chest. The man brushed his blond hair away from the nape of his neck. "I won't hurt you," he promised, his voice suddenly intoxicating in the boy's ear.

But the man lied because the pain did come, and it was intense. But it did not come where he expected as something sliced into his neck. The boy could not struggle in the man's iron embrace and his arms were pinned to his side.

The boy's vision began to swim and he felt light-headed. He stopped struggling and leaned back against the man, no longer feeling the pain. The feeling now was not entirely unpleasant.

The man held him for awhile longer, then violently pushed him away. He himself staggered to his feet. "I must stop. You are too young."

The boy lay on the ground, feeling the ache in the side of his neck. He did not know what the man had done to him, nor what was causing the man's intense, internal struggle. He began to drift in and out of consciousness. He had the impression the man sat him up and placed something to his lips, water, perhaps.

His next memory was of being upside down on the horse, jostled from side-to-side as the horse trotted into his village. He had an inverted view of his hut just prior to being dumped unceremoniously on the ground. After that, he remembered nothing.

Susan would not leave the woman. She had been sitting in front of the window for well over 12 hours, now. During that 12 hours, the right side of the woman's face had almost completely healed. All outward signs of her ordeal had disappeared. She had even lost the preternatural paleness in evidence earlier; her skin now glowed with health.

The sheet continued its slow rise and fall. Respirations were approximately 10 per minute, slow for an adult, but reasonable. Heart rate hovered around 40 beats per minute; again, extremely low for an adult but possible for a well-conditioned athlete in deep sleep.

Susan studied the woman's face. Now that it was whole, the high cheekbones, the full mouth, the slender nose all lent themselves to the striking beauty she and Mason had speculated on earlier. The woman truly had the face of a sleeping angel.

Susan crossed her arms on the console in front of her and rested her head. Her eyes drifted closed.

The boy recovered from his ordeal, as he had done before. But this time he seemed to be left with a craving, a hunger for something that wasn't food.

He could not explain it but the mundane life of the village began to chafe at him. The restlessness he felt invaded his entire world, and he realized how small that world was.

He thought about the Man often, but his questions to his mother were met with mute silence. This silence only added to his frustration, a frustration that finally culminated in his decision to leave the village.

He did not know why, but he did not wish to tell his parents he was leaving. He said nothing but made his plans in secret. Then, one moonless night, he packed everything he owned in his bag, took the horse, and set out in the general direction of the brightest star in the night sky.

CHAPTER 11

WEEKS PASSED, PERHAPS MONTHS. THE BOY TRAVELED FROM village to village, exploring the smallest part of a world he had not known existed. On this cool afternoon he saw smoke from one such village from a distance. He kneed his horse and the beast started in that direction.

His entrance into the town caused little interest; everyone seemed to be drawn to a commotion down the street. He tied his horse to a post and went to see what everyone was looking at.

A woman, blood running from a cut on her temple and a bruise on her cheek, staggered in the center of the throng. A man, evidently her attacker, kicked her again and she went to her knees.

"You adulteress!" The man shouted, kicking her again.

"Liar!" The woman screamed. She struggled to her feet. "Is there no one who'll stand witness for me?"

The woman was met with taunts and raucous laughter. Men and women threw clods of dirt at her in response. She struggled to protect herself from the missiles, but could not escape the man's meaty fist as he struck her in the side of the head. She moved out of his range, pleading with the crowd.

"Won't someone speak for me?"

When she was still met with nothing more than taunts, she pulled a bag of coin from her cloak. "I have coin!"

The crowd grew silent. It was common to challenge the veracity of witnesses by challenging them to combat. Mercenaries made good money selling themselves as champions of truth. One could literally buy one's innocence, if only someone would fight for them.

No one seemed inclined to accept the woman's offer. The man snatched the bag from her hand and threw it in the dust. "No one wants your sinful money, you adulteress bitch."

"How much money is it?" the boy asked, stepping from the crowd.

There was a murmur from the townsfolk at the cloaked stranger. It turned to laughter when the boy pulled his hood down.

The woman eyed the beautiful youth uncertainly. He was small, but he had been the only one to speak up. She picked up the bag of coin and handed it to him. He hefted the bag, then handed it back to her.

"I will speak for you."

The crowd was now in high spirits. This was great drama, all the better because it would include violence and death, and probably humiliation.

The man spat contemptuously, barely missing the boy. "Choose your weapon, boy. I have no patience for these games. I'm going to kill you, then I'm going to kill my unfaithful bitch of a wife, and then I'm going to take her money and buy much drink to celebrate with."

This declaration brought loud cheers from the crowd. The man threw off his cloak, revealing a barrel chest and thickly muscled torso. The boy inwardly sighed. He carefully removed his own cloak, neatly folded it and set it in the dust. A man moved from the crowd and kicked the garment into disarray.

The boy removed a small dagger from his waist. It was the only weapon he had, and the only one his father had taught him to use. The barrel-chested man laughed loudly at the weapon. "You challenge me with that? It delivers only a little prick."

The crowd laughed at the joke, but the boy cut the laughter short with his terse reply.

"You should know. Perhaps that's why your wife's eye wanders."

The man turned crimson as the crowd laughed even more at his expense. He drew his own dagger and stood ready. "Come on, boy," he growled, "I'll cut that sharp tongue of yours."

"Not likely with so dull a wit."

The man's face appeared apoplectic and he charged. The boy easily sidestepped him and he went barreling into the crowd, which caught him and pushed him back into the clearing.

The boy watched the man warily. He was large and strong, but he was clumsy and slow. He charged again and the boy easily sidestepped once more, this time snaking the knife outward and drawing blood from the man's side.

The man howled in fury and pain as the crowd laughed. The boy stood staring at the blood pouring from the man's side. It made him feel lightheaded and strange, as if his body was suddenly weightless. He stood rooted as the man charged him.

It appeared to the crowd the boy was frozen in terror. They leaned forward expectantly, awaiting his comeuppance. The barrel-chested man charged forward, screaming obscenities at him.

The boy felt as if he were moving in slow motion. Indeed, his movements appeared almost languid to the mob as he gracefully side-stepped once more, this time slashing out and upward at the man's throat.

The big man stopped abruptly, clutching the suddenly gaping wound on his neck. Blood spurted between his fingers as he crumpled to his knees, then went facedown into the dirt.

Loud cheers erupted from the crowd and the boy was surrounded by congratulatory men and women who pounded him on the back. The woman he had spoken for pushed through the crowd and they all stepped back, creating a small clearing.

"Here you are, boy." She held the small purse above her head and eyed the crowd. "Let it be known I am innocent of all charges!"

"Yeah right, Gert, until next time!" someone yelled from the crowd. This comment was greeted by much laughter and the woman herself cackled as she handed the purse to the boy. She winked at him and smiled a toothless smile. "Perhaps a lad as handsome as you would like a greater reward."

The boy took the purse and simply nodded to the crone, then pushed his way through the crowd. It appeared Gert was immediately forgiven because everyone knew the Lord worked in mysterious ways. She went off to drink with her accusers-turned-exculpators.

The boy went to the stalls in the small marketplace to buy supplies. He eyed some fresh bread and was just about to make an offer when he noticed the proprietor.

The man was short and completely bald, but that was not what attracted the boy's attention. The boy was staring at the stump where the man's right hand used to be. The man was trying to hide it within his clothing, but the knob protruded. The boy glanced back up into the man's eyes. He knew dismemberment was often the punishment for perjury; obviously this man had no one to fight for him, or the champion he had chosen had lost.

The boy looked back down at the bread. That was probably why the man had so much fresh bread. People were horrified by any type of deformity. Those unlucky enough to be deformed or dismembered were often killed; at the very least they were shunned.

The boy did not share this horror, but he was not above taking advantage of it. He offered the man but a few pence for the lot, knowing the man had little choice but to take it.

CHAPTER 12

Susan thumbed through various charts, glancing at the woman through the glass. She had found so many unique things about her anatomy that just about any randomly performed test would yield a surprise.

"Mommy, what are you doing?"

Susan glanced over at her red-haired son patiently. She felt so guilty about being away from him on the weekend that when he asked to come to work with her, she consented after only a little cajoling. She packed a bag full of toys and books and brought them to the lab with her. He had spent the last few hours alternately napping, playing, reading, and asking her what she was doing.

"I'm trying to find this woman's digestive system."

Jason wrinkled his brow. "Oh," he said thoughtfully, "She's pretty."

Susan glanced at her son fondly as he returned to his blocks. He had a 5 year-old's gift of understatement. She glanced at the woman sleeping peacefully in the other room. She was strikingly beautiful. Susan turned her attention back to the documentation of the woman's internal anatomy.

Although she could find little that was identifiable in the digestive system, the renal system was remarkably similar to what it should be. Both kidneys were functioning, although they did not appear to be doing what normal kidneys did.

To Susan's knowledge, the woman had absorbed no nutrients from the feeding tube and therefore elimination had not been necessary. Beyond the fact that Susan had no idea how the woman survived without eating or eliminating waste, she could not decipher exactly what the kidneys were doing.

Until she had glanced at the charts in front of her. The levels of erythropoietin were sky-high in the woman's kidneys. Erythropoietin was a substance synthesized by the kidneys to increase red blood cell production in bone marrow. This rather pronounced increase of red blood cells would boost endurance by promoting elevated oxygen delivery to muscles. It was the theory behind "blood doping" which athletes often attempted to increase performance.

The problem was that the level in the woman's body should have created too many blood cells. She should have "polycythemia vera," or in layman's terms, blood the consistency of glue. Susan glanced at the sleeping woman. Her blood should be too thick to supply oxygen delivery and thick enough to at least cause a stroke, if not death.

But instead, she just slept peacefully on.

Susan sighed and sat down.

Susan glanced at the EEG. It was the same pattern as always; the only difference was the degree. The glowing line traced out alpha waves, signaling alertness. Susan glanced in at the woman, who appeared asleep as always. Rarely did theta waves show up on the monitor, and never beta waves. Susan sat down heavily. What she wouldn't give to know what was going on in that woman's head.

It was nearly three years before the boy returned to his village. He was taller, though still slender, and he had been hardened by the life he had led. His sword had been instrumental in many battles, and although he was but 18 years old, he was proclaimed a man among men.

He was dusty and tired, and his horse was thirsty. Judging by the position of the sun, his village should be another hours ride.

He stopped at a stream and allowed his horse to drink. He waded into the water, fully clothed, and doused himself. He remounted his horse and continued on his way.

Although his senses were always keen, perhaps it was the stench of battle still in his nostrils that at first caused the scent of smoke and death to elude him. The smell finally intruded upon his awareness, and a look of concern crossed his features. He kicked his horse into a gallop.

He topped the rise above his village, but the familiar sight of the huts was not what greeted him. Instead, he was welcomed by burned out hulks and smoldering ashes. His jaw clenched, he rode slowly down into his home. He had not missed this act by more than a day.

Bodies were strewn amongst the wreckage, and although he had seen carnage in battle, none of it affected him the way this did. He moved to where his hut had stood, and although he did not recognize the burned corpses, he knew them to be his mother and father.

The cry of a nearby winged scavenger attracted his gaze and he dismounted and chased the bird away. The body the bird was attempting to feed off was that of a young woman. It took the boy a moment to recognize the young girl he had saved from the priest seasons ago. Her body was not burned, but she had been run through with a sword. Judging by the blood between her legs, she had been run through by more than a sword before dying. The boy clenched his jaw tighter.

The sun was nearly setting by the time the boy finished. He buried the young girl; everything else he burned to the ground. His fatigue left him, replaced by an icy coldness much stranger than the fierce anger he felt in battle.

He examined the immediate area. It was not difficult to find the trail of the men who had committed this act; no one in the village owned horses. He started out in the black of night, following a sparse trail that seemed as clear as day to him.

The sun rose and set twice more before the boy caught up with the men. He had not slept and did not feel the need to. It was early morning and the men were breaking camp as the boy peered at them from the bushes. Their laughter increased the coldness inside of him.

He recognized one of the men. It was the one called Derek who had tried to kill him when the Man had stepped in and taken him away. The boy knew he had found the band that had destroyed his village.

As a soldier, he had learned to count the number of the enemy. He counted twelve now. One man approached the underbrush near the boy and began to relieve himself. The boy slipped up silently behind the man, placed his hand over the man's mouth and then slit his throat from ear-to-ear with his short sword. He quietly lowered the dead man to the ground.

The boy worked his way through the brush to the horses. One man was tending them. He moved silently behind the man and again slit his throat. His killing was so efficient the horses barely stirred.

The boy returned to his own horse and removed the longbow he had stored there. He strapped the quiver of arrows to his back and returned to the clearing. No one seemed to notice the two missing men.

The boy scaled a tree so he had a clear view of the encampment. He thought he could get off two, maybe three arrows before the alarm was sounded. He would try and pick off as many of the band as possible, then chase them down as they fled in the confusion.

The boy braced his back against the tree. It took tremendous strength to draw the string on his bow, but it seemed effortless to him. He closed one eye, and aimed for two men standing closely together.

The arrow sped through the air, making its distinctive flitting noise. It flew true and with such force that, not only did it pierce the first man, it continued forward and impaled the second man. The two soldiers were pinned chests to chest, forced to look into the dying eyes of one another with little more than confusion on their faces.

The boy was already fitting another arrow to the bow, and as the men tried to make sense of the sudden, deadly embrace of their comrades, another fell, his chest exploding into crimson before his eyes.

Instinct kicked in as the men began to run for cover, trying to identify their assailants. But the boy was fitting another deadly missile and another fell before he could reach cover.

The boy slid down the trunk of the tree, knowing the men would run for their horses. He was there before them, and another arrow flew, knocking a man from the horse he had just mounted. This spooked the horses as they began to run away.

The boy gave a fierce cry and charged, his sword drawn. The man nearest him was so startled he could barely get his sword from his sheath. It did him no good as the boy knocked the sword from his hand and ran the man through.

Three of the men ran in terror, disappearing into the forest. The boy let them go, his eyes searching for the one called Derek. Another man charged him and the boy blocked his sword thrust, locking the two hilts together. He pulled the man's own dagger from his belt and thrust it into his stomach. He crumpled to the ground.

The boy sensed a presence behind him and instinctively ducked. The sword whistled through the air above his head. He head-butted the figure behind him and it stumbled backward.

Derek was furious. "You arrogant little bastard. I should have known it was you, hiding in the forest like a coward."

The boy was also furious. "Oh, and was it so manly to attack a defenseless village?"

Derek smiled cruelly. "Yes, we did accomplish some manly deeds there."

The boy remembered the body of the young girl and attacked in fury. Derek parried the boy's blows, but not easily. It was obvious he was astounded by the boy's strength, which appeared to anger him even further.

"Victor believes you to be special, but I don't think so."

The boy smashed his sword down. "I have no idea what you're talking about," he said through clenched teeth, "Nor do I care."

The boy smashed Derek's sword out of his hand and in a tremendous blast of fury, drove his sword into his midsection clear to the hilt. Disbelief was on Derek's face as he sunk to his knees, grasping the hilt of the sword.

The boy stared down at Derek, his fury unabated. He didn't want to simply kill Derek; he wanted to utterly destroy him.

Derek coughed blood, still clutching the sword handle. He had difficulty speaking, but he choked out his last words.

"It doesn't matter, boy. It doesn't matter." Derek coughed again, and this time the blood came up black. He looked up and the boy saw a deep bitterness in Derek's eyes. "Hell will wait for you, anyway."

Derek died.

The unexplainable bitterness Derek held for him and his strange last words finally cooled the boy's fury. He pulled his sword from the dead man and wiped it on his tunic. He resheathed it and staggered back to his horse.

His fatigue finally overcame him. He pulled himself onto his horse and laid down on the beast's neck. The animal sensed its master's exhaustion, and quietly picked its way through the forest.

The boy was shaken awake and sat upright on his horse. A rosy-cheeked farmer was gently pulling on his leg.

"Are you all right, boy?"

The boy nodded, trying to shake his exhaustion. It was no use and he nearly fell off his horse. The farmer caught him halfway down. The farmer was joined by his equally rosy-cheeked wife, who helped the boy to their wagon.

"Would you be wanting a ride for a ways?"

The boy had a natural distrust of anyone who would do a good deed without compensation, but his exhaustion was too great. He nodded dumbly, not even bothering to ask where the two were going. It no longer mattered to him.

The farmer tied the boy's horse to the rear of the wagon, and the horse began to happily munch on the hay there. The farmer's wife helped the lad into the bed of the wagon, and he collapsed into the heap of warm hay. The farmer's wife clucked to herself and covered him with a heavy wool blanket. The boy was too tired even to thank her, and collapsed into a deep and dreamless sleep.

The Man watched the cart pull into his courtyard. The heavy gate clanged closed behind it. He moved down the steps to greet the farmer and his wife, nodding his thanks. He glanced into the rear of the cart, knowing what was there before he did so.

The figure was sprawled in the hay, only the tousled hair peaking out from underneath the blanket the farmer's wife had laid upon it.

Soldiers stepped forward to assist but he waved them back. Effortlessly, he lifted the figure from the hay and much to the surprise of everyone present, carried the figure himself. All watched in silence as the dark-haired man carried the prone figure in his arms, across the courtyard, then all the way up the stone stairs.

He laid the figure down on the hard bed amongst the soft coverlets. The figure stirred but did not waken. He nodded to the nursemaid who had followed him into the room.

"This is your new charge. A hot bath and clean clothes will make a good start."

The nurse eyed the prone figure. "Is the boy ill? Will he awaken soon?"

The man smiled. "The 'boy' is not ill, but sleep will not release this one anytime soon."

The nursemaid nodded and the man left for an adjoining room. A brief time passed, and he was not surprised to hear screams echo down the stone hallways. She came rushing into his room.

"My lord, you must come quickly. The boy has suffered some grievous injury!"

The man smiled, not the least bit perturbed by her hysteria. "And what type of injury would that be?"

The woman swallowed hard. This would be difficult. "I'm afraid he's lost his manhood, my lord."

The man shook his head. It continually amazed him that this people would accept the extraordinary over the obvious. "Miriam, he has not lost his manhood, because 'he' is not a 'he'."

Understanding was slow to dawn on Miriam. She had to repeat his lordship's words several times silently to herself before she realized what he was saying.

Victor nodded when he was certain she understood his meaning, but he wanted to clarify it just in case. "I am quite aware the boy in the next room is not a boy, but a girl. Her name is Rhian. Now, please continue your care for her."

Susan awoke, her head on the console in front of her. She panicked for a moment, thinking she had forgotten Jason, then remembered that Neda had picked him up hours ago. She stared groggily at the clock, mentally ticking away the hours she had been asleep. She glanced through the window at the prone figure. She might as well have gone home.

She left her lab, nodding to a security guard who was making his rounds in the hallway. She plucked self-consciously at her hair, wondering what it looked like after her lengthy nap. She went into the women's lounge and washed her face. The hair was not as bad as she expected.

She dried her hands and tossed the paper towel into the trash. She walked the length of the hallway a few times to get the blood flowing, then ran her security card through the reader and re-entered the lab.

The control booth door whispered closed behind her as she sat down heavily in her chair. She leaned forward to pick up her glass of water, an act she would not complete.

Her hand hovered in the air, grasping a phantom glass of water, its image reflected in the glass separating the console room from the sterile room. But it was not the reflection of her hand that Susan Ryerson was staring at, but rather what was in the room beyond it.

The woman was standing upright, naked, facing away from the window. She was easily six feet tall with broad shoulders and a muscular back. The back tapered to a slim waist and slim hips in an almost boyish figure. It was easily one of the most beautiful physiques Susan Ryerson had ever seen.

The woman moved with a lithe, animal-like grace and seemed unconcerned with her nudity. She gazed down at the EKG with mild interest, then removed the electrodes from her torso and draped them over the machine.

The woman turned and for the first time Susan looked into her eyes. They were an indeterminate color and harbored a look of devilish amusement. Susan felt her heart begin to pound violently. It seemed almost as if the woman could sense this because her amusement increased.

Susan froze as the figure began to come toward her. The woman covered the distance in a few strides and leaped. Susan ducked as the human projectile came hurtling through the window. Susan sprawled onto the floor to escape the spray of glass. Shards flew everywhere as the woman landed in a graceful crouch.

The woman stood upright, no injury apparent from her violent exit. With little more than a glance down at Susan, she began moving toward the door. She was halfway there when the MRI image of herself on the wall caught her eye. She paused, examining the picture with obvious interest. She then shrugged, the gesture more of an impression than a physical act, and was gone.

Susan stared up in shock from her position on the floor. It took her a moment to regain her senses and scramble to her feet. She slipped on the glass fragments, struggling for balance, then ran to the door.

The hallway was empty.

She ran to the elevator, but the lights indicated it was motionless on another floor. She ran to the end of the hallway, but there was no sign of the woman. She ran to the other end and it, too, was empty.

There was nowhere the woman could have gone, and yet she had disappeared.

Susan walked slowly back into her lab. She surveyed the damage to the observation cubicle in a daze.

How could she just disappear? How could a patient in a pronounced vegetative state with life-threatening injuries just get up, smash through two inches of glass, and then just disappear?

Susan turned back toward the hallway, as if to find reason there. It seemed impossible that no alarm had been sounded, that no one had spotted a nude, six-foot woman fleeing on-foot from her research lab.

Susan turned back to the carnage in front of her. The ultimate medical find of her lifetime just smashed its way out of the equivalent of a maximum-security wing. She stared at the smashed glass, at the MRI image, at the computer that blinked at her. She had no idea what to do.

The security guard wandered down the hallway. He thought he heard a noise ahead of him, but as he peered into the darkness, he saw nothing. He walked beneath low hanging pipes and ducked out of habit, even though he was not tall enough to strike his head.

The woman was a study of concentration, balanced on the pipes above the security guard's head. Her body was stretched out to its full length and appeared to almost levitate in the air, supported only by her grip on the pipes beneath her. Her forearms were corded and the strain on the shoulder muscles was obvious, but her face was serene. Once certain the man was gone, she swung down from the pipes, landing like a jungle cat.

In an instant, she was through the service entrance and gone.

The Mercedes convertible was exactly where she had left it. She glanced upward at the skyscraper she had leaped out of weeks earlier. The top floor was scaffolded and boarded shut, the signs of fire damage still evident.

The woman shrugged and leaned down to remove the soft, protective cover on the car. She punched in a security code on the door lock. Once inside the vehicle, she pulled the ignition key from the glove box and fired the engine to life.

As the engine warmed, she pressed a button and the convertible top smoothly retracted into the rear of the vehicle. Even though it was completely dark, she removed a pair of sunglasses from the glove box and put them on. She leaned forward and thoughtfully selected a song on the CD player, then put the car in gear and pulled smoothly away from the curb. The convertible's tires made crunching noises in the newly fallen snow.

Susan slumped down onto her Queen Anne sofa. She was not normally one to slump, but the three glasses of wine she had consumed aided her in her lack of decorum.

Her thoughts were no clearer for the wine, but they had been so unclear to begin with she didn't see the harm.

The woman was gone. The patient who could not possibly be alive had gotten up, smashed through a two-inch thick glass window, and then just disappeared. The woman with the internal anatomy and blood profile of something from another planet had just casually exited both her hospital and her life.

Susan sighed, eyeing the remaining wine in the bottle. Mr. Earl circled her uncertainly, sensing her distress. He finally determined she needed him and leaped up onto her lap, purring. Susan stroked the cat, settling for the softness of his fur over the draw of the remaining wine, her thoughts distant from both.

She heard a commotion at the front door and then Jason came tearing around the corner. He was in mid-leap when he saw the glass of wine she was holding. He came to a screeching halt.

"Mom," he said with disapproval, "You're not supposed to have juice on the couch."

Susan suppressed a smile as Neda rounded the corner behind him. The matron took in the wineglass and nearly empty wine bottle. "Here," the older woman said, grasping the wine glass, "I'll take that."

With her hands free, Susan pulled Jason onto her lap. She hugged him tightly, wishing his warmth could wash away the disappointment and confusion inside her. Neda glanced at the few remaining drops in the wine bottle, then went to boil some coffee. It was not like the young doctor to drink in the middle of the afternoon.

Jason sensed her distress as well. "What's wrong, mom?"

Susan sighed, "Oh, nothing, munchkin. I just had a long day at work."

Jason's countenance suddenly darkened. "The lady didn't die, did she?"

Neda froze in the doorway at the young boy's words, and Susan quickly responded. "Oh no. She didn't die." She stopped. Her inebriation made her want to disclose more than she normally would and she could not hide her disbelief. "She just left."

Jason wrinkled his brow, but decided this was an appropriate outcome. He was still somewhat concerned. "Oh, okay. So she was all right then?"

Susan could picture the woman standing upright in the lab, her physique rivaled only by that of Michelangelo's David. "Oh, I think she was quite all right."

Neda listened quietly in the doorway. By the young doctor's tone of voice, it was evident there was much she was not saying. She hurried to make the coffee.

CHAPTER 13

Susan stepped from her car door, wincing at the bite of the cold. It had been three months since the first snow of the season, and the weather had been frigid ever since. She shut the car door behind her and began moving carefully up the slippery walk towards the hospital doors. Although her proximity to the emergency room would lessen the danger of a fall, it would not make it any less painful, nor any less embarrassing.

Susan's attention drifted away from her struggle to negotiate the slushy terrain. Three months, she thought to herself, three months since the golden-haired woman had disappeared. Ninety days, during which Susan Ryersons's career had changed forever. The hospital doors slid open silently upon her approach and she entered the building with a heavy sigh.

She walked down the hallway of the hospital, her focus on the elevator ahead of her. Safe passage was denied, however, when Stanley Meyers, the hospital's chief administrator, stepped into her path.

"Susan," he said, attempting to convey warmth, "Let me be the first to offer my congratulations."

The attempt to convey warmth was not entirely successful, but Susan smiled politely and grasped his hand anyway. "Thank you, Stanley, I appreciate your support."

Stanley nodded. "I've always been in your corner, Susan." He leaned forward, giving the impression of shared confidence. "Even a few months back when accounting was in an uproar over some of your 'expenditures,' I told them to give you free reign. And look what it brought me."

Susan smiled politely, removing her hand from his. She highly doubted this version of events, but accepted it anyway. He stepped back, beaming. "You won't believe the number of phone calls we've received since your publication."

Susan nodded. "I can only imagine."

Stanley leaned closer, lowering his voice in confidence. "Of course, they all want to know how you did it. But you were smart not to publish that portion of your research. Can't let everyone know our secrets, eh?"

Susan nodded uncomfortably and Stanley continued. "I think 'Newsweek' magazine will be running a story on your discovery. This may be one of those medical stories that make the jump from medical journal to popular press. And we all know what that means."

Susan nodded, her discomfort now overwhelming. Yes, that meant big money for the hospital. She extricated herself from Stanley Meyers and continued on to the elevator under his beaming gaze. Her focus on escape caused her to miss David Goldstein's baleful eye, who watched the exchange from the gift shop.

Once in her lab she shut the door quickly behind her, leaning against it as if to shut out the outside world. She had never felt like such a fraud.

Three months ago, after the woman had disappeared, Susan had been at a loss. She had no direction or inspiration in her work and was nearly in despair when she finally decided to continue her analysis on the woman's remaining blood samples.

The implications of the chemical make-up of the blood had been too much to resist. Longevity, immunity, strength, energy, all would be affected by the chemical "imbalances" that existed in the woman's system. Susan would never publish anything about the woman's anatomy because it was too unbelievable, not to mention she had no proof. But the possibilities within the blood sample were irresistible.

Susan had never stated in the peer-reviewed journal article that she had balanced the L-gulonolactone enzyme within the blood, but of course everyone assumed she had. As Stanley had so aptly put it, it was expected for her to hide the details of her methodology. The biotechnical community was already salivating at the prospect of genetic engineering that would allow humans to produce their own Vitamin C. No researcher in her right mind would publish the process describing how to do so.

Susan moved into the console room. But she hadn't designed a process; she had simply described what had been in the woman's system, and only a very small part of it at that. Susan tried to rationalize her actions, to tell herself that the potential benefits to humankind far outweighed any procedural ambiguity in the article.

But the rationalization weighed heavily on Susan as she gazed through the replacement window into the sterile, empty room. She wondered uneasily if she were not selling her soul to the devil, one small piece at a time.

Susan glanced in on Jason, who was sleeping soundly. She smiled at the sight of his redhead cushioned on the flannel pillowcase, marveling at the sleep of the innocent.

She shuffled down the stairs, debating whether to have the cold chicken in the refrigerator. Neda had cooked dinner for them earlier, then left for the evening. The leftovers were now calling her name.

Susan walked into the kitchen. It was dark, but the light from the full moon shown through the window. She opened the refrigerator door and the interior light provided more illumination. She began to peruse the contents. There was fried chicken, potato salad, a slice of chocolate cake...

Susan settled for her original thought, the fried chicken. She pulled the foil-wrapped plate from the shelf and set in the cabinet next to her. She closed the refrigerator door, turning as she did so....

And walked full into a large, immovable object.

Susan screamed and tried to step back, but her arm was encased in steel. She started to scream a second time but choked it back as her thoughts flew to Jason. She did not want to wake him.

So great was the strength of her attacker that not only could Susan not escape, she could not even move. The power of the person holding her was inhuman, and she could not push or pull her arm even a fraction of an inch. The force generated by the grip and the unwavering balance of the person maintaining that grip was uncanny, so strange that Susan actually stopped struggling.

The golden-haired woman stepped into the light, maintaining her effortless grasp on Susan's arm. Her face was impassive as she stared down at Susan. With a measured gaze, she slowly released her grip.

Susan stared up at the woman, disbelief evident on her features. She was so stunned she would not have been able to flee had she wanted to. Her arm fell heavily to her side.

"You," the woman said, nodding at the kitchen table, "Have made a terrible mistake."

The woman's voice was melodious, strange. Far too old and polished for the youthful face it represented. It took a moment for her words to register, and Susan turned to see what the woman indicated when she spoke.

The medical journal with her most recent publication was lying on the table. Susan felt a wave of guilt wash over her. The fact that this woman had broken into her house and accosted her became secondary to defending her integrity.

"I never said I created the process," Susan began defensively, "I was simply explaining what I found. If people-"

"No," the woman interrupted softly, amused, "You don't understand." There was the faintest trace of ridicule in her voice. "I care nothing for your findings, or the ethics of your publishing." The woman paused, glancing around the room. Her gaze returned to Susan. "You have placed yourself in great danger."

Susan caught her breath and took a step backward. As if in response, the woman glanced upward at the ceiling, then back at Susan. "You have a child in the house, do you not?"

Susan still was not breathing as the woman murmured, almost to herself, "I can hear his heartbeat."

Susan turned to run, but no sooner had she made the decision, then the woman was in front of her, looking down.

"I will not harm you," she said.

Susan's own heartbeat was so loud now she was sure the woman could hear it. There was no way humanly possible the woman could have moved so quickly. Susan tried to still the tremble in her voice. "But you just said I was in great danger."

The woman shook her head. "Not from me." The woman turned, as if she were unconcerned at Susan's attempt to escape. Susan debated a second attempt, but the woman was now between her and the staircase. She would not leave Jason.

The woman kneeled to look at an antique rocker. "I used to have one of these," she said absently. She glanced around the room with interest, then stood upright once more. Her tone changed from conversational to deadly serious as she turned her full attention on Susan.

"There are others like me," the woman said. "They will know you've studied one of their Kind, and they'll come for you."

"What are you talking about?" Susan asked fearfully. "What do you mean, 'others like you'?"

The woman smiled, a smile revealing no teeth. "You studied enough of my body to at least partially understand my words, Dr. Ryerson. I have no inclination to stand here and try to convince you of their truth. The fact of the matter is, you have placed your life and the life of your son in danger. And," she added, as if this were an even greater consequence, "You have inconvenienced me."

Susan was flabbergasted, momentarily speechless at the woman's arrogance. The woman took this silence as acceptance of blame, and turned to leave.

"Wait a minute," Susan said, her anger finally overcoming her fear, "You can't just break into my house, threaten me, then just walk away. I'm calling the police."

The sudden coldness in the woman's eyes stopped Susan dead in her tracks. Her face took on a strange expression: aloof, dispassionate, predatory. It was completely incongruent with her youthful beauty, yet somehow fit perfectly on her features.

"Dr. Ryerson," the woman said patiently, as if addressing a child, "You will find I can and will do anything I want."

And with that, she was gone.

The outer gates opened silently inward to admit the Mercedes convertible. An invisible guard stared through darkly tinted windows from within the guard shack. He nodded deferentially, although he could hardly be seen through the blacked-out windows at night.

The car pulled smoothly up the long driveway lined with maple trees. Hidden cameras whirred quietly as they tracked the vehicle's approach. The car whispered to a stop in front of a marble staircase that led upward into the brightly lit mansion. No sooner had the vehicle come to a stop then a man in uniform appeared seemingly out of thin air to open the driver's door. The golden-haired woman stepped from the car, paying little attention to the servant who bowed to her. Her disinterest was not interpreted as disrespect, but rather as expected. Indeed, the man would have been shocked and perhaps a little afraid had the woman showed him any attention at all.

She moved gracefully up the steps and had no sooner reached the top when the front doors whispered outward as if on command. Without breaking stride she stepped into the huge foyer. The butler in the doorway kept his head bowed deferentially until she passed, then closed the doors behind her. A young man in black pants and a starched white shirt stepped forward to offer her service, but she waved him off, barely slowing. She walked into the den, a dark-paneled room lined with shelves and thousands of books from floor to ceiling. She picked up some mail from the desk, her back to the shadows.

"What news, Edward?" she said casually over her shoulder

The older man stepped from the shadows. He knew she was aware of his presence, but would not have stepped forth until she acknowledged him. His patrician features were expressionless as he answered her query.

"Nothing yet," he replied in a clipped, British accent. He set a copy of a popular newsmagazine in front of her. "But now it's only a matter of time."

The woman glanced at the magazine, feigning unconcern, but Edward knew her too well. "Yes," she said calmly, "This could cause complications."

The golden-haired one sprawled in the chair and Edward moved to the front of the desk. He chose his words carefully.

"My lord," he began, "Have you considered the possibility of simply killing Dr. Ryerson?"

Neither the startling suggestion nor the odd, incongruent title that preceded it seemed to draw her attention. She stared at the magazine in front of her.

"I have considered that option," she replied calmly, using the same dispassionate tone he used. She looked up at him. "And what of her boy?"

The thought of orphaning the boy apparently did not faze Edward. "He would be cared for the rest of his life. It is a small price to pay."

The young woman was silent for a long moment. When she glanced up at the older man, her words were many-layered.

"Then the boy would have no mother."

This momentarily brought the valet to silence. Only his great concern for his master caused him to continue.

"You could bring Dr. Ryerson and her son here, where they would be safe."

The woman now gazed at him with amusement. "And imprison her? I hardly think that's an acceptable solution, either. No," she said, lifting the magazine then replacing it on the desk, "I think perhaps we will just wait for now. What comes," she said fatalistically, "Will come."

Edward inwardly sighed. He would not argue with her, indeed, could never even bring himself to cross her. But as he stood with a distant look in his eyes, his senses straining the night, he knew that no good would come of this situation.

CHAPTER 14

JASON PRESSED HIS FACE AGAINST THE WINDOW OF THE PET store in the mall. Tiny puppies frolicked in the warm hay and he desperately wanted to hold them. The shopkeeper peered out the window at the youngster, sensing his desire. He motioned Jason in.

Jason looked over at his mom who had taken a seat nearby. Susan waved him on and he disappeared inside. She could see him from where she sat, and smiled when the wriggling puppy covered his freckled face with kisses.

The smile did not remain on her face long, however, and her gloomy thoughts returned.

Susan had not told anyone about the woman's break-in. Indeed, the incident seemed so unreal to her that she considered the possibility she had dreamed it. But she could not maintain that illusion for very long; she knew it had happened.

There were so many things about the incident that baffled Susan. How had the woman gotten into her house? Why? How had she moved so quickly? How could she be so strong? What did her strange warning mean?

Susan rubbed her wrist, feeling the woman's vise-like grip even now. The incident terrified her, yet curiosity was beginning to compete with that terror. The woman could have hurt her if she wished, probably even killed her. Yet beyond bruising her wrist to keep her from fleeing, she had not harmed Susan. She had not broken anything, nor had she stolen anything.

She had simply appeared out of nowhere, issued her warning, then disappeared.

Susan thought about the woman's words. The woman was aware of the journal article, but was not upset that Susan had performed research on her without her consent. Nor did she seem disturbed by the fact that Susan was receiving credit for the findings. She was concerned only with the "danger" that Susan had allegedly brought upon herself. And based upon her statement of her own "inconvenience" outweighing that danger, it did not seem the woman was greatly disturbed by even that.

"Can we get a dog, mom?"

Jason's voice intruded into her thoughts. Susan stared at her son, brushing the thoughts away. She was nearly moved by the longing in her son's voice. She stiffened her resolve, however, and shook her head. "You know we don't have any room, Jason. We don't even have a backyard."

Jason turned as if to reason with his mother. "It could live in the house. It could live in my room with me. I'll take care of it."

Susan smiled at her son's attempt at persuasion.

"They're clever at that age, aren't they?

Susan turned at the voice. She had been so engrossed in her thoughts she hadn't noticed the figure that now sat next to her. Surprising, since he was extremely handsome.

"Yes," she replied, trying not to stare at him, "They certainly are."

The man turned to her and smiled and Susan felt her heart flutter. He was probably ten years younger than she was but that didn't seem to matter at the moment. He stood, straightening his pants, then nodded to her, "Have a nice day."

Susan watched the young man's retreating back, disappointed at his abrupt departure. She thought it odd he had initiated so brief a conversation and wondered how long he had been sitting there. She shrugged and reached down to grasp Jason's hand.

"Come on, kiddo, maybe next time."

Jason immediately brightened at the thought. "For real, mom? We might get a puppy some day?"

Susan glanced down at him. "I'll think about it. How about that?"

This seemed to satisfy him and he hung on her arm as the two walked to the exit of the mall. They were outside in the brisk air only a moment before entering the parking structure. It seemed to get cold as soon as the sun went down these days. They walked up the ramp toward their car.

"Smells like gas in here, mom."

Susan smiled at his inquisitive nature. Actually, it smelled strongly of emissions, but he was close enough.

"I see our car, I see our car," he began chanting. He broke away from her and began running toward it.

"Jason," she called out, "Be careful."

She caught up with just as he reached their Lexus. He tapped the bumper. "I win."

Susan removed her keys from her purse. "Okay," she said, "You win." She turned to place the key in the doorlock, bumping the figure that was there. She stepped back, startled. "Oh, I'm sorry," she said, stepping back, "I didn't see you."

The figure stepped forward and Susan was surprised to see it was the handsome young man. He smiled at her but it was a cold smile and Susan had sudden misgivings. It seemed entirely too coincidental that he had been in the mall and was now here.

"No problem," he said smoothly, "Can I get that for you?"

Susan took a step backward, unconsciously clutching the keys to her body. "No," she said, "That's all right. Thank you."

Susan took another step back and the man took another step forward. Susan held out her purse. "Look, if this is what you want, you can have it." She realized she was clutching the keys, and held them out as well. "If you want the car, you can have that too."

The young man's eyes flickered up and down her body and his tone was insolent. "You don't seem to realize I can have anything I want."

The words were oddly familiar. Susan pushed the irrelevant thought away, trying to concentrate on the situation at hand. She tried to steady her voice, hoping and praying that someone, anyone, would appear in the deserted parking structure. "And what is it you want?" Susan asked, attempting another step backward

The man's arm flashed out, grabbing her by the throat and yanking her to him with incredible strength. He leaned down to look in her face. "You should never have written that story," he said between clenched teeth. "Who did you find? Who was the one who betrayed us?"

Susan shook her head in denial, her eyes wide. Thoughts of the golden-haired woman flashed through her mind. "I don't know what you're talking about," she managed to croak out. The man's grip tightened, beginning to crush her windpipe.

"You lie," he snarled through gritted teeth, "Who was it?"

Susan could see Jason's head peaking from behind the car. The thought of her son made her both afraid and brave. She began wildly struggling. The man holding her seemed surprised at her sudden surge of strength, but this merely caused him to tighten his grip.

Jason chose that moment to launch his assault. He ran forward and kicked the man in the shins. The man, without removing his eyes from Susan, shoved the little boy into the side of the car, knocking him unconscious. Susan desperately tried to catch sight of him as he fell, but wasn't able to because the man was holding her so tightly.

"That wasn't very nice," came a voice from the shadows.

The voice was smooth, melodious, the tone offhanded. The figure sounded almost bored, completely unmoved by the scene before it. Susan recognized the voice immediately.

The golden-haired woman stepped from the shadows. She was taller than the young man and stared down at him. The dangerous glint in her eye belied the lack of concern in her voice.

The young man underwent a startling transformation. The arrogance on his features disappeared and was immediately replaced by terror. He released Susan and she slumped to the ground next to Jason's prone body, rubbing the bruises on her throat. The woman moved closer, glancing down at the two then back at the young man. Her words were unconcerned.

"I think you should pick on someone your own size."

The young man tried to bolt but the woman's arm flashed out. She now held the young man by the throat and dragged him effortlessly to her. She gazed down at him as he began pleading.

"Oh my god," he sobbed, "I didn't know. I couldn't have known. I was told to come here by-"

The woman silenced him by placing her fingers on his lips. "It doesn't matter," she whispered to him. "It's too late."

She reached her arm around his head and snapped his neck. The move was so quick and unexpected that Susan did not have time to turn away from the violent act. The man's head now hung at an odd angle and his lifeless eyes stared down at her.

Susan turned away, clutching Jason to her breast. She did not want to watch the incomprehensible scene before her.

The golden-haired woman stared down at her, seemingly unperturbed by the corpse she now held in her hand. "You had better go," she said to Susan.

Susan scrambled to her feet, trying to hold Jason and retrieve her keys at the same time. She fumbled with the keys, dropping them, then kneeled to pick them up, still clutching her unconscious son. The woman took the keys from her patiently, effortlessly supporting the corpse with one hand. She unlocked the door then held it open in a chivalrous gesture, holding out the keys.

Susan snatched the keys from the woman, practically threw Jason in the car, then climbed in and slammed the door behind her. Her hands were shaking as she placed the key in the ignition. She started the car, slammed it in reverse, then went screeching backwards. She slammed it into drive, then went screeching toward the exit.

The woman watched the Lexus recklessly leave the parking lot, her face expressionless. She glanced down at the body in her grasp, then pulled it into the shadows. She held the lifeless corpse, focusing her senses in the darkness: not lifeless just yet. She shrugged. Easy enough to rectify.
Rather than kneel down, the woman pulled the body upward. She removed a dagger from inside her coat and with surgical precision, sliced the man's throat from ear-to-ear. Blood began to spill out onto the ground.

Although the neck of the corpse still hung at an odd angle, the man's eyes fluttered open. He tried to speak, but could not because of the damage to his throat. The woman held him dispassionately, allowing the blood to pool on the ground. He struggled feebly for a few moments, then went limp. She sensed that his life force was still present, but this did not concern her. It would just take the right combination of technique.

She smashed her fist through the glass window of the vehicle next to her, the violence as quick and easy as before. She shoved the body through the gaping hole, then walked to the rear of the car. She placed her fingertips under the edge of the trunk and popped the trunklid upward with a flick of her wrist. She was pleased to find a gas can in the storage space. She shook the can, noting the sloshing sound inside.

She removed the cap and splashed the gasoline on and underneath the car. She moved a few feet away, then removed the small case from her pocket. She took a small cigar from the case, expertly lit it, then turned to walk away. As she turned, she tossed the match over her shoulder.

The gas caught quickly and within seconds the car was fully engulfed. Her body was momentarily silhouetted by the flames before it disappeared into the darkness.

Susan stared down at her son in the hospital bed. His head was wrapped in a bandage and he was lightly sleeping. After ensuring there was no bleeding inside the skull, the doctors suggested he be kept in the hospital for observation. Susan, understanding how serious a head injury could be, agreed without hesitation.

Susan had rushed Jason to the hospital immediately following the attack in the parking structure. He had awakened in traumatic care and fortunately the first thing he had seen was her. He stayed awake all through the examination, and only moments ago had finally drifted off to sleep. He clutched the stuffed dinosaur Neda had brought from home.

The thought of the older woman made Susan glance up. She could see Neda seated outside clutching a box of tissues. There were dark circles under her eyes. Susan's eyes drifted to the left. A refined-looking gentleman sat three seats down from her. He was dressed in a three-piece suit with a cane leaning against the seat next to him. A hat was perched neatly atop the cane.

Susan stared at the man. There was something about him.

She stood up abruptly and moved toward the door with purpose. The man glanced up from his magazine as she came through the door. Neda started to speak but the words died on her lips as Susan brushed by to confront the man.

"Where is she?"

The man gazed up at her in some confusion. "Excuse me, ma'am?" he asked politely in a clipped, British accent.

Susan was not to be deterred. "The woman. The one with the golden hair. Where is she? I want to speak with her."

The older gentleman's expression was still perplexed, but now laced with a little sympathy. "I'm afraid I don't know what you're talking about, ma'am. And I believe you must have me confused with someone else."

Neda stood and took Susan's elbow but Susan pulled away. She was adamant. "There are no other patients on this floor. I know. I work here. There's no reason for you to be here."

The gentleman's expression changed to one of concern. "Oh, then I must be on the wrong floor." He stood, gathering his belongings. "How unfortunate. Thank you so much for telling me."

To Neda's dismay, Susan reached out to grab the man's sleeve.

And he was gone.

Susan turned and there he was, to her right, several feet away. He gazed at her with an unwavering gaze, his air of grandfatherly concern gone, his face now expressionless.

Susan was slightly afraid, but her anger and fear for her son were making her brave. "I want to see her. I want an explanation."

The man shook his head. His words were unequivocal. "This is not her fault. You should not have published your work. You brought this upon yourself."

Neda was desperately trying to follow the conversation between the two, but this brought her up short. She took a threatening step toward the man. "How dare you accuse her of bringing this upon herself. As if she would ever do anything to-"

Surprisingly, it was Susan who stopped Neda's tirade. She watched the man, trying to steady her voice. "I don't care," she said, "I want an explanation."

The man was silent, giving no reaction to her words. If he was contemplating them, he gave no indication he was doing so. Susan was discouraged but continued anyway, playing her last card.

"I don't think you would be here if she didn't feel at least partially responsible."

Her words seemed to have no impact on him. He simply stood there and for a moment, Susan was afraid he was going to walk away.

He did not. "Very well," he said stiffly, his accent even more pronounced. He lowered his voice so that Susan could barely hear it. "If it were up to me, I would not let you anywhere near my master."

The expression caught Susan by surprise. It seemed so archaic, so ancient, so out of place in the ultra-modern hospital corridor. The man continued. "I would not even have come here were it not for her direction. But I know her well, and I believe she will receive you."

The man abruptly turned and began to walk down the hallway. He now moved fluidly, in complete contrast to his earlier stiffness. Susan watched him walk away. She glanced indecisively through the window at her comatose son, then made a snap decision.

"Stay with him, Neda. I'll be back."

Neda stepped forward as if to try and talk her out of it, but then relented. She watched the young redhead disappear into the elevator with the older man. She then moved to the window to look down into the receiving area of the hospital. A sleek, black limousine pulled up to the curb and within minutes, Susan's red hair could be seen next to it. Both she and the elder man climbed into the rear seating area and the limousine pulled smoothly away from the curb.

Neda watched it disappear, feeling a shiver make its way up her spine. Although not a particularly religious woman, she crossed herself for good measure.

Susan rode silently in the back of the limousine. The windows were blacked out so she could not see where they were going. Other than a few directions to the unseen driver, the older man did not say a word. He sat staring at the opaque window, almost as if he could see through it.

After an indeterminate amount of time, Susan felt the vehicle slow, then begin to drive up what seemed a curvy road. This part of the drive was much shorter, and it seemed only a few minutes before the vehicle came to a stop. Immediately the door opened and the man gestured for her to get out.

Susan stepped out onto the entranceway to a mansion. Light streamed from every window into the night beyond. She stood at the base of the stairway, staring upward in astonishment. She had been to many opulent houses, but this was a castle.

The man took her elbow and began guiding her up the stairs. Normally she would not stand for such a patronizing gesture, but she was overwhelmed at her surroundings and was actually glad for the guidance.

Double doors whispered outward and she was led through the entranceway into a luxurious foyer. The furnishings were elegant, but simple as well. Servants kept their eyes downcast as she passed. If they were curious, they did not show it.

Susan was led through another set of double doors into what appeared to be a small version of the Smithsonian library. A large fire burned in a huge marble fireplace set in the wall. The golden-haired woman sat behind a desk, reading the Wall Street Journal. She did not look up at Susan's approach.

The man stopped several feet from the desk and Susan stopped as well. He did not speak, and Susan shifted uncomfortably. The woman didn't appear to notice their entrance, and did not acknowledge their presence in any way. Susan quickly became impatient and took a step forward.

In a flash, the elder man was in front of her, blocking her path. Susan was startled by the quickness of his movement and retreated the step she had taken forward. He still did not speak, merely looked down at her with disapproval.

"Let her pass, Edward."

The voice was sardonic, almost resigned. After an imperceptible hesitation, Edward stepped out of Susan's way. He moved some distance away, maintaining his vigil.

The woman finally looked up. For the first time, Susan noticed the strange color of her eyes, a combination of gray, blue and green. They seemed to shift hues with the flickering firelight. Her gaze was mesmerizing and her words, although polite, were a decree. "Won't you have a seat, Dr. Ryerson?"

Susan moved numbly to the seat the woman indicated. Strangely, her anger and urgency disappeared at the sound of the woman's voice. Susan noted the undefinable quality she had noted before, the depth that belied her youth.

"It seems you have me at a disadvantage," Susan said, referring to the fact that the woman knew her name.

"Yes," the woman interrupted smoothly, "I do."

Susan flushed at the slightly mocking tone in the woman's voice. She had come here with the intent of demanding answers. Yet now all she could do was sit and stare at the young woman who stared back at her with an unblinking gaze.

"Do you have a name?" Susan finally asked, unable to completely disguise her sarcasm.

The sarcasm did not escape the woman, nor did it offend her. There was a devilish glint in her eye when she replied. "Yes, I have a name."

She turned in her chair, her unblinking gaze resting on Edward for a moment, then turned back to Susan. "My name is Rhian."

Susan was not certain she had heard the name right. It had a slightly different inflection than she had heard before. Evidently, the woman picked up on Susan's confusion and elaborated. "An acceptable equivalent would be 'Ryan.' Now what can I do for you this evening?"

The events of the last few days came flooding back to Susan and she felt her anger stir again. "You could start with an explanation. My son is in the hospital."

Ryan nodded. "I am well aware of the condition of your son. I warned you that you were in danger."

Susan felt her anger flare. "I think you owe me more than a warning. I want some answers. Who the hell are you? Why did that man come after me? And why did you kill him? Couldn't you have just stopped him? Turned him over to the police?"

Ryan looked at her with an expression that bordered on exasperation, as if what she were suggesting were incredibly naive. Susan was just beginning to vent, though, and now the questions and accusations came pouring out.

"You show up in my lab a corpse and I watch you come back to life, only to have you smash your way out of the hospital. You show up three months later, break into my house, leave some obscure warning, then disappear again. Three days after that, some madman attacks me, and you pop up out of nowhere and break his neck. In the meantime, my son is in the wrong place at the wrong time and nearly gets his head cracked open."

Susan finished her tirade, catching her breath. Her chest heaved with the emotion of her words. She felt tears sting her eyes as Ryan gazed at her, expressionless. The golden-haired woman spoke at long last.

"I am sorry about your son."

Susan lashed out at her. "Well, wonderful. I want you to be more than sorry. I want some answers. Who are you?"

The words hung between them for a long moment. Susan did not think it was a question requiring so much thought.

Ryan pushed back from the desk and leaned back in her chair, crossing her long legs in front of her. She folded her hands, her elbows on the armrests of the chair. She gazed at Susan Ryerson in the flickering light.

"Do you know how old I am, Dr. Ryerson?"

Susan didn't see how the question was relevant. "No, I don't," she said impatiently, "I would think late 20's, maybe early 30's."

The woman's eyes shifted to Edward who was standing in the shadows.

Whatever unspoken advice he transmitted to her, she ignored. "Late 20's, early 30's," she repeated. She picked up the glass of red wine from her desk, swirling the contents. "I don't have a record of my birth," she said, "But as near as I can tell, I should be reaching a century mark sometime soon."

The woman's words were conversational, as if she were discussing something as mundane as the weather. Susan wasn't certain she had heard her correctly.

"Are you telling me you're almost a hundred years old?"

Ryan shook her head, her gaze on Susan. "No," she said, "Almost seven hundred."

Susan caught her breath. Obviously what the woman was suggesting was impossible. Extraordinary anatomy or not, she could not possibly be that old. Even as Susan mentally denied the possibility, though, her own words came back to her: longevity, immunity, strength....

It seemed as if the woman could read her mind. "Don't you believe your own research, Dr. Ryerson? Can you explain any of your findings? What did you say? 'The patient appears to be suffering from some type of genetic abnormality, or perhaps a state of advanced pathology. The heart is enlarged to nearly three times normal size. The lungs are shrunken, as are the liver and the pancreas...'"

Susan was stunned. The woman was repeating word-for-word what she had documented on her computer. "How did you get access to my records?"

Ryan shook her head. "I didn't need to, Dr. Ryerson. I overheard you."

Susan shook her head, still feeling numb. "You couldn't have. You were unconscious, and out of hearing range."

Ryan's reply was softly spoken. "Having not actually tested my hearing range, I would think that's a rather premature statement."

Susan was taken aback at the gentle reproof.

"You see, that's a problem," Ryan said, continuing her mild rebuke. "Your scientific method analyzes everything, explains nothing. It is blind to everything outside itself. You're a product of your time. You've been taught to distrust everything you cannot measure with your senses. Which amazes me, " she added as an afterthought, "Because humans have notoriously poor senses."

"What do you mean 'humans'?" Susan said with skepticism, "Are you saying you're not human?"

Ryan gazed at her. "I would not think so, noting the very fundamental differences between myself and human begins. I think I was once human, but that was a very long time ago."

"Seven hundred years ago?" Susan asked, unable to hide her sarcasm.

Ryan just smiled, amused at the sarcasm. "Seven hundred years ago," she replied.

"Then what are you, if you're not human?"

Ironically, this gave Ryan pause. She turned to stare into the fire. "I don't have a name to describe my Kind, because I speak with the language of humans. And humans have no name for my Kind, any more than people who live in a black and white world would have names for colors."

"What year were you born?"

Ryan laughed, aware of Susan's attempt to trap her. "Again, that shows me your inability to step outside your time. Only in this century has time been divided into such discrete little quantities." She continued to gaze into the fire. "As if the ebb and flow of life were so constrained." She turned to Susan, raising an eyebrow. "I read history books and they give the illusion that the human race has always measured itself with calendars and clocks and the dates of important events. When I was a child, we didn't even know of such things."

Susan did not try to hide her incredulity. "So how do you know it's almost seven hundred years?"

Ryan had a gleam in her eye; she saw through the skepticism to the beginnings of genuine interest. "I know I was born in the first part of the 14th century, my best guess would be around 1325, if your history books are even close to being correct."

"Why 1325?"

"When I was 16 seasons," Ryan paused, correcting herself, "I mean 16 years old, I fought for Edward, the Black Prince."

Susan thought furiously, trying to remember her history. She would shatter this illusion yet. "Would that have been the Hundred Years War?"

Ryan looked at her mockingly. "Well, yes, I guess, but it was not called the Hundred Years War until later because, when it started, no one knew it was going to last a hundred years."

Susan stopped, startled. She hadn't thought of that. Ryan continued her rumination.

"Actually, it lasted exactly two for me, at which time I ran away from service to return to my family."

Susan thought she had her now. "How could you be allowed to fight in the 14th century as a woman?"

Ryan shook her head. "I couldn't. Women were little more than chattel at the time I was born, which is why to this day I sometimes have difficulty respecting them."

Susan shook her head. "I examined you, remember? I know you're female."

Ryan's gaze settled on Susan. Susan felt warmth gather at the back of her neck and realized she was blushing. Ryan's words were soft, amused. "Yes, I am well aware of your examination, Dr. Ryerson." The words hung in the air, and then Ryan raised her voice once more. "Technically, I was born a female. But until I was 19 seas-, years old, I was raised as a man. In fact, for the first 400 years of my life, I lived as a man."

Susan's disbelief was evident. "Why?"

Ryan laughed. "You have to remember, Dr. Ryerson, things were not as you think they were. I would have been at a tremendous disadvantage had I been raised female, and perhaps would not have survived. As a male I was given many privileges and freedoms that would have been questioned were I female."

For the first time, Ryan turned her attention fully to Susan

"I've watched your moving pictures, your films, and I've seen the portrayals of both my time and of other times, of this world, and of other worlds. And I can tell you, in every portrayal I've seen, even the wildest fantasy or science fiction, I have never seen a world more alien than the one from which I came."

This statement silenced Susan, simply because it had the profound ring of truth.

Ryan stood, moving to the fireplace. "You have to remember that when I was born, the only light in the world was fire." She turned back to Susan. "There was no running water, no bathroom facilities, no supermarkets. Food had to be grown or killed." Ryan gestured to a picture of a wolf that sat on her desk "There were no photographs, no paintings for the common man, no drawings, no likenesses of any kind." She pointed to the shelves and shelves of books. "There were no books, no written communication of any kind. And it wouldn't have mattered anyway because we were profoundly ignorant. No one could read or write other than the clergy and whatever they said was taken at face value." Ryan glanced down at the Wall Street

Journal. "Higher math was unknown because few people could even count; they had no need to. Life was simple and harsh."

Ryan returned to her chair, reclining once more. "A horse was the most rapid transportation known to man, and if a person traveled more than a 100 miles from their place of birth, they might as well have seen the whole world." She shook her head. "No one knew anything of political events, so the myths you read in history books about the peasants rising up to fight for some noble cause are just that: myths. We were profoundly ignorant about everything, and the 20th century forgets that when they try to imagine what it was like."

Susan was drawn into the account against her will. If the woman were making it up, she certainly had an amazing amount of detail, details that Susan had never considered. Susan chose her words carefully, reluctant to give any ground. "My grandmother talks about how difficult it's been to live through changing times. If you truly are 700 years old, how have you survived that change? It would be as if you came from another world."

Ryan nodded. "That's exactly my point. I would imagine your grandmother had to heat water over the fire in order to take a warm bath. "

"Yes," Susan nodded, remembering their conversations, "And you had to do the same?"

"No," Ryan laughed. "We did not bathe. I'm amused by your 'historical' depictions. I never saw anyone that clean. The filth we lived in would have been considered obscene by 20th century standards."

Susan thought back to the earlier conversation.

"So how did you end up fighting for the Black Prince if you were politically ignorant?"

Ryan shrugged. "It was very common for the poor to be 'conscripted' into the army. I fought as a mercenary. I fought for two years, never knowing what I was fighting for. I returned home when I was perhaps 18, 19 years old, at which time my life changed forever."

Victor watched the child in the bed. Now that she was clean and her golden hair was untangled, she did indeed look more female than male. He frowned. At some point in time, his instructions for her to take the waters every day had been ignored. Perhaps at the same time the instructions for her to stay in the village had been ignored.

Victor controlled his anger. Years of planning had nearly been destroyed; he had taken his fury out on the village. He cared nothing that the child had exacted her revenge against Derek and the others. He cared only that she was now here.

The child moaned slightly in her sleep and rolled over. Miriam eyed her carefully for signs of awakening, then returned to her stitchery.

"Child" was probably not the appropriate term for the figure in the bed, Victor reminded himself. She was nearly two decades old now, and by common standards, a fully grown woman.

Victor gazed again at the figure, this time with misgivings. To his mind she was still little more than a child, far too young. He sighed his frustration and Miriam glanced over at him beneath raised brows. Victor waved towards the door and Miriam nodded primly and disappeared.

Victor began pacing about the room. He knew it would be difficult once he was in her presence; he had underestimated how great that difficulty would be.

No he hadn't, he reminded himself. That was why he had kept her away for nearly two decades. It would have served no purpose to take her as a child.

And she is still a child, he told himself.

The figure stirred in the bed once more, and he moved to her side. He stared down at the perfect features, the golden lashes, and his jaw clenched. In a sudden fury, he stormed from the room, slamming the door behind him. He stalked down the halls of his castle and through the courtyard. He took the reins of his favorite stallion and, throwing one long leg over the horse's back, galloped from the castle into the night.

Miriam watched him from the window, a candle in her hand. Her face was expressionless as she watched her master flee.

Victor stayed away several days until he felt he had regained control. His reappearance was greeted with the usual lack of reaction from his staff; he had chosen them well although he could hear their whisperings even from great distances.

He spoke briefly with the stablehand on care for his horse then left for his own quarters. The girl's room was adjacent to his own, and he wondered if she was still sleeping. He cocked his head to one side as if listening to something that no one else could hear; he didn't think so.

When he walked into the room, the bed was empty. He glanced to the window, then to the far corner. The room was empty.

He frowned, more annoyed than concerned. He again cocked his head to one side as if listening to a far-off noise. He started down the passageway to the great hall.

He entered the great hall and caught sight of the figure on the far side. She looked like a young boy once more, dressed in leggings and an oversized shirt. She was balanced precariously on the hearth, reaching for a sword hung ceremoniously on the wall. She came down, sword in hand. She turned, startled to see Victor a few feet from her.

"I don't think you need that."

The lithe figure gazed at the Man with supreme distrust. She did not know where she was or why she was here, but she recognized this man. She raised the sword in front of her.

"I'll judge that."

The man smiled ever so slightly and the next thing she knew, the sword was out of her hand and in his. She had not even seen him move and wondered what sort of magic this was. He tossed the sword aside as if it was inconsequential. She felt for the dagger concealed in her shirt. The man saw the movement.

"Why don't you give me that as well?"

She removed the dagger from its hiding place then made as if to hand it to him. Instead, she dodged to the right and fled from the hallway.

Victor simply stood there, sighing. He didn't know why he had assumed this would be easy.

The girl fled down the hallway, accidentally tackling the nursemaid, Miriam, in the process. Miriam screamed and the girl continued to flee. Victor came striding down the hallway, unperturbed. He glanced at Miriam, who was attempting to gather the basket of spilled yarn. He continued after the girl.

The girl was completely unfamiliar with the layout of the castle and found herself going up when she wished to go down. She wanted to backtrack down the spiral staircase, but was uncertain how much of an alarm had been sounded in the castle. It seemed to her as if no alarm had been sounded at all.

To her frustration, she wound up exactly where she had started, which was on the level of her original quarters. She heard footsteps behind her and had no choice but to enter the bedroom she had so recently left.

She hid herself behind the doorway, the dagger clutched in her hand. She had never feared any man, nor ever found one she could not do battle with. But for some reason, this man seemed different.

The door opened and the dark-haired one walked in. She lunged forward with the dagger and he turned and caught her easily. She surprised him with her strength, however, and broke her wrist free, slicing forward with blinding speed.

It was only Victor's own preternatural speed that allowed him to deflect the blow. The dagger glanced off his leather jerkin and caught him just above the collarbone, nicking the skin. A drop of blood welled in the cut, then began to trickle downward, staining his white shirt.

The child stared at the bloodstain, feeling the strange lightheadedness that had overcome her at other times. But this time it was different. A knot began to twist and uncoil inside of her. Breathing became difficult and her mouth was suddenly unaccountably dry. She stared at the bloodstain as if mesmerized, unable to draw her eyes from it.

Victor watched the reaction and felt his self-control begin to crumble. A thousand arguments formed over hundreds of years tumbled through his mind and none of them seemed to matter. His words were an anguished whisper.

"You are still too young."

The girl looked up at him, but her eyes were drawn back to the blood seeping from the wound. She took a step forward and Victor no longer cared about her age. His passion for this young one was all-consuming.

She reached up and touched the wound, fascinated at the blood she came away with on her fingers. She could not understand the compulsions filling her as she touched her fingers to her lips.

The sensation was strange and thrilling. An odd pleasure shot through her, beginning on her lips but spreading throughout her body. She had tasted blood before, but it had been salty and metallic. This tasted different, and was not so much a taste but a feeling.

She raised her hand again but Victor caught her wrist and pulled her toward him. He sat down on the bench and pulled her onto his lap so she was facing him. She wanted to ponder the strangeness of this position, but her attention was attracted to the blood seeping from his neck. It was much nearer her face, now, and she leaned forward to touch her lips to the wound.

A shudder went through Victor at the touch. He entangled his fingers in the golden hair and pressed her head to him.

The girl's mouth filled with blood but it was neither salty nor metallic. With a certain horror, she swallowed and felt a powerful warmth spread throughout her body. It was as if an old hunger was suddenly satisfied, but the satisfaction only increased the hunger. She began to drink.

Victor leaned back, knowing the child had no understanding of what she was doing. She had the appetite of an infant, instinctive and undiscriminating. Her own neck was exposed to him in this position and he fought to control himself. But he had waited so long and had shown such extreme patience that his control was slipping. The combination of her power and her vulnerability was intoxicating to him, and he was tired of waiting.

He grabbed her by her shirt collar and lifted her forcibly off the ground until her feet dangled in the air. He slammed her backward against the stone wall, pressing the full length of his body against her lithe, muscular form. He could feel her powerful heart beating in her chest and it was the final sensation that pushed him over the brink.

Pinned against the wall, her feet dangling above the ground, she felt the familiar slicing to her neck. But now it was agonizing. She felt warmth run down her back and down her chest, and realized it was her own blood she was feeling. She also realized this was not the first time this man had fed off her in this fashion.

She tried to feebly struggle against him, but she was locked in his iron embrace and growing weaker by the minute. She kicked at him but it had no more effect than would the kick of an insect.

Her head was swimming and she could no longer focus on the objects in the room. Her eyelids grew heavy and she fought to keep them open. Her head grew heavy and she rested it on the man's shoulder.

Victor felt the girl's limbs grow heavy and fought for control. It took everything in his willpower not to kill her, because oh, what a sweet consummation that would be. Instead, he forced himself to pull back from her and lowered her feet to the floor.

She was unconscious and for a moment, Victor simply held the limp body, still grasping her by her shirt collar. He felt her blood race through his veins and felt powerful, more powerful than he had in ages. He lifted her body and carried her to the bed. He lowered her bloodied form onto the pile of coverlets, then went to the door and locked it. He settled into a chair by her bedside and began his long vigil.

She swam through a strange world on the border of life and death. She had been here before, but never so close to death's side. Her mother and father were there, and she wanted to join them, but the Man was standing in her way.

He did not speak but his piercing black eyes spoke for him. He would not let her cross the border, not now and not ever. She was so very tired and wanted to cross that border, but was not strong enough to fight him.

She awoke, feeling lightheaded and nauseous, too weak to even lift her head. She was no longer wearing bloody clothes but was wearing another oversized shirt. Several blankets were piled over her to keep her warm.

She slowly turned her head and the pain in her temples was excruciating. She closed her eyes but white light flashed behind her eyelids and she wondered if this was a vision from god. She re-opened her eyes and focused upon the Man, and her thoughts were that it might be a vision from Someone Else.

The man gazed at her, unperturbed and with a hint of amusement in his black eyes. She wondered why her mouth was so dry, and why the thought of water did not appeal to her.

Victor stood and moved to the bedside. His passion was not completely satisfied, but he felt more controlled now. He felt the risk of killing the child had passed, and now it was time to complete the act. He sat down on the edge of the bed.

She tried to move away from him, but did not have the strength. Her feeble attempts seemed to amuse him even further, and this angered her.

"What kind of monster are you?" she whispered with hostility.

"I am no more a monster than are you."

She was preparing a scathing retort but something in his words made her pause. He still looked at her with desire, but it was a much different type of desire than that which had caused him to attack her. It was not like the desire of men who had tried to rape her, thinking she was a young boy, nor was it like the desire of men who took women forcibly. It was not like that of his mother and father in their crude wooden hut, nor was it like the lust of the priest in all his wants.

It was a desire that had nothing to do with sex and everything to do with power. And she looked within herself and saw the same longing, although she had no idea what she was longing for.

She turned away from him, swallowing hard, but he had seen what was in her eyes. He placed his hand beneath her chin and turned her head so that she was again looking at him. She could feel her heart in her chest, although beating weakly, beating rapidly.

"Ah, little one, I have waited so long for you I cannot wait any longer."

Victor took the knife from the bedstand and in one quick movement, sliced a thin cut through his neck. Blood began to seep from the wound.

She was startled by the self-infliction of the wound, but her eyes were drawn to the blood that began to run down his shirt. She dragged her eyes away from the wound to look in his.

"I cannot do this, this abomination."

Victor shook his head. "It is too late, my dear. It is already done."

She looked away, at the floor, at the wall, at the ceiling, at anything but the blood on his shirt. He kneeled at her feet and she swayed towards him, catching herself. She tried to stand but he grabbed her wrists, pulling her to her knees as well. She could not resist now, the blood was too close to her mouth and all she had to do was lean ever so slightly forward...

And then her mouth was on his neck and he was holding her tightly as she fed. But this time it was different. Sensations raced through her body as his blood coursed through her veins. Pictures, disjointed and nonsensical fluttered through her mind. Pictures of things she had never seen and places she had never been.

Her hand rested languidly on his cheek and he gently turned her wrist. She felt a slight pain and knew that he was now feeding off her as she fed on him. But again, this time it was different. She had felt only pain before at his touch, but now a flush of pleasure spread out over her body, radiating from the wrist he held so tightly in his grasp.

The sensations that went tearing through the girl were extraordinary. Her entire being was flushed with blood, first with his and then with her own as he returned what he had taken. She had no concept of how long they were locked in their deadly embrace. She only knew that the sensations continued to build and pulsate until the pleasure became unbearable, and she broke from his grasp.

He released her, sated for the first time in centuries, and reveled in the power coursing through his veins. Nothing in all the known world provided such completeness, such satisfaction. He gazed down at his unholy child, knowing all had come to fruition.

Susan shook her head, trying to clear it. She felt as if she were coming out of a trance. She and the woman had been having a conversation, but at some point in time she forgot that they were talking. It seemed almost that she stopped listening and began seeing, although that of course was preposterous.

Susan glanced around the study. The images were so vivid the study seemed strange, incongruous. But when she tried to picture faces or details, the vividness of the picture faded away until all she could see, or rather hear, were the words that had obviously passed between them.

Ryan gazed at her. It appeared she herself was unaffected by the conversation, but not surprised by Susan's numb state. Susan wondered if she had placed her in some type of hypnotic state.

"So," Susan began carefully, "What you're telling me is that you're a vampire."

Ryan's hand stopped in mid-air, not quite reaching her wineglass. Susan heard a muffled chuckle behind her and glanced back. She had forgotten about Edward.

Ryan had a look of exasperation and annoyance on her face. She seemed completely surprised at the reference. "Of course not. What an idiotic suggestion."

Susan was taken aback. She felt compelled to apologize without really knowing why.

"I'm sorry. But from what you were describing-"

"Dr. Ryerson," Ryan interrupted smoothly, "Do you believe in vampires?"

Susan was slow to reply. "No, no I don't."

"Well neither do I," Ryan said, "And I've been around quite a bit longer than you have. Vampires are a result of over-active human imaginations. People of my time believed in them, but people of my time held trials in which kitchen appliances were charged with witchcraft. I thought you were a little more sophisticated than that."

Again, Edward's attempt to muffle his laughter failed. Ryan shot him a dark look. Susan did not know how she had ended up on the defensive end of this conversation. "Well, of course. But from what you were describing, it seemed a logical conclusion."

"What I was describing was what happened," Ryan said, "Whatever conclusions you drew were your own."

Susan felt oddly chastised as Ryan continued, now speaking almost to herself. "Besides, I could eat Dracula for dinner."

The words were spoken so casually and with such confidence that Susan abruptly raised her head. There was a subtle sense of danger around this woman that at times could be extremely unsubtle. Ryan glanced up at the antique clock, which now read 4 am. "You should be leaving."

Because the sun will be up soon, Susan thought before she could stop herself.

Ryan smiled knowingly at Susan's expression. Susan noticed Ryan did not show her teeth when she smiled, another thought she attempted to brush off.

The thought of leaving, however, brought her reasons for coming back into focus.

"I'm not certain I believe even a word of what you're saying," Susan began, "But that doesn't change the fact that my son is in the hospital, and that you're responsible."

Ryan did not deny the responsibility, although Edward cleared his throat. Ryan's eyes shifted to him once more and he quieted. She turned her attention to Susan.

"How exactly," Ryan asked slowly, "Would you have me absolve myself?"

Oddly, this momentarily silenced Susan. She was careful in framing her reply. "You have self-healing abilities I've never seen before, " She felt a tinge of desperation in her voice which she tried to disguise. "I would like to continue studying you."

Ryan was silent for a long moment. Susan was hopeful that the silence meant contemplation. Her hopes were dashed by Ryan's reply.

"No."

Susan tried to reason with her. "Why not? You have things in your blood that could change the world."

Ryan took a sip of her wine. "I don't want to change the world."

The tinge of desperation was a little more obvious. "Why not? Your body chemistry could provide all sorts of insight into immunology. If I could recreate your blood chemistry, I could conquer disease. You could save the human race."

This appeared to amuse Ryan. "It's been my experience that the human race is not particularly worth saving."

The scathing indictment caused Susan to spring to her feet in anger. Edward was instantly there. Susan tried to calm herself, tried to sound reasonable.

"Then let me study you for myself. I've spent my entire life looking for something like this."

"Ah," Ryan said, sitting back, "The truth at last. I fail to see how this would benefit me in any way. I'm not motivated by altruism."

Susan controlled her anger. She knew she was about to be dismissed and grabbed at one last final straw. "Then do it for yourself."

Susan saw a flicker in Ryan's eye and pressed on. "You're curious. I saw you hesitate in front of the MRI image. You were studying yourself. I can help you."

Edward took a step back, still guarding his master. Ryan smiled a slight smile, twirling the stem of the wineglass between her fingers. "Self-interest. The last appeal."

Ryan glanced down at the desk in front of her. Her reply startled Edward. "I will consider it," she said.

Susan released her breath, unaware she had been holding it. Up until that moment, she had not known how important an affirmative response was to her. Although Ryan had not said "yes," she had not ruled out the possibility.

Edward moved to Susan's side, and she realized it was time for her to leave. Ryan confirmed this realization. "Please ensure Dr. Ryerson is given safe passage to the hospital."

Susan simply nodded because there was nothing left to say. Edward began escorting her out. She felt self-doubt and a little guilt gnaw at her as she left the study. She wasn't certain if her desire to study Ryan was entirely due to her concern for the human race.

Ryan sat gazing into the fire. She wondered if Edward would personally escort the doctor back to the hospital. Her question was answered when a few moments later Edward returned. Although normally restrained, on this occasion he would not hold back.

"You cannot possibly be serious."

Ryan glanced up at him, then returned to her contemplation of the fire. "I see little harm in it, as long as she does not publish anything."

"I see little benefit in it. And surely you realize Dr. Ryerson is exceedingly ambitious."

Ryan turned to him, and although her demeanor was calm and her features expressionless, Edward knew he had crossed a line.

"Are you doubting my judgment, Edward?"

Edward bowed his head, immediately repentant. He was truly regretful. "I apologize, my lord. Of course not."

Ryan began to turn back in her seat.

"But-"

She raised an eyebrow.

"-You often act without due self-regard."

Ryan hid a smile. Edward was stubborn, but few could deliver so clever an admonishment. It reaffirmed the reason he had been her personal servant for nearly three centuries. She allowed him to wait in silence for what seemed an interminable amount of time.

"I will keep that in mind."

Edward bowed stiffly from the waist, then left the room. Ryan glanced out the window. It would be dawn soon. She stood, stretching, then followed Edward's path. She took the sweeping marble staircase into her suite. She switched on the soft lights, only slightly disturbing the Cockatoo who was sleeping on his perch. He opened one eye sleepily, then yawned. Ryan scratched his head and he fluffed himself, settling back down. It was far too early for any respectable bird to be rising.

Ryan switched off the light and then stripped off her clothes, grabbing a robe from the bathroom. She went onto the balcony, then down another sweeping set of stairs into the pool area. She reveled in the cold on her skin; there had been snow out here a few days earlier, but the groundskeepers had cleared the area. She removed the robe and dove into the water.

By the time she was done, the sun was peeking over the hills in the distance. She wrapped herself in the robe and eyed the sun without concern. She reentered the house, then returned with the newspaper, settling into one of the cushioned chairs poolside. She glanced through the paper, wincing a little as the sun cleared the distant hills. It had that cold morning glare only a winter sun can have.

She reached for her sunglasses that were lying on the nearby table. She remembered the look on Dr. Ryerson's face when she had begun discussing vampires. Ryan laughed as she put the glasses on, her only concession to the daylight.

CHAPTER 15

SUSAN WATCHED AS JASON'S PUPPY CHASED HIM THROUGH the park. He ran through the dewy grass, squealing as the tiny beast caught up with him and nipped at his heels. Jason had a bandage on his forehead, the only reminder of their recent ordeal.

And the puppy, Susan thought to herself with irony. She had capitulated on that almost immediately. She knew it was mostly from guilt. In the last few days she had begun to feel a heavy responsibility for recent events. Although initially she blamed Ryan, she finally admitted to herself that it was her own breach of ethics that had endangered her son.

Susan became aware of the concern in Jason's voice.

"Randy! Here boy! Randy!"

Susan glanced over. Jason had moved some distance from her and she could barely make him out in the lengthening shadows. She called to him. "Jason, don't go any further." She stood up and started towards him.

"Randy," Jason called out, "Where'd you go boy?"

Susan picked up her pace. Jason was still moving away from her, and now she could only see his white tennis shoes. "Jason," she called out, trying not to sound alarmed, "I'll be right there, stop where you are."

Jason stopped, but then heard a yelp from the shadows. The plight of his puppy was probably the only thing that would make him disobey his mother. He disappeared into the shadows.

Susan began running, truly afraid now. "Jason!" she cried out, "Jason, come back here!"

Jason reappeared from the shadows, he himself shaken at the darkness. He tried to muster his courage to re-enter the blackness to search for the puppy. He took a deep breath to do so, but Susan caught his arm just in time. She yanked him backward to her. She crouched down, clutching him tightly. She could feel her heart beat against his chest and tried to calm her irrational fear.

A shadow fell over her.

Susan felt nausea leap up into her throat, so quickly did her fright return. She slowly turned her head to look upward, uncertain of what she would find.

Ryan stood gazing down at them. She was gazing at the boy. She held the puppy out toward Jason. "Is this your dog?" she asked in her silvery voice.

Susan was so relieved she couldn't be angry. Jason seemed enthralled as he stepped away from his mother. He reached up to take the puppy from her. "Thank you," he said, then continued uncertainly, "You're the lady from the hospital."

Ryan nodded. "And who might you be?"

Jason put on a mock-serious face. "I'm Batman," he stated sternly. He glanced up at the golden-haired woman. "And you," he stated with some authority, "Will be Robin, the Boy Wonder."

Susan's tired relief immediately transitioned to mirth as she muffled laughter in her hand. Out of all the things her son could say to this creature in front of him, that had to be the most inappropriate. Ryan simply stared down at him with her unblinking gaze.

"I don't think so," she said.

Susan controlled her laughter. It was hard to judge this woman at times. Susan revised her last thought. It was hard to judge her all the time.

"How long have you been here?" she asked.

Ryan turned her attention to Susan. "Not long," she said. She glanced over her shoulder in the shadows. "I don't think you should be out here, though."

Susan felt a cold chill of fear once more. She wondered what Ryan saw in the shadows that she could not. Ryan did not elaborate. "I will walk you home," was all she said.

It did not take them long to reach Susan's house. Jason, against his protestations, was put to bed. His puppy slept in a box next to his bunk, and when Susan glanced in on him five minutes later, both he and the puppy were asleep in the bed.

"I once slept like that," Ryan said, gazing over her shoulder at the sleeping child.

Susan jumped. She wished Ryan would make a little more noise when she moved about. She closed the door behind her. "Would you like some tea or something?"

To her surprise, Ryan accepted her offer. While Susan made the preparations, Ryan leaned in the doorway. Susan rattled some pots and pans for a minute, then began boiling the water. She was actually glad Ryan had showed up this evening. The story she had told in her study had haunted Susan, to the point where she even dreamed about it. She still wasn't certain if she believed the woman, but she wanted to hear the rest of it, anyway.

"What happened after you drank that man's blood?"

"Victor?" Ryan asked, slightly surprised Susan had asked. At her affirmation, Ryan said, "After that, I slept for a very long time."

Susan wondered if that was what she had been talking about earlier. "How long is a 'long' time?"

Ryan's eyes became distant. "I slept for nearly 14 years, which was about half the expected life-span of a peasant like myself at that time."

Susan pulled the boiling teakettle from the stove. "Well, other than the fact that what you're saying is impossible, sleep is needed for physical regeneration." She poured the water into two cups. "Sleep deprivation causes all sorts of physical and psychological problems." She was suddenly struck by the memory of the continual REM Ryan demonstrated while unconscious. "Do you dream?"

Ryan glanced at her sideways, a charming smile tugging at the corners of her mouth. She appeared to possess a sudden and remarkable innocence. "You'd better be careful, Dr. Ryerson. Despite your qualifying statements, you sound as if you're in danger of believing me."

Susan frowned, but without anger. "Well," she said, attempting to be as noncommittal as possible, "I'm a scientist. I try to be open to new experiences."

Ryan took the cup from her hand and followed her into the living room. "Yes," she said, "I dream. And I dream with the eyes of anyone I've ever Shared with as well."

Ryan used that word in such a strange context. Although Susan thought she had a pretty good idea what Ryan meant by "Share," she still wasn't certain. She wasn't ready to address that just yet.

"What happened when you awoke?"

Ryan settled into the rocking chair. Her eyes were distant and it was evident she was reliving the moment. "It was very strange," she said, "And difficult to describe because there are no words for it in the human language. It was as if I was suddenly bombarded by sensations I had never experienced before." Ryan shook her head. "No, that's not quite right."

Susan tried to help her. "Your senses were enhanced?"

Ryan again shook her head. "No, not just enhanced. It goes far beyond that." Ryan glanced over at the silk shirt that Susan was wearing. "When you first put that shirt on today, you could feel the silk against your skin, could you not?"

Susan nodded, thinking back to the experience as Ryan continued. "And yet, within minutes of wearing the shirt, you became deadened to the experience, and now you can no longer feel it."

Susan moved the shirtsleeve against her arm, trying to recreate the initial feeling. Ryan was correct, even now it was difficult to consciously feel the softness of the shirt.

Ryan continued thoughtfully. "I read in 20th century literature that this 'deadening' was a product of human development, that without it, human senses would be overwhelmed, and you would be so distracted with the feel of the silk against your skin you could not protect yourself from danger."

Ryan's gaze was distant. "When I awoke, it was almost as if that protective mechanism had been removed. Not only were my senses enhanced, but I was no longer capable of filtering out unwanted stimuli, or any stimuli for that matter."

Susan shook her head, but more in disbelief than disagreement. "How could that be? How could you keep from going immediately insane? How could you even walk across a room if you were so flooded with sensation?"

"It was not easy," Ryan said, "At the time, of course, I did not know any of this. I simply woke up seeing and feeling things I never knew existed. And I dealt with them, with a great deal of help from Victor." She then added as an afterthought, "My Change was not an easy one."

Susan was retracing their conversation, trying to organize the questions that were flying about in her head. Ryan was still thinking aloud.

"Perhaps that's why I slept for so long. At the time I had no idea what had happened to me. With 14th century eyes, I thought perhaps my soul had been stolen or I had become one of the walking damned. But looking at it now with eyes that have seen the 20th century, I think perhaps I slept so long because my brain was reworking itself to deal with what I had become."

"Is it unusual for you to sleep that long?"

Ryan nodded. "I have not slept nearly that long since. It's not unusual for me to sleep for weeks, or even months. But years, years is extremely rare, and I have never approached 14 since."

"So what do you see? What's so different about your perception?"

Ryan looked around the dimly lit living room. Her gaze settled on the cinnamon candles burning on the mantle. "I would have as much luck describing what I see as you would have describing colors to a blind man. You could say that red is 'hot' or blue is 'cool,' but that simply reinterprets what you see. It never allows the blind man to actually see it."

Ryan glanced back at Susan. "Did you know that heat is a color, and it's not red?"

It was Susan's turn to look over at the candles. That certainly made sense, but it was difficult to imagine. All of the different wavelengths of light probably had corresponding colors; humans were only capable of seeing the "visible" spectrum.

"I suppose your hearing is the same?"

Ryan nodded. "I can hear your heartbeat from across the room." Ryan smiled her shark's smile. "And it just skipped a beat." Susan blushed as Ryan continued. "You would feel ultrasound; I can hear it. I can feel things you can only hear, and I can see things that you can only feel."

"As I grew older, my senses became more powerful, more refined. I began to feel forces swirling around me. It was not until science described the earth's magnetic field that I had a name for these forces." Ryan shrugged in her impassive way. "Of course, placing a label on what I was feeling did not alter the experience."

"Having had the luxury of many, many years of study, I would have to say that eastern mystics are probably the closest to having a perception like mine."

"How is that?" Susan asked.

Ryan contemplated the room around her. "I see everything as a whole.

It's the only way to process the information my senses draw in. There is no separation, no division until I consciously draw it. Human development chose a different path, chose to divide things, to alter reality to increase your chances for survival." Ryan looked at her for the first time with something close to disapproval. "And then your race forgot they did so."

This approach was interesting to Susan, but she thought she saw a weakness in Ryan's reasoning. "So you believe you have the one true perception of reality?"

Ryan laughed, easily anticipating the coming argument. "Absolutely not, I just think my version is a good deal closer to the mark than yours."

Ryan abruptly stood, and it was evident their conversation was at an end. Susan thought for a moment that Ryan was simply going to disappear, but she stopped, appearing thoughtful.

She turned to Susan. "I enjoy our conversations, Dr. Ryerson. There is a courage about you that I admire."

Susan was embarrassed at how pleased the statement made her. Ryan glanced down at her. "Against the counsel of my manservant, Edward, I have decided that I will allow you to study me."

Her voice hardened and her unblinking gaze locked with Susan's. "But you must not publish anything else."

Susan nodded her agreement. "Of course," she said glancing down, "Just the knowledge alone-"

Susan glanced back up, realizing that she was speaking to an empty room.

Ryan was gone.

Ryan climbed into the back of her limousine. Edward could not hide his disapproval.

"So you have done this deed?"

Ryan nodded, oddly tired from her conversation with Susan. She realized she was not completely recovered from her injuries. The healing process took incredible amounts of energy and she would require much more sleep than normal until she was completely recovered.

"Yes, Edward, I have done this deed."

Edward turned away and stared out the window. He brooded over this turn of events in silence. It was Ryan who finally broke that silence.

"Edward," she said firmly. It was both a request and a command. Edward turned to his youthful master. She chose her words carefully.

"It is only a matter of time before my past actions catch up with me. Dr. Ryerson has, without intent, now accelerated this process. I think it would be foolish for me to overlook her as a resource."

Edward vented his frustration. "You could just as easily force her to do your will. Or seduce her. You don't have to allow her to study you."

Ryan's demeanor did not change. "She will work much harder if she is driven by her own ambition. She may give me the clues I need to withstand what will come."

Edward was unswayed. "She may sow the seeds of your destruction."

Ryan shrugged. "So be it," she said.

Edward turned away. He knew the conversation was over, but his concern for his master would not let him stop.

"You have brought up the specter of your past. The Others may consider this as great a crime."

Ryan's look turned sardonic. "I sincerely doubt that, Edward. I am damned a thousand times over for that. I don't think consorting with a human will add to my sentence."

"It is not consorting with a human they will charge you with, but rather violating the code of secrecy. Our Kind has not survived for thousands of years by winding up on the front page of Newsweek Magazine, nor by becoming medical experiments for those whose ambition might betray us."

Ryan's anger was evident, perhaps fueled by the knowledge that Edward was right. "I," she said with emphasis, "Have been around for a great many of those years. I know the punishment for revealing our Kind. If I felt I was jeopardizing our secrecy, I would never submit to Dr. Ryerson's examination. It is why I forbade her to publish anything else."

Edward turned away from her to stare out the window. "It may already be too late," he said, resignation in his voice. "The Others sent their first 'emissary' when the dear doctor had done no more than publish a few cryptic results in an obscure medical journal. Their willingness to take immediate action should convince you this is a most serious matter to them."

Ryan, too, gazed out the window. "It will be a more serious matter to them if they choose to take me on."

Edward did not reply.

The limousine came to a stop and Ryan exited onto the marble staircase. Tired or not, she took the stairs three at a time, strolling into the foyer. Edward entered behind her, and she turned to him. He sighed, then bowed, knowing how utterly strong-willed his master was.

Ryan went upstairs to her bed. She undressed, then pulled the goose-down comforter over her. She was momentarily lost in the sensation of the fabric against her skin, and it took several minutes for the sensation to pass. Her senses were such that the tiniest of pleasures, unnoticed by most humans, was sufficient to create considerable bliss. It had taken years for her to learn not to be driven to distraction by such stimuli.

Ryan felt sleep steal over her quickly, as it always did. She knew she would dream vivid dreams that were less dreams than pure memories.

The girl awoke, feeling an extraordinary sense of peace. She glanced around, thinking the Man would be here, but he was not. She was in the same room, but now an old woman sat at the foot of the bed.

The girl stared at the woman, thinking she looked strangely familiar. Perhaps it was her daughter she had seen earlier.

Victor entered the room, knowing his charge was now awake. "Miriam, you may leave now."

The girl looked closer at the woman as she hobbled out of the room. She still looked remarkably familiar. Victor watched her expression with amusement. "Do you know how long you've been asleep, Rhian?"

Ryan looked up at the man. She knew that she had a name yet had not heard it but once or twice in her life. She had always been known simply as "the blacksmith's son," or some variation thereof. She had forgotten she had a name. She shook her head.

"Have I slept more than a day?"

Victor laughed. "Yes, I would say more than a day."

Ryan looked about the room. "What's wrong with my eyes?"

It seemed as if she could see every little crack in the wall, and there were colors coming from the fire in the hearth, colors she had never seen before. She pulled herself from the bed, and was surprised at how light on her feet she felt. She moved to the fireplace and put her hand in the color. It was warm, and the darker the color, the hotter it became.

The sensation of heat on her skin was nearly overwhelming as she felt it in every part of her body. She pulled her hand away, startled.

Victor watched his prodigy begin to adapt to her new senses. They would continue to change over time, but it was generally this first adjustment that was the most difficult.

Ryan stood staring into the fire, her mind a jumble of events. Something within her had radically altered, but she was not certain what it was.

"How long have I slept?" she asked quietly, her back to Victor.

Victor was silent a long moment, then responded. "Fourteen years."

Ryan turned to him, stunned. "That is not possible."

Victor shrugged. "You saw Miriam. She has not aged as well as you have."

Ryan looked down at her hands, and except for her sudden, extraordinary clarity of vision, they looked exactly the same. She touched her hand to her cheek, and it was as smooth as it had been before. Ryan looked at him.

"You have not changed, either. How can this be?"

"I do not change. Nor will you. Ever."

Ryan was suddenly desperately afraid of this man and darted for the door. She was inhumanly fast but he was more so. He picked her up and she struggled with him.

"You," he said, grappling with her, "Are already too strong." His tone was not at all displeased and Ryan even sensed a trace of pride as he fought to gain control of her. She realized how futile her position was and settled.

Victor looked down at her. "You will not change. You will not grow old, and you will not die."

Ryan pulled away from him, now even more afraid. "This is blasphemy. If I do not die, how will my soul be redeemed?"

Victor's sarcasm was evident. "I care nothing for the redemption of your soul. If you do not die, then it is no concern."

Ryan ran to the hearth and plucked the dagger from the wall there. She held the knife to her throat, threatening.

"If I cannot die, then this will not hurt me."

Victor elegantly sprawled into a chair, unconcerned. "Oh, it will hurt you. But it will not kill you. Go ahead," he challenged, his eyes gleaming, "Cut your throat."

Ryan swallowed hard. She had never been afraid of death and did not fear it now. She would wake up tomorrow in the afterworld and this sacrilege would be gone. She took a deep breath, then raked the knife across her throat.

Blood spurted out and Victor, although feigning indifference, could not contain himself. In seconds he was on his knees holding his dark child. The blood flowed freely into his mouth.

Ryan lay there, realizing she had played into his hands. Although mild dizziness overtook her, death was nowhere near as the warmth began to spread throughout her body. Because of where Ryan had slit her throat, Victor's neck was at such an angle that his throbbing neck veins were nearly pressed against Ryan's lips.

Ryan nearly moaned in despair. What madness and depravity was this? That she should crave something so unholy, so unnatural?

"Do it," Victor commanded through gritted teeth. His own passion was consuming him.

Ryan could not fight the strange desire and leaned forward, biting him. She was surprised at the ease with which her teeth pierced his skin, but her surprise gave way to ecstasy as his blood flowed into her body.

The strange pictures came to her again, almost as if she was seeing through someone else's eyes. But the pictures were fuzzy and unclear and made no sense to her. Once more, it was different; this time more powerful, more painfully beautiful. She could stay at that peak of pleasure longer, but again in the end, had to pull away.

She collapsed on the floor, her heart pounding.

A scream startled Ryan from the floor and she sprang to her knees, but not as quickly as Victor sprang to his feet. Miriam was standing in the doorway, her eyes wide with terror at the sight of the two covered in blood. In two quick steps, Victor was at her side and broke her neck.

She fell to the ground with a thud.

Ryan looked at the dead woman on the floor. She looked at Victor standing over his faithful maid, covered in blood with an expression of mild exasperation on his face. She looked down at herself, her white shirt a crimson red.

Victor watched the girl on the floor. He knew this was a pivotal moment. It would be quite possible for her to break, and although he could make her as physically powerful as possible, he could do nothing to strengthen her mental state.

Ryan very carefully stood, as if the act itself could bring her stability. She glanced at the woman on the floor. She glanced at Victor, covered in blood. She glanced down at her soiled clothing.

"Do you," she said, steadying herself, "Do you have another shirt I can wear?"

Victor's face was impassive but he inwardly smiled. He had chosen well.

CHAPTER 16

SUSAN PACED AROUND THE OBSERVATION CUBICLE IN HER laboratory. She was not expecting Ryan for another hour, but she was impatient to begin. Not only was she driven by the possibility of medical knowledge, now there was an alien, medieval world flitting through her mind.

Susan glanced in at the empty bed where Ryan had once laid. What did one do when faced with the impossible? In the movies, the characters made one or two objections, then settled upon the most unlikely of explanations. These explanations never caused the mind-altering, life-changing experience they would in reality. Most people could not accept something as simple as death without months of an adjustment process called grief. Yet characters on television accepted UFO's, beings from space, aliens, supernatural experiences, etc., without them making so much as an indentation on their mental landscape.

What did one do when faced with the impossible?

Susan would like to have discounted Ryan as mentally unstable. But other than her fantastic story, she demonstrated no signs of mental instability. In fact, she was extremely articulate and intelligent. Susan actually enjoyed listening to her, if she could just get past her discomfort over the content.

And then there were the physical aspects of Ryan that were, well, also impossible. Her anatomy was completely foreign. She had healed from injuries that would have killed anyone else, and had done so in a matter of days. She had already demonstrated levels of strength far beyond those of a normal human.

Susan stopped herself. This was going nowhere, because she was trying to think of Ryan in comparison to a normal human. Ryan was not a normal human, if she could be considered human at all.

Susan felt an odd sense of relief at having finally, even if silently, voiced the thought. Perhaps Ryan wasn't human. There were a lot of different species on earth. Perhaps she was a different form of primate, an offshoot of humans or a different branch of the family tree. Evolution said it could happen, humans just didn't think of it as happening to them.

Susan mentally went over what she knew about Ryan. She had to admit, if she were going to create a being with an extended lifespan, she would certainly include all the ingredients in Ryan's blood. And if she were going to genetically engineer a vampire, it really would not have need of a stomach, and its esophagus should certainly be connected to its heart.

This thought was extremely sobering to Susan.

But Ryan had treated the idea of a vampire with disdain. Was it just a matter of semantics? Could it be possible that such a creature could exist, living off the blood of others? Mosquitoes did, as did leeches. Would it be possible for a creature the size of a human to adapt in such a way? What chemical interactions would be involved? What nutrient breakdown of the blood could support such a creature?

The complexity of the questions was mind-boggling. It was as if all rules were broken and re-written for Ryan to exist. Susan was overwhelmed by the possibilities.

She shook her head to clear it. No sense in becoming overwhelmed before she even got started. She leaned around the corner to peer out into the hallway. The portion she could see was empty. She glanced at her watch and decided to make a dash for the restroom before Ryan arrived.

She stared into the bathroom mirror, plucking at her red hair. She saw many of her son's features staring back at her: the green eyes, the light sprinkle of freckles across the nose, the rosy cheeks. The thought of her son brought a smile to her face. Although Jason had gotten most of his looks from her, he had Brent's gentleness and irrepressible sense of humor. She was glad Jason seemed to get the best of both of them. Susan washed her hands, dried them on a towel, then exited the restroom.

She was straightening the cuff on her lab coat as she entered the hallway and almost missed the figure ducking into the elevator. She was not certain she had seen what she thought she had seen, so she hurriedly moved to the closing doors. She was too late, though, and the doors whispered shut in her face. The numbers began to light up as the car dropped to the ground floor.

Susan turned and was startled by another figure coming down the hallway. She relaxed when she saw it was the security guard.

"Albert," she asked, "Was that Dr. Goldstein who just got on the elevator?"

The security guard nodded. "Yes ma'am," he said. He seemed a little puzzled. "I don't know why he left so quickly, though. He said he came up here to see you."

Susan was both thoughtful and suspicious. "He did, hmm. Did you let him into the lab?"

Albert shook his head. "No ma'am," he said emphatically. "I've been told that the only one who goes in your lab is you. I brought Dr. Goldstein up here, but I told him he'd have to wait in the hallway for you. He was kind of impatient, but I don't know why he wouldn't wait."

Susan was no longer thoughtful, only suspicious. She had a pretty good idea why he wouldn't wait, and she was doubtful that Goldstein had come up here to see her. In fact, he was probably hoping she was gone. Fortunately, Stanley Meyers had agreed to all of her requests for added security, and there was no chance Goldstein could go snooping through her lab.

Susan re-entered the lab, and within minutes perked her head up. She heard another set of footsteps coming down the hall, but this time it was someone with a casual gait and long strides. Susan knew the identity just from that leisurely stroll.

Susan went to the security door and opened it. Ryan stood outside of it, her hands casually thrust in her pockets. Susan was struck again by the power of her physical presence. She actually felt a little flustered, and then was both angered and mortified by the feeling. This caused her to be a little brusque.

"Please come in."

Ryan smiled her predatory smile, not the least bit perturbed by Susan's blunt manner. She followed Susan into the observational cubicle.

"This is a picture of your internal organs." Susan laid out the hard copy of the MRI and Ryan leaned over it with interest.

"Are you familiar with normal human anatomy?"

Ryan did not look up from the picture. "Quite."

Susan nodded, all business. "Good, then you'll understand what I'm saying." She pointed to the heart. "This is about three times the normal size of a human's heart. It's probably developed this way to accommodate the large amount of blood your body sometimes holds."

Ryan nodded. "I notice the entire circulatory is extremely developed. That makes sense."

Susan nodded her agreement. "You said you don't eat. That also matches your anatomy. I don't see a stomach or any digestive organs. Your esophagus," Susan tapped the drawing, "Appears to be attached here, so it's become a part of your digestive system..."

Susan removed some more readouts. "Now the strength test you gave me the other day yielded some very interesting results."

Ryan stared over her shoulder as Susan continued. "I think I can explain at least some of your strength ."

Susan set the charts on top of the MRI readout, then turned to look up at Ryan. "Normal strength levels or strength increases are generally due to muscle hypertrophy, or an increase in muscle size. Even though you're very muscular," she said, "Your size can't account for your incredible strength."

Ryan nodded her understanding and Susan continued. "Muscle hyperplasia, the splitting of muscle fibers, could account for normal strength increases. But your strength increases are so far outside normal ranges that, even though an analysis of your muscle tissue indicates extreme hyperplasia, it's not even close to being an explanation."

Ryan again nodded. "So if you're telling me it's neither of these things, I assume you have another explanation?"

Susan bobbed her head excitedly. "I didn't really key on it until I was looking at your charts. It's not anything particular to the muscle itself, but rather the muscle's neuro-efficiency."

Ryan examined the charts. "So what you're saying is, it's not the way the muscle and nerves are firing, but the rate at which they're firing."

Susan was surprised at the remarkably accurate summary. She looked up at Ryan. "Exactly. The nerve impulses in your body are firing so quickly my equipment can't measure it." She glanced back down at the charts. "But it's definitely thousands of times faster than a normal human being."

Ryan was thoughtful. "I read somewhere that bone can withstand 20,000 pounds of pressure and it is the limitations of human connective tissue which limit strength."

Susan agreed. "Right. That and the body's own safety mechanisms which keep it from injuring itself." She then qualified the statement. "But you may not have either of those limitations. And," she added, "Your bones may be even stronger."

"Speaking of bones," Susan said, her tone of voice changing slightly, "Let me take a look at your teeth."

Ryan smiled, neither perturbed nor fooled by Susan's unsubtle request. Susan thought for a moment that Ryan was going to refuse her, but then the golden-haired woman simply shrugged and opened her mouth slightly.

Susan moved forward cautiously, and her caution seemed to amuse Ryan. She pulled a penlight from her pocket and shined it into Ryan's mouth, still unable to see her teeth. She took another step closer, trying to peer in without actually getting too close. She had a tongue depressor in her left hand, and she used it to widen Ryan's jaw ever so slightly.

Ryan snapped her teeth together and the wooden depressor splintered at the pressure. Susan jumped backward and laughed nervously.

Ryan stared at the other woman with her unblinking gaze. "All you have to do, " she said with emphasis, "Is ask."

Ryan smiled, revealing two rows of perfect teeth. There were no fangs, nothing out of the ordinary, just two rows of gleaming bicuspids.

Ryan picked up the piece of paper the strength tests were recorded on. She ran it lightly over the front of her teeth. It made a shearing noise as it split in two, a noise similar to that of sharpened scissors passing through notebook paper. The human occupant of the room stared as the papers fluttered to the floor.

Ryan gazed at Susan with her unwavering gaze, then did something Susan had never seen her do. She blinked.

Susan stared up at her, not certain she had seen what she thought she had seen. Although Ryan had blinked, she had done so without closing her eyes.

Susan moved in closer, fascinated. "Do that again."

Ryan obliged and again blinked. Susan brought the penlight back into operation and stood on tiptoe. "One more time, but this time leave it closed."

Ryan obliged and Susan stepped back in amazement. "You have a second eyelid, just like a shark." She waved her hand in front of Ryan's face. "It's nearly translucent. Can you see this?"

Ryan's hand flashed out and she seized Susan's wrist. "I can see fine."

"That's amazing," Susan murmured, thinking aloud. "Shark's developed a second eyelid because they're such fierce predators, I wonder why...."

Susan's words trailed off and she felt a huge discomfort at the implications of her own words. She also suddenly realized how close in proximity she was to Ryan. She stepped back. Ryan released her wrist, smiling her tight smile, now revealing no teeth.

"I should probably leave now, Dr. Ryerson," she said, gently mocking, "I have other business I have to attend to."

Susan nodded dumbly and stood there while the woman let herself out. She felt disoriented and could not even generate anger at herself for the way she was acting. Ryan had the strangest mixture of power and vulnerability, of self-confidence and reticence, as if she possessed an extraordinary ability that she herself fought to keep under control.

Susan looked down at the strength chart that was now sheared in two. She glanced over at the tongue depressor that was now in splinters.

She had a pretty good idea what Ryan used that second eyelid for.

CHAPTER 17

Ryan watched Victor move through the courtyard, admiring his grace and physical beauty, unaware that she looked and moved the same way. He spoke to her, and in even the simplest interaction, his desire for her was subtly present.

"Take your sword, 'boy,' or I shall slay you where you stand."

Ryan mimicked his mocking manner. "I should like to see that, my lord." Her sword was on the ground in front of her and she flipped it upward with the tip of her boot, catching it easily in her hand. Although the sword was heavy and looked far too large for her slight frame, she wielded it easily. She took a couple of practice swings through the air, then lunged toward her mentor.

Victor deflected the blade and the fierce engagement was on. Many stopped their chores to watch the Master and his young charge battle, marveling at the savagery of the fight. It was said that few could match the ferocity of their mock engagements, even in the heat of battle.

Rumors had spread when the boy had appeared from nowhere. Many felt his lordship had sired a bastard and was training him for warfare so the boy could raise his station in life. Others felt there was another, more sinister motive, that his lordship had tired of women and had taken a liking to boys. Most shrugged, buggery was not acceptable, but not uncommon either.

Whatever the boy's purpose, few would speak aloud of it for fear of the

Master.

Ryan fought skillfully, parrying Victor's thrusts and counterattacking.

Once Ryan had begun to adjust to the Change, Victor began to educate her in everything from reading and rudimentary mathematics to the art of warfare. He himself had traveled much of the known world and beyond, and he set out to pass on his formidable knowledge to his prodigy.

Victor was never disappointed in Ryan and if anything, was continually amazed at her. He had chosen far better than he could ever have wished. Born into a world where stability was prized and change was abhorred, she faced the unknown with an astounding insouciance.

Victor performed a complex series of maneuvers that Ryan struggled to defend against. She had lost her sword previously, but she had also learned from her mistake. Although the defense was awkward, it was successful and she pushed him back.

Victor laughed, pleased. His "boy" was one of the most skillful swordsman he had ever seen, and he had seen many. Victor sheathed his sword. And he had killed as many.

Victor threw his arm about Ryan's shoulders as the two walked into the castle. Once inside the main hall, Ryan loosed her hair and let it fall about her shoulders. No one would trespass within these walls unless called, and both she and Victor would be aware of an intruder's presence long before they were aware of theirs.

Victor removed his leather jerkin, revealing a white, embroidered shirt beneath. Ryan removed her mesh, revealing similar dress. She hung the chain mail on a rack. The metal shell was not so much heavy to her as unwieldy, and she was learning to fight in the cumbersome garb.

Victor cocked his head to one side and motioned to Ryan. Ryan stepped back, disappearing into the shadows. It was another skill Victor had taught her, one she was quick to perfect.

The knock came at the door and Victor took his seat.

"Enter."

The messenger came through the great doors, followed by two of the castle guards. The messenger bowed low as the guards took their posts close by, eager to protect their master.

The great Lord needed little if any protection, the messenger thought to himself. He fought to still his trembling.

Even as a child he had heard stories of the great Lord of the east, a man from a line of warriors so powerful that no King dared conscript them and no Prince dared demand tribute. The King had never asked for this man's help, but his father had.

The messenger stood. "Your skill in battle is well-known, my lord, and your family is legendary. His royal majesty, Henry the III requests your allegiance."

The messenger leaned forward to hand Victor the parchment. Victor examined the document and the seal. He appeared unimpressed, both by the letter and the man's announcement.

He rolled the parchment and returned it to the man. "My skill is not known to this King. I have never stood at his side."

The messenger nodded. "This is true, my lord. But your father fought for Edward, the Black Prince, as did your father's father. Henry knows your family, and feels you can help him gain his land back from the French."

Victor laughed mockingly. "I am but one man. I have no armies, no foot soldiers. I have nothing to offer the King but my sword."

The messenger bowed his head once more. "That is all he requests, my lord."

Victor pondered the man's words. He had foreseen such a request. Each King had approached him over the years, all drawn by the legend of his family's prowess in battle. He had been careful that none should see him in their old age, and each new King thought he was his father's son, asking him to stand by England's side.

He had no wish to fight for this King's cause, nor any man's. But he had learned over time that denying a King's request was more trouble than it was worth. He did not fear the King, but had found it fruitful to respond to the throne's wishes. It generally brought him much reward, and enough respect and fear that he and his own were left alone in his remote lands.

Victor glanced down at the still-bowing man. And of course, he thought to himself, he did so ever love a good battle.

"You tell your King I will be in Agincourt before the new moon."

The messenger stood, surprised that his lordship knew of the King's location. It had been an unplanned destination as Henry had intended to march to Calais, but had been thwarted by the flooded Somme. This man somehow already knew where the King was headed. It was enough he said he would be there.

"Thank you my lord, and godspeed."

The messenger and two guards exited as Victor sat thoughtfully on his dais. Ryan moved from the shadows to his side. She waited expectantly for him to say something, and when he did not, she drew a dagger and began sharpening the edge with a flint. The silence became too great for her and at last she spoke.

"You will, of course, take me."

Victor looked at her with a raised eyebrow. "Right now, my dear? You are so demanding."

Ryan's brow furrowed in anger, and with a flick of her wrist she sent the dagger sailing towards his throat. His hand moved too fast for even her eyes to see and he plucked the knife from the air.

Ryan stamped her foot. "I meant 'take me with you.' And if you do not, you will not be 'taking me' any time soon, either."

"Oh really," Victor said, fingering the blade, "As if you had any say in that."

As he finished his last word, his wrist flicked and the dagger flew back towards its owner, swifter and as true as she had thrown it. She cried out in pain as the knife impaled her just below her collarbone. She gazed down at the hilt of the dagger, her eyes burning with anger.

Victor was immediately mesmerized by the blood that began pouring from the wound, staining the white shirt. Once again he had underestimated the effect she had on him. He had to forcibly restrain himself from leaping from his chair.

"Come here," he commanded through clenched teeth.

Ryan gazed down at the blood on her hands and at the growing crimson stain on her shirt. She looked up at him defiantly. "I will not."

Victor felt his hunger as if it were a thing alive. He could not take his eyes from the scarlet stain. There was a growing hoarseness in his voice.

"If the distance between you and I is too great even at this moment, what makes you think I could travel further without you." Victor dragged his eyes from the blood to stare into her own. His words were evenly spaced and brooked no further disobedience. "Now, come here!"

Ryan moved toward him, knowing she could not further defy him. But she lingered, still angry, and he snatched her from her feet, dragging her to the chair with him. She was seated on his lap, facing him and he yanked the dagger from her chest. He buried his face in her bloody shirt and covered the wound with his mouth.

The pain from the wound was intense, but the pleasure from Victor's feeding was more so. As soon as her blood began to pulse through his veins, she began to see the visions.

She had seen them before when they had Shared, and each time they became clearer. She saw them vaguely when Victor fed upon her, more clearly when she fed upon him, and most clearly when they Shared together. She did not understand what she was seeing, nor did she have any control over the apparitions. The pictures came to her as dreams.

She could feel Victor's pleasure intensify as he was reaching satiety, and was so attuned to him she did not hesitate when he pulled away and leaned back, opening his throat to her. Ryan leaned forward, allowing her razor sharp teeth to whisper over the skin on his neck. Blood began pulsing into her mouth, giving Victor's engorged veins the release they needed and feeding her hunger.

The visions became startlingly clear and she nearly pulled away from him in her dismay. He had anticipated her reaction and held her close, forcing her to continue.

Ryan saw a young peasant boy, fair-haired and fair-skinned. She saw her mother standing by the boy, and then her father pounding away at an anvil. They looked as they had decades before, long even before they had been killed in Derek's raid.

The vision changed and now she was chasing someone through the forest. It appeared to be an older boy, but still a child. The boy was agile but she was catching him easily. She leapt upon him, dragging him to her.

In shock, Ryan pulled away from Victor and the vision slipped away from her. She stared at her mentor in horror and dawning understanding.

"That was me, wasn't it?"

Victor stared at the youngster on his lap. She was nearing her eighth decade, but to him she was still a child. He wiped the blood from his mouth.

"Yes," he said calmly, "That was you."

Ryan still did not completely understand. "How could I see myself," she stopped, struggling for words, "In that way?"

Victor readjusted her weight, sitting up slightly. "Because you are looking through my eyes."

Ryan now pulled completely away from him, standing up. Victor let her go.

She stared at the man in front of her, a man who knew everything about her, but who suddenly seemed a stranger to her.

"You fed on me when I was a child."

Victor nodded, unperturbed. "I Shared with you when you were an infant, and then again as a young child. I gave you my blood when you were still human."

Ryan looked at him accusingly. "You tried to kill me. You made me deathly ill. My father thought I had sinned against God to bring such a plague on myself."

"It is what saved your life time and time again," Victor said angrily, "And gave you strength that no mortal could have. It lessened the pain of your Change because you had already begun to Change long before I took you."

Ryan stared at him, realizing a further implication. "Then you planned my Change long before it ever took place. You planned everything."

Victor looked at her with his unblinking gaze and a fire burned there that wasn't all anger. "You were perfect in every way. I could not take the chance you would fall prey to some disease or be killed by some outlaw. I made certain you would survive until you could be Changed, and even then I could not wait and Changed you too soon."

Ryan wanted to ask him what he meant by "too soon," but another question fought its way to the surface. "How did you know I would be 'perfect'?"

Victor's face became impassive, and he wore a dispassionate expression normally reserved for his underlings. "I just knew," he said.

Ryan was suddenly uncertain. Victor rarely kept things from her, but as she watched him walk from the room she had the distinct feeling he was doing so now.

CHAPTER 18

Susan pulled into the 24-hour mini-market. She normally didn't shop here and rarely even came to this neighborhood, but Neda had called and asked her to pick up some milk on the way home. She didn't see the harm in running in and running out.

She stepped from her Lexus. The parking lot was dirty. The trash bin was overflowing with garbage and the surrounding area smelled strongly of urine. Susan glanced up at the sun, relieved that she still had another hour or so of sunlight. She set the car alarm, then walked across the parking lot to the store.

The odor of mildew from the refrigeration unit was nearly enough to end Susan's search. But a few milk cartons with expiration dates indicating they were fairly fresh caught her eye. She snatched one, quickly paid for it, then exited back into the parking lot.

She was nearing her car when she sensed a presence behind her. She glanced back and saw two men following her, then a third behind them. Oddly enough they were dressed in business suits. Any other time she would have been relieved by their attire. But it was so inconsistent with this neighborhood that she quickened her step, her heart picking up pace as well.

She was too far from the store entrance now and didn't think she could get into her car before the men caught up with her. She briefly contemplated standing her ground, but then decided that three against one were not good odds. In a hasty decision she would regret, she walked past her car in the hope that there was an establishment nearby that she could duck into. She turned the corner and was alarmed to see there were no storefronts along this row of buildings, no crowds for her to disappear into. She quickened her step until now she was almost at a jog. A glance back told her the men were keeping pace with her, removing any remaining doubt they were indeed stalking her.

Susan broke into a run and she heard an exclamation as the men behind her began to give chase. She was surprised they did not catch her immediately. In fact, she managed half a block in high heels before the closest one caught her. She started to scream, but the man quickly put his hand over her mouth.

"Don't make this difficult on yourself, Dr. Ryerson."

Susan's eyes were wide. One of the men removed a roll of duct tape from his pocket and Susan began struggling. A black Lincoln town car with tinted windows pulled to the curb, and the man holding her tried to pull her toward the door. Susan resisted, stomping her heel down on his instep. He swore and released her. The larger of the other two wrapped his arms around her in a bear hug. He lifted her off the ground while the other tried to tape her kicking legs. The scene up until that moment had been almost comical. But then the one who had received the spiked heel stepped forward and slugged Susan in the face. She instantly stopped struggling and hung limply in the large man's arms.

A strange, tuneless whistle drifted over the sounds of distant traffic, and the men, as one, turned to look up the street.

A tall figure dressed in dark clothing came strolling down the sidewalk, hands in pockets. The approaching woman did not seem overly concerned with the scene ahead of her, and that in itself was enough to give the men pause. They seemed confused by her presence, uncertain what to do.

Ryan removed her hand from her pocket and began to run it along the chain-link fence bordering the sidewalk. Without removing her eyes from the three men, she let her hand drift up the fence. As she walked, she began casually brushing it along the barbed wire. She appeared almost to caress the wire, then gripped it in the palm of her hand, still moving. The barbs sliced into her flesh as she slid her hand down the wire and blood began to flow down her arm. As she stepped away from the fence she clenched her fist and snapped the wire from the post, wrapping the barbed strand around her knuckles.

The men were frozen, stunned by the act of self-mutilation and the fact it appeared to have no effect on the woman walking towards them. A very primal fear began to grow in all of them, but not soon enough for it to save them.

Ryan hit the first man with her makeshift brass knuckles and drove him into the ground. She turned on the next man who tried to strike her, but she easily blocked the blow and raked the barbs across his cheek. He was the one who had struck Susan. Ryan palmed his face in her hand and with little more than a shove, threw his entire body backward, headfirst through the passenger window of the towncar. The car squealed off, the man's limp body hanging from the window.

The last man huddled behind Susan and Ryan reached down, grabbing the man's shirt collar. She picked him up contemptuously and threw him like a rag doll against the wall. He fell into a crumpled heap.

Ryan tossed the barbed wire aside and with her other hand leaned down. In her oddly chivalrous manner, she helped Susan to her feet. She touched the bruise that was forming on Susan's cheek.

"So tell me, dear doctor, is your research worth this?"

Susan was shaken, but also angry. "How long is this going to go on?" she asked accusingly. "How many of your 'kind' are going to come after me?"

Ryan shook her head. "Oh no," she said, glancing down at the unconscious man. "These are not my Kind."

Ryan's reply brought Susan up short. "Not your kind?" She, too, looked down at the unconscious man. "Then who are these people? What do they want with me?"

Ryan shook her head, holding out her arm to Susan. "I do not know." Her eyes swept the deserted street. "But I will find out."

Susan took the proffered arm, then brushed at her skirt in embarrassment. "You're quite strong."

Ryan smiled without revealing her teeth. "Fight or flight syndrome, I'm sure." She turned to look down the block, her amusement evident. "But I never flee."

Susan noticed the damage to Ryan's hand. The physician in her, and possibly some sort of mothering instinct came into play. She removed her arm from Ryan's and took the damaged hand in her own.

"That wasn't very intelligent," she said, examining the hand.

Ryan pulled her hand from the doctor's grasp and raised it to her own lips. "It's not as if it's going to kill me," she said, looking at Susan over the hand and gently sucking the blood from the wound.

Susan watched her with a sense of morbid fascination. It was an utterly self-sensual act, and it seemed to slow the bleeding.

"What are you doing?" Susan asked, not certain she wanted to know.

The blood had stopped and Ryan wiped her lips. "Well, I've heard the act of Sharing is similar to sex, so this must be akin to masturbation." She turned on her heel. "So glad I could share that with you," she said over her shoulder.

Susan watched as the woman began to stroll unhurriedly down the street once more. "Is that what you call it," Susan asked when she caught up with her, "Sharing?"

Ryan shrugged, hands in pockets once more. "For lack of a better term. It is appropriate."

"Well, the ones who are killed might object to it," Susan said.

Ryan glanced over at her. "I have killed a lot of people and have very little moral objection to it. But I have never killed anyone in the act of Sharing."

Susan was confused. "Then how do you feed?"

Ryan stopped in her tracks. "What do you mean, 'feed'? Are you still caught up in your vampire fantasies?"

Susan was slightly embarrassed. "Well, I just assumed from your story that-"

"That what? That I roam the night seeking innocent victims so I can suck their blood?" Ryan had a look of distaste on her features. "How disgusting."

Now Susan was really confused. "Well, I was just trying to come up with a hypothesis that fits the information you've given me, which you have to admit is pretty sketchy."

The look of distaste was still on Ryan's face as she began walking again. "But human blood would do nothing for me. And it tastes like salt. Try downing a salt shaker and tell me if that's enjoyable for you."

Susan did not think she would accept this particular challenge. "Then why was Victor different? I don't understand."

They were now back at her car. Ryan indicated that Susan should give her the keys. Susan did so, not exactly certain why.

"Victor was not human, nor am I. We don't feed on humans, but on our own Kind."

Ryan opened the passenger door and held it open for her. She then walked around the rear of the vehicle and let herself in the driver's door. She moved the seat rearward then examined the keys carefully. She chose the correct key for the ignition and started the car. She pulled the Lexus smoothly away from the curb.

Susan wanted to continue their conversation, but Ryan's driving was now taking all of her attention. Although her driving was extremely skillful, she was traveling a good 30 miles per hour over the speed limit. In no time at all, they were pulling into Susan's driveway. Mr. Earl was on the porch.

Wordlessly, Ryan exited the vehicle and rounded the car. She helped Susan from the vehicle and handed her the keys. She turned and began to walk down the street.

"So tell me," Susan called out after her, "Are you spending all your time just following me around, waiting for me to get into trouble?"

Ryan turned. "No, not exactly, I've just been lucky."

Susan unconsciously lifted her hand to the bruise on her cheek. Ryan nodded her farewell and turned away. Susan watched as the woman disappeared into the dusk.

Goldstein was startled to see two men in business suits push their way into his office. It was late, and he was not expecting them to return. Upon closer inspection, he realized that these were not even the same men who had been there earlier.

"Who's the other woman?" the first one asked.

Goldstein shook his head. "What are you talking about? What other woman?"

The first man looked to the second and some silent communication passed between the two of them. He turned back to Goldstein. "Our employer is not going to be happy at this turn of events."

Goldstein was exasperated. "What in the hell are you talking about? I tried to get you whatever information you wanted, but I can't even get into the goddamned lab. The only other thing you asked me to do was call you next time Susan Ryerson left work. Which I did."

The two men glanced at one another once more. The first nodded stiffly. "Very well. Perhaps you won't be of much use to us after all. We will relay your lack of competence to our employer, and he may decide he no longer has need of your services."

Goldstein watched the door close behind the two men. He silently cursed Susan Ryerson under his breath. That bitch would be his downfall yet.

He pushed away from his desk and stood up. He moved to the coat rack near his door and snatched his overcoat. He grabbed his hat, inadvertently wrinkling it, and struggled to put his coat on. He started to put his hat on, then paused. He looked back at his desk. He stood there for a moment, contemplating. He turned away from the desk angrily and crushed the hat onto his head. He reached for the doorknob, but again paused.

Frustrated by his own indecision, he snatched the hat from his head and threw it on the ground. He removed his overcoat and tossed it in the general direction of the coat rack, ignoring the fact that it fell to the floor. He marched back to his desk.

He pulled the false panel from underneath the desktop and leaned down to dial the combination to the safe. He dialed it incorrectly the first time and swore under his breath. The second time the lock released with a barely audible click and Goldstein opened the door. He carefully removed the object within and settled into his chair.

Goldstein stared into the vial of blood. Although it was not refrigerated and no attempt had been made to preserve it, the blood had not coagulated, dried, or changed color as it was supposed to. He inverted the vial. The bright red liquid flowed from one end to the other. He uprighted it, and the liquid flowed back to the other end. He sat back in his chair, holding the vial up to the light. The thick red fluid coated the glass, then pooled at the bottom once more. He stared at the blood, as if his observation alone could unlock the secrets it held.

David Goldstein would sit that way long into the night, his hat and coat forgotten on the floor.

CHAPTER 19

EDWARD STEPPED FROM THE LIMOUSINE AND GLANCED upward at the glass and steel skyscraper. What an utterly soulless piece of architecture, he thought to himself. No sense of grace, beauty, or refinement. It was all metal and right angles. He walked up the steps, swinging his cane. The automatic doors swung inward to admit him.

Edward crossed the lobby and stepped into the waiting elevator. He pressed the button to the top floor, ignoring the curious gazes of the other passengers. By the time the conveyance reached his destination, he was the sole occupant of the car. He stepped out into sumptuous surroundings and sniffed disapprovingly. These furnishings were as garish and tasteless as the building itself.

He approached the receptionist, who eyed him from her workstation. Two large men in dark suits stood a few feet away from her on either side. Edward smiled graciously and extended his card to her. He spoke in his utterly refined way.

"I believe Mr. Grant is expecting me."

The receptionist glanced at the card, and her demeanor changed immediately. "Oh yes, Mr. Evans. Mr. Grant is waiting for you now."

Edward was ushered into the huge corner office. He was not surprised that his large, dark-suited escort did not leave when the door shut behind him. The chair behind the executive desk swiveled around, and Alan Grant replaced the phone receiver in its cradle.

"Mr. Evans," he said without rising, "Please take a seat."

Edward stepped forward and settled into the chair. He leaned back, at ease, and folded his hands in front of him.

Grant stared at him for a long moment, then cut to the chase. "Why don't you tell me why you're here, Mr. Evans. I don't normally see anyone. But when I receive a message from one of the most prestigious law firms in town telling me that it would be in my best interest to grant you an audience, it piques my interest. Especially when they won't tell me why I should I meet with you, or even who you are."

Edward was silent for awhile longer, allowing Grant's irritation to grow. He finally spoke. "I am here on behalf of Dr. Susan Ryerson."

If Grant was surprised at the statement, he hid it well. Or he would have had the person sitting across from him not heard the increase in his heart rate. Grant attempted a mocking laugh, but Edward heard the hollowness in that as well. He smiled a tight smile, revealing no teeth. He continued.

"I understand you have attempted to purchase the rights to Dr. Ryerson's research and that the hospital has refused you."

Grant shrugged. "Grantech International is the world's largest pharmaceutical company. We would be very interested in Dr. Ryerson's research. But this is not the first time we've been turned down."

"And is it your policy to pursue alternative methods to obtain what you want?" Edward asked smoothly.

Alan Grant's face was expressionless, and in fact his demeanor would have been frightening to someone who had any reason to fear physical harm. But Edward could hear the unevenness of his heartbeat, sense his agitation. He was not fooled by the calm arrogance of Grant's reply.

"I certainly hope you're not falsely accusing me of something, Mr. Evans. I would regret having to send my attorneys after you."

Edward very slowly smiled, gazing at Grant with his unblinking stare. "Yes," he said simply, "You would." He abruptly stood, the action so quick it startled the bodyguard by the door. He placed a card on the desk in front of Grant, bowing from the waist.

"I just wanted you to know that Dr. Ryerson is currently under contract with my employer. Any further attempt to obtain her services will be viewed with some hostility. Good day, Mr. Grant."

Grant was dumbfounded. But before he could signal his bodyguard, the elderly gentleman was gone. Although he hadn't appeared to move in any great hurry, he had simply disappeared.

The bodyguard went out into the hallway, which was empty in both directions. He leaned back in the door, shaking his head. Grant waved him off, furious.

How dare that British buffoon come in here, threaten him, then just disappear. He picked up the card, then threw it down. "Timeless Enterprises," what kind of stupid name was that. He picked it up again. There wasn't even an address or a phone number on the card. It said simply, "If we need you, we'll call."

Grant's anger burned. He was not used to anyone competing with him in terms of arrogance, let alone beating him at it so soundly. He sat down heavily in his chair, fuming. He was tempted to send his men after the Brit, ordering them to drag him back here and beat him senseless.

He turned his chair to look out over the city. He would not admit to anyone, not even to himself that it was not restraint that kept him from doing so, but perhaps the tiniest trace of fear.

Ryan sat gazing into the fire in her den. She cocked her head to one side. Although the gate was a quarter of a mile away, she could hear the limousine coming up the drive. That would mean Edward was returning.

She listened patiently as the footsteps came up the staircase. Within moments, her faithful servant came through the doors. He bowed his head in subservience, but his tone was chiding.

"It is worse than we thought."

Ryan sighed. "No, Edward. I am certain it is worse than I thought. But nothing is ever as bad as you believe it to be. What news?"

Edward began without preamble. "The men are employees of a biotechnical and pharmaceutical firm known as Grantech International. I obtained a meeting today with the owner, a Mr. Alan Grant. He is a man most impressed by his own limited capabilities."

Ryan smiled at his editorializing as Edward continued.

"He is quite interested in Dr. Ryerson's research and apparently quite willing to go to great lengths to obtain it."

Ryan leaned back, stretching her neck. "Is he as ruthless as I am?"

Edward shook his head. "I have yet to meet your equal, my lord," he said dryly.

Ryan again smiled. "Enough of your flattery. Did you convince him of the error of his ways?"

Edward was thoughtful. "I left him an oblique warning. There is nothing more dangerous than a petty man with power. I did not wish to corner him, but to let him know that Dr. Ryerson is not without allies."

Ryan absorbed this information, silently pondering Edward's words.

"Who is watching Dr. Ryerson and her son now?"

"There are three of your best men guarding her as we speak. There are another four standing by should a situation develop."

Ryan was thoughtful. "Well, it seems that if anything is to happen to Dr. Ryerson, it will happen on my watch. I have had sentries posted on her 24 hours-a-day from the moment I saw that article, and yet twice now I have been the one to defend her."

"I don't believe you would have it any other way, " Edward said. He glanced at her shrewdly. "And I think these fortuitous events are due to more than fortune."

Ryan glanced at him from beneath lowered brows, but did not speak.

Edward continued. "I have long been aware of your ability to look back in time with such acute perception. I wonder if you do not look forward as well."

Ryan was quiet for a moment, then shook her head. "That is not my gift."

The odd inflection caused Edward to look over at her. It was obvious, though, that she was not going to elaborate, so he did not ask.

Both settled into silence and Ryan's thoughts drifted to the events of the night before. She was slightly angry with herself. In her attempt to remain at a distance from Dr. Ryerson, she had allowed her to be injured. She pondered what other mistakes she had made in the confrontation.

"I should not have let those men live," she said at last.

Edward did not disagree with her. "One of the men has already succumbed to his injuries. One is still unable to speak. But the third has told his story many times. Fortunately he is incoherent, and has very little credibility at this time. But who knows what time will bring?"

Ryan nodded. "I concur." She turned to him. "Will you see to it that neither lives to see the dawn?"

Edward bowed. Now this was the Ryan he knew. "I live to serve you," he said, a gleam in his eye. "And the leader of Grantech?"

Ryan took the silver case from her pocket. She stared at the inscription on it. "Leave him be. I trust your warning will be enough for the time being. If he persists in this misguided direction, I will deal with him myself."

Edward nodded, then left to carry out her bidding.

Ryan turned her attention back to the fire. Details, details.

CHAPTER 20

Jason pressed his face against the glass to get a closer look at the mummy's remains.

"Ahem," the museum attendant said, clearing his throat loudly. Susan stepped forward and pulled her eager son back.

"Not so close, kiddo, they don't want you to wake him up."

Jason squealed with laughter, moving on to the next exhibit. This one held artifacts and talismans the mummy had been buried with. The carved alligator particularly fascinated him.

Susan glanced around her, searching for Ryan's face in the crowd. They moved from the Egyptian exhibit to one covering the Middle Ages. Jason wasn't much interested in the cooking pots or farming equipment, but he was fascinated by the suits of armor and weaponry.

"Do you think you could lift one of those?"

Susan turned, surprised to see Ryan standing right next to her. Jason's eyes grew wide in recognition. He turned back to the broadsword she referred to. "I don't know," he said doubtfully, "It looks kind of heavy."

Ryan nodded. "It's very heavy." She pointed to the suit of armor. "So are those." She glanced at Susan. "In hindsight it seems a very silly way to fight." She bowed in her somewhat chivalrous manner. "Thank you for meeting me here, today."

Jason raced on to the next exhibit. "What do you know about these?" he asked.

Ryan glanced at the display case. "Those swords are for thrusting. See how they're narrow at the end? They're not that great for chopping," Ryan accented this comment with an imaginary swing, "But they're great for slipping right between here." Ryan leaned down and poked Jason in the ribs. He giggled, a little nervously.

A small crowd of people was gathering around a carpeted platform where one of the museum curators was speaking. Ryan, Susan, and Jason moved closer. Ryan eyed the ancient weapon the man held in his hands. It was nearly as long as he was tall.

"An English longbow," Ryan whispered to Susan, "Or at least a good replica."

The museum curator was speaking. "These were used around the first part of the 14th century and were the deciding factor for the English army against the French."

"Until gunpowder," Ryan said somberly. Susan glanced over at her tone of voice, then turned back to the man.

"It takes over a hundred pounds of pull to even draw the string," the curator intoned, "And there's no guarantee of accuracy even if you can pull it."

The curator made a valiant effort and drew the string back to perhaps half its capable distance. He let the string go with a twang. A few in the crowd clapped. He turned back to the crowd. "Is there anyone here who'd like to try?"

Two younger men had been watching the display with interest. They wished to try their hand at the bow. The curator waved them onto the platform to the polite applause of the crowd. The curator handed the first the bow. "Now be careful. But go ahead and try."

The first young man grasped the bow and with a great show, pulled the string back perhaps a little further than the curator. He handed it triumphantly to his partner, who repeated the effort, pulling it back a little further than his friend. The crowd again politely applauded.

Ryan watched them, her ever-present amusement in her eyes. "It helps if you use correct technique," she murmured to Susan. Jason tugged on her shirt.

"Why don't you try?"

Ryan shook her head. "I don't think that's such a good idea."

Susan turned to her. "No, why don't you give it a try? It would be interesting."

Ryan looked from one to the other. "I really don't think I should."

Susan raised her hand, waving to the curator. "Here's someone who'd like to try!"

Ryan sighed in exasperation and cast Susan a baleful look. The curator waved her on. "Certainly. We're equal opportunity employers. Come on up here and give it a try."

The curator's comment was met with good-natured laughter from the crowd. When Ryan stepped up onto the platform, however, the crowd grew oddly silent. She took the bow then held it, testing its balance. She turned to Jason who gazed up at her expectantly.

"This is much easier to do," she said, "If you do it correctly."

The curator glanced from the woman to the boy, feeling he had just been subtly insulted. "I've studied some of the finest scrolls available from that time period. James of Avalon described in detail the use of the English longbow. I've never had anyone come in here and pull it to its full length."

Ryan ran her hand down the length of the bow, testing for any imperfections. "And I never met James of Avalon," she said.

The curator started to reply to the ridiculous remark, but the woman's next actions stopped him cold. Ryan reached over and removed an arrow from the wall. She notched it expertly and glanced at the curator. "The longbow," she said in the voice of instruction, "Is dependent not so much on the strength of the bowman, but on the length of his arms."

Ryan took a slight breath, held it, then, instead of pulling the string towards her she pushed the bow away. The curator, as well as the crowd, was stunned. Holding the string in place, she continued to speak.

"The trick is to utilize the full length of your arm, by doing this." The bow was now pulled taut and the arrow was ready to fly, tremendous force behind it. Ryan turned it directly on the curator, who was suddenly quite nervous when faced with the formidable weapon on the verge of being loosed.

"And as for accuracy," Ryan said, turning slightly to his right, "That just takes practice."

She loosed the arrow and the it flew past the curator's head. The projectile flew true, impaling an ancient brass pot on the wall nearly 200 feet away. The arrow had flown with such force it pierced through the bottom of the pot and embedded itself into the wall a good three inches. The pot dangled from the arrow.

The curator was stunned by the display. No one had ever been able to fully draw the longbow, let alone use it with such deadly accuracy. The crowd was stunned as well, and it was Jason who finally broke the silence.

"Yay!" he cheered.

Led by the boy's example, people in the crowd began to clap, hesitantly at first, then louder.

"Oh my," Ryan said, eyeing the pot with slight chagrin. She set the longbow down and removed some money from her pocket. She counted out several thousand dollars and handed it to the flabbergasted curator. "I think that will cover the damage," she said, "If not, I know where I can find you another one."

Ryan stepped down from the platform, rejoining Susan. Those who might have been moved to pat her on the back rethought the impulse. A few were brave enough to mumble congratulations under their breath and move on.

Ryan glanced down at Jason. "There. Are you satisfied?"

Jason gazed up at her in devotion. "You could never be Robin," he said.

Ryan looked at him in puzzlement. "What?"

Jason shook his head at his own miscalculation. "You could never be Robin," he said, "You would have to be Batman."

"Oh," Ryan said in understanding, "I see. Well, then you'll have to be Robin."

"Really," Jason asked excitedly. "I could be your sidekick?"

Apparently Ryan was highly amused by this suggestion. "Hmmm. I think you'll have to ask your mother."

Susan was not certain she wanted Jason worshipping a person this dangerous. Jason was oblivious to his mother's misgivings.

"Maybe we should buy you one of those," he continued thoughtfully, staring at the longbow.

Ryan glanced at the bow and laughed. "No thanks," she said, "Too many bad memories."

Ryan climbed the steep cliff behind Victor. Neither climbed with difficulty and Victor reached the precipice only a short time before Ryan. He stood gazing out over the valley below.

Needing neither food nor sleep, he and Ryan had traveled alone for three days and three nights. They had traveled on foot at a speed which Ryan would not have imagined possible. She had needed to stop occasionally, not being as strong as Victor, but she understood why Victor had left his menservants behind with the horses. Even the horses would not have kept up with them, and they would have needed to stop and rest. They would catch up, perhaps in several days, bringing with them their supplies and armor. All Ryan and Victor carried were their weapons.

Ryan stood, also gazing out into the valley below. There was a light fog covering the scene, but even without her preternatural eyes, the sight was an awesome one.

Tents were spread the entire length of the valley, thousands of them. Ryan had not known there were that many people in the entire world, let alone gathered in one army. It made her wonder why this King needed Victor's help.

Victor smiled down at his charge's wonder. He had seen larger armies, and would so again. He returned his gaze to the valley below and frowned. It was not a strategic position for an army. Either this King was utterly foolish or in too great a hurry. Victor motioned for Ryan to follow and started down the hill.

Ryan frowned for her own reasons and let her hand rest comfortably on the hilt of her sword. She started down the hill after him.

They approached the edge of the camp and an alert rippled through the encampments nearest them. Their approach was greeted with much interest and men began to gather as they neared. It seemed odd that a man and a boy should appear out of nowhere, on foot, carrying with them nothing but their swords.

Ryan could see the awe in the men's faces, but even then it was difficult to imagine how the two of them appeared.

The soldiers saw a man, taller and broader through the shoulders than nearly any man they had ever seen. A man who moved with an unusual grace and power, a man whose image seemed to ripple with the mist that he walked through. His companion was tall as well, but slender, and as fair as the man was dark. Both possessed an unnatural beauty, a beauty that even the comeliest of lasses would not wish to compete against.

A sentry stepped forward as if to challenge the pair but a single icy glance from the dark-haired man froze the man in his tracks. The guard felt his innards seem to liquefy and he could do little but step back as the two passed.

The word of their coming continued to ripple through the camp and it was not long before a knight came forward to escort Victor to the inner circle. Ryan waited patiently outside as Victor was ushered into a resplendent tent.

Ryan was preoccupied with her own thoughts and ignored the stares of the men around her. She fingered the hilt of her sword, drawing comfort in its familiar feel. She wondered idly where they would sleep as they had not carried tents with them.

"Where are your horses, boy?"

Ryan turned to the man who was standing too closely to her and staring. She could smell the alcohol on his breath and wondered if the rest of the army was in the same state of readiness.

Ryan gazed at him silently for a long moment, and just when the man was beginning to squirm in discomfort, she replied coldly. "They will catch up."

This brought much laughter from the surrounding crowd that was watching the exchange. They thought the boy had made a clever reply, not realizing Ryan was telling the truth. The man muttered something to himself and stumbled off.

Victor pulled the flap of the tent aside and exited. He bent down, whispering in Ryan's ear.

"We will bed with the King's company tonight, and until our company arrives. Tomorrow I will meet with the knights to plan strategy. We may be in Agincourt before the new moon."

Ryan kept to herself over the next few days. She could hear the whispers of the men, as loudly as if they had been shouting in her face. There was much discussion revolving around the dark Lord and his fair companion. Some of it was ribald speculation regarding their relationship. Ryan was more amused than angered by this talk; the truth was far more illicit than even they could imagine. Other talk circulated about the Lord's alleged fighting prowess; some spoke in awe, their tone hushed. Others professed doubt, no matter how imposing his appearance.

Ryan overheard others speak of the two's strange behavior. They had no horses, no one had seen them eat, and neither appeared to sleep, roaming the camp at all hours of the night. The two would also disappear into the darkness together, which would generally circle the conversation back to crude speculation.

In truth, both Ryan and Victor were restless and the two would roam for miles around the encampment, both exploring and scouting the area ahead of them.

They reached Agincourt on a frosty morning and it was then that Ryan realized how truly small the English army was. The French barred the way to Agincourt, blanketing the horizon with their superior numbers. Word reached their camp that they would attack the next day.

The following morning men stood in the long shadows shivering from both cold and fear. Both armies stood in the open, perhaps a stone's throw from one another. The English, however, were flanked by thick woods on both sides. They had no reserve and lined up in a single line of dismounted knights and men-at-arms, with the archers between them and at their flanks. The King stood at the center, as did Victor and Ryan.

Victor and Ryan wore only mail, unlike the knights behind them who wore full armor. Neither wore helmets, or the leather headdress of the archers. They were the only two on the field uncovered.

Victor turned and smiled at Ryan, and it was the smile of a predator. Ryan felt a shiver of excitement run up her spine, and she could not help but smile as well, the smile of a hunter ready for sport.

The two armies stood facing one another, neither liege willing to sound the attack. Hours passed as Ryan paced impatiently, and the sun was nearly overhead when they finally received the word to attack.

The English marched forward and Victor restrained Ryan, whispering they would halt when within bowshot. Ryan whispered that she was already within her range and Victor suppressed a smile. The men-at-arms in front of them stopped and began planting stakes to repel a calvary charge. The opposing army began to move towards them.

Victor watched the battle with keen eyes. Because of their position, they were safe from a flank attack, and because of the stakes, they beat back the frontal attack. As soon as the front wave of French calvary began to retreat, he pushed Ryan forward to chase them down.

The retreating calvary flung their own advancing infantry into confusion that was worsened when the second division began to advance. The two waves of humanity came clashing together and it was quickly evident the French army was being pushed back. Victor searched the line for the weakest link in the chain of men; that would be where the two would go.

Victor ran forward, easily outdistancing his line. Ryan kept pace with him and the two loped across the field to the spot Victor had chosen. Ryan knew her duty; she and Victor would fight back-to-back, entrusting no one else to protect them.

Victor reached the line first and with a tremendous blow, cut a man in two with his sword. The surrounding soldiers were so stunned at the feat, they could not protect themselves from Ryan's flashing sword. She quickly dispatched three before a fourth could raise his sword, and even this act did him no good. Ryan impaled him, chain mail and all.

The world became a mad swirl of blood and flailing bodies, of dust and screams and amputated body parts. Everything appeared in slow motion to Ryan; the men surrounding her moved as if their limbs were frozen. The only person who appeared to be moving at a normal speed was Victor, who fluidly cut a swathe through the sluggish masses.

Ryan followed Victor as he moved forward. She had the brief impression they were surrounded by enemy soldiers, but this sea of humanity flowed to their deaths as the two cut them down as easily as the previous ones.

There seemed to be a pause in the fighting and Victor glanced over at Ryan with warning. To the surprise of those around them, Ryan sheathed her sword and moved closer to Victor, gazing far off into the distance. She stepped in front of her mentor, waiting patiently.

She did not have long to wait. The sky was suddenly blackened with arrows as enemy archers let the missiles fly. The rain of arrows fell to the ground, blanketing both friend and foe alike. Screams of agony filled the air as men cried out when the arrows found their mark.

But they did not fall to the ground near Victor, nor did they come near him. Ryan stood in front of him and in a study of concentration, began to snatch the missiles from the air. Her hands moved with blinding speed as she knocked them to the ground or deflected them to the side.

At the same time, Victor was dispatching any enemy still standing. It was only a matter of moments before he and Ryan were the only two still standing within a great distance.

The hail of arrows ceased and Victor turned his gaze to the enemy line. The ground began to shake as knights on horseback rode down the hill toward the battleground. The ground behind them also began to shake as the English knights began their charge. Ryan again drew her sword.

The two calvaries clashed with a horrendous noise and Victor and Ryan were trapped between sweaty, wide-eyed horses and unseated knights who struggled to their feet in their bulky armor. On horse or on foot, the enemy knights were no match for Victor's sword as he cut through their mail or smashed them to the ground, armor and all.

Ryan was separated from Victor, but she was only slightly concerned. Her sword flashed out, smashing a lance in two and knocking the horseman from his mount. She beheaded him and turned to block another blow.

Ryan was beginning to feel fatigued. She had lost all sense of time or the number of men she had killed. She was covered in blood and the heat was beginning to wear on her. The noise of battle and the screams of death of both men and animal seemed endless. Although the surrounding men still appeared to move in slow motion, she herself began to feel as if she was slowing down.

She heard the sound of hooves behind her and whirled, her sword held ready. But she had not turned fast enough and the tip of the lance passed beneath her sword and pierced her chest above her heart.

The pain was immediate and intense as the lance traveled straight through her. Her vision blurred and in fury she grabbed the lance and leaned backward, lifting the startled knight from the back of his horse. The horse galloped by her as she held the knight suspended, dangling helplessly, and then she smashed the lance in two with her sword. The knight came crashing to the ground toward her and her sword flashed out, cleaving him in two.

Ryan dropped her sword and staggered away from the dead man. She grasped the lance and tried to pull it from her body, but she was weakening and had poor leverage. The battle seemed to be waning, but Ryan did not notice. Unable to free herself from the lance, she decided she would attempt to jar it loose. She took a deep breath and fell backward, jamming the lance into the ground and pushing it back up through her body as she followed it to the ground.

Ryan laid on the ground staring up at the sky. The pain was enormous, blocking out all sound and all sight. She still was not free of the lance and now the tip was embedded in the ground beneath her. She tried to pull the lance upward once more, but now she was weaker, and effectively pinned to the ground.

A shadow fell over her and she noted distantly that an enemy was standing over her. With a cry of triumph, he thrust his sword into her lower torso and Ryan felt the searing pain cut through her. He yanked his sword loose and prepared to stab her a second time.

With the same dispassionate interest, Ryan watched as blood spread over the front of the enemy's torso. The tip of a sword appeared through the man's chest and he screamed as he was lifted from his feet.

Victor swung his sword, dislodging the man and throwing him to the ground. Ryan turned her head to look into the dying man's eyes. He gurgled once, then his eyes were lifeless. She turned her head once more to stare up at Victor.

Victor stared down at his charge, mentally noting her injuries. He inwardly cursed himself for not staying closer to her, but outwardly he was unconcerned.

"Must I always keep an eye on you?"

Ryan stared up at her mentor, uncertain whether she should feel fear. She glanced at the lance protruding from her chest. "I guess someone has to."

Victor shook his head and placed his foot on her sternum. He grasped the lance firmly in one hand. "I guess that would be me, then."

With one swift move he yanked the lance from Ryan's body. Ryan gasped at the pain and closed her eyes. Victor threw the weapon to the side and leaned down and grasped Ryan's collar. He lifted her effortlessly, holding her upright with one hand. He stared at the wound, even now feeling his hunger stir.

Ryan opened her eyes, catching the glint in his. "I hardly think now is an appropriate time," she said through clenched teeth.

Victor did not speak but instead lightly bit his own lip. He placed his lips on Ryan's and she tasted his blood in her mouth. Strength immediately flowed through her and the pain, although still present, suddenly seemed manageable. All she wished to do now was sleep.

He ended his kiss, still holding her close to him. With his free hand he thrust his sword into the ground and then lifted her into his arms. The battlefield was littered with dead as he began to pick his way through the bodies. Men stared in awe as the dark lord stalked from the grounds into the forest, carrying his mortally wounded companion.

It was not simply the common man who stared. The King sat on the back of his horse on a nearby hilltop. He had been mesmerized from the beginning of the battle by the ferocity and skill of the two warriors. He stared at the lone sword standing amongst the piles and piles of bodies, by far the greatest number slain anywhere on the field. He had witnessed in disbelief and fear as the lad had plucked arrows from the sky. He had watched as the dark lord had cut men in two, armor and all. He had watched the lad suffer the grievous injury, and still slay his attacker. And he had watched that strange, sensual kiss between the man and his dying boy.

Henry the III had never seen anything like it before, nor would he ever again.

CHAPTER 21

The three left the museum and continued to walk downtown. Susan felt as if all eyes were upon them as they strolled the street, glancing in shop windows. Both Ryan and Jason seemed enamored with the sights: huge wheels of cheese and hanging sausages in a delicatessen, a candy store in which every color imaginable was represented, book stores with hundreds of different books in the windows.

Susan was interested by people's reaction to the tall, golden-haired woman. Ryan definitely attracted a lot of attention although she seemed unaware of it. Susan was thoughtful. Ryan did not seem particularly interested in people. She was far more interested in the aesthetics of buildings, the play of light and shadow through the trees, the different colors in the candy store. She seemed to live in a world where human beings were not the principle visual attraction, indeed, were not even contenders. Susan glanced around her. By following Ryan's gaze, she began to see things she had never seen before.

Susan was surprised when Ryan paused, staring intently ahead of her. She looked, trying to see what Ryan saw.

Ryan was staring at a young man about a 100 feet ahead of them. He was surrounded by several female companions, not surprising since he was extremely handsome. He seemed unaware of Ryan's scrutiny, although it was quite marked.

Ryan turned to gaze into the window of a bakery, staring at the rows of bread and pastries.

"Is something wrong?" Susan asked her.

Ryan glanced back at the young man, who seemed to sense something and looked about him with confusion. He apparently did not see Ryan, who was still examining him at length. Ryan nodded toward him, addressing Susan.

"The young man ahead of us, he is one of my Kind."

Susan was startled and swiveled her gaze back toward the young man. He did seem to have some of the presence Ryan possessed, although not nearly to the degree. He continued to look around him in confusion, and continued to miss Ryan.

Susan watched the man. "You can sense one another, can't you?"

Ryan gazed back down at the pastries. "Yes. Sometimes from miles away. But he can't sense me because I'm not allowing him to."

The young women with him pretended to be upset over his momentary inattention and he appeared to shrug off his feeling. He returned his full attention to his companions and they set off down the sidewalk.

Susan grabbed Jason who was pressed against the bakery window. He glanced up at his mother, sensing her unease.

Ryan began to follow the young man from a distance and Susan, clutching Jason's hand, fell back. Ryan waved for her to catch up, and she pulled Jason along.

"I'm assuming you're more powerful than him?" Susan said, a little fearfully.

Ryan laughed a short laugh. "Oh yes. He's a Young One, and not particularly powerful, although I imagine he's extremely compelling to his human companions."

Susan noted the derisive quality in the comment. "And you're able to block his ability to sense you?"

Ryan nodded, easily keeping pace with the group in front of them. The sidewalks were crowded with the evening throngs of people, but everyone seemed to move out of Ryan's way. "I'm clouding his mind. He senses me, but that's more a result of my power than his ability."

Susan watched as the young man began to glance over his shoulder. He still seemed unable to spot Ryan, and he was becoming increasingly agitated. His companions complained as he began to hurry them along.

Ryan had picked up her pace as well and Susan's unease increased.

Jason was struggling to keep up, practically running at her side. Susan had the distinct impression that Ryan was stalking the young man. She seemed to take no particular pleasure in what she was doing but rather was coldly methodical, like a shark circling its prey.

The young man's agitation was peaking as he glanced wildly around him. He could not pinpoint what was following him, but he knew it was strong and that it was hunting him. Susan felt Ryan tense, and the young man bolted.

In little more than a flash of dark clothing, Ryan was gone. She left only the impression of movement, and even that Susan caught only out of the corner of her eye. Susan stood on the sidewalk, the man's bewildered companions a few feet in front of her. She turned and was startled to find Edward at her side.

"I believe you should come me with me," he said calmly. A limousine pulled to the curb.

Susan made a snap decision, realizing it was probably foolish. "Take him," she said, thrusting Jason's hand into the older man's grasp. Edward started to object, but Susan was already running down the street after Ryan. The older man glanced down at the youngster now in his care and sighed.

Ryan chased the Young One down the sidewalk, effortlessly keeping pace with him. She felt his fear and knew he would quickly make a mistake.

He did so, attempting to cut into an alleyway and instantly Ryan was upon him. She held him by his collar and his eyes grew wide with terror as he realized how Old the one was in front of him.

"Please," he asked, begging for his life, "Let me go. I'll do anything for you."

Ryan gazed down at the Young One. "You'd do anything for me, anyway."

The young man swallowed hard, knowing the words to be true. Old Ones were always seductive, but this one was absolutely hypnotic.

"Who made you?" Ryan asked.

The Young One spoke a name but it meant nothing to Ryan and she was relieved. However, she did not wish her presence to be known. She could block her image from the Young One's mind but the magnitude of her power alone would leave an imprint. There were still a few who would recognize that imprint. She looked into the Young One's eyes, and realized he was flawed and weak anyway.

The young man realized he had been weighed in the balance and found wanting. He closed his eyes. "Oh god," he sobbed.

Ryan snapped his neck expertly, without anger but without remorse. She stood holding him, wondering if his life force would remain. She did not sense it and knew her judgment to be correct; if he had been killed so easily he should not have been made.

A gasp at the opening to the alleyway attracted her attention. She had been aware of Susan's approach and had not been particularly concerned by it. She now realized the picture she presented, holding the dead man in her arms.

Susan's eyes widened in horror as she took a step back.

"Susan...", Ryan began warningly.

Susan stumbled and turned, fleeing from the scene in the alley behind her. Ryan rolled her eyes in exasperation and tossed the body behind a dumpster. She gave chase to Dr. Ryerson.

She caught Susan easier than she had caught the Young One and bodily picked her up. Susan had the impression of air rushing by her and the next thing she knew she was teetering precariously on a windowsill near a fire escape, three stories above the ground.

Ryan leaned casually against the building, crossing her arms in front of her.

Susan was desperately trying to remain calm. This was the first time she had been genuinely afraid of Ryan, and knew she had badly underestimated her.

Ryan simply gazed at her with her unblinking gaze. "I would think you'd be getting used to this by now."

Susan shook her head, feeling nauseous. "I could never get used to the way you kill."

Ryan's voice was suddenly cold. "Do not judge me by your standards, Dr. Ryerson. You know nothing of my Kind, and you know very little of me."

Susan steadied her voice, trying to ignore the fact she was 35 feet above ground, standing on a ledge less than a foot wide. "Are you going to kill me?"

Ryan wrinkled her brow in confusion. "Why would I do that?"

"You don't seem to have a lot of respect for life."

Ryan shrugged noncommittally. "You're correct. I do not. But I was raised in a world full of people who had no respect for life. My disrespect is more a result of the two decades I spent as a human than of the seven centuries I have spent as I am."

Susan inched away from the edge, pressing herself against the building. "Why did you kill him?"

Ryan again shrugged off the act. "He was weak, and he was flawed, and he would have told the Others."

"Why don't you wish to be found?"

Ryan looked out across the city. "My Kind are attracted to me," she paused, as if searching for words. "In the most inconvenient way. I want to be left alone."

Susan had the feeling Ryan was leaving some very important details out. She was reluctant to ask her next question.

"Why didn't you Share with him?"

Ryan laughed without humor. "After what I'm used to, he would not satisfy me."

Susan wanted to pursue this line of questioning, but not as much as she wanted to get off the ledge and down on the ground. Susan gestured towards the fire escape and Ryan nodded in acquiescence. Instead of helping her, however, Ryan leaped onto the ladder and slid the entire length to the ground.

Susan inwardly cursed her, silently arguing that she was too old for this type of stunt. Ryan watched her carefully, however, and Susan knew instinctively that the woman would not let her fall.

Once on the ground, Ryan set out for the alley where she had dumped the body. "Edward is outside the alley, tell him to pull in here, I'll get this for you," Ryan instructed over her shoulder.

Susan was dumbfounded. "What?"

Ryan paused, slightly impatient. "Bring the car around. I'll retrieve the body for you."

Susan was astonished. Not only had Ryan committed a crime, she now was nonchalantly returning to the scene to retrieve the body.

Ryan put her hands on her hips, looking at Susan as if she were a dimwitted child. "You said you wanted to study my Kind. Here's a perfect opportunity for you."

Susan still did not move and Ryan now left no room for discussion. "Get the car," she said firmly.

The command finally had its desired affect and Susan, in a daze, went to find Edward. She hoped Jason wouldn't see any of this.

Once the body was safely in the trunk, the limousine was on its way. Jason was fascinated by the buttons, the television, the refrigerator. Edward eyed him with some disapproval.

"Well, how do you expect to get that bo-," she stopped, glancing at her preoccupied son, "That 'thing' upstairs to my lab?"

Ryan looked at Edward, and some sort of private communication passed between the two. Ryan sighed, turning her attention to Susan.

"You won't be going back to your lab. Nor will you be going home."

Ryan's words were slow to sink in. "What?" Susan said, "What are you talking about?"

Ryan spoke with a rare hesitation. "It is why I sought you out today. Things," she paused, searching for the words, "Have become much more complicated."

"What do you mean by more complicated?"

Ryan stared at her. "The Young One today was not searching for you, but he was here. That means that Others are here, or will be coming."

Susan shook her head. "No, you were looking for me before that. What else has happened?

Ryan glanced at the elder man. "Edward?"

Edward turned to face Susan. "The men who attacked you the other day were not our Kind. They were employees of an international pharmaceutical company extremely interested in your work. The risk that they will find you is too great."

"So what if they find me? So what? You don't have to keep protecting me. Jason and I can go somewhere else."

Edward managed to express his derision of the remark without saying a word. Susan turned to Ryan, who was watching Jason play with the buttons on the television "So you're just going to imprison us?"

Ryan sighed. "Well, for the time being, yes. My hope is that it will be a temporary situation."

Jason was finally beginning to follow the conversation. "What about my puppy?"

Edward turned to him, his demeanor still firm. "Your dog has already been moved. He will be there when you arrive." Edward turned to Susan. "As well as most of your possessions, some of your lab equipment..." he paused as if forgetting something. "Oh yes, and your housekeeper as well."

Susan was speechless. "You kidnapped Neda?" she finally sputtered out.

Ryan seemed almost embarrassed by the admission, but Edward was unmoved. "In theory, yes. She was not exactly a willing participant in the move."

Susan was flabbergasted. Just when she thought that nothing would surprise her anymore, these two managed something new.

CHAPTER 22

JASON IMMEDIATELY ADAPTED TO THE OPULENT surroundings, impressed and curious about everything he saw. He was happily reunited with both his puppy and a frightened and angry Neda. Susan tried to calm her caretaker, telling her it was a temporary move and that she would explain everything later. She left the two in Jason's suite, then stalked into her own. She paced about the luxurious room, but felt her anger dissipating. It was hard to be incensed when surrounded by such beauty, especially when she knew Ryan had brought them here to keep them safe. Susan glanced around the room. They were required to stay here, but Ryan had said nothing about her staying in her room. She started down the hallway. She felt many eyes upon her as she moved through the house, but no one tried to stop her.

Ryan was in the den where Susan expected to find her. She sat in front of the fireplace as she had before. The golden-haired woman glanced up at her. "Would you like a glass of wine?"

Susan started to refuse, then changed her mind. "Why not?" she said.

Almost before the words were out of her mouth, a young man was at her side with an empty wineglass. He held up the bottle for her inspection. Out of habit, Susan looked at the label. She then did a double take.

"This is 1961 Cheval Blanc, St. Emilion."

Ryan glanced over at her. "What?"

Susan shook her head. "Nothing." She took the glass of wine from the young man and settled into the chair next to Ryan's. She took a sip of the wine, savoring it. She had a fine appreciation for wine, but she had never tasted any that went for $750 a bottle. She was silent for awhile, enjoying the fire and the drink. Perhaps it was the alcohol giving her courage, but she finally spoke what was on her mind.

"When are you going to tell me what's really going on here?"

Ryan glanced over at her in surprise. "What do you mean by that?"

"Why did you kill that young man? He didn't know you were there. He wasn't any threat to me."

"You're not entirely correct," Ryan said. She took a drink of her wine. "Granted, he didn't know I was there, nor was he any threat to you. But he did sense me. I couldn't let him live with that imprint."

Susan wasn't entirely sure what she was talking about.

Ryan sensed her confusion. "Perhaps I owe you an explanation of sorts since I have so disrupted your life. But I cannot really explain anything about myself unless I explain to you more about my Kind." Ryan lapsed into silence for a moment, then continued. "And I really can't do that unless I explain to you how I met the Others for the first time."

Ryan gazed into the fireplace, a far-away look in her eye. "I guess I was perhaps a hundred years old. Old for a human, no doubt, but young for one of my Kind. I did not realize there were Others. I thought Victor and I were the only two of our Kind in the world, off fighting our battles and wandering the world. It never occurred to me there might be Others, nor did I realize how meeting them would change everything."

Ryan whipped the horse harder. Although it was in a lather and on the verge of collapse, she drove the beast on. She considered dismounting and continuing on foot, as she could now run nearly as fast as the horse. But she continued on horseback.

They had only been in France a few weeks and Ryan did not particularly care for it. It had been Victor's idea to leave the rolling hills of England. Although they traveled away on many occasions, it had generally been to fight in some battle or another. She had spent half her life battling the French, and now she was supposed to forget all that and act civil.

Ryan did not know why Victor had chosen to leave, she simply knew he had been watching her thoughtfully one day, and abruptly made the decision. Ryan had not been happy with the decision but did not argue with Victor, indeed, did not even question the reasons behind it.

They traveled without fanfare and without entourage through a land filled with bands of criminals. And they did so without incident. No one stopped and asked them for their papers; no one stopped them for any reason.

And they had arrived in this city, the largest city Ryan had ever seen. It was teeming with life, but the stimulation quickly tired Ryan who was overwhelmed by the sights and sounds picked up by her ever-increasing senses.

To give herself respite, she would take long rides in the surrounding countryside. On this particular day she had been gone since early morning light. Victor had watched her leave, unconcerned at her destination but directing her firmly that she should return by evening as he had plans for them.

Unfortunately Ryan had completely lost track of time and with a certain amount of misgiving realized the sun was going down when she was a long way from home.

She could feel Victor's displeasure from a distance and in her mind's eye, could see him pacing impatiently. She spurred the horse onward and although it whinnied in protest, it picked up its pace.

She wheeled the horse through the gateway and quickly dismounted. A servant rushed forward to take the beast, which stumbled badly in its exhaustion. Ryan hesitated a moment, wanting to care for the horse, but she had no choice.

"Take care of him," she ordered the stablehand, then headed up the walk, taking the stairs two at a time. She brushed by the servant in the foyer and then burst into the dining hall. Victor was at the other end, aware of her arrival and obviously waiting for her. She moved towards him, hurried yet graceful as ever.

She bowed slightly, out of breath. "I'm, I'm sorry my lord. I'm late." Ryan became suddenly acutely aware that there were many other people in the room as well. She glanced down at her disheveled appearance. "And I am not properly dressed."

Victor himself was dressed in formal wear, but when he looked down at his young companion who was quite fetchingly dressed as a stableboy, any anger he felt evaporated. "I don't think anyone is concerned with what you're wearing."

There was a languid quality to his voice and Ryan tried to decipher his words. She glanced around her, realizing the room had become completely silent and all eyes were on her. She turned back to Victor and he stared intently in her eyes.

Stay close, came the voice inside her head, and guard your thoughts.

Ryan was suddenly aware of an immense number of competing sensations and was stunned to realize that everyone in the room was like her and Victor. She could feel them.

And they could feel her.

Victor reached down and brushed a lock of hair from Ryan's forehead. No one in the room missed the significance of the sensual gesture, or the possession behind it.

Abigail observed the gesture from behind her fan. As one of the oldest and most powerful of their Kind, she was well respected. Her appearance was that of an elder matriarch because she had been Changed when physically older. This lent her a certain dignity even among a people where physical appearance was misleading.

Abigail leaned towards the beautiful, dark-haired woman to her left. "It appears Victor has made himself a child."

A mixture of emotions flitted across Marilyn's face as she watched the young woman. She struggled to control them, outwardly preserving her icy demeanor. "Ce n'est pas possible."

Abigail watched the child and mentally reached out to touch her. She was startled at the power she felt. She smiled behind the fan. "Yes, impossible. But it appears he has done it."

Marilyn was younger than Abigail in appearance, but they were nearly the same age. Marilyn's power easily rivaled that of Abigail's, perhaps even surpassing it. She stared at the silent interaction between the two.

Abigail could not resist baiting Marilyn further. "It almost appears as if he speaks to her with thought."

Marilyn's jaw again tightened. "That is impossible. Even if she is his offspring, she is too young to have such abilities."

Abigail smiled. "Yes, of course my dear."

Marilyn bridled at Abigail's condescending tone but the elder woman had already risen to her feet and was gliding across the floor toward Victor.

Victor turned toward the matriarch and bowed slightly. Abigail bowed to him as he took her hand. "Victor. Let me be the first to congratulate you," she said with a significant glance at Ryan. She then turned to the younger woman. "And the first to meet this exquisite creature."

Ryan was overwhelmed by the older woman's presence and felt herself immediately physically drawn to her. Victor watched the reaction, entertained but cautious with his charge.

Abigail was also aware of the reaction and was immeasurably pleased by it. It normally meant nothing to her to attract a Young One, but this one was so simultaneously powerful and vulnerable, the feeling was intoxicating. She held Ryan's hands while looking deep into her eyes, gauging her. Yes, this one bore Victor's mark as surely as she was standing before her.

Abigail pulled back but did not release Ryan's hand, instead sweeping her away from Victor. "I will introduce her to everyone, my lord."

Victor was not completely pleased at this turn of events, but neither was he concerned. No one would touch Ryan. Still, as others came and went, paying their respects to him, he kept Ryan in his sight.

Ryan was swept around the room in a whirlwind, surrounded by faces with names she would never remember. There seemed to be some unspoken hierarchy, some hidden social order. They were greeted with enthusiasm and people pressed closer to meet and pay their respects to both of them.

Ryan sensed, however, that not all were pleased to see her. She felt the weight of a pair of eyes and turned to a dark-haired woman across the room. Although surrounded by admirers, she had eyes only for Ryan and what was in them was not pleasant.

The dark-haired woman turned away and Ryan turned her gaze to Victor, who had watched the entire scene. There was an iciness about him right now that Ryan had never seen, and it was not directed at her but at the dark-haired woman. Abigail had also watched the drama play itself out, finding it extremely diverting. She placed her hand on Ryan's elbow, gently guiding her back towards Victor.

"Come my dear, we mustn't push our luck."

Ryan had little idea what that meant. In fact, there was an undercurrent throughout the room of which Ryan had little if any understanding. She was actually quite relieved when she returned to Victor's side, taking comfort in his nearness.

"Oh my," Abigail whispered behind her fan as she fell in beside Victor.

Her eyes were on Marilyn who had started towards the trio. Marilyn swept across the floor and her admirers fell to the wayside as she neared Victor.

Ryan felt herself drawn to the woman as she approached, much like with Abigail. But Victor apparently found this reaction less than entertaining as he put his hand on Ryan's shoulder.

Marilyn sensed the reaction and her eyes narrowed slightly in surprise. She, too, felt what Abigail had felt and mentally revised her opinion of the whelp. She grasped the free hand Victor extended and leaned to kiss him chastely on the lips.

"Hello my dear, I've missed you."

Victor bowed slightly. "Hello Marilyn," he said politely, "It has been too long."

"Yes, of course." She turned immediately to Ryan. "And who, pray tell, is this?"

Victor's response was guarded. "This is Rhian." He glanced at Ryan as he spoke, "Marilyn is a very old friend of mine."

Marilyn was quite openly examining Ryan from head to foot.

"Yes," she agreed, "Very old friends." To Ryan's surprise, Marilyn reached out and grasped her hands, pulling her towards her and out of Victor's grasp. Marilyn pulled her close so that they were face to face, and then the dark-haired woman leaned down to kiss her.

Many had kissed her in greeting during the course of the evening, but none like Marilyn kissed her. The kiss was prolonged and anything but chaste, and Ryan felt herself nearly swoon in the beautiful woman's embrace.

Marilyn released her and stepped back, causing Ryan to stumble backwards into Victor. Victor caught her by her shoulders and did not release her. There were several titters about the room at Marilyn's action and the Young One's reaction. Abigail smiled once more behind her fan. Marilyn gazed at Victor, half in triumph, half in fury. Victor returned her gaze, not pleased with Marilyn's action but not as displeased as she would have wished. Marilyn's desire for his dark child was a victory in itself.

Ryan was extremely confused. There were too many competing sensations right now, too many things she did not understand. She pressed backwards into Victor, wishing she could saddle another horse and leave.

A stabbing pain suddenly raced through Ryan's head, followed by a mind-shattering silent scream. She stood upright, stunned by the mental onslaught, and more stunned by the lack of reaction around her.

Few people seemed to even hear the silent scream, and fewer seemed to care. It was the Old Ones who tilted their heads slightly at the sensation, and their responses ranged from mild regret to amusement. The younger Ones appeared oblivious to the sound, neither hearing the cry nor feeling the pain that Ryan did.

She turned to Victor who knew what she was feeling and what she had heard, but he could not comfort her right now. He simply lifted two fingers and pressed them to her lips to silence any questions that might be forthcoming.

Ryan kept her tongue and turned back around, only to find Marilyn watching her closely. She had not missed Ryan's reaction, nor had Abigail. Abigail fluttered her fan in front of her face, but her eyes were locked with those of Victor, full of the knowledge of the implications of Ryan's reaction.

Victor was unperturbed. He, too, knew the implications of Ryan's abilities. He kept Abigail's gaze, however, for he did not care.

Ryan sensed a restlessness in the room, especially amongst the Old Ones. Some unseen chain of events had just been set into motion. People began to draw near to one another, and there seemed to be some sort of hidden order to the pairing. She sensed Victor's restlessness and turned to him in question. She heard the voice in her mind.

We must leave.

Ryan nodded imperceptibly and made ready to leave. Victor addressed Abigail and Marilyn.

"If you ladies will excuse us, we will be retiring."

Abigail nodded, a knowing look on her face. She would be retiring herself shortly.

Marilyn watched Victor lead Ryan from the room, and Abigail watched her. A mixture of emotion was on the dark-haired woman's face: anger, jealousy, but mostly desire.

Abigail turned to the young man who approached her. He was not an Old One, but neither was he terribly young. It would be a coup for him if she accepted his invitation, but he might make for an interesting evening.

Abigail accepted his proffered hand and she began to leave. She nodded to Marilyn, who was still standing as if frozen in place. Marilyn was already surrounded by those vying for her attention, and more than likely would accept more than one invitation.

But for the moment Marilyn stood unmoved by the attention. She returned Abigail's nod, her face returning to its icy repose. But her eyes returned to the now-empty door and the dangerous desire still burned within them.

Abigail's final fleeting thought as she left the room was one of curiosity. She knew Marilyn's bloodlust was for Victor, as always.

But she also wondered how much of that bloodlust was now directed at Victor's dark and bewitching child.

Victor spirited Ryan away from the gathering and they fled on foot into the night. When they reached the outskirts of the city it was evidently Victor's intention to stop.

But the gathering had left Ryan with a strange, pent-up energy. She did not wish to stop and continued on foot, laughing at Victor's stern orders to halt.

Victor watched his wild prodigy run into the night with exasperation. The gathering had left him with pent-up energy as well, but he knew what release he needed. He set out after Ryan.

She was fast, Victor thought to himself, and agile. Although this annoyed him as he had to chase her, it was coupled with a sense of pride.

Ryan sensed that Victor was not angry with her and increased her speed. She knew if she could reach the trees, she might have a chance at escaping him in the undergrowth. She could then take to the treetops and possibly outdistance him.

Victor sensed her intention and decided he was tired of this game.

Ryan was running full-tilt now but seemed to lose contact with Victor. She turned her head because she no longer sensed him behind her.

She ran headlong into an object that did not move, knocking her to the ground. Victor was no longer behind her because he was standing in front of her. Although she was knocked backward several feet, the collision did not move him.

"That's not fair," Ryan said, brushing herself off with feigned irritation. In reality she was fascinated when Victor revealed the full scope of his abilities.

She leaped to her feet but again he was there. She made as if to dodge around him but he grasped her by her shirt collar and lifted her effortlessly off her feet.

Denied of all leverage, she could do little but struggle in his grasp. He drew her close, gazing into her eyes with his preternatural amusement.

"Just so you have no doubt who is the master here."

Ryan held his gaze, cunning in her own. "I have none," she said.

In a lightning movement she leaned forward and fastened her arms about his neck, slicing into the flesh with her razor-sharp teeth. The move was unanticipated and Victor was so simultaneously startled and aroused, he could do little but wrap his arms about her as she began to drink.

Her hunger was so overpowering to him he staggered backward until he found a seat on a nearby stump. He intertwined his fingers in her hair as she fed off him, and he felt her mind become one with his. The sensation was one of ecstasy, almost as much an ecstasy of the mind as of the body.

He could control how much access she had to his Memories, to a degree. But the link between the two of them was powerful and grew more powerful each time they Shared.

Victor's own hunger was immense and as soon as he sensed she was sated he pulled her from his neck and set upon her own. He had near-absolute access to her mind and he saw the events of the night through her eyes. The blood flowing back into his body was powerful, and each time they Shared it became more so.

CHAPTER 23

Victor watched Ryan move up the walkway away from his carriage. Abigail waved to him from the doorway and he nodded to her before he slapped the reins onto the horse's back.

He had misgivings about leaving Ryan, but he knew she would be safer with Abigail than by herself right now. He did not completely trust Abigail, but he trusted her more than any of the Others. And he could not take Ryan with him.

Ryan had her own misgivings, but they had nothing to do with Abigail. She did not understand why she could not accompany Victor. She had been apart from him in the past, often for long periods of time. But her introduction to the Others filled her with questions and feelings that Victor had not yet had time to address. His absence right now was at the very least inopportune.

Ryan tried to tell herself that was all there was to it as she walked up the steps. She was dressed in her usual attire, an oversized shirt tucked into leather breeches which in turn were tucked into high boots. Ryan cared little for fashion and generally went about dressed as a man.

Abigail, on the other hand, was dressed in her usual finery. She eyed the youngster coming up the walk. Of course, if she looked the way Ryan looked in her clothing, she probably would dress that way, too.

Abigail was like most of her Kind, appreciative of all that was aesthetic. It explained why most of their Kind were extremely pleasing to the eye;

they were attracted to only the most handsome of humans. Abigail watched the lithe figure come up the stairs; Victor had chosen well.

Ryan greeted Abigail, very much aware of the woman's presence. Abigail watched the flush creep into the girl's cheeks and felt her own inner response. This was going to be more difficult than she had imagined, and she mentally reminded herself of both her promise and loyalty to Victor. It might be a good idea to set the girl on her own for a little while.

One of the servants showed Ryan about the grounds. The huntmaster's bitch had just given birth to a litter of pups and Ryan spent some time playing with the tiny hounds. When she had finished her tour, she returned to the house, seeking Abigail out.

Abigail was seated in the salon working on some stitchery. She raised her eyebrows upon Ryan's entrance, but continued her work. Ryan sat down restlessly on a nearby settee, watching Abigail's fingers fly.

It was not Abigail's duty to entertain Ryan, but she felt some obligation to keep the youngster occupied. Abigail smiled at that thought. Youngster, the girl was probably over a hundred years old.

It was Ryan who broke their silence however, and she did so with a question that was surprisingly blunt.

"Abigail, what did I feel at the gathering the other night?"

Abigail's fingers paused. "You do not know?"

Ryan shook her head. "No, I have no idea."

Abigail's fingers began to move once more, but now more slowly. "How much do you know about our Kind?"

Ryan shrugged. "Very little. I did not know there were Others until Victor and I came here."

Abigail's fingers stopped again and this time she had to make a grab for her tapestry as it began to slip to the floor. "You know nothing of our Kind?"

Ryan sensed the surprise and disapproval in Abigail's voice. She shook her head.

Abigail began stitching again, thoughtfully. She knew why Victor had kept Ryan ignorant of their Kind. She glanced sideways at the girl; she probably would have done the same if Ryan belonged to her. Abigail returned her attention to her stitchery. Victor's instructions had been quite specific, but he had mentioned nothing about educating the child.

"Do you remember the Young One, Jacque? I introduced him to you early in the evening."

Ryan had a vague recollection of the blond-haired young man. She nodded.

"What you felt was his death."

Ryan's head jerked up. "What do you mean his death? Who killed him?"

Abigail smiled. "He chose to Share with someone much more powerful than himself, and that person chose to kill him."

Ryan was dumbfounded. "But why?"

Abigail continued to stitch, indifferent to the topic at hand but entertained by Ryan's reaction. "Because we are predators, my dear. Like the wolves and the bears. But unlike these animals, we prey on our own Kind, and there is nothing in the world more pleasurable than Sharing unto death."

Ryan attempted to absorb this information. It seemed so strange to hear these words from a woman who had the air of a nurturing matriarch. "Then he was killed for someone's pleasure?"

Abigail again smiled, a very predatory smile. "It is our way."

Ryan was silent and Abigail casually continued. "But you should not have felt his death."

"Why not?" Ryan asked.

Abigail thrust the needle through the tapestry. "Because you are too young. No one within a hundred years of you even felt a whisper of his cry, and yet you felt it as strongly as an Old One." She looked pointedly at Ryan. "And it affected you much more than an Old One because you are so young and not ready to deal with such things."

Ryan again sensed disapproval in Abigail's voice, and this time she gave voice to her observation. "You seem to bear some sort of reproach for me."

Abigail delicately threaded another needle. Her words were still casual, but full of meaning. "I don't know if reproach is the proper term. I am curious because," she paused, seeking the right words, "Well, simply because you should not exist."

Ryan was more baffled than offended. "Why should I not exist?"

Abigail began stitching with her red thread. "As we grow older, we become more powerful. After a certain age, we can no longer reproduce because the blood becomes poisonous to humans. Victor is the oldest One of all, and he is many centuries past where he should be able to have offspring."

"And yet here I am," Ryan said.

Abigail nodded, her words significant. "Yes, here you are."

Ryan was silent, but it was a silence filled with questions and one she could not keep. "Why are there not more of us?"

Abigail smiled. "There are many reasons why our numbers are so small. First off, very few of us can reproduce. Young Ones are not powerful enough to initiate change, and Old Ones are too powerful. Only those occupying the middle ground are capable of initiating the Change." Abigail glanced up at Ryan, her words layered with meaning. "Under normal circumstances."

Ryan shifted uncomfortably as Abigail continued. "Secondly, the Change is tremendously difficult on humans, and most do not survive the process." She glanced up from her tapestry. "I imagine yours must have been particularly horrifying.

Abigail watched Ryan pale and knew she had hit upon a truth. She continued. "And finally, as I said, we are predators by nature and have a bad habit of destroying our Young simply for the pleasure of it."

Ryan looked at her. "If so many Young are killed, how does anyone survive to grow Old?"

Abigail shrugged. "Ours is a strange hierarchy. The humans who survive to become Young Ones are often killed. There are some who initiate the Change simply so they can then kill them." There was neither approval nor disapproval in Abigail's tone; she was simply stating a fact. "Some of the Young have powerful mentors who are capable of controlling their own passion to allow their progeny to grow up to become their companions."

A servant entered, setting out a flask of wine and some goblets. Ryan absently poured a glass of wine for herself, deep in thought. She sat back and put the glass to her lips, unaware of how closely Abigail was watching her.

Good god, Abigail thought to herself. This child had a sensuality about her that was as devastating as it was unintentional. Ryan sipped the wine, lost in her own thoughts. She finally became aware of Abigail's scrutiny, and blushed.

Abigail had to concentrate for a moment on her tapestry. Ryan took this opportunity to form another question.

"So age determines how powerful one becomes?"

Abigail tilted her head to one side thoughtfully. "To a degree. There are really three things that determine how powerful one is, and how powerful one can become. Foremost, of course, is age."

"And the other two?"

Abigail glanced over at Ryan. "The first is a matter of chance; the second a matter of politics."

Ryan waited patiently as Abigail carefully formed her reply, watching for Ryan's reaction. "The more powerful the person who created you, the more powerful you are and will become."

Ryan digested that bit of information. "And the political?"

Abigail examined her tapestry. "If you Share with one more powerful than yourself, you yourself will become more powerful."

Ryan began to understand the interaction at the gathering. "What advantage would there be, then, to Share with anyone less powerful than yourself?"

Abigail made a languorous gesture. "There is always the seduction, which can be exciting. And Sharing in and of itself is always pleasurable, with the exception of first contact when they are still human. But the greatest pleasure is either to kill, or to Share with one more powerful."

Ryan was quiet for a long while, absorbing the implications of Abigail's words. She suddenly understood some of the reaction to her presence, and why she was considered so unusual. Abigail was not content to stop with mere implications.

"Victor was responsible for your Change, yes?"

Ryan nodded slowly and Abigail probed further.

"And you have Shared with him, probably on a regular basis, have you not?"

Ryan did not know if she should be answering these questions, but knew that the heat in her cheeks had already given Abigail the response she wanted.

Abigail's mood, one of calculated disinterested, suddenly changed. Her gaze was now intense and her words were spoken very deliberately. "Victor is the oldest and greatest of our Kind. You do not seem to realize that Victor is our King, and you do not seem to understand that you are now our crown prince."

Ryan was taken aback at the suggestion, no, the command. "Victor has no other offspring?"

Abigail held her gaze unblinkingly. "None."

Ryan was stunned by this revelation, although a search of her mind told her she had already known it to be true. Abigail seemed to follow her train of thought and her mood of calculation returned.

"Do you have Victor's Memories?" Abigail asked casually.

Ryan seemed unaware of the undertone in Abigail's voice, and answered truthfully, musing. "Sometimes. I see pictures, but they are not clear."

This time Abigail had to struggle to maintain her own composure. The child should definitely not have this ability, and the fact that she announced it with such naiveté told Abigail she did not understand the significance of the admission.

Ryan continued her silent contemplation as Abigail watched her. Her lack of self-consciousness was disarming.

And extremely dangerous, Abigail reminded herself. She could not afford to allow herself to become entranced with this child. She examined her most recent stitchery, and Ryan posed another question.

"If I Shared with you," Ryan began curiously, "Would I have your Memories?"

This time the tapestry slipped to the floor unchecked. Abigail stared at her across the room and Ryan felt she had just inadvertently crossed some line.

Abigail searched Ryan's face, seeking any sort of knowledge of the implications of her question. She found none.

"You must never," Abigail began carefully, "Never speak of such things to me."

Ryan felt as if she had committed some terrible faux pas, but was not certain what it was.

Abigail eyes lingered on Ryan's lips, then on her throat. Her eyes were dark as she regained control, and her predatory smile returned. "You must not suggest such things, my dear. Even I am tempted by you." She carefully picked up the tapestry from the floor, and her eyes flickered back to Ryan's. "You sorely test my loyalty to Victor. It would take very little encouragement for me to seduce you."

Ryan swallowed hard. She could not hold Abigail's gaze and looked down at her hands. Abigail watched her for a moment more, then returned to her tapestry. Ryan sat in silence for a long while, chastened.

But her thoughts swirled, returning to all they had spoken of. She realized how truly vulnerable she was in this violent and erotic world. This brought other questions to mind, questions she felt she had to ask.

"What would happen to me," Ryan began hesitantly, "If something happened to Victor?"

Abigail glanced sideways at her. "Nothing will happen to Victor."

"Yes," Ryan pressed, "I know. But what if something did?"

Abigail shrugged. "There would be a great fight for you amongst the Old Ones," she said, as if it were of no consequence.

"And would you fight for me?" Ryan asked.

Abigail smiled her preternatural smile. "Yes my dear, I would fight for you."

Ryan was not appeased. "And who would win this fight?"

Abigail shrugged, as if it were no matter. "Probably Marilyn. She is very strong."

A thought occurred to Ryan. "Did Marilyn Share with Victor?"

Abigail looked at her shrewdly, but she answered offhandedly. "Yes, I believe she has in the past. But it has been a long time."

Ryan digested this information and Abigail continued casually, watching her. "Marilyn has always wanted Victor, but I watched her at the gathering and I believe she has found something she wants more."

Ryan looked at her blankly, so Abigail spelled it out for her.

"I believe Marilyn's desire for you is nearly as great as her desire for Victor, perhaps even greater."

This was another startling revelation to Ryan, who had perceived none of this. She thought this through, returning to her original question. "And so Marilyn would fight for me and would win, and I would be killed."

This gave Abigail pause and she was thoughtful for a moment. "I do not believe so." She shook her head. "No, I am not certain that you can be killed. You may already be too powerful."

This disclosure was finally enough to silence Ryan. She sat quietly while Abigail's fingers flew over the tapestry. Abigail glanced up from her work, aware of the child's deep contemplation. Again, Ryan's lack of self-consciousness was disarming. Abigail reached out to mentally touch her.

Ryan's head jerked upward, unsettled by the contact. Abigail let her eyes linger on Ryan's throat once more.

"You know, my dear," she said softly but not gently, "I think the most precarious part about taking you would be not knowing who was seducing whom."

"I don't think I would have any difficulty answering that question."

The voice from the doorway startled Ryan, but Abigail had sensed Marilyn's presence a long way off and was unperturbed. She was not pleased with Marilyn's presence but like most of her Kind, any type of stimulation was irresistible, no matter how dangerous.

"Why Marilyn," Abigail said, making no attempt at subtlety, "Whatever brings you here?"

Marilyn moved gracefully to Abigail's side. She leaned down and kissed her lightly on the cheek. "I came to pay my respects, of course."

She turned to Ryan as she said this and Ryan felt herself getting to her feet, apparently not of her own volition. Marilyn moved to her side, her movements languid. She grasped Ryan's hands in her own.

Ryan gazed deep into Marilyn's eyes and it seemed to her the dark-haired woman's influence over her was like something alive. Ryan gazed at her lips, at the long, lustrous black hair, and tried desperately to clear her mind.

There was wicked glint in Marilyn's eyes and Ryan knew the fury directed at her the other night had been displaced by other, more powerful emotions.

"Marilyn," Abigail said with warning, "Do not toy with the child."

Marilyn released Ryan's hands and Ryan sat down heavily on the settee. Marilyn sat down next to her, smoothing her flowing skirt.

Abigail watched the two, warring with herself. She knew she should not allow Marilyn here with Victor's progeny, but she was also immensely enjoying the sensations present in the room. She inwardly shrugged. What harm would there be in allowing Marilyn to trifle with the girl?

Ryan sat on the couch stiffly. She felt very much in over-her-head. Marilyn was not only powerful, she was also extremely beautiful. Ryan was conscious of her rough attire next to Marilyn's elegance.

Marilyn in turn was very aware of the effect she was having on the girl and found it captivating. Young Ones normally did little more than annoy Marilyn, but this one was special. She reached over and took a lock of Ryan's hair in her hand, twirling it around her finger.

Ryan looked to Abigail, who was dividing her attention between her stitchery and the scene. Ryan realized she would receive little help from the older woman. Abigail had laid out boundaries but she would do nothing until Marilyn crossed them, leaving her plenty of room to torment Ryan.

Marilyn was now stroking her hair, which had a hypnotic effect on the young woman. Ryan's head began to feel too heavy for her neck and she had to lay back and rest it on the cushions. Her eyes became heavy and she fought to keep them open. All of the stiffness left her body and her limbs became leaden as she was forced to relax. Her eyes closed.

Abigail paused in her stitchery. She could not help but stare at the child who appeared drugged on the couch. Abigail tried to ignore the sudden ache inside of her and Marilyn looked at her knowingly.

You could have her too, came Marilyn's voice inside her head.

Abigail looked at Marilyn in fury, angry that the woman had chosen to invade her mind without her permission. But the taunt was in Marilyn's eyes as well, and Abigail knew that Marilyn had manipulated her into a dangerous space. How could she stop Marilyn if it took all of her willpower just to keep from joining her?

Marilyn returned her attention to the girl. Ryan was already half-leaning on her and it was a simple enough maneuver to gently guide her head so that she was lying on Marilyn's lap. Marilyn ran her thumb lightly over the veins in Ryan's throat, feeling a kindle of excitement at the strong pulse. This would be satisfying, but far too easy. Perhaps the girl was not as powerful as she thought.

Abigail felt as if time had stopped. She was powerless against her own voyeuristic passion. Their Kind was ever more motivated by instant gratification over abstract concepts such as consequence, and she could no longer contemplate Victor's wrath. She wanted nothing more than to see Marilyn's teeth on the Young One's throat, and to watch the blood spill.

Marilyn lowered her head and brushed her lips lightly across the girl's veins. The throb of the pulse against her lips aroused her even further and she parted her lips so that she could brush her razor-sharp teeth against the skin.

But it was not to be because Marilyn felt a hand at her own throat, holding her head away.

Ryan looked up at her, her limbs still leaden but her eyes quite clear. Her hand was wrapped around Marilyn's throat and it took all of her strength to hold the woman away. Marilyn stared down at the child in stunned disbelief.

Ryan held Marilyn's gaze, watching her carefully. She slowly loosened her grip until her hand was merely resting against Marilyn's throat, and now it was her turn to gently caress Marilyn's veins with her thumb.

Fury flashed in Marilyn's eyes and her hand moved swiftly. Ryan could barely deflect the hand away from her and just managed to grip the wrist, which she could barely hold onto. Marilyn's other hand moved faster than her eye could see and she just managed to get a weak grip on the forearm to protect herself.

But she was no match for Marilyn's strength and Marilyn easily pressed her arms downward, pinning her. Ryan realized she should have left one hand at Marilyn's throat.

"You impudent whelp," Marilyn said through clenched teeth. "Any others, even Abigail would welcome my attention."

"Oh, yes dear," Abigail said, highly amused. She had returned to her stitchery, still entertained by the unfolding drama, but now for different reasons. It was characteristic of their Kind to switch allegiances without hesitation, and apparently without the slightest bit of self-reproach.

Ryan stared up at the furious woman. She forced herself to remain calm, and gathered her strength.

No, came the soothing voice inside Marilyn's head. You will not do this.

Marilyn was stunned, and in her surprise, she loosened her grip on Ryan. Ryan did not move, but simply stared up at the woman, holding her gaze intensely.

"You will not do this," Ryan repeated softly, this time aloud, "Because it is not your way."

"What do you know of my way?" Marilyn asked through still-clenched teeth.

Ryan again stared at her intently, and she spoke as if remembering. "You have never forced anyone," she said slowly, "They come to you because they want you." She cocked her head to one side, as if listening. "Even Victor came to you because he wanted you."

Marilyn was so astonished by the girl's ability and insight that she fully released Ryan. Ryan sat up and moved away from her on the couch, straightening her clothing. She gave off an aura of outward calm but was inwardly struggling to maintain her composure.

Marilyn was not fooled by the girl's outward display and quickly regained her own icy poise. Her hand flashed outward and she snagged Ryan's shirtfront. With a snap she dragged Ryan toward her and Ryan found herself half on her knees and half on Marilyn's lap, face-to-face with the dark-haired woman once more.

Marilyn stared down at the Young One, searching her eyes. Ryan tried not to look at her, but found her own eyes lingering on Marilyn's lips. Marilyn did not miss the involuntary attention.

"So," she said with satisfaction, "You are only half-right."

Ryan was flustered. "What do you mean?"

Marilyn smiled, and it was not a pleasant smile. "You are right. It is not my way to force anyone. But you are wrong if you think that will save you."

Ryan swallowed hard, desperately trying to hide her emotions. But she could hide nothing. Marilyn saw the flicker of desire in the girl's eyes, saw the confusion intermixed with longing.

Ryan tried to turn away but Marilyn would not allow her to do so. "You do want me," she whispered to her, her dark eyes flashing triumphantly.

Ryan could not deny her words and closed her eyes, as if that could lessen the woman's hold on her right now. Marilyn leaned close to whisper in her ear.

"You will come to me one day."

"Well isn't this a pleasant domestic scene," Victor said dryly from the doorway.

Abigail glanced up from her stitchery, unruffled by his presence. She had sensed Victor's approach, and knew that Marilyn had not. "Greetings, my Lord, I trust your journey went well?"

Marilyn responded to Victor's presence by releasing Ryan, causing her to sprawl backwards onto the floor at Abigail's feet.

Victor raised an eyebrow. "I thought I left fairly explicit instructions, Abigail," he said mildly.

Abigail glanced down at the dazed youngster. "She is unharmed, my Lord. I believe that is all you asked of me."

Marilyn stood and smoothed out her skirt. "Why Victor, I did not expect you to return so soon," she said coolly, contrition absent from her voice.

Victor watched as Ryan staggered to her feet. "Yes, that's quite obvious."

Ryan sat down on Abigail's stool, holding her head in her hands. The strain of resisting Marilyn had taken its toll. Marilyn watched the exhausted child through narrowed eyes. She had been so close.

"Ryan and I were simply becoming better acquainted."

Victor also noted Ryan's signs of exhaustion, and the blatant look of calculation on Marilyn's face. He had felt from a distance what had transpired; what he saw before him was only confirmation.

"Ryan," he said firmly, "Leave us."

Ryan glanced up at him and stood. She was too exhausted to provide a defense and simply obeyed. She walked from the room without a backward glance while the three Old Ones watched her leave.

Marilyn stood abruptly, smoothing her skirt. "I should be leaving as well, my lord."

Victor said nothing but watched her as she approached the door. She paused in the doorway and turned back to him. "Thank you for such a delightful afternoon," she said suggestively, "It has been years since I have so enjoyed myself."

She started to turn again but paused when Victor spoke.

"Marilyn," Victor said mildly, "Do not follow my child."

Marilyn left, not foolish enough to ignore the warning. The sound of a carriage pulling away could be heard.

Victor turned to Abigail with a look of reproach. "Abigail, I do not trust Marilyn but I had hoped for better from you."

Abigail shrugged, continuing her needlepoint. "I did not ask to be placed in so difficult a position." She looked up at him shrewdly. "Can Marilyn be accused of desiring that which you yourself covet so greatly?"

"And you as well," Victor added.

Abigail's only concession was a slight nod. "But I live to serve you, my lord," she murmured.

She placed her needlepoint down and looked Victor straight in the eye with the unblinking gaze of their Kind. Her words were thoughtful.

"But now perhaps I should fear for you, as well."

Victor looked at her with surprise. "And why is that, my lady?"

Abigail glanced off into the distance and Victor knew she was mentally reaching out to touch Ryan. She made the contact and her attention returned. Her countenance darkened as she thought of the girl, and the darkness was reflected in her words.

"I fear you have created something you cannot control."

Victor's response was also dark and thoughtful, but his words were surprising. He, too, mentally gazed out into the distance before he spoke.

"I certainly hope so."

Susan was mesmerized by the story. She was having the same experience she had the first time Ryan had begun to speak of her past, almost as if she were in a trance. Susan felt she could see what was happening. Ryan told the story in an odd manner, though, almost as if from multiple perspectives.

"You sometimes speak from Victor's point of view."

Ryan nodded. "It's because I have his Memories." Ryan crossed her long legs in front of her. "It's a very strange feeling, and one that takes getting used to. Even now it's odd at times because I'm not certain whose mind I'm looking through. I see places I've never been and remember things I've never seen."

Ryan glanced over at Susan curiously. "So what do you think?" she asked.

Susan was surprised. "What do I think about what?"

Ryan shrugged. "Well, now that I've weaned you off your vampire fantasies, what do you think of me and my Kind?"

This was a subject to which Susan had given a lot of thought. She wasn't certain, though, exactly how to frame her ideas.

"Well, when I was first examining your anatomy, I kept having the thought that, if I were going to create a perfect human being, I would have created you."

Ryan was silent.

Susan continued to think aloud. "I wonder if you're not a form of accelerated evolution."

"Well that's a new one."

"What do you mean by that?"

Ryan shrugged. "I don't mean to disparage your beliefs, but I've been called many things. A demon, an angel, a monster, a witch. And I've been called all these things by people who believed them just as sincerely as you believe what you're saying now."

Susan was at a loss. "I don't see how that's the same...."

"That's exactly my point." Ryan said, staring into her wineglass. "It is the same. Every century has given me a name, and all believed they had the answer to what I am. The people of my time believed me to be a monster with the same certainty you believe me to be 'accelerated evolution.' There is no difference. Two hundred years from now they will have a new name for me, and they will be just as certain as you are now."

Ryan's words brought silence to Susan. The silence stretched into minutes until Ryan asked, "Do you have any idea what time it is?"

Susan pulled herself out of her reverie and looked to the French windows. She was surprised to see it was dark. She glanced around the room, searching for a clock, but there were none. She glanced down at her watch. It was almost 2 am.

Ryan stood. "I think I'm being a bad influence on you. I forget you don't do as well without sleep as I do."

Susan stood and the young man appeared at her side, taking her empty wineglass. "Well, I'm going to check on Jason and Neda, and then I'll head to bed."

"Good night," Ryan said, sitting back down.

Susan was almost to the door when she stopped. Ryan was aware of the pause even though her back was to both Susan and the door. Susan had one last question she wanted to ask and Ryan, ever perceptive, braced herself.

"Could I see your Memories if I tasted your blood?"

The question hung heavy in the air. Ryan stared into the fire. Susan thought for a moment that Ryan was not going to answer her, but then she spoke distinctly.

"I am the most powerful of my Kind," Ryan said slowly, without boasting. "And my blood would kill you instantly."

Although Susan could no longer see Ryan, it seemed as if a great heaviness settled over her. Susan turned to leave, not completely certain why she had asked such a question.

Ryan gazed into the fire, taking the last sip from her wine. She stood, threw another log upon the fire, and poured herself another glass of wine. She settled into the chair once more, pulling a blanket over her legs to ward off an imaginary chill, one she had not felt in reality for centuries.

She enjoyed her conversations with Susan Ryerson, although the Memories the conversations stirred were disturbing. It was bad enough Ryan dreamed vividly of both her Memories and Victor's; now she spent hours awake thinking of her past.

The fire crackled loudly and sparks flew as the log slipped, then settled. Ryan gazed at the wine in her glass. It was times like these when she could see Victor's face, inhumanly beautiful.

Odd, when one thought about it, how easily Victor had maintained his illusion over so many years. In the world she had been born into, there were no photographs, no way of recording events other than in writing. Only the very wealthy could have paintings commissioned, and even those were a poor reflection of the person sitting for the picture. It was easy for Victor to move through centuries without being noticed, without being tied to another place or time, without being discovered as immortal.

It had been as easy for Ryan to do the same over the years, but it was not as simple now. The first time Ryan had seen a photograph, she had not seen a miracle of technology, but rather the beginning of a new danger. She often wondered if this latent fear had not revealed itself in the myths of their Kind; it was not that they could not see their reflection in a mirror, it was that they did not wish to. If there was no reflection, there was no record.

Prior to her life with Victor, Ryan had so seldom seen her own reflection she did not recognize herself the first time she gazed through Victor's eyes. It had taken her awhile to realize that Victor also saw through her eyes, and longer to realize she could hide nothing from him.

Ryan had no pictures of Victor. No paintings, no photographs, no film, no images of him whatsoever. But it did not matter, because the Memories were etched into her mind forever, as clear as the day they were recorded.

CHAPTER 24

"Well, what do you think?"

Ryan leaned over the railing of the ship. They were still miles from shore, but she could just barely make out the land in the distance. A seaman next to them snorted, he could see nothing.

Ryan pushed away from the railing. Victor had tired of war, and tired of their leisure in France, and then tired of his castle in England. But he never tired of showing Ryan the world. It had been his decision to travel across the channel, then south through France, but Ryan's to take a ship through the Mediterranean. Their destination was the Papal States themselves, and ultimately Rome.

"I can't tell. It certainly doesn't look like England."

Victor laughed. No, it certainly wouldn't be like England.

They landed in port and Victor left instructions to restock the ship with supplies. He and Ryan had needed little on the trip over, but the crew required food and water. The captain leaped to do his master's bidding. After all, his lordship owned the ship.

The two began their journey to the city. They were to meet Marilyn in Rome, but Victor was in no hurry, moving with the leisurely gait of their Kind.

Ryan knew they were going to join Marilyn, and she had mixed emotions. It was difficult for her to remember how long it had been since she had seen the dark-haired woman. After their initial meeting, she and Victor had seen the woman at various social engagements. But Victor tired of the whirlwind of parties with the Others, and once he felt Ryan had received enough exposure, he spirited her away. Ryan remembered that Marilyn had watched her leave with a gaze that made her shudder for many reasons.

Ryan thought back. With her long, strange sleeping patterns intermixed with months of staying awake, it was difficult to judge time. Days blended into weeks which blended into years. Ryan was surprised, perhaps it had been several decades since she had seen Marilyn.

Ryan glanced over at Victor. She was curious why Victor accepted Marilyn's invitation. She knew he did not trust Marilyn around her; she gathered that much from his Memories. But she also knew Victor enjoyed the challenge of Marilyn's presence. Ryan inwardly frowned, perhaps he found her company lacking.

Victor glanced down at his young companion knowingly. She could not know the reservation he had about bringing her within Marilyn's grasp, nor did she realize his reasons for doing so were strictly political. There were strange winds blowing within the papacy, winds that would affect him were he not to take action first. He had not survived for centuries without knowing when he could keep to himself, and when he had to act.

Victor glanced down at Ryan, who was still lost in thought. She was correct; Marilyn did stimulate him. But not to the degree that she herself did. One of Ryan's most endearing qualities was her complete unawareness of her own allure.

It had been a wise decision to keep Ryan cloistered before meeting their Kind. During that first century, Ryan had little to judge herself by except Victor, giving her no concept of how truly powerful she was.

Victor was thoughtful. Even once Ryan had become aware of her place in the hierarchy of their Kind, it seemed to have little affect on her. It wasn't as if she didn't know how powerful she was, it was as if she didn't care.

Victor inwardly smiled. Each passing year told him he could not have planned or chosen better.

Ryan realized Victor was immensely pleased with himself for some reason, and she wondered if it was because they would soon see Marilyn. She tentatively touched his mind, feeling only for impressions.

She didn't think so.

Marilyn glanced out the window of the alcove at the two figures below. Victor was speaking graciously to a young woman who was fluttering her fan about her face. Humans, both male and female found Victor devastatingly handsome, and Marilyn herself could hardly disagree. She turned her attention to the girl and her eyes narrowed. As usual, the whelp was dressed as a man.

Ryan possessed the peculiar androgyny of their Kind, and although all were essentially sexless, Ryan seemed to epitomize this genderless quality. Dressed now in breeches, boots, and a loose shirt, it was difficult to determine if she made a more beautiful girl or boy. Even Marilyn had to admit Victor's progeny was stunning.

Marilyn reached out to touch the girl and Ryan immediately looked upward. Marilyn was startled to feel the girl's strength. Although she was still no match for Marilyn's own immense power, the girl was already beginning to demonstrate signs of a rare maturity. So many of their Kind at Ryan's age were drunk with their own power and failed to grow into it. Ryan's power was phenomenal for one less than two centuries, and yet she seemed to be adapting gracefully.

Marilyn's eyes narrowed again. Once more, the girl seemed to be the exception.

As if sensing her thoughts, Victor turned his gaze upward. The young lass, realizing she had lost his lordship's attention, turned her fan to the young, fair-haired gentleman. But he, too, was looking upward and the young lady realized petulantly that she could not compete with the beauty of the woman in the window.

Victor grasped Ryan's arm and the two entered the villa. Ryan tried to calm herself but she felt a fluttering inside as Marilyn swept down the staircase towards them.

"Hello darling," Marilyn said, taking Victor's hands into her own. She leaned forward and kissed him chastely on the lips, lingering perhaps a little too long. She released Victor and turned to Ryan, who had the sudden urge to take a step backward.

Marilyn sensed Ryan's trepidation and was both entertained and enticed by it. She could not let such a moment pass.

"Hello, little one."

The endearment was subtly insulting and the amusement in Marilyn's eyes told Ryan it was so intended. But before Ryan could react to the slight,

Marilyn stepped close to her and pulled Ryan to her. She embraced her and Ryan felt Marilyn's lips brush her neck with a kiss.

The caress sent a shock through Ryan and she stiffened. She pulled backward, staggering into Victor who caught her easily. He sighed.

"I see you haven't changed, Marilyn."

Marilyn smiled, her dark eyes still on Ryan. "But she has, my lord." She turned her gaze to Victor. "And in other ways, she has not."

To Ryan's relief, Victor and Marilyn settled to discuss business. Ryan was not interested in the politics of their conversation, although she knew she should be. Instead, she turned her attention to the contents of her bag. She carefully removed an object wrapped in soft leather and set it upon the table in front of her. She removed the leather coverlet and folded it, setting it aside.

Ryan stared down at her prize possession. It was a copy of Le Morte d'Arthur, printed in Latin. Victor had given her the book as a gift, and although she had read it hundreds of times, it was still her favorite.

Books were extremely rare and Ryan had seen very few of them. But every one she had seen, Victor had bought. She had a beautiful copy of Chaucer's Canterbury Tales, but that story, although humorous, did not enthrall her the way King Arthur and his knights did.

Ryan could now speak several languages, but could read only in Latin. It was something of a shock for her to read the Bible for the first time. The actual words of the scriptures were far different from those told to her as a peasant boy, several lifetimes ago. Ryan realized the local clergy had based their sermons on many things, but few that were found within the text of the Bible. It made her realize how powerless the people had been because of their ignorance; they had no choice but to believe whatever the priests told them. Ryan understood how important books were, and how important they would become.

Ryan traced the words on the cover in front of her, then opened the book and began to read. She was engrossed in the tale when she realized someone was speaking to her. She raised her head to find both Victor and Marilyn looking at her.

"I'm sorry, what did you say?"

Marilyn turned to Victor. "Don't tell me she has hopes of becoming a scholar."

Forty or fifty years ago, the comment would have caused Ryan to blush. Now she calmly returned Marilyn's gaze. "No, I don't wish to become a scholar. But I do enjoy reading."

Marilyn was thoughtful for a long moment. "I'm not certain I know anyone else who knows how to read. Did Victor teach you?"

Ryan nodded. She had the feeling Marilyn was contemplating something, although she was not certain what. She was surprised at the woman's next words.

"Then perhaps you could teach me."

Marilyn's words were not directed at Victor, but at Ryan. Ryan glanced at Victor uncertainly. It would be rude for her to refuse Marilyn, but agreeing to tutor her would put her in the woman's company far more than she liked. It could also place her in situations where she would be extremely close to Marilyn, and Victor might not always be present.

From the calculated look in Marilyn's eye, that was exactly what she intended. But whatever her motives, Ryan could not find reason to refuse her.

"I guess I could do that," Ryan said hesitantly. "I'm certain you would find reading enjoyable."

Marilyn's words were laced with double meaning. "I'm certain I'd find it most enjoyable."

Victor was not completely happy with Marilyn's games with Ryan. But Ryan would have to learn to deal with her sooner or later, so it might as well be under these circumstances. He made a mental note to himself, however, to stay close when the "lessons" took place.

Ryan carefully repacked her book and stood to leave. Victor noted the lengthening shadows and reminded Ryan of their evening commitment.

"Do not forget our engagement. We must leave before sundown."

Ryan nodded. She might as well get dressed now. It would be one of the few times Victor asked her to dress in garb beyond that of a stable boy. She started up the stairs, her thoughts filled with irony.

Who knew that a peasant boy, born in poverty and filth, would nearly two centuries later dress in the clothing of kings? And who knew that such a boy, raised in complete ignorance of all but his village, would one day travel to foreign lands and be one of the first to read the works of scholars?

And who knew that this peasant boy, who had never received more than passing attention from the local priest, would one day be summoned into the presence of Rodrigo Lanzol Y Borgia, otherwise known as Pope

Alexander VI?

Ryan pulled the embroidered doublet over her pleated undershirt. Both were a deep indigo, contrasting with the black silk hose and ankle boots she wore. The sleeves of the blue shirt were split and embroidered with black thread. The outfit was simple but elegant, and Ryan was pleased with her appearance.

Victor was more than pleased with her appearance. Ryan possessed a lithe muscularity that was rare if not non-existent in the nobility. Few could wear the clothing she did, and none could wear it as well.

Victor pulled his own doublet on, then the knee-length coat. Of course with Ryan traveling as a man, it would once again bring into question their relationship. He smiled grimly to himself.

With what he had heard about the man currently heading the Church of Rome, it would not matter what anyone thought of them.

Marilyn watched the two leave, against her will admiring the pair they made. Ryan looked the part of a young prince and Victor that of a reigning king, the former angelically handsome and the latter devilishly so. The two, accompanied by a fair-sized entourage carrying gifts, set out for the Vatican.

Ryan was not particularly excited about the evening ahead, but as they approached the papal palace, an odd tension overtook her. She was becoming ever more attuned to the emotions of humans and wondered what was causing such a tautness in the air.

As they neared the grounds, flags embossed with a red bull on a field of gold stirred in the mild breeze. Once inside the gates, they were surrounded by statues in various erotic poses sprinkled throughout the garden.

Ryan glanced around curiously at the "statues." They were actually young men and women who had painted their bodies and were now frozen in various acts of debauchery. The acts ranged from the mildly deviant to the incomprehensible. Ryan marveled at the acrobatic nature of some of the sexual scenarios, but was otherwise unimpressed. Victor appeared equally unmoved, in direct contrast to the titillated crowds surrounding the still-life actors.

Victor pushed his way through the throng, aware of the attention they were attracting. Heads turned and he could easily overhear the whispers of those present as they both subtly and unsubtly tried to get a glimpse of the beautiful strangers. Humans had always been drawn to their Kind, and few of their Kind had the overwhelming presence of he and his fair companion.

They moved into the great circular hall that was set up for a banquet. Tables with chairs and recliners were set in a roughly circular pattern between the pillars, leaving the middle of the hall open. Victor ignored the murmur that went through the room at their entrance, his gaze sweeping the hall. His eyes settled on the raised dais at the far end of the room where a richly dressed man was seated. The man nodded to Victor.

Victor glanced down at Ryan who was coolly examining the room, ignoring the illicit conversation their arrival had sparked. She nodded to him in understanding, following his lead.

Alexander sat upon his papal throne. Although over seventy years old, he was still a fleshy man of huge appetite. He took the measure of the two men coming toward him with a practiced eye.

Although well known for his insatiable lust for women, he had an unabashed appreciation for virility. The tall, dark-haired man approaching him had to be one of the most virile men he had ever seen. Dark-eyed with high cheek bones and an aquiline nose, the Medici's would have a hard time finding so perfect an ideal in their vast collection of art.

Alexander turned his attention to the boy. He himself had no predilections in this particular area, but had he access to so beautiful a youth, he felt he could be persuaded. It was unlikely there was as comely a person, male or female, in the entire room. He was pleased with this addition to his banquet.

Victor bowed and took the hand of the Pope, kissing his ring. Ryan followed suit and stepped back to Victor's side.

"I am honored at your invitation, your Holiness."

Alexander gazed at the man in a certain languor. "Of course you are." He paused, a certain significance in his words. "This is the first time you have had the pleasure of our company at such an event?"

Victor nodded as Alexander continued. "I trust you will participate fully. I am unhappy when my guests are not pleased."

Victor understood the implied warning and bowed gracefully. He guided Ryan to the far side of the room, almost directly across from the papal throne. The two sat down at a table between two pillars, ignoring the inviting looks of those around them.

Ryan leaned close to Victor. "And what, pray tell, are we to participate in?"

Victor looked down at his young charge, a youth who was 10 decades older than the next oldest person in this room. He brushed the hair from her eyes. "You will have to trust me."

From across the room, Alexander watched the sensual exchange between the two and was oddly excited. It normally took the depths of depravity to elicit any type of response from him, yet he felt his groin stir at this simple interaction between these two. He settled back on his throne; this night would prove to be even more interesting than he had thought.

Ryan settled back, not the least bit appeased. She glanced curiously around the room, trying not to make eye contact with those so obviously trying to do so with her. She was successful until her gaze wandered to the woman seated next to the Pope.

The woman stared boldly back at Ryan, a naked hunger in her eyes. Ryan estimated the girl to be 19 or perhaps 20 years old. She had long golden hair, a shade lighter than Ryan's, framing the sweetest of faces. The innocent countenance did not match the unbridled lust in her eyes.

Ryan carefully let her eyes continue about the room, but her gaze was arrested by the very next man she came to. He was bearded and handsome, clothed in the robes of a cardinal. But there was no Christian charity in his eyes on this night. He gazed at Ryan in hot fury.

Ryan decided to cease her perusal of the room as it was having unintended consequences. Victor leaned close to speak in her ear.

"Her name is Lucrezia, and the man next to her is her brother, Cesare. They are both Alexander's children."

If this was not shocking enough to Ryan, his next words were more so.

"It is rumored she has been both her father's and brother's lover. She had another brother, Juan, whom Cesare apparently killed in a jealous rage."

Ryan suddenly understood why the bearded man looked at her with such fury. Lucrezia's attention was quite overt. Ryan's misgivings about the entertainment ahead dramatically increased.

As if on cue, great platters of food were brought in. There were gasps from the guests as entire stags were brought forth, the meat stuffed within the hide of the beast. Great boars, tusks and all, were brought in a similar fashion. Every type of exotic fruit and vegetable was available, and the people began to eat ravenously.

Alexander noted that the handsome pair were not eating. They also appeared disinterested in the proceedings around them. He was aware of Lucrezia's interest in the boy, although he had the feeling the boy would not be interested in her. He glanced at his temptress of a daughter; he did not see how that could be possible.

The food was whisked away as quickly as it had been brought in. A small ensemble in the corner began to play music and a group of 50 to 60 men and women came pouring into the hall. They danced around, playfully picking partners from the seated guests. The guests eagerly leaped to their feet and began to dance with the courtesans.

The wine and rich food were obviously beginning to have an affect as the dancers gaily began to shed articles of clothing. The more they danced, the more clothing was removed until several dancers on the floor were nearly nude.

Alexander clapped his hands and a group of servants rushed in bearing candelabra. Chestnuts were thrown amongst the burning candles and the courtesans began to snake their way through the impromptu maze, picking up the chestnuts. Ryan could see no rhyme or reason for this display, other than it put the courtesans in the correct positions for what was to follow.

Guests began to run out on the floor, shedding the remainder of their clothing. They grabbed the prostitute of their choice, which was sometimes whoever was closest, and began to vigorously copulate.

Ryan, who had seen many things in the last two centuries, was startled by the display. She glanced across the room at Alexander who seemed immensely pleased by the exhibit, and indeed, was even cheering some of his favorites on.

Every type of sexual act imaginable was present. Although the vast majority took place between men and women, there were a scattered few amongst same sex partners. Oral copulation, anal copulation, copulation with parts of the body that seemed incapable of copulation, all were performed with orgasmic abandon. Those who were not immediately engaged in the sexual act were voyeuristically preparing for it. Servants appeared to be keeping count in some bizarre contest.

Alexander felt his eyes drawn to the handsome pair, and was displeased. They were not participating, and indeed, did not even appear to be enjoying the show. As if he sensed his scrutiny, the dark-haired man turned towards him.

There was a knowing, sensual look in the man's eyes. It was almost as if Alexander heard the man's voice inside his head.

I know what you want.

Alexander's eyes narrowed, but he did not turn back to the orgy in front of him. Instead, he watched the man across the room brush the boy's hair away from the nape of his neck with a languid gesture.

Ryan turned in surprise to Victor, who was partially reclined on a sofa. With little indication of his intention, he grasped the front of her shirt and pulled her effortlessly to the recliner in front of him. She tried to pull away but his grip was suddenly like iron and she was trapped, laying stiffly in front of him facing away.

Victor stared across the room at the Borgia Pope who was suddenly oblivious to the carnal display in front of him. He watched in fascination as the dark-haired man pinned the youth in front of him. He somehow had the feeling he was about to witness something far more extraordinary than a simple sexual act.

Ryan was angered by Victor's actions. He rarely used his strength against her other than in play.

Relax, came his voice inside her head.

Ryan was further angered that Victor would use his power in such a way. His influence over her was extraordinary, but he rarely forced her to do anything. Against her will she felt her limbs relax and a peculiar languor steal over her. She rested her head against his chest.

Alexander watched the youth's expression. The boy suddenly appeared drugged as he relaxed in the man's embrace. The man, his eyes still locked with Alexander's, rubbed his thumb against the pulse in the boy's throat.

Alexander felt his excitement quicken. Although cries of ecstasy were all around him, he had eyes only for the pair across the room. He felt himself actually leaning forward in his chair.

The man gazed mockingly at Alexander and Alexander felt his frustration build. He did not think he spoke the words aloud, but he knew the man heard them.

Show me.

The man had a knife in his hand that glittered from across the room. The man appeared to toy with it, caressing the boy's throat with the flat of the blade. The boy did not appear frightened by the weapon, and in fact, appeared almost to be aroused against his will.

Ryan struggled feebly in Victor's grip. "Why are you doing this to me?" she whispered through clenched teeth.

Victor knew why he had initiated the act. But his reasons for continuing had nothing to do with the Borgia Pope and everything to do with his hunger for this dark child.

The knife whispered across the boy's throat and Alexander could see the crimson of the blood from across the room. Never taking his eyes from him, the man lowered his lips to the wound and began to drink.

Alexander felt his passion strain the confines of his holy raiment. The boy's eyes closed briefly and the perfect lips parted. The eyes reopened but now they were distant, focused on a place that all of Alexander's depravity had never succeeded in taking him.

The man's eyes were closed now as well, locked in his unholy embrace. He no longer seemed concerned with satisfying Alexander's voyeuristic passions, intent only on satisfying his own passion. Alexander finally had to look away.

He gradually refocused on the couples in front of him, but their straining and grunting seemed somehow sordid now, pathetic. He turned his gaze back to the dark-haired man, but he was not surprised to see he was gone.

Alexander would not know how few years he had left alive. But in the ultimate retribution for his sins, he did know he would never again be satisfied.

Victor did not wait for a carriage but spirited Ryan away in his arms, on foot. She was nearly unconscious because he had bled her completely. It was unfortunate he could not have warned her of the night's events. He knew how headstrong she was, and she probably would not have complied with his wishes. He could have forced her, which is ultimately what he did, but keeping her ignorant had been much simpler.

Victor had been at the mercy of the Church before, and knew that sometimes the best way to fight it was to join it. It had been Marilyn's idea to toy with the Borgia Pope, well aware of his perversion. She knew if Victor could gave him the ultimate gift, sexual excitement, the Pope would leave both Victor and his lands alone.

Victor glanced down at Ryan. He knew she would be angry upon awakening. She would not understand why Victor chose to do such a thing. Ryan's way was to break a man in two, but Victor had learned that although effective, force was not always successful. If it were truly counted, Victor's wealth would be unmatched in the known world, but wealth and power sometimes bred enemies of the envious.

Ryan knew she was being carried but was too dazed to open her eyes to see by whom. She was laid gently to rest on a soft coverlet and heard the murmur of voices. There was a ringing in her ears so she could not make out to whom they belonged.

She rolled over onto her side, wishing the pounding in her head would dissipate. Images from the night swam through her mind, coupled with Memories stirred from her own blood. Her skin felt flushed.

A cool hand startled her out of her feverish thoughts. She turned instinctively and sat upright, seeking a sword or a weapon to defend herself. But Marilyn was much faster than she and easily captured the flailing wrist.

"It's just me," Marilyn said, as if that should comfort her.

Ryan stared at the woman, still half-upright with her arm still in the defensive gesture. She slowly lowered the arm. Marilyn pushed her gently but firmly back onto the mattress and stretched out beside her.

"Victor sent me to watch you, he is concerned about you."

Ryan turned her shoulder slightly, speaking under her breath. "He must be concerned if he sent you."

In a flash, Marilyn pulled Ryan to her, her face so close to Ryan's cheek could feel her breath on her neck. "Be careful, little one," she whispered into her ear.

Marilyn released her, settling comfortably behind her. But Ryan was anything but comfortable, pressed up against the other woman. She lay stiffly for a few moments, but finally her fatigue began to overcome her and the stiffness seeped from her body.

Marilyn felt the girl relax and reached over to stroke her hair. Normally Ryan would not suffer such attention, but she was too tired to pretend the cool caress was unwelcome.

Marilyn was once again amazed at the effect this girl had on her. Under normal circumstances, a Young One, especially one who had just been bled, would hold no attraction for her. But Ryan's vulnerability only seemed to heighten Marilyn's desire. She knew the girl lying on the bed could offer her only token resistance in her current exhausted state.

Marilyn toyed with Ryan's hair. She wondered why the girl was so feverish. Normally those who were bled were cold and pale. This one felt as if she were on fire. Marilyn put her cool hand on Ryan's arm and felt a tingle of excitement at the heat emanating from her.

"And how was your evening?" Marilyn asked idly, still fingering her hair.

Marilyn felt the girl stiffen again. Ryan slowly turned to her and Marilyn saw fury in her eyes, the fury that was stoking the fire in her body.

And Marilyn saw something startling within that fury. A distance between Ryan and Victor that had never been there before.

It was the slightest whisper of invitation, a vague, sensual promise that Ryan would turn her considerable charm on Marilyn were the circumstances ever right and Victor ever wrong. It was astonishing for Marilyn to see because, in that instant, she understood how truly powerful Ryan would become, and how magnetic her attraction would be.

And then the whisper was gone and the veil behind Ryan's eyes was replaced, leaving only the vaguest of impressions that anything had been there at all. She was once more a Young One who was simply angered and exhausted. Ryan turned onto her side once more, and within minutes was asleep.

Marilyn lay next to the sleeping girl and stared into the darkness, her eyes thoughtful.

Victor returned sometime before the morning light. He raised an eyebrow at Marilyn's proximity to Ryan in the bed, but Marilyn seemed unwilling to engage in her typical banter with him. She gazed down at the sleeping girl next to her.

"It is her one weakness."

Victor removed his outer coat, laying it at the foot of the bed. He glanced over at the contemplative woman. "And what might that be?"

Marilyn brushed a lock of hair out of Ryan's eyes. "Her need for sleep.

She sleeps much more than any of our Kind."

Victor shrugged. "She has greater need of it than any of our Kind. She withstands more strain than most Old Ones could bear."

Marilyn turned her attention to the handsome dark-haired man. "Yes, I'm well-aware of how demanding you can be."

Victor ignored the innuendo in her voice, although he knew her words to be true. "I don't think Ryan is nearly as vulnerable as you believe her to be. I did not ask you to stay here tonight so much to protect her as to keep her in check. Ryan can be very temperamental."

Marilyn was thoughtful, thinking back to their earlier wordless exchange. Temperamental was an understatement. For the first time she wondered if Victor could indeed control the hot-blooded creature he had made.

Marilyn smiled ever so slightly. And she wondered if she could be strategically near if he failed.

CHAPTER 25

Ryan swung the ax in a smooth, practiced motion. The wood split cleanly down the center, each piece falling to the side. Jason sat a few feet away, watching the rhythmic motion.

"Can you teach me to do that?" he asked between chops.

Ryan set up another piece of wood on the block. She swung the ax up over shoulder in a graceful arc and brought it hurtling downward. She made it look effortless, but the speed with which the ax-head traveled was extraordinary.

"Maybe when you get a little older."

Ryan set another piece of wood up. She had learned to chop wood when she was about his age, but children were raised differently these days. She paused. She had also had a few "advantages" that other children did not.

The ax came swinging downward once more, splitting the wood down the center. She bent down to pick up another block of wood when Jason's next words stopped her in her tracks.

"I wish I had a dad like you."

The incongruent phrase gave her pause. Ryan turned to look at the little boy. "Why a dad?" she asked, curious but not insulted.

"Because I already have a mom," he replied with a 5 year-old's logic.

"Oh," Ryan said. She picked up the block of wood and set it on the stump. She glanced over a the boy. "What happened to your father?"

Jason looked down at the ground. "He died when I was little. In a plane crash."

"Oh," Ryan said in understanding. "My parents are dead, too." Ryan hefted the ax handle, gazing at the blade. "I don't think you'd want me to be your dad. I don't think you'd like your new relatives."

Jason was silent for a moment and Ryan set another piece of wood up. She was bringing the ax over her shoulder when he spoke again.

"Was your dad a lot like you?"

Ryan stopped the swing in mid-air. She turned away from the boy, fighting against the sudden loss of control. But the battle was quickly lost and with incredible force, she hurled the ax across the yard toward a large oak tree. The ax hurtled end-over-end until it embedded in the tree with a tremendous crack, splitting the tree down the middle. Jason stared wide-eyed as Ryan stalked across the yard.

Susan had been watching the two from the glass door. At Ryan's startling act of violence, she ran out to Jason. Edward was right behind her. She picked Jason up, clutching him to her breast, but he was not upset. He stared at the tree in wonder.

Edward watched as Ryan's back disappeared into the afternoon shadows. He sighed and glanced to the pile of wood she had stacked, and to the tree she had destroyed. Ryan only chopped wood when something was bothering her.

Susan carried Jason back to the house, setting him down once they were inside. Jason was less frightened than concerned that he had upset Ryan. He looked up at Edward as the elder man re-entered the mansion.

"I didn't mean to make her mad."

Edward rarely acknowledged either of them so it surprised Susan when he paused, then actually sat down next to them.

"It's not your fault," he said in his very British accent, "Ryan has something of a bad temper."

Susan was further surprised by the remark. Edward had never shown anything but unswerving loyalty to Ryan. The remark was not so much a criticism as an observation, but still, Susan had never heard him speak against her in any way. She had a sudden insight.

"You care for her a great deal, don't you?"

Edward's stiffness did not diminish in any way, but a fierce light burned in his eyes. "Ryan is my King. I live to serve her."

Susan was a little taken aback at the fierceness of his reply, but she nodded. She was struck by the incongruous title. "Queen" would have seemed more appropriate for Ryan's sex, yet somehow less appropriate for Ryan.

Jason seemed to have processed Ryan's androgyny with little difficulty. "I want her to be my King, too."

Edward looked down at the boy, and for the first time gazed at him with something akin to approval. "I think Ryan would commend you as a subject." Jason smiled happily, then pushed himself off Susan's lap to run and find his puppy. Edward turned back to Susan. "Although your presence here is problematic."

Susan bristled. "Problematic? Remember, we are not here by choice. It was Ryan's decision to bring us here."

Edward's face remained impassive. "And a wise decision it was. At least your presence here guarantees she will no longer place herself in danger trying to protect you."

Susan could not disguise her sarcasm. "I find it difficult to believe that Ryan is in danger from anything."

Edward glanced out the window toward the toppled oak tree. Several gardeners were already removing the debris. "Perhaps endangered is not the appropriate expression. You have placed her at a strategic disadvantage."

Susan was angry. "What do you mean by that?"

Edward turned to her and his reproach was evident. "You set a chain of events in motion when you published your work. Ryan has no equals; she has no weaknesses. You," he said emphatically, "Are now her weakness."

Susan stood up. "I don't have to listen to this."

But Edward stood up as well, firmly grasping her elbow. "Listen to me, Dr. Ryerson."

The urgency in his voice made Susan pause.

"I encouraged Ryan to kill you, but she would not because she felt sympathy for your son. Now I believe she holds a certain fondness for you. That does not change the fact that you are a liability to her."

Susan pulled her arm away. She stood up to her full height, although she was still considerably shorter than he was.

"My son and I are ready to leave anytime you wish to disobey your 'master'," she said cuttingly.

She turned on her heel and stormed from the room. Edward watched her retreating back, his face impassive.

Ryan knocked on Susan's door several hours later. Susan let her in, noting something odd about Ryan's appearance. She finally realized what it was. Ryan looked tired.

"Is Jason all right?" Ryan asked.

Susan motioned for her to come in. "Yes," she said, "In fact, he's ready to swear his undying loyalty to you."

Ryan smiled, running her hand through her hair. The gesture was so uncharacteristic, it made Ryan look even younger than the 19 years she had claimed at one time.

"I understand you and Edward exchanged words."

"Ah yes," Susan said. She sat down. "He feels that we are a 'liability' of sorts."

Ryan sat down as well. "That does not surprise me. That's the lawyer in him talking."

Susan was surprised. "Edward is a lawyer?"

Ryan nodded. "Oh yes, Edward is many things to me. But he's primarily my attorney. He runs my business affairs and my estate. He is quite excellent, and knows more about the law than any person on this planet."

Susan digested this information and Ryan continued. "I used to be a lawyer."

This seemed to be some sort of private joke to Ryan.

"What do you mean by that?" Susan asked.

"When I was young, it was very common to challenge witnesses by battle. You could literally accuse someone of lying, and if you beat them in combat, then they were lying. On the other hand, if you lost, then you were lying. Truth had very little to do with it." Ryan was thoughtful. "The legal system really hasn't changed that much."

"And how were you involved in this?"

Ryan leaned over and picked up an elaborate letter opener from the table between them. She hefted the weight of it in her hand.

"It was quite lucrative to freelance as a 'champion of truth,' if you will. All of justice became a fight between mercenaries. Those who could hire the best mercenaries, those were the ones justice favored." Ryan replaced the letter opener. "Like I said, things haven't changed that much."

Ryan glanced around the room. She saw a rosary lying on the nightstand. "You're not catholic, are you?"

"Yes," Susan admitted, "Actually I am, though not practicing. I had a strict religious upbringing that I rebelled against when I married. My husband was Protestant."

Ryan stood up. "You could have been killed for that years ago," she said, walking to the nightstand. She picked up the rosary, fingering the beads in her hand. "I met a pope once," she murmured.

This was more than enough to attract Susan's attention and her next words even more so.

"And I killed his son."

Susan was too uncertain at her words to be shocked. "How could the pope have a son? Don't they take vows of celibacy?"

Ryan turned to Susan and her eyes were dark with devilish laughter and perhaps a little scorn. "You don't know much about the history of the catholic church, do you?"

Susan tried to hide her defensiveness. "Well, it's not that. It's just that it's hard for me to think of the Pope as having a son."

Ryan clicked the beads together in her hand. "Well, this particular Pope had at least two sons, and a daughter, and probably many more that he didn't know about. In all my very long life, he was one of the most perverse individuals I ever met, as were his children."

Susan was in disbelief, but curious all the same. "Why did you kill his son?"

Ryan replaced the rosary, thoughtful once more. "Cesare was a vicious and evil-tempered man, which in itself was not unusual. It was rumored he killed his own brother out of jealousy over his sister."

Susan was shocked. "They were lovers?"

"Oh yes. Unfortunately, his sister took a particular liking to me, an infatuation that continued for several years. Cesare finally attempted to ambush me in a back-alley fight, and I ended up killing him."

Ryan did not appear too upset by this ending and in fact, recounted it almost as if it were a fond memory. "Poor Cesare," she said without the slightest bit of sympathy.

Susan stared at the tall woman with her back to her. It was times like these when she suddenly saw Ryan in a new light. She could see how some young girl could be infatuated by such a figure, a creature with such mesmerizing qualities. Poor Cesare indeed.

Ryan left Susan to her own devices and on a whim, Susan went to the computer Edward had provided her. She turned the machine on and brought the on-line encyclopedia to the screen. She was thoughtful for a moment, then began her search, typing in the information.

"Let's try 'Popes'."

This brought 87 different matches, so she narrowed her search by time. "Let's try 1300-1600."

That narrowed the search further. Susan paused for a moment, then on a guess, she linked the search to the name Ryan had used, "Cesare."

To her surprise, she got an immediate hit and brought the information up on screen. She began to read aloud.

"Cesare Borgia, Cardinal, son of Pope Alexander the VI. Brother to the infamous Lucrezia Borgia..."

Susan stopped for a moment. Now that was certainly a name she recognized, although she had always thought the stories were exaggerations. She was stunned. Was that the sister Ryan was talking about who had become infatuated with her? She continued reading.

"Cesare Borgia was a violent and bloodthirsty man who met his demise in sordid circumstances in the first part of the 16th century. It is unknown exactly how Cesare was killed, but it is speculated he died in a bar room brawl."

Susan paused for a moment, then kept reading. "Cesare is best known for the deviance surrounding his family, but also is recognized as the model for 'Il Principe'."

Susan switched off the machine and sat back, staring at the darkened screen. Ryan had certainly told an interesting story this time. If what she had said was true, Ryan had killed the man whom Machiavelli had immortalized in "The Prince."

Ryan walked into the great room of her mansion. A low fire was burning in the hearth. She settled into the large, comfortable couch, feeling the vaguest sense of ennui.

That was the worst part about being who she was, she thought, the occasional lapse into boredom. For many of their Kind it was much worse, and as time went on they would go stark raving mad. Fortunately, those who were most affected by this boredom were also the weakest. They could still be killed before they became a liability.

Ryan could do anything she wished, could go anywhere she wanted, could have anything in the world. She had wealth beyond imagination that continued to compound over decades, then over centuries. She could move the course of entire economies if she wished, and could bring governments to their knees. It was a power that many longed for. It was a power Ryan cared little about.

The truth of the matter was Ryan was rarely bored. She was interested in almost everything, and in those times when she could find little to occupy her time, she could spend time in her Memories, or time thinking about the future. She hoped she would one day travel to the stars.

She stared into the fire, her countenance darkening. That was if these idiots did not destroy themselves first. She had never been much concerned with the ebb and flow of human events until they had taken on such a global scale. Ryan was fairly certain she could survive a nuclear war, but wasn't certain she would want to.

Despite her outward detachment, Ryan had grown increasingly angry at this race of people. Human beings were short-sighted because they were short-lived. They were unwilling to make changes that would not benefit them in their lifetimes, indeed, would not benefit them immediately.

They were nearly incapable of truly great change unless it was thrust upon them, and each generation acted as if it were the first on earth. Each generation also acted as if they were the last, compounding the misery of future generations.

Ryan wondered if humans would treat the earth the way they did if they were to live as long as she, forced to reap what they sowed.

It seemed to go beyond shortsightedness, however. Human beings seemed incapable of grasping simple cause-and-effect when it occurred over any length of time. Ryan could feel the changes in the environment that had occurred over the last hundred years. She could feel the increased electromagnetic frequency in the air because it had not existed for much of her life. She could also feel her body adapt to it. She knew that humans would not adapt as well, if at all.

She could feel the increased virulence of diseases, the strength of infections. She could feel her immune system take on more and more powerful predators. She could feel many changes that her system adapted to effortlessly, and watched as humans began to blindly die from things that had not existed when she was a child.

Humans were overwhelmed by time, which stretched reality beyond their capacity to see. They continually drew erroneous conclusions from the simplest of data, then completely missed the obvious. They were incapable of thinking about the way they thought. They lived with the specter of death, oblivious to it. They were driven by greed, which made no sense to Ryan as none seemed to live long enough to enjoy the fruits of it.

Ryan switched on the large-screen television at the end of the room. She rarely watched it because it appeared as little more than colored dots to her. Her mind worked entirely too fast to blend the pixels into a single picture. Films were even worse as she could actually see the frames going by. But she would occasionally turn on the set and, if she turned her head at just the right angle, she could form a picture out of her peripheral vision.

A national news program sent Ryan back to her musing. Humans were frightened of the spectacular and the extraordinary, but they died from the mundane.

Ryan thought of Susan Ryerson, fighting her diseases. Once Susan grasped the fact that Ryan was truly immortal, would she long for such an immortality herself? The fact that she had already asked Ryan the question about being able to see her Memories told Ryan the thought had already crossed Susan's mind. Ryan could not Change Susan; she was too powerful. Not even Edward could do it. Although 400 years younger than she, he was still considered an Old One. Ryan could have it arranged, however, but that would entail contacting the Others.

Ryan's countenance darkened again. She didn't want to think of that.

Her thoughts returned to Susan. Ryan had spent much of the last two centuries alone, yet had not been lonely. She did not normally cultivate human companionship because humans changed, they grew old and they died. But Susan Ryerson had stumbled into her life and Ryan felt a certain responsibility to her and her son.

Ryan chastised herself. It went beyond responsibility. She had to admit she was beginning to enjoy the woman's company. Ryan had never Changed anyone and thus had no offspring. With the possible exception of Marilyn, she had no equals amongst her Kind and did not encourage their company. Susan Ryerson was possibly the closest thing to a friend she had ever had.

Ryan entertained that pleasant thought for awhile, trying and failing to ignore a far less pleasant reality. Edward was correct. If Ryan befriended Susan Ryerson, then she had inherited a liability.

Although Ryan was invulnerable, Susan Ryerson and her young son were not.

This thought was met with deep foreboding. Ryan had been placed in that situation before, and it had not turned out well.

CHAPTER 26

RYAN STRODE THROUGH THE FOREST, ENJOYING AN ODD sense of freedom. She had set out several months ago at Victor's suggestion. He had sensed her restlessness and suggested she travel as he was occupied with business affairs. She packed little and set out the next day.

She was not certain where she was, indeed, was not even certain what country she was in. She was fairly sure she had passed from France into the Holy Roman Empire, but there were few maps available as accurate as her own sense of direction.

It was a simple matter for Ryan to travel. Needing few supplies and little sleep, she could cover large distances without stopping. She traveled on foot because a horse would only slow her down, needing both food and water. She generally slept under the stars, unafraid of wild animals or outlaws. She carried papers indicating her identity as an English noble, and enough gold in a pouch to purchase several small villages.

She carried a sword and dagger, eschewing pistols and gunpowder. It had been her experience she could dispatch far more men with the former without ever having to reload. She also carried a bow and quiver of arrows. The arrows had been specially made, designed with an extremely hard wood and sharp flints. Ryan could drive one through a tree if the shaft of the arrow did not snap.

Ryan glanced up at the sun filtering through the trees. She was extremely attuned to cues of light and could identify both time of day and season if she had a fair idea of her location. Ryan shrugged. Not that it ever mattered.

Ryan suddenly stopped, her senses straining the forest in front of her. The breeze had shifted and she caught the wisps of distant odors. She smelled smoke and fecal matter, indicating there was probably a village miles ahead. She could also hear the vaguest hum of voices, although she was still too far away to make anything out.

She started in the direction of the distant village and then stopped. She cocked her head to one side. There was something else, a strange, metallic odor she had not smelled since battle. She grasped the hilt of her sword out of habit and started through the forest once more.

The voices became clearer and the odors became stronger as she neared the village. The smell she was most concerned with came from north of the village, however, and she changed course.

Ryan stepped from the trees into the edge of a clearing, her mind having difficulty grasping what she was seeing.

Dozens and dozens of stakes were driven into the ground and bodies hung from the stakes in various grotesque positions. Limbs were askew, broken in multiple places. Heads hung limply from necks that had been snapped in a hanging. Intestines hung from opened body cavities and blackened skin bore the marks of torture.

Ryan stood there trying to comprehend what she was seeing. She had been witness to many horrors in war, and had been responsible for perpetrating just as many. But she had never seen anything like the scene before her.

The bodies were all children.

Infants, toddlers, youths, young girls, none of who looked to be older than 13 or 14 years.

Ryan moved into the clearing, walking between the rows of stakes. The smell was hideous, decaying, rotting flesh and fecal matter from the disembowelments. Blood, some dried and some not, was everywhere. Birds of prey feasted, insolently disregarding Ryan's presence.

Ryan mentally counted the bodies, and stopped when she wished to count no more. There were nearly thirty bodies in the field.

She heard a whimper and turned toward the sound, making her way through the rows of stakes. She came to the body of a young boy, pierced through his stomach by the stake from which he hung. His open eyes gazed lifelessly up at the sky, but his body still trembled with the life force that would not let him go.

Ryan stared down at the youth, remembering another youth she had struck down long ago in a stockade. She reached out and laid her hand over his face, closing his eyes. His body still trembled and jerked as Ryan gazed down at him dispassionately. She carefully placed her hand at the base of his skull and then twisted his head, snapping his neck.

The body went limp, freed at last from its prison of pain. Ryan turned away from the boy, feeling a fire begin to burn in her chest. She saw a flash of movement out of the corner of her eye and in a fraction of a second was upon it at the edge of the forest.

She held a young girl dangling in her hand. The girl was terrified, pushed past the point of screaming. She looked up at Ryan in a wordless horror.

Ryan set the girl on her feet, not releasing her. She forced the girl to look in her eyes. "What happened here?" she commanded.

The girl felt herself relaxing against her will. There was a mesmerizing quality to this beautiful young man's speech, although she didn't understand it. The girl wondered if God had sent an angel to save her, but shouldn't the angel know what had happened?

This thought caused the girl to begin trembling again and tears began to well up in her eyes. Ryan loosened her grip on the girl. On a hunch, this time she spoke to the little girl in German. "Where do you live?"

The little girl pointed across the clearing in the direction of the village. Ryan nodded. "What is the name of that place?"

The little girl sobbed, a catch in her voice. "Wurzburg."

Ryan stood, releasing her physical but not mental hold on the girl. The girl stood quietly at her side. Ryan leaned down and picked her up. "Let's leave this place."

Ryan carried her through the forest away from the village. She found a small, secluded clearing and set the girl on her bedroll. She started a fire because she was not certain if the girl was shivering from fear or the cold. The girl huddled near the warmth of the flames.

Ryan sat down on a nearby rock, uncertain how to start. "What's your name?"

The girl looked up at her. "Amelia, and my brother's name is Franz."

"Where's your brother?"

Amelia stared down into the flames, trembling once more. "I don't know."

Ryan thought about the bodies in the clearing. She had a pretty good idea where Franz was. "Amelia, look at me."

The small girl looked up at the handsome, golden-haired man with the strange eyes. She felt a calmness settle over her and concluded that this must be an angel sent to test her.

"What happened here?"

There was an emptiness in Amelia's young voice, a voice that even despair had been leached out of. "They took Erin and Gertrude and Patience, and all the others."

Ryan was patient. "Took them where?"

"To the town square for trial."

Ryan didn't understand. "Trial for what?"

Amelia looked down. "Because they're witches," she paused, "Or at least that's what they say."

Ryan sat back in amazement. Witches. She had heard of the different witchhunts over the last few decades, but she had considered them anomalies, aberrations of ignorant people. She looked down at the young girl in front of her. Apparently they were not as rare as she had thought. She turned her attention back to the young girl.

"Why were you hiding in the forest?"

There was a profound sadness on the little girl's features, and a sense of shame. "I thought at first, when they took Patience, that it was a good thing. I didn't like Patience. But then they began to take more and more, and now I'm afraid they'll take me." She turned imploringly to Ryan. "But I'm not a witch, really I'm not."

Ryan rubbed her eyes. "And so what if you were," she said, more to herself than to Amelia.

The little girl glanced up at the man. That was a strange thing for an angel to say.

Ryan was about to ask another question when a noise to her right attracted her attention. Faster than the little girl could see, she disappeared into the forest and returned, dangling a small boy from her grasp.

"Franz!" Amelia cried.

Ryan released him and the boy ran to his sister's side in terror. Ryan briefly concentrated and the boy calmed. He gazed up expectantly at the angel, waiting for salvation.

Ryan gazed down at the two in consternation. She had heard the boy in the thicket from a distance. She had judged him to be small and was correct. He could have been Amelia's twin. Ryan frowned. If they were twins, that could be enough of a sign for these village idiots to accuse them of witchcraft.

Ryan sighed. It wouldn't be the first time she had been accused of being in league with the devil.

Apparently Franz and Amelia were exhausted because they quickly fell asleep in the fading glow of the fire. Ryan gazed at the embers far into the night, keeping vigil over her two new and inconvenient companions.

By morning light, Ryan had decided on a course of action. She easily captured two hares and rekindled the fire. By the time the children awoke, their breakfast was ready. They ate as if starving.

When Ryan informed the two they were all going to return to the village, the children's eyes widened in terror. Amelia, however, decided she would put her trust in the angel and Franz followed his sister's lead.

Ryan had to pick her way through the forest because the children moved so slowly. At one point, she picked them both up and covered the remaining distance quickly, setting them down at the edge of the town. Each child clutched a hand, glued to her side.

Ryan's acute gaze swept the village. Her arrival was immediately noted and villagers gathered.

Ryan gazed at the dirty peasants. They clutched various farm implements as if holding weapons. An odd light glowed in their eyes, a combination of fear and madness.

The burgermeister stepped forward and examined the stranger. He noted the beauty of the man with suspicion. Looks such as those did not come from god, but from Satan. Ironically, the burgermeister had made the same rationalization for the malformed in the past.

Ryan cleared her throat. "I came through the forest. I couldn't help but notice the children in the clearing."

The strange, musical quality to the stranger's voice caused the burgermeister's eyes to narrow. He motioned to Franz and Amelia.

"Children, step away from that man."

Amelia clutched Ryan's hand tightly but Franz was uncertain. The burgermeister attempted to capitalize on the boy's wavering.

"Franz, this man is a witch, step away from him!"

Ryan inwardly sighed. She had a feeling this would happen. She released the boy's hand. "I'm not holding them. They came to me in the forest, out of fear. They're afraid for their lives."

"They should be afraid for their souls," a crone said from the crowd. She spat into the dust. "The devil walks these lands, seducing children." The crone eyed Ryan warily, "Perhaps he walks in the guise of a pretty boy today."

Ryan shook her head. "I am not the devil. I'm a simple traveler."

The crone eyed him. "Then where's your food and water? Where's your horse?"

A murmur swept through the crowd at this obvious lack of sustenance. Ryan heard the whispers. Only Satan or one of his minions could walk so unencumbered.

Apparently this was enough to convince Franz and he made a run for the crowd. Amelia still stood clutching Ryan's hand. The burgermeister spoke to Ryan, eyeing the girl.

"And you walk in the company of one accused."

Ryan looked down at the little girl, then back at the burgermeister. She had a hard time controlling her anger. "Accused of what?"

The crone spoke out, shaking her broom. "Witchcraft, of course. The girl is a witch, just like the others."

Ryan shook her head in amazement. "Where's this girl's mother?"

The old crone spat again, and Ryan thought it ironic this woman looked more like a witch than anyone she had ever seen. The crone grimaced, revealing toothless gums. "I'm her mother."

Ryan was stunned at the madness that had overtaken these people. There was a maniacal anticipation in their eyes, as if the world had become one huge witchhunt demanding participation lest one become the next accused.

Ryan decided it was probably best if she just left. She would take the girl to another village and find safekeeping for her. She grasped Amelia's hand and turned to leave.

Amelia called to her brother. "Franz, come with us. Don't stay here!"

The boy appeared to waver once more as the crone grasped him by his shoulders. Ryan stopped, aware of his indecision. Amelia pulled from her grasp and moved a few steps toward him. The crone pulled the boy back towards her filthy skirt.

The burgermeister lunged towards Amelia, but Ryan moved quicker. She intercepted the man, knocking him to the ground.

The unnatural speed and strength the stranger possessed was enough to convince the crowd that this indeed was a witch. Ryan was undecided whether to move for the boy or for Amelia. In that split second of indecision, a man at the edge of the crowd snatched a hot poker from a nearby fire and thrust it in Franz's direction. Another brave soul wrapped an arm around Amelia's neck, placing a knife at her throat.

Ryan was furious at herself. If she had simply reacted, she could have had both children out of harm's way. Now she wasn't certain she could move quickly enough to save them both. She stopped in her tracks.

The man holding the poker waved it in Franz's face and Ryan wondered uneasily if he was going to accidentally burn the child. He spoke to the crowd.

"'Tis proof enough both of them are in league with this demon. They follow his commands."

The crone joined in. "You saw his strength. 'Tis not the strength of a mortal man. This could be Satan's son himself we're dealing with."

Ryan rolled her eyes. Her father Hans the blacksmith was probably turning in his grave at the accusation. Ryan tried to exert her influence over the crowd, calming them.

"I'm not Satan, or one of his minions. I'm just a simple traveler and I'll be on my way if you promise not to hurt the children."

"How do we know you won't come back for them?" the man with the poker said, waving the poker in Franz's face again.

Ryan eyed the poker. That was exactly what she intended to do. But she certainly wasn't going to announce that to this mob. Her subtle influence appeared to be working because she noticed the man with the knife was relaxing his grip on Amelia. If he would lower the knife just slightly further, Ryan knew she could get to the poker, then the knife before either man could react.

The crone shook her head as if clearing it from sleep. She began screaming. "Don't you see what he's doing? He's clouding our minds. This is Satan!"

Ryan was chagrined to see the man with the knife snap to attention and the poker begin waving wildly. The red hot metal brushed the boy's cheek and he cried out. Ryan took a step toward him but saw the knife move out of the corner of her eye.

"Wait!" she cried, stopping once more. The knife shook in the man's hand, nicking Amelia's throat. She cried out in pain, her eyes wide and her mouth trembling.

Ryan stopped, feeling an incredible frustration. If she moved in either direction, one of the children would be seriously injured or killed. She saw blood on Amelia's neck and smelled the small boy's burnt flesh.

The burgermeister had recovered from the blow and was struggling with a coil of rope. "Help me," he cried to several men joining him, "We must bind Satan."

The men approached Ryan warily and she tensed. She watched the poker wave around the boy's face and her frustration intensified. With misgivings she allowed the men to wrap the cords around her. She was not concerned for her own safety, but knew now she would be even slower to act because she would have to break the bindings before she could move. She only hoped the crowd would turn its attention towards her and relax their vigil on the children.

It was not to be. The crone sensed the only thing keeping the stranger in check was Franz and Amelia. "Hold the children tight," she admonished, a mad gleam in her eye.

Even Ryan's feet were bound and she was lifted up onto the shoulders of the crowd. They seemed surprised at how light she was given her earlier display of strength. It was one more confirmation of the stranger's unholy status.

The mob screamed and began to run as one towards the river, carrying the demon. They taunted the stranger with curses and obscenities even as they made the sign of the cross to ward off this devil's influence. As they reached the bank of the river, the men carrying Ryan rushed to the front of the crowd and without hesitation, threw her into the water.

Ryan plunged into the icy depths with a sense of relief. At least down here she could not hear them scream. She saw the legs of several peasants as they waded in to hold her under the water. She did not resist as they drowned her.

Or at least tried to. Ryan gazed at the bottom of the river trying to think of a course of action. Perhaps if she played dead she could catch them off guard. She let her body go limp.

The burgermeister and several other men dragged her from the water, yelling triumphantly. They dragged her limp body onto the dirt shore.

"Cut the demon's head off," the crone shouted from the crowd.

Ryan was startled. She had not anticipated this turn of events and rolled just in time as the ax came whistling down, thudding into the damp earth beside her.

The mob screamed in fear, but their terror only fed their hatred. Both children were still held captive and the knife and the poker sprang to positions of readiness once more.

Ryan had never felt so helpless in all her long life. Once again, she was not concerned for her own safety but rather frustrated by her inability to help both children. She glanced up at Amelia who, although now afraid of her, was still praying for the stranger to come to her rescue.

"Trial by fire!" the crone shouted, and Ryan inwardly cursed the bitch. She was lifted and unceremoniously carried into the center of town where another hot poker was acquired. The man holding the iron spat on Ryan as the crowd leaned forward in anticipation.

The red-hot tip seared Ryan's cheek and she could smell her own flesh burning. The pain was intense but she refused to cry out. This seemed to incite the man and he laid the iron against her thigh.

This was too much for Ryan and her foot flashed out, snapping the man's thigh in two. He fell to the ground, screaming in agony, the bone protruding through the flesh.

"Burn the boy!" the crone screamed.

Ryan turned to see the poker descend on Franz's cheek. The boy screamed in pain.

"Stop it," Ryan shouted, "I won't fight!"

The poker moved away and Ryan could see the burned flesh. She closed her eyes, feeling absolutely impotent.

Ryan was again lifted onto the shoulders of the mob. She wondered what they had planned for her now. She could see Amelia being dragged along, the hairy arm still pinned around her throat. Franz was half-dragged, half-carried along as well, his tears flowing unchecked down his burned cheek.

Ryan was dragged to the center square where two horses were held in check. The already agitated steeds were frightened by the mob and began struggling against their harnesses.

Ryan was unbound and ropes were quickly slipped around both wrists. The ropes were attached to the harnesses and the slack taken out, causing Ryan to stand upright with her arms spread wide. She stared at Franz and Amelia who gazed back at her in wordless terror. Ryan felt a sense of helpless resignation about what was to come.

"Hiya!" the burgermeister yelled as he slapped the rump of one horse. Another man slapped the other horse and they began running in opposite directions.

Ryan stared at the children as the crowd leaned forward in anticipation. The horses covered the short distance at breakneck speed, spurred on by the jeers of the mob. The sound of their hoofs was drowned out by the screaming crowd.

Both ropes went taut simultaneously, but the crowd did not get their anticipated dismemberment. Instead, Ryan held fast and both horses were stopped in their tracks, toppling backwards as their heads jerked rearward from the force. Both steeds fell to the dust as Ryan stood unmoved.

The crowd was suddenly mute as Ryan slipped the ropes from her wrists, still standing. She raised her head, finally facing the inevitable.

Amelia cried out as the man holding her slit her throat in fear. Ryan closed her eyes as the girl slid to the ground, choking to death on her own blood. Similarly, the crone grabbed the poker and thrust it into Franz's small torso and he collapsed to the ground, screaming from the burning iron impaled in his gut.

They were petty and impulsive acts of revenge from a mob angered by the denial of their vengeance. The crowd turned to the stranger standing silently in the square, their eyes filled with a rabid hatred and fear of this monster that would not die.

Ryan opened her eyes, and those standing in the forefront of the crowd took a step back. Even those standing in the rear shifted uneasily.

There was a look in the beautiful man's eyes the villagers had never seen. It was a look of fury that could stoke the fires of hell, as if death itself had taken physical form and was now staring at them across the town square.

Ryan reached up and loosened her hair, causing the blonde locks to fall about her shoulders. This strange act and its effect on her appearance caused much muttering amongst the crowd and more shifting of feet.

Ryan slowly drew her sword, hefting the weight in her hand. She gazed at the blade, then back at the crowd. Regret was intermixed with resignation in her voice, and she shrugged her shoulders.

"You're right," she said, "I am Satan."

Some attempted to flee while others were cut down where they stood. Ryan's fury fed her already preternatural speed and strength as she began her slaughter. The few villagers who made it into the forest were quickly hunted down by the demon who spared no one, not even the few remaining children.

Ryan leaned against the hilt of her sword, her rage dissipating. Her clothing was covered in blood. She walked to the river and waded into it up to her waist, scrubbing the blood from her arms.

She walked through the now silent village, grabbing a stick from an untended fire. She threw the stick onto the thatched roof of a hut. It crackled for a moment, then caught quickly and spread to the neighboring huts.

Without a backward glance at the conflagration behind her, Ryan walked into the forest. The burn on her cheek and thigh had already begun to heal.

CHAPTER 27

Susan walked down the hallway of the mansion, feeling her excitement build. She opened the door to her makeshift lab and was surprised to find it was anything but. She walked into the room, stunned. Her lab had been almost perfectly replicated in one of the wings of Ryan's manor.

Susan walked around the room, gazing at the equipment. Edward had told her the room was ready for her, but it had taken several days for her to wander over here. Now she was angry with herself for delaying.

She moved to the table. Her final readouts from the lab were laid out. She glanced over to her desk. There was her computer, the display blinking her final words at her. Susan was amazed. This was not a duplication of her lab, this was her lab.

"I hope this is acceptable," Ryan said from the door.

Susan turned to Ryan. She could see Edward standing behind her. "This is incredible," she said, "How in the world did you get all of this stuff?" She gestured around the room. "The hospital would never part with this equip-" Susan stopped. "You didn't steal this, did you?"

Ryan laughed. "No, Edward is much more inventive than that."

Edward stepped in the room. His face was as impassive as ever, his demeanor as stiff as always, but Susan sensed he was pleased with himself.

"The hospital was reluctant to part with any of the equipment, and certainly were not going to part with any of your research, so we had no other option."

Susan looked from one to the other in confusion. "So what option did you take?"

Edward deferred to his leader. Ryan shrugged. "I bought the hospital."

"You did what?" Susan asked in disbelief.

"I bought the hospital," Ryan repeated, as if it were the only logical solution. "They were particularly unwilling to bargain for your publishing rights, so I bought the hospital right out from under them."

Susan was flabbergasted. She had no idea how much something like that would cost, but she knew it would be hundreds of millions, if not billions, of dollars. And Ryan spoke as if she had just purchased a new car.

Ryan moved to the table. "It also removed the possibility of any pharmaceutical company using your patents. I don't think Grantech International has ever met the likes of Edward before."

Edward was willing to give credit where credit was due. "I don't think Mr. Grant has ever played hardball with the likes of you, my lord. He will be quite surprised on the morrow."

Ryan glanced down, controlling a smile. She looked at the paperwork on the table. "I noticed you were doing some more work here," she said to Susan.

Susan moved to her side, refreshing her memory. "Oh right." She turned to Ryan. "I was curious how you can drink liquids without them entering your bloodstream. I took a closer look at the original MRI and I think I discovered why."

Susan pointed to the picture, indicating an area of the throat. "Here where your esophagus and your aorta fuse, there's a bifurcation."

Ryan looked to where she pointed. Edward leaned over her shoulder, interested despite himself. "It does appear to branch there," he said.

Both women looked at him and he had the grace to appear embarrassed. He did not leave, however.

Susan returned to the picture. "Correct. It does appear to branch. I haven't been able to trace its destination, but it does seem you have at least vestiges of a digestive system. You could probably eat, although I've never seen you do it, and your body would shuttle the food through this second pathway."

Ryan was puzzled. "Then where would it go?"

Susan looked over at the blonde-haired woman. "Well, that's what I'd like to know. It seems you'd need some way to eliminate waste products. But you don't," Susan paused for a moment, then continued, "Which is why I have another theory."

Ryan raised an eyebrow. "It doesn't have to do with accelerated evolution, does it?"

Susan frowned at her. "No, not exactly. It has more to do with a perpetual motion machine."

This definitely piqued Ryan's curiosity. "What do you mean by that?"

Susan was thoughtful for a moment, framing her reply. "I think you burn everything you take in, whether it's oxygen, alcohol, blood products, whatever, you burn it as fuel. I've taken your temperature when it was a good 20 degrees higher than any human could withstand."

"So what happens when I don't take anything in?"

Susan was quiet for a moment. "I think you shut everything down, just as if you were dead. But your consciousness doesn't leave. In fact, your body begins running off that."

Ryan had the distinct feeling Susan was heading somewhere significant. "Why do you think it doesn't leave? What makes it stay?"

Susan looked at Ryan without wavering. "You do," she said simply.

Ryan looked at her with her usual polite curiosity. "I'm afraid I'm not following you."

Susan set the chart down on the table. "One of the first things I noticed about you while you were unconscious was your brainwave pattern. It was very unusual for sleeping. At first I didn't think much about it because there was so many other things about you that were unique. But I kept returning to it because there was something about it, something I couldn't quite put my finger on."

Ryan was silent, knowing Susan would continue.

"I was thumbing through my books the other day when I came across a text on 'psychoneuroimmunology,' also known as the brain/body connection."

Ryan nodded. "A much neglected topic in western medicine."

Susan did not disagree. "I think I discovered one of the most important differences between you and a normal human."

Ryan was cautious. "And what would that be?"

"You never sleep."

Edward snorted, reminding Susan of his presence. Ryan raised an eyebrow at him, then turned back to Susan. "I sleep all the time. I sleep more than any of my Kind. I sleep for years at a time."

Susan shook her head. "You're not sleeping," she said, pausing. "You're meditating."

This statement silenced both Ryan and Edward. Susan picked up the chart. "Your brainwaves, they never represent sleep, even when you're dreaming. I didn't recognize the pattern at first because it shouldn't have been there. Then I saw the same pattern in that book. Your brainwaves show the classic configuration of relaxed alertness, or a perfect meditative state."

Ryan still did not speak as Susan continued. "They've done studies with Buddhist monks who've shown remarkable improvement in awareness and visual acuity after meditating." She changed the subject. "How's your sense of taste?"

Ryan glanced at Edward. She was thoughtful. "I never really noticed any difference from my Change."

Susan nodded as if this were further validation. "Taste is the one sense not enhanced through meditation. No one knows why."

Susan went to search for a book on her desk. "Before I left the lab, I went to pick up a medical text on meditation." She pushed some papers around. "Ah, here it is. Remember when we talked about your senses crossing over? When you see heat or hear colors?"

Ryan nodded and Susan thumbed through the book. "It's called synesthesia. It's a byproduct of meditation."

Ryan slowly took the book from Susan's hand as Susan continued. "If the greatest mystics of all time could meditate as you do, over the span of centuries, they might have some of your abilities. All your senses are amplified, your sight, your hearing. Do you know the primary result of meditation?"

Ryan shook her head.

"It controls blood flow."

Ryan stared down at the book in her hand. "What exactly is 'psychoneuroimmunology'?"

"It's a fairly new field of medicine which believes that thoughts can physically affect the body."

Ryan smiled wryly, turning to Edward. "It's not new. They once called them 'humours'."

Susan continued. "At first I thought your resistance to pain might be a result of certain hormonal responses. For example, your thymus gland secretes an incredible amount of thymosin fraction 5, which powerfully stimulates certain adrenal hormones that effect your central nervous system."

"I take it that's not a sufficient explanation?" Ryan asked wryly.

Susan shook her head. "No. Like I said, I thought that way at first."

"So," Ryan said, "Why don't I feel pain the way you do?"

Susan pointed at the book. "The decrease in pain stimuli is not due to chemical processes, but rather mental ones. Your body feels the same pain as anyone else, but your mind has altered the way it perceives it."

Ryan stared at her own hands in puzzlement, as if they were suddenly foreign objects.

Susan continued. "A lower pain threshold is not necessarily a good thing unless an organism can heal itself the way you do. Then pain is simply an unnecessary nuisance, one your body has obviously dealt with."

Edward cleared his throat and Ryan realized it was time for them to go. She bowed to Susan. "We must finish the paperwork on the acquisition of the hospital." She turned to leave, then stopped.

"Oh, and by the way?" Ryan said casually, "A transition team is already in place in the hospital. The majority of the staff will be kept on. However, initial interviews with the nurses in ER revealed that there is one gentleman who is particularly disliked by all colleagues. I hope you're not too disappointed that Dr. David Goldstein will no longer be a member of the faculty."

Susan tried to appear unconcerned, as if it were no matter to her. "It's your hospital."

Ryan gave a short bow. "Very well," she said, and disappeared.

Susan looked down at the MRI printout in front of her. She wondered what it would be like to be Ryan, to wield that much power. She wondered what it would be like to be at the top of the food chain.

Susan stared at the paperwork. That analogy wasn't completely correct, she thought to herself. Ryan wasn't at the top of the food chain, she was outside of it entirely.

Alan Grant sat brooding in his corner office. He had left explicit instructions not to be disturbed, so the knock at the door did nothing to improve his mood.

A man in a dark suit leaned in the doorway. "I have news I think you'll want to hear, Mr. Grant."

Grant glowered at him. "I hope for your sake that you're correct. I told that feeble-minded receptionist of mine that I wanted no visitors."

The man pushed his way into the room. "We received word this morning that St. Mary's Hospital was purchased by a private bidder."

Grant was astounded. "What? Are you telling me the hospital was purchased by a single person? Who the fuck was it, Bill Gates?"

The messenger shifted uncomfortably. "Uh, no sir. From my understanding, Bill Gates would have had to take out a loan to finance the purchase, and this was a cash deal."

Grant could not hide his astonishment. "Impossible! No one has that much money. There aren't very many people in the world with that kind of capital. No one else was interested in this hospital."

"Well sir, apparently someone was. The transaction is complete."

Grant's face turned apoplectic. He picked up a paperweight and hurled it at the messenger. It barely missed the man, and he quickly scurried through the door, pulling it shut behind him.

Grant picked up another paperweight and started to hurl it after the first one, but stopped himself. He glanced down at the marble block, hefting it in his hand. He carefully set it back down on the desk.

He settled into his cushioned chair, patting his shirt pocket. He felt the reassuring outline of the solid, cylindrical object and unbuttoned his shirt pocket. He removed the blood vial and held it up to the light. The plasma swirled, then settled into a smug, tranquil inertness.

CHAPTER 28

VICTOR FELT RYAN'S RETURN EVEN THOUGH SHE WAS STILL a great distance away. He sensed something in her mood, a sort of despair he had never known to plague her. Although he knew she was still far away, he put his things aside and waited for her.

Ryan could see the castle from a great distance. It had been modified many times over the last decades, but the primary structure still stood. The hills surrounding it were dark green from spring rain.

Ryan began climbing the steps that were cut into the green hillside. She sensed eyes upon her and looked upward as she climbed. Victor waited for her at the castle gates, his white shirt opened at the collar, revealing his tan throat. The sight of him was achingly beautiful, and Ryan welcomed the comforting pain it caused her.

Ryan bowed her head, unwilling to share or confront the burden she had carried with her from Wurzburg. Although in a sense she had been dead for many years, this was the first time she truly felt so.

She came to the castle gate and went to move past Victor when he stepped in her path. They stood at an impasse for a moment, Ryan with her head still stubbornly lowered. Victor grasped her chin and raised her head so she was forced to look up at him.

There was none of the usual sardonic humor in his dark eyes, no hint of mocking. Instead, there was a deep compassion, as if he knew the road she traveled because he himself had been there before.

Ryan gazed into his eyes and the ache in her heart flared. There were times when she had little understanding of their strange, powerful relationship, and other times when such understanding was not even necessary.

Victor pulled her to him, comforting her as he would a child.

Ryan joined him later in his quarters as he stood gazing out at the sudden spring shower. The sky was dark with thunderclouds and the rain fell in heavy, fat drops. Victor sat in the sill of the window and Ryan moved to settle in front of him. They moved as one, as they had for centuries, and no outward communication was necessary. Ryan leaned back against his chest, melding her body against his.

Ryan allowed Victor's influence to settle over her like a cloak. Her eyes drifted closed as she sought peace in the blackness only he could give her. She felt the slightest pain as his teeth brushed her neck.

Although Victor always hungered for her, it was not his intent at this moment to satisfy himself. As her blood flowed into him, so did her Memories, and her pain. He saw her failure at Wurzburg, saw the deaths of the children, saw the revenge she had taken against the town.

Ryan had seen many, many things over her lifetime. She had been witness to the worst of atrocities, and been little affected by them. She had killed hundreds, maybe thousands of men, and had done so indiscriminately in battle and in brawls.

But Victor sensed something different in Ryan this time, and it took him a moment to identify what it was.

She had lost hope for this people.

Ryan had always faced the world with an astounding nonchalance, as if nothing affected her. It was the mark of her time, the mark of her people. It was the mark of the powerless, and even after Ryan was no longer powerless, she still bore the attitude. And beneath that attitude was the belief that one day things would be better, either in this life or the next.

Ryan no longer believed this. She had no next life, only this one, and it was filled with short-lived, brutal people who existed soullessly and mindlessly. Victor gazed into her mind's eye and saw her shattered faith.

Victor raised the arm that held her and Ryan took the proffered wrist. His blood poured into her, offering an unholy salve to her soul. She saw he had no faith in this people, and therefore no faith to lose. He held himself apart from the human race because to embrace humanity was to embrace their weakness.

CHAPTER 29

RYAN SPRAWLED, BOTH CASUAL AND ELEGANT IN THE oversized chair. Susan watched her, examining the fine features. She had become aware of how people watched Ryan, and were drawn to her. Ryan greeted this continual interest with a profound indifference; she was aware of it but did not care.

Susan examined the woman, trying to figure out what exactly it was that attracted so many people to her. Certainly Ryan was physically attractive but there was much more to it than that. She had a subtle sense of power about her, a charisma that could be devastating when fanned from spark to flame.

"What?" Ryan asked her, slightly bemused at the attention from her companion.

Susan shook her head as if clearing it. "Nothing," she said.

Ryan gazed at her for a few seconds with her unblinking gaze, then turned back to her own thoughts.

A large bird of prey landed on a statue outside. Susan thought at first it was a raven, but it was larger than a raven and not as darkly colored. It preened itself for a moment, peering into the French doors as if it could see the occupants inside.

Ryan's parrot stretched itself to its full height, then fluffed all of its feathers in indignation. It settled back down, pretending it was unruffled by the raptor's intrusion. The falcon flew off.

Ryan gazed at the parrot fondly. "It's just a kite, Teddy."

Susan thought about the woman's words. She had never heard "kite" used in that sense, at least not in spoken language. She thought about Ryan's voice, the way she spoke so smoothly and melodically, like polished stained glass. It was a young voice with an old inflection, as if the mouth had tried billions of words and now a multitude of sounds poured forth effortlessly

Susan Ryerson came to a startling conclusion. It was one she had superficially accepted, one she had discussed and acted upon, one she had supposedly already grasped. But it was only at this moment she grasped the idea in its totality.

"You really are 700 years old."

Ryan glanced at her with amusement, realizing Susan had just reached some private epiphany.

"Why yes," she said, "Yes I am."

Susan sat back in her chair, unaware she had sat bolt upright. Ryan gazed at her curiously. "What?"

"They missed it," Susan said, half to herself, "They all missed it."

Ryan sat patiently, allowing Susan to continue.

"All the writers, all the filmmakers, all the people who ever tried to envision what you would be like, they all missed it."

Ryan shrugged, as if Susan were stating the obvious. "I believe I already told you that."

"No!" Susan shook her head, unwilling to let Ryan minimize her sudden prescience. "No, you don't understand. It's not the obvious things," Susan trailed off, then spoke to herself, "And of course, it wouldn't be."

Susan looked over at Ryan and Ryan maintained her polite silence.

Susan's thoughts raced furiously. It wouldn't be the obvious melodramatic things humans always tried to envision. It wouldn't be the hopes and dreams that mortals projected onto immortals, nor would it be human weaknesses manifested and magnified over time.

It would be the subtle things. Things like a certain way of speaking. From a voice that had been shaped by hundreds of languages, from a mouth that had articulated nearly every sound possible. It would be a certain way of moving, from muscles and joints untouched by the ravages of time, and yet blessed with centuries of neuro-muscular development.

It would be a sense of time fundamentally different from human beings, a temporal sense tied not to 70 or 80 years on this planet, but to an unlimited number. It would be a total lack of fear, not the bravado demonstrated by so many immortal caricatures, but a genuine lack of fear.

Because Ryan had nothing to fear.

Susan gazed at her, at last understanding. "You're never in a hurry, are you?"

Ryan shook her head. "Why should I be?"

Susan was quiet for a long moment. "You must find 'Dracula' pretty amusing."

Ryan shrugged. "It's a morality play. I found it interesting, but not particularly accurate. It seemed very much tied to the time and place in which it was written, not the time it was supposed to have occurred. But it's always this way with human writing. It's easy to write about dates and places in history because those are recorded. What it was really like is much more difficult to capture."

Ryan was thoughtful a moment. "I'm always struck by human portrayals of immortality. I have nothing in common with these characters. Why do they always long for their mortality? Is this simply a human's idea that there is some sort of nobility in death? It seems to me they're trying to convince themselves. And why do these characters always whine so?"

Ryan was silent for a moment, amused by this thought. She continued in a more serious vein. "I don't comprehend how this entire race marches blithely towards a blackness that none truly understands, and yet all live as if they will never die. 'Waste time' has no meaning for me, but I understand it. It has a very specific meaning for humans, yet very few grasp it." Ryan turned to look at Susan. "Even you will one day walk into a blackness and not return, and you don't know if you'll come out the other side."

Susan did not wish to contemplate her mortality at this moment. "So you don't 'long for your humanity,' like so many of these tortured characters?" she asked, attempting to bring back the lightheartedness of their earlier discussion.

Susan's question was lightly phrased, and she was unprepared for Ryan's reaction. Ryan looked almost as if Susan had struck her. She looked away, her eyes filled with sudden unwanted memories. Susan was not certain if it was the question itself which elicited such a response, or if the question simply triggered some deeper battle within Ryan.

Ryan turned her unblinking gaze back on Susan, but this time her eyes mirrored a rare indecision. When she finally spoke, her words were quiet.

"I was never human."

Susan was startled. Ryan had told her much of her past life, and yet she had never given her any indication of this revelation. Susan did not understand how this could be, considering the stories Ryan had told her. Once again she had the feeling Ryan was leaving significant parts of her life out of her account. Susan had a sudden suspicion. She knew she would be treading on dangerous ground probing into Ryan's past, but the question began to burn inside her, demanding to be asked.

Ryan turned to her in resignation, waiting for the question she knew was coming.

"Ryan," Susan asked quietly, "What happened to Victor?"

Ryan stared at her for a minute, then in a completely uncharacteristic gesture, covered her face with her hand, rubbing her forehead. After a long moment, she raised her head and the unblinking gaze returned. All indecision was gone from her eyes and her voice was devoid of emotion.

"He's dead, " Ryan said simply, "I killed him."

Susan stared at the woman, stunned. Everything Ryan had told her had just been contradicted by this single statement. And although Ryan seemed perfectly aware of the paradox she had just presented her companion, she stood and left the room without another word.

Susan was gone by the time Ryan returned, and she was left to stalk through her mansion alone. She whirled on her heel, staring into the licking flames of the fireplace.

"Time is the fire in which we burn," she said bitterly to the flames, "But it does not burn me."

Her anger grew and she was unaware her language was returning to an earlier time. "Nor does it provide me any heat or any light."

She whirled on her heel again, stalking the shadows as her Memories began to stalk her.

She remembered the first time she had felt any anger at Victor, the time he had taken her against her will in front of the Borgia Pope. Although she had seen through his mind later that he had sufficient reason for doing so, she never completely forgave him for his deception. He in turn had seen the subtle invitation she had offered Marilyn, and had been furious at her.

Although Ryan had felt a pronounced sense of fear at Victor's fury, she also felt the slightest sense of power over him because of his jealousy. This did her no good, however, as he sensed everything she felt and could take her thoughts simply by feeding off her. He took these thoughts from her and laughed, giving her nothing in return. He was not weakened by his jealousy; it only made their bond more powerful.

But as the bond between them grew, Ryan began taking Victor's thoughts as well. Much of his Memory was unclear to Ryan, as Victor thwarted her efforts when he felt it necessary.

But Ryan continued to probe his mind over the years and their second great fight occurred when she discovered he had been the instrument of her parent's destruction. She had always assumed Derek had acted alone. But in one unprotected moment, Ryan peered into the recesses of his mind and discovered he had sent Derek to find her.

Victor had not understood her anger. In a way, Ryan did not understand it herself. She had felt no great love for her parents, and Victor had given her much more than Hans and his wife ever had. Even at her young age several centuries ago, Ryan was already accustomed to death and destruction.

For years, Ryan was uncertain why she had reacted so violently to the knowledge that Victor was responsible for the death of her parents. She did not understand the rage that circulated through her body like the blood of a stranger, a stranger that neither she nor Victor had ever Shared with.

This thought infuriated Ryan and she sprang to her feet, lifting a vase from a nearby table. She threw the vase with such force against the hearth it shattered into dust.

As quickly as it had come, the fury vanished, replaced by a sadness so profound it would have killed a normal human being.

Ryan collapsed onto the couch, her head in her hands. She reached out, as she often did, into a void that would never be filled again. All that greeted her was a black emptiness.

Even from a great distance, many of the Others would feel an anguish that none would understand. Only a dark-haired woman, one of the greatest of their Kind, fully understood and gazed thoughtfully into the darkness.

CHAPTER 30

The rain had stopped. Susan was glad because between the foul weather and the luxurious accommodations, she was not inclined to get out of bed.

She went downstairs and found Ryan sprawled in the great room. Her clothing was wet, as if she had been outside. She seemed unconcerned with her damp attire and sat gazing mutely into the fire.

Apart from the wet clothing, Ryan looked no different from any other time Susan had seen her. But it appeared almost as if Ryan were tired, although Susan had seen her like this only once before, recently. If she did not know better, she would say Ryan had been spending a few "sleepless nights."

Susan moved to her side and on impulse, put her hand to Ryan's forehead. Susan was shocked at the temperature. "How are you feeling?"

Ryan looked at her curiously. "I'm fine, why?"

Susan shrugged. "No reason, I just thought I'd ask."

Ryan started to say something, then stopped.

Susan looked at her expectantly. "What is it?"

"Actually," Ryan said slowly, "I have a headache."

The significance of Ryan's admission did not register on Susan, but Ryan seemed oblivious to this as she puzzled over the malady. "I have not had a headache in over 200 years."

Susan's concern deepened as Ryan settled deeper in her chair, shivering slightly. "Not even when you were recovering from your injuries?"

Ryan shook her head, then shrugged the entire matter off. "I'm probably adapting to something my other senses are unaware of."

Susan was not satisfied with Ryan's explanation, but Ryan did not seem to want to pursue the subject further. Besides, the conversation had led in a direction that Susan had wanted to explore for some time.

"What exactly happened to you the night you wound up in the morgue?"

Ryan turned her unblinking gaze on Susan, and for a moment Susan thought she would not answer. When she finally did, her tone was expressionless.

"I had contact with some of the Others."

"Contact?" Susan's words were filled with slight dismay. "Is that what you would call it."

Ryan gave a short, bitter laugh. "We are predators, remember? The reunion was not particularly joyous." Ryan was silent a moment, then said off-handedly, "Besides, most of my wounds were self-inflicted."

Susan turned to her, incredulous. "What do you mean, self-inflicted?"

Ryan was patient with her. "Surely I've told you enough of myself for you to realize there's no one out there who could do that to me."

"I have been curious," Susan admitted, "But I still don't understand."

"I came in contact with some of the Others. I don't think they realized who I was, but I was not taking any chances. Not only did I destroy all of them, but I faked my own destruction as well."

"Why would you do that?"

Ryan was contemplative. "Although none of these knew me, word could get back to those who might. Those whom I could not destroy."

Ryan settled into silence, and Susan recognized she would say no more on the matter, so she changed the subject. "When did you first come to the United States?"

"The Americas?" Ryan was thoughtful, "Probably around the middle 1600's, I've never been very good at keeping track of time."

"So you were one of the first settlers here."

Ryan laughed, a short sarcastic laugh. "If you don't count the several million people who were already living on this continent, yes, I was one of the first ones here."

Ryan seemed very bitter right now, and Susan pressed her for more information more to get at her mood than to get at her story. "I guess I didn't realize there were so many," she prompted.

Ryan glanced at her sideways, as if she knew what Susan was doing. She went along with it anyway. "There were millions, at least until we Europeans landed, bringing every sort of pestilence imaginable. I thought the Black Plague was bad, but it killed only one out of every three in my time. The plague here killed 9 out of every 10 Indians."

Susan was astounded at the number. Ryan continued. "And after they welcomed us with open arms." Ryan shook her head. "The settlers never battled any great uncharted wilderness. Large portions of the land were already cultivated by the native people, and once we came with our diseases, they all conveniently died out and left the cleared land to us."

Ryan's voice took on the mesmerizing quality it always did when she began to tell her stories.

"I watched white men acting in the name of their Christian god, desecrate Indian gravesites, destroy villages, cornfields, whatever they felt like. In all my 700 years, I can't think of a single people so mistreated by history."

Ryan glanced at the empty television screen. "I've watched modern westerns, watched even so-called 'politically correct' depictions, and none of them are even close."

"What were the Indians really like?"

"They were a very noble people. I spent a lot of time with them. They were one of the only people to realize that Victor and I weren't human, and they did so almost immediately."

"They weren't afraid of you?"

Ryan shook her head. "The Indians were very civilized, far more civilized than their barbaric invaders. They had religion, philosophy, art, music, they were excellent linguists, often speaking three or four languages."

Susan nodded. "I remember the stories from World War II, how the Hopi tribe used their language as an unbreakable code."

Ryan glanced over at Susan, cocking her head to one side. "Did you know there's a far more sinister connection to World War II? Adolph Hitler was a great admirer of the concentration camps the colonists used to round up the Indians. They were very efficient and he admired that."

Susan fell silent, unaware of that fact.

Ryan continued. "The colonists enslaved the Indians, of course, just as they enslaved everyone. That fact doesn't find itself in many textbooks, either." Ryan sighed. "Modern history could at least give credit where credit is due. The Iroquois nation had a confederacy that lasted over 150 years. It showed how to control a large, disparate area and is probably the model that the United States was built upon. The US was a grand experiment, no monarchy, no religion. Yet history acts as if the founding fathers plucked the idea from the sky."

Ryan pulled a coin from her pocket. "Even the great seal of the United States bears the mark of the Iroquois confederacy: the eagle and the arrows. But again, this fact finds itself in few textbooks."

"Did you practice a trade?" Susan asked.

"Victor and I were wealthy beyond belief, even then. We still had all our lands in England, which had grown. We were in every type of commerce imaginable. Shipping, mining, farming...."

This thought brought a slightly mischievous smile to Ryan's face.

"What?" Susan prompted her.

"I used to own a hemp farm."

"You grew marijuana?"

Ryan shook her head. "No, hemp, probably the most versatile plant on this planet. A good hemp plant grows twenty feet in a year. You can make paper, clothing, fuel, all sorts of products from it. It was quite respectable back then. Both Benjamin Franklin and Thomas Jefferson grew hemp, although I didn't know them personally."

Ryan was always a wealth of interesting information. "When did it become illegal?" Susan asked.

"Not until the middle part of this century, and then mostly for political reasons. It had nothing to do with any 'war on drugs.' It had a lot to do with very powerful companies making products which hemp could make cheaper and more efficiently. Hemp became 'marijuana' right after the Spanish-American war, when anything Mexican was bad." Ryan sighed, "Leave it to the United States to morally cloud an issue that's about nothing more than money."

Ryan stopped suddenly, putting her hand to her temple.

"Your headache?" Susan asked.

Ryan nodded. "It seems to have returned."

Susan was concerned for Ryan, concerned about the unusual headache and her subdued demeanor.

Ryan stood up abruptly. "Perhaps we should go out. Perhaps I have been trapped in this place too long. The rain has stopped, the sun is coming out. Let's go into the city."

Susan went to fetch Jason. Neda had dressed him and combed his hair. The older woman declined to join them, and Susan had the suspicion that the older woman would be in the heated spa before they left the driveway. Edward, on the other hand, was not pleased with their expedition. It was evident to Susan that he, too, was concerned about Ryan's strange mood.

Ryan took Susan and Jason to a French restaurant. Edward took a post outside while they were escorted to a table. Susan and Jason ate the three course special and Ryan drank only wine.

Too quickly the meal was over and the three set out for a walk in the cool night air. Ryan did not see Edward upon their exit, but this did not concern her. Jason held Susan's hand as Ryan loped along beside them, hands thrust casually in her pockets.

They walked to the outdoor mall adjacent to the park, which was now closed for the evening. Streetlights threw soft light on the benches and planters, creating long shadows of the shop corners. Their footsteps echoed on the cobblestones, which were slightly damp from the night air, and their voices and laughter drifted gently through the settling fog.

Susan was surprised there were no other people in the mall. Generally, the walkways were filled with young couples pushing strollers, or older couples out for an evening walk. She glanced at her watch. It was getting late, but usually there were people out far after midnight. The normal security guards seemed to be missing as well. Were she not with Ryan, Susan might have been concerned.

Jason was talking non-stop and his voice echoed eerily in the empty mall. Susan glanced over, catching an uncharacteristic gesture from Ryan out of the corner of her eye. Ryan raised her hand to her forehead, a slight grimace of pain on her face.

"Are you all right?" Susan asked.

Jason stopped, concerned he had missed something. Ryan shook her head. "It's nothing, I'm fine," she said. Apparently another stabbing pain struck her as she again grimaced. "This is so unusual for me," she murmured.

That was exactly why Susan was so concerned. The three started forward but had only taken three steps when Ryan abruptly stopped, raising her hand.

Jason and Susan also abruptly stopped. Susan started to say something, but the sudden tension in Ryan's body stopped her. She and Jason both stood silently, watching her, then glancing around them.

Ryan's senses strained the darkness in front of her. She cocked her head to one side, as if listening to some sound that only she could hear. Susan watched the woman with growing premonition and fear. Ryan had a look of dawning recognition on her face, intermixed with anger. Her next words did not allay Susan's fears.

"Stay close," she ordered in a whisper. Her words were casual, unconcerned, but her posture was alert as she gazed into the darkness around them. There was almost a sense of resignation about her.

The first figure slipped from the shadows to the left of them. A young man, dark-haired and handsome, moving with a lithe and preternatural grace. A second figure appeared next to him, an Asian woman, both stunning and exotic.

A pair of platinum-haired twins stepped from the shadows to the right, and then a red-haired, green-eyed beauty next to them. The auburn-haired one was accompanied by an ebony Adonis, a man so dark he appeared as one with the night.

Figures began to step from the shadows in every direction until Ryan and her companions were completely surrounded. All possessed an unnatural beauty and moved with the lithe grace Susan had come to associate with Ryan. Susan realized with great trepidation that these people were Ryan's Kind.

They were the Others.

Ryan watched impassively as they revealed themselves, the slightest trace of anger the only emotion on her face. Susan unconsciously moved closer to Ryan, noting that although they were surrounded, none of the Others dared come too near. They were aligned as if standing outside some hidden boundary, some line of demarcation they dared not cross.

Ryan turned, gazing into the nearby shadows. She had an air of expectancy about her, as if she already knew who was there.

On silent command, the figures in the circle parted and a dark-haired woman moved into the circle, not hesitating at the line of demarcation.

Susan stared at the raven-haired beauty, stunned. The woman was ravishing, so beautiful there seemed to be a radiance about her. The silence in the courtyard was complete. Ryan simply stood there and Susan knew who the woman was before Ryan spoke the name.

"Hello Marilyn," Ryan said dryly. There was the faintest hint of mocking in her voice, and a trace of amusement.

Marilyn stood there for a moment, taking in the sight of Ryan. She took the girl's measure from head to toe, and there was an overt sensuality and subtle insolence to the inspection.

Ryan would not allow herself to rise to Marilyn's baiting, and the dark-haired woman started towards her. It was with a certain annoyance she realized Marilyn was still slightly taller than her. She was also acutely aware of how much physically younger she looked than Marilyn and most of those surrounding her. In a people where appearances could be deceiving, Ryan decided they could also be incredibly inconvenient.

Marilyn stopped only inches from Ryan, gazing down at the girl. She very slowly raised her hand to Ryan's chin, tilting it upward. She leaned down and kissed her chastely on the lips, lingering slightly before she raised her head. Her eyes danced with her usual wicked humor.

"Hello, little one," she said.

Ryan again suppressed the reaction Marilyn sought, but Marilyn felt the suppression and smiled knowingly.

"And to what do I owe this pleasure?" Ryan asked with thinly veiled sarcasm.

"As much as I always enjoy your company," Marilyn began, her emphasis on "enjoy" pronounced, "I'm afraid this is strictly business."

The false regret in Marilyn's tone set off a warning for Ryan. She cocked her head to one side. "What kind of business?"

There was the smallest hint of satisfaction, even triumph in Marilyn's tone. "I have been ordered to bring you before the Grand Council."

"I was unaware of the existence of a 'Grand Council'," Ryan said, her sarcasm now evident.

"It was convened out of necessity," Marilyn said with a significant pause, "After the death of our leader."

Ryan's jaw tightened imperceptibly, but Marilyn noted even this facial gesture. Her tone cooled and became vaguely threatening. "The Grand Council requests your presence to answer for the death of your mentor, Victor Alexander."

If Ryan was moved by the accusation or the implied threat, it was not evident. Nor was any sign of repentance. She lowered her voice until it was a seductive whisper, heard by all but meant for Marilyn alone.

"Since when is murder a crime amongst our Kind?"

The enticement in the girl's voice pulled at Marilyn and she was startled at the strength of it. Startled and pleased. She gazed at Ryan knowingly and she too lowered her voice to barely a whisper.

"You will not be tried for the crime of murder, but for regicide. That, and your failure to take his place."

The Others were quite aware of the war the two Old Ones were waging. It was mesmerizing, giving them a glimpse of power few dreamed even existed. Even the human woman sensed the power struggle between the two, a struggle as much about seduction as it was about strength.

"And do you intend to take me by force?" Ryan said mockingly.

Marilyn smiled, the double entendre not lost on her. "No my dear," she said with her false regret, "As enjoyable as that might be, I don't believe it will be necessary." She glanced meaningfully at Susan Ryerson, then down at her son. "Although I'm quite convinced of your invulnerability, I don't think your human companions would survive the struggle."

Ryan felt cold fingers creep around her heart. She glanced at Susan and Jason. She had known better. A lesson ignored was a lesson unlearned.

Susan stared at Ryan, stark realization in her eyes. Edward had been right.

Ryan stared at Susan for a long moment, then turned back to Marilyn, her words casual but with no sense of defeat about them.

"Very well, I will come with you. But I want you to know this," she said, pausing. Something very subtle changed in Ryan's demeanor and those in the shadows shifted uncomfortably. "If anything happens to Dr. Ryerson or her son," she said casually, glancing around the circle with mild contempt, "I will destroy everyone here." Her icy, unblinking stare returned to Marilyn.

"Including you."

The silence was complete. No one moved, no one breathed. There was no mocking in Marilyn's eyes, no sarcastic retort. She nodded in understanding, almost in deference, and gestured for Ryan to accompany her.

Ryan preceded her through the opening the Others made in the circle, and the circle collapsed behind them. Susan and Jason were drawn along behind in the crowd. When they exited onto the street, Susan was reminded of the material power these people wielded.

Jason stared in amazement at the line of limousines that stretched in both directions as far as the eye could see. The long, sleek cars gleamed blackly under the streetlights, reminding Susan uncomfortably of an infinite funeral procession.

Susan watched as Ryan approached the door that was held open for her. She was struck by the deference with which Ryan was being treated. Prisoner or not, the awe in which she was held was evident.

Susan started to follow Ryan and she was grabbed roughly from behind by a young woman. Faster than the eye could see, Ryan was there between them, holding the Young One off the ground by her throat.

In the same instant, Marilyn was behind Ryan, slipping her arm about her waist and pulling her to her. She leaned over her shoulder, brushing her lips against Ryan's throat, then whispering in her ear.

"Let her go, Ryan, she's young and stupid and she forgets herself."

Ryan stared down at the Young One, her fury and frustration threatening to explode. But the combination of Marilyn's touch and the whispered reasoning distracted her. Her grip on the wide-eyed girl loosened.

Marilyn's hand brushed Ryan's hair from the nape of her neck, and the gesture was so familiar and seductive, Ryan closed her eyes against the sensation. She released the girl, who staggered backwards.

Marilyn held her for a moment longer to make certain Ryan's temper had indeed cooled. She gazed past Ryan to where Susan Ryerson was standing. There was no fear in the Susan's eyes, but rather the beginnings of a suspicion.

Susan, watching the scene, was again struck by the deference with which Ryan was treated. Marilyn had twice chosen not to confront Ryan, but rather to beguile her. It made her wonder if Marilyn chose the path of least resistance out of necessity, if she was indeed powerful enough to defeat Ryan.

Marilyn stared at her impassively, as if reading her mind, then slowly smiled.

Susan mentally added another option. Or perhaps Marilyn chose that path simply because she enjoyed it.

Ryan relaxed and Marilyn released her. Ryan stepped away from the dark-haired woman into the waiting limousine. Marilyn motioned for Susan and her son to ride in the same vehicle, then she herself climbed in after

Susan.

Susan sat next to Ryan and Jason sat between them, clutching his mother. He wanted to go to Ryan, but her body language was closed to him. She gazed out the window at nothing as they began moving.

Marilyn's attention was fully on Ryan. She examined the girl's features. Physically, Ryan had hardly changed. She was taller, her shoulders broader, but she was still slender. She still had the face of an angel, with the high cheekbones and the too perfect mouth.

Marilyn's eyes narrowed. On the other hand, Ryan had changed dramatically in other ways.

It had taken all of Marilyn's composure to appear unruffled at the first sight of Ryan. She thought back centuries before as she lay by the girl's side, when Ryan had first displayed her formidable temper. Marilyn remembered her premonition at how powerful Ryan would become, how great her magnetism would be.

Marilyn's first thought upon mentally touching Ryan this evening was how badly underestimated that prediction had been. Ryan's charisma was staggering. Although Marilyn sensed that she herself was still the more powerful of the two, it was not by as great a margin as she would have wished, especially considering the disparity in their ages. The whelp had made up considerable ground in the last two centuries.

Ryan turned her gaze upon Marilyn, and her expression was unreadable. The dispassionate expression irritated Marilyn, who allowed her eyes to drift to Ryan's lips, then to her throat. Her gaze lingered there, caressing the artery.

Ryan, as always, was aroused against her will. She carefully maintained her poise, however, and returned her gaze out the window. Marilyn smiled.

In some ways, the girl hadn't changed at all.

CHAPTER 31

Susan stood at Ryan's side in the alcove. Edward stood at her other side. Jason had been removed from their presence at Susan's objection, but Edward had assured her the boy would not be harmed.

Susan looked over at Edward. His demeanor had changed dramatically. She had seen him as subservient before, but she now him as a warrior standing at the side of his King, ready for the battle for which he had prepared for centuries.

Ryan also looked composed, as if she had steeled herself for what was approaching. She had spent the last few hours isolated, aware of the Others' presence, but immune to it. She stood calmly in the shadows, as if awaiting some hidden command.

A figure slipped from the shadows and Susan saw that it was Marilyn. The dark-haired woman approached Ryan and Ryan did not at first acknowledge her presence, keeping her own counsel. She finally turned to Marilyn, nodding. Marilyn gestured for Ryan to lead the way.

Ryan stepped from the alcove into a great subterranean hall. The room was longer than it was wide and the ceilings were so high they could not be seen in the blackness. The walls were covered with huge tapestries stretching up into the darkness. The light from thousands of candles flickered across the faces of those leaning out of the balconies to glimpse the procedures below. Pews lined both sides of the central aisle, filled with hundreds of people. The hall was less a courtroom than an underground cathedral.

Ryan briefly paused at the entrance to the hall as all eyes turned towards her. Susan could feel the sudden tension, as if the room had drawn its collective breath. Electricity suddenly danced between every occupant of the room, and Susan realized she was the only human present.

Ryan began walking forward, allowing her eyes to briefly skim the great crowd of Others as if they were of no consequence to her. And indeed, they were not. She could feel their shock at her presence, feel them reach out to her and withdraw in terror. She could feel their desire intermixed with their terror, their longing intermixed with an ancient fear.

Ryan strolled leisurely down the aisle, coming to a stop at the table set before the judge's stand. She was not surprised to see the identity of the One who would sit in judgment of her. She gazed at the matriarch standing on the dais before the great hall.

"Hello Abigail," Ryan said softly and sardonically.

Abigail examined the young woman in front of her, a young woman who was no longer young but truly one of the Old Ones. Abigail noted the slight physical changes in Ryan that Marilyn had noted, and the non-physical ones as well. She smiled her slight and enigmatic smile.

"Hello my dear."

Susan had a very good idea who the older woman was, just by Ryan's previous tales. But there was much Ryan had failed to convey in her stories.

Each of these people had distinctive characteristics that were magnified by a devastating eroticism. From Marilyn's earthy sensuality to Abigail's matronly seduction, they all wore their lust on their sleeve with little if any contrition. Even now, in her position of objective judgment, Abigail did not hide her admiration for Victor's protégé.

With great show, Abigail seated herself behind the huge desk, smoothing her robe. She picked up the paperwork in front of her.

"The courtroom may be seated."

Susan Ryerson started to sit but then caught herself awkwardly halfway. No one else in the great hall had moved, so she as subtly as possible stood upright once more. Edward stood rigidly upright, unmoving.

Abigail's rustling papers were very loud in the silence, a silence that became even more pronounced when the rustling slowed, then stopped.

Abigail glanced around the great hall. Not a single person moved. All stood stiffly as if involuntarily at attention. Abigail turned to look at Marilyn, whose gaze flicked upward to those in the balconies, then around the room. She turned her attention to the accused standing in front of her.

Ryan stood at the head of the great hall, only the slightest trace of tension about her. Very slowly and with deliberate casualness she took her seat. She took a moment to settle into the cushion, then crossed one long leg over the other. Without taking her eyes from Abigail, she languidly raised her hand, and with a casual gesture, allowed the rest of the room to take their seats.

There was much whispering as people settled into their chairs; no one in the room missed the significance of the gesture. Abigail herself was aware of the message Ryan had sent her. She gazed down at the younger woman with the ambiguous emotions of their Kind. She was impressed but not surprised; exasperated but unmoved; and, as always, stimulated by the casual display of power. She looked down at her paperwork.

"Please state your name for the record."

"My name is Rhian."

Susan glanced over at Ryan. She spoke her name with that curious inflection, as she had the first time she had met her.

Abigail peered expectantly over the papers. "Your full name, my dear."

Ryan shifted in her seat, a look of discomfiture passing over her features. She took a deep breath. "My name is Rhiannon Alexander."

This brought a slight murmur as Abigail nodded in satisfaction. "Rhiannon," she said, "The goddess of the dead. How appropriate."

Susan at last understood. Ryan spoke her name so curiously because it was a shortened version of her true name, a name that she had never spoken.

Ryan sat back in her chair, arms folded. Abigail gazed at her a few moments longer, enjoying the implications of the name. Her gaze drifted over to Susan. "But I do believe you are now called 'Ryan'."

Ryan nodded curtly. "That is correct."

Abigail turned her attention to the paperwork in front of her, from which she began to read aloud.

"You have been brought here today to be tried by a jury of your peers."

"Then I move for a mistrial," Edward said, interrupting her.

Abigail peered over the paperwork. "On what grounds, counsel?"

Edward turned to Ryan, who gazed at Abigail with her unblinking gaze. "I have no peers," she said.

The silence was very loud as Ryan's words hung in the room. Susan gazed up at Abigail, expecting to see the older woman angered at Ryan's insolence. Instead, Abigail was having difficulty controlling a smile. She regained her composure and waved her hand.

"This is inconsequential."

The omission in Abigail's words was greater than the content, and silence again settled upon the room. Ryan spoke softly.

"But not untrue."

Abigail herself did not break eye contact this time. "No," she agreed, nodding ever so slightly, "Not untrue." She drew herself up. "But it is still immaterial, motion denied."

The gavel came down, startling Susan so she jumped. She glanced over at Ryan, then back up at the judge. She wasn't certain what was going on, but it seemed Ryan had just won two small victories in a row. She could not tell if this judge wanted to destroy the defendant or eat her for breakfast. Somehow she had the feeling the magistrate wanted to do both.

Abigail continued to read from the paperwork. "You are accused of killing your mentor, Victor Alexander. How do you plead?"

The expectancy in the room was in sharp contrast to Ryan's nonchalance. "I plead not guilty," she said firmly.

A murmur went through the crowd and Abigail raised an eyebrow. "You deny killing Victor?"

Ryan shook her head. "No, I plead not guilty because my actions were justified."

Another murmur swept the crowd as Abigail gazed down at the defendant. "An interesting defense."

A distinguished looking black man stood. Apparently he would be serving in the role of prosecuting attorney. He turned to Ryan. "So you admit killing Victor Alexander."

Edward stepped forward. "Objection, my client admits nothing."

The prosecutor turned to Abigail, speaking over Edward's continued objections. "If the defendant wishes to stipulate to certain details of the crime to-"

Ryan interrupted. "So stipulated," she said impatiently, silencing them both. Her gaze drifted to Marilyn. "It is well-known I killed Victor."

The prosecuting attorney seemed surprised at his own victory, and settled back into his chair. Edward sat down, unperturbed at this turn of events. Abigail continued.

"In order to judge the validity of your defense, we must examine the events surrounding the incident. I will allow the prosecution to begin its case."

The prosecuting attorney stood. "Very well, your honor, I would like to call to the stand my first witness, Dr. Susan Ryerson."

Ryan's head jerked up in surprise. Edward sighed. Susan looked over at Ryan, then stood uncertainly. Marilyn gestured Susan towards a seat next to the judge's stand.

Susan settled into the cushioned seat, very aware of Abigail's proximity. Abigail gazed down at Susan with a sort of motherly sympathy. "There's no need to swear you in, Dr. Ryerson. We will know instantly if you're lying."

Sympathetic or not, Susan did not miss the threat lurking in Abigail's words. She nodded her understanding, remaining remarkably poised. She turned her attention to the prosecuting attorney.

"Dr. Ryerson, can you describe the circumstances under which you first came to meet Ryan Alexander?"

Susan was silent for a moment, gathering her thoughts. Were they asking her if she stole the body from the morgue? She didn't think so. "Ryan came to the hospital as a patient." She stopped. "No, that's not entirely correct. She came to the hospital as a corpse. The coroner discovered her in the morgue and determined she was not dead, but rather comatose."

The prosecutor nodded, willing to let this version of the truth stand. "And can you describe the defendant's physical condition at that time?"

Edward leaned forward and began to take notes as Susan continued.

"Ryan was in a deep vegetative state. She had no vital signs, no blood pressure, no heartbeat, no respirations. She had sustained several 'mortal' injuries, including fractures to both her skull and femur. Even so, she exhibited an extraordinary amount of brainwave activity, which is why I put her in intensive care."

Ryan smiled as Susan's heartbeat jumped up, indicating the lie. Abigail turned to look down on her as Susan desperately tried to calm herself.

Edward fingered his pen, scratched something on his pad, then abruptly stood. "Your honor," he began, "I object to this line of questioning based upon relevance, or rather lack of relevance, to the case at hand."

Abigail appeared entertained by this early conflict. She turned to the prosecutor expectantly. "Well counselor?"

The handsome black man was unperturbed. "Your honor, I'm simply laying a foundation for my future argument, which will reveal itself as I continue."

Abigail turned back to Edward. "I will allow it for the time being, counsel." She smiled down at Susan. "You'll have to be patient, we're rarely if ever in a hurry."

Edward returned to his seat and the prosecutor turned his attention back to Susan.

"Please continue, doctor. How did Ryan's healing progress?"

Susan looked over at Ryan as she spoke. "Ryan's healing was remarkable. Once she received a blood transfusion-"

The prosecutor interrupted her. "A blood transfusion? Human blood?"

Susan nodded and a slight murmur went through the courtroom. Susan felt the need to explain. "It was human blood at first, but it quickly took on properties I'd never seen before, properties I came to associate with Ryan."

The prosecutor was helpful. "Properties such as-?"

Susan shrugged. "Heightened immunity, predatory blood cells, an extraordinary adaptive system...."

The prosecutor nodded his understanding as Susan trailed off. "And how long did it take Ryan to heal completely?"

Susan was thoughtful for a moment. "I would say it took about three weeks."

This time the murmur in the courtroom was more pronounced. Edward himself was caught off guard, if such a thing were possible. Three weeks was unexpectedly short. He stood.

"Your honor, the prosecution has failed to show the relevance of this line of questioning. I'm going to have to object once more."

The prosecutor started to interject his counter-argument, but Abigail waved him off, her eyes on Ryan. "I see little objection coming from your client, counsel, which leads me to believe she herself understands the relevance of this line of questioning."

Edward turned to Ryan. Ryan's reply was casual. "I have a feeling I know where this is going."

Abigail nodded, her eyes gleaming. "I'm going to allow him to continue."

Edward sat down, the beginnings of a suspicion forming. Two hundred years to prepare for this moment, and apparently his client hadn't told him everything.

The prosecutor turned his attention back to Susan. "I believe you had the opportunity to examine another one of our Kind," he said, pausing for effect, "A Young One."

Susan's eyes shifted to Ryan and her sudden uncertainty was evident to all in the room. Ryan waved her off. "By all means, Dr. Ryerson, please be truthful." She turned her head, addressing no one in particular. "Yes, yes, I killed him, too."

Susan looked around. Neither the prosecutor or the judge seemed startled at this admission, nor did they give any indication it was significant. She glanced over at Marilyn, who seemed to be presiding in some sort of bailiff position. Marilyn actually appeared amused at the admission.

The prosecutor gently prompted Susan. "Doctor?"

Susan began slowly. "Yes, I examined another one of your Kind. I performed a complete post-mortem examination, as well as an autopsy."

The prosecutor nodded, his words thoughtful. "And how would you compare his anatomy to Ryan's? And please keep it in layman's terms, Dr. Ryerson," he interjected before Susan could begin. "Very few of our Kind are doctors because we have little need of them."

This brought a few chuckles from about the room, allowing Susan to gather her thoughts. Even with the additional time, however, she could think of only one thing to say.

"They're different."

Silence abruptly settled on the room once more. Ryan herself leaned forward, for the first time demonstrating any interest at all in the proceedings. The autopsy had been so recent, they had not discussed Susan's findings.

Susan looked at Ryan, gathering strength from her. "The anatomy of the Young One was very different from Ryan's."

The prosecutor shrugged. "You say different. How different, doctor? Significantly different?"

Susan seemed oddly hesitant. "I don't know much about the anatomy of your Kind..."

The prosecutor became abruptly firm. "Doctor, in your medical opinion, was Ryan's anatomy significantly different from the Young One?"

Susan stared at Ryan, who was waiting for her reply. "Yes," she said at last, "Significantly different."

Susan could see the next question coming before the one word slipped from the prosecutor's lips.

"How?"

Ryan was waiting for Susan's answer, as was the rest of the room. Susan released her breath, unaware she had been holding it. "The Young One's anatomy was more similar to a human being's. He lacked many of the adaptations Ryan possessed, adaptations which made her so unique."

"Unique," the prosecutor said, savoring the word. "And did you form any opinion as to why this difference existed?"

Edward stood. "Objection, your honor. Calls for speculation."

Abigail's eyes were not on the attorney but on his client. For once Ryan did not hold her gaze, but rather looked down at her hands. Abigail turned her attention to Edward. "Overruled. Susan Ryerson is a medical doctor and capable of rendering an expert opinion on this matter."

Edward took his seat, his misgivings growing. Ryan turned her attention back to Susan.

"I thought perhaps it was because Ryan was so much older," Susan began, "That she had changed over time-"

"Oh really," the prosecutor interrupted smoothly. He strode across the room to Susan and leaned against the railing in front of her. He lowered his voice, and his words were slightly mocking. "Is that what you really think?"

Susan held his gaze for a moment, then looked past him to Ryan. She shook her head. "No," she said simply, "That's not what I think."

The prosecutor maintained his position a moment longer, then abruptly stepped back from the railing. He bowed slightly.

"Thank you Dr. Ryerson, that is all I have."

Edward was surprised by the abrupt ending. Evidently the prosecution did not wish to pursue their line of questioning any further although he was uncertain what they had just established. He wrote on the pad in front of him, knowing any whisper would be heard throughout the hall. He handed the message to Ryan. It read, "Is there something I should know?"

Ryan shook her head. "Ignorance is bliss," she said aloud. Abigail stared down at her, eyes gleaming. Edward stood.

"I have no questions for the witness, your Honor."

Edward took his seat Susan vacated the stand. Ryan glanced over at him. "How much do I pay you for such brilliant cross-examination?" she asked wryly.

He pushed his chair into the table. "Not enough," he said briskly.

Susan took the seat on Ryan's other side, glancing over at her apologetically. Ryan shook her head as if it were no matter. But as she glanced up at Marilyn, who was now regarding her thoughtfully, she knew the damage had already begun.

The prosecuting attorney stood and addressed Abigail politely. "Your honor, I would now like to call to the stand Marilyn de Fontesque."

Marilyn moved to the stand with elegant grace. She settled comfortably into the seat, her eyes on Ryan.

The prosecutor bowed to her. "Madam," he began respectfully, "Would you please describe the circumstances under which you first came to know the defendant."

Marilyn smiled, as if the memory gave her great pleasure. "Yes, I remember it as if it were yesterday. It was in France during the first part of the 15th century." She turned to Abigail. "We had not seen Victor in some time when he suddenly appeared out of nowhere with this half-wild creature in tow."

Abigail nodded in agreement, as if the memory also gave her pleasure. Evidently joining in on Marilyn's testimony did not seem improper procedure to her.

The prosecutor saw no problem in it, either, and addressed his questioning as much to Abigail as he did to Marilyn. "And can you describe your impression upon seeing her?"

Both were thoughtful, and it was Abigail who responded first. "I thought she was exquisite. So young, and yet so powerful," she remembered fondly. She shrugged. "And of course, so impossible."

The prosecutor raised an eyebrow. "Why impossible?"

Marilyn fielded this question. "Victor should not have been able to Change her. He was too old and too powerful."

Abigail nodded her agreement. The prosecutor nodded as well. "For the record, your honor, would you state why Victor was too old? We all, of course, know why, but I think it should be explicitly stated for the record."

Ryan did not hide her derision. An explicit statement had nothing to do with procedure. An explicit statement had everything to do with creating an impact.

Abigail gazed at Ryan knowingly. "Certainly, counsel. Procedure dictates." She smoothed her robes and began to tell her story.

"Ours is a hierarchy of power. Unlike normal man, who grows more frail as he ages, we grow more powerful. The more powerful we become, the less capable we are of being destroyed, until we come to a point where death is no longer a threat."

Abigail took that moment to glance at Ryan. "At least in theory." She turned back to the courtroom, continuing. "We also become more powerful through the act of Sharing. To Share with One more powerful than yourself is the greatest pleasure because the younger is strengthened by the blood of the elder." Abigail appeared to momentarily digress, "Although sharing with a Young One is a pleasant experience, nonetheless. And it is one of life's greatest pleasures to Share unto death."

"In fact," Abigail said mildly and without remorse. "Quite often, the younger ones are killed. Only the very strong of the Young will survive. They are either seduced by their mentor or others, and are killed or enslaved. Even if they are enslaved they may not survive the passions of their masters. It is only when they reach a certain age, usually several centuries, that they move beyond death and are not threatened with destruction."

"Victor was too Old to Change Ryan," Abigail said simply. Abigail was thoughtful for a long moment. "The politics of Sharing are complicated beyond belief, and the power amongst our Kind is determined by many things, the most important being who created you."

Abigail took that moment to cast a significant look at Ryan before she continued. "The older the mentor at transformation, the more powerful the Young One will be. However, after a certain point, we are no longer capable of reproducing because as we age our blood becomes too powerful for humans and is toxic to them." She shrugged. "So although the Old Ones would create the most powerful of our Kind, they are completely barren. The task of procreation is left to those who survive their infancy but who are not yet Old Ones. The very Young cannot reproduce because their blood is not powerful enough and the very Old cannot because their blood is too strong."

Abigail paused to impart another significant glance toward Ryan. "Again, this is in theory."

Edward took this opportunity to stand. "Then how could Victor have possibly created my client?"

A heavy silence hung over the courtroom. Abigail's eyes did not leave

Ryan. "That is what we all want to know."

Ryan rolled her eyes as Edward took his seat. "That was a marvelous move. Thank you."

Edward felt no regret over the question; Ryan had brought this upon herself by not giving him all the facts. He realized there was much beneath the surface of this trial.

The prosecutor stood, turning his attention back to Marilyn. "Madame de Fontesque. Now you stated you felt Ryan possessed an unnatural power for her age. Were there any other incidents where you were again struck by this 'power'?"

Marilyn nodded, her eyes on Ryan. "Yes. It was shortly after Ryan had the pleasure of meeting the Borgia Pope."

Ryan's jaw tightened imperceptibly, but Marilyn saw it. Her pleasure at the reaction was evident in her tone. "It was the first time I saw the extent of Ryan's temper." She turned to Abigail, speaking conversationally. "Oh, I had seen it before. Ryan could be quite deadly when angered. She once cut a man in two, springing to defend my honor."

Susan was surprised to see that Ryan actually looked embarrassed at this revelation. Abigail nodded in agreement, as if this incident did not surprise her. Marilyn continued.

"But Rome was the first time I had any premonition of how powerful she was," Marilyn paused, growing more serious, "And how powerful she would become. Even fully bled her body was heated by a fire that had no source."

For whatever reason, many in the courtroom turned their attention on Ryan, as if trying to see what secret her physical form could reveal.

Ryan was staring at Marilyn, an enigmatic expression on her face. In a seemingly purposeless gesture, she raised her hand and stroked her chin. She began tapping her teeth with her fingernail, as if deep in thought. But her eyes were clearly focused on Marilyn.

"Ouch," Ryan said softly, her hand jerking away from her mouth. Her attention was now focused on her index finger, which she slowly drew away to look at.

A single drop of crimson rolled down the edge of the finger towards the palm. Ryan gazed at the drop with a slightly concerned expression on her face.

Susan felt the tension in the room increase a thousandfold. Every eye in the great hall was now riveted on the tiny drop of blood rolling unchecked down Ryan's hand. Even Edward turned and physically moved himself away from the wound.

Ryan watched the blood continue its downward descent as she held her hand upright in front of her face. She appeared bemused by the injury, as if uncertain how to care for it. She looked past her hand to Marilyn, who had frozen at the sight of the blood. Marilyn tore her eyes from the scarlet to look at Ryan, but the blood was still between them.

Ryan held Marilyn's gaze, the slightest trace of a smile about her lips and a knowing look in her eye. She very deliberately moved the finger to her mouth, touched the red to her lips, and began to gently suck the wound.

It was too much for Marilyn, who turned away.

Ryan turned her attention to Abigail, who was as aroused by the scene as Marilyn. She knew how close Marilyn was to being completely out of control, because she herself was as near. She was also aware of the considerable unrest in the room.

"Dr. Ryerson," Abigail in a dry but strained voice, "Would you please attend to your patient?"

Susan glanced around the room, then picked her purse up from the floor. She retrieved a large Band-Aid from the back of her wallet, then turned in her chair. She knew full well the game Ryan was playing, but she wondered if Ryan knew how close these people were to attacking her.

She took Ryan's hand in her own, staring at her across the short distance. Ryan gazed at her with cool amusement.

She knew.

Susan quickly and efficiently bandaged the finger, wiping the excess blood with a gauze pad and shuttling the pad immediately into her purse. She snapped the latch, never having known a handbag to attract so much attention. She settled back into her chair, smoothing her skirt.

Ryan turned back to Abigail, highly amused over her little triumph. Abigail, as always, was more entertained than displeased by the child's antics.

Marilyn, however, was not the least bit amused. Her fury was evident.

Susan glanced at her friend. It seemed Ryan did not have the good sense to mask her relish of the situation. Ryan gazed at Marilyn, fairly taunting her.

It appeared the prosecuting attorney was not immune to Ryan's considerable charm, either. He stood at a loss until Abigail gently reprimanded him.

"You may continue, counselor."

The prosecutor shook his head to clear it. "Yes, of course. Umm, Madame de Fontesque..." He trailed off, then gathered his thoughts. "Can you describe the next time the defendant demonstrated her formidable temper?"

Marilyn's words were icy. "Why yes, yes I can. I believe that would have been the night Victor was murdered."

Ryan stiffened as if stabbed, and all traces of amusement disappeared. Marilyn settled back in her chair, pleased at the control she had regained.

"And could you describe the events leading up to that night?"

Marilyn nodded. "But of course. I have recounted them for the council on several occasions." Marilyn turned her attention to Ryan.

"It was in the early part of the 19th century. Ryan and Victor had established quite an estate in the northwestern United States. I came to visit them on numerous occasions."

The prosecutor nodded. "And did you sense anything between them, any strife?"

Marilyn shook her head. "Not at first. Everything seemed well between them. They always thought, acted and moved as one. They fit one another as if they were two parts of the same whole."

Marilyn continued to stare at Ryan icily as she spoke. Ryan swallowed hard and looked away.

"But I began to sense something between them, a type of tension, and I didn't know what was at the root of it."

"And did you ever have occasion to speak with Victor about the tension?"

Marilyn shook her head. "Not directly. Victor was ever one to keep his own counsel and I was wont to question him."

Susan noted how Marilyn, much as Ryan did, slipped into an older version of the language at times. Marilyn continued.

"But Victor did once refer to the growing distance between he and Ryan."

The prosecutor leaned forward. "And what did he say?"

Marilyn looked at Ryan, even now her interest evident. "He said there were things Ryan did not know, and he feared the day she discovered them."

Abigail raised an eyebrow as she looked over at Ryan. Ryan stared resolutely forward at nothing, her posture unyielding.

"And did you ever find out what Victor referred to?"

Marilyn again shook her head. "No."

The prosecutor stepped back, looking over his shoulder at Ryan. Ryan's eyes flickered upward to him, and he stared at her a long moment before he spoke.

"And can you describe the events surrounding Victor's death?"

Ryan's eyes flickered to Marilyn. Marilyn held Ryan's gaze and for once there was no game playing, no layered meanings. Marilyn spoke simply and clearly.

"I was not at the estate the night Victor was killed. I was hundreds of miles away, yet I felt it as if he died next to me."

Ryan bowed her head slightly, closing her eyes, but Marilyn did not see the gesture. She seemed lost in her own memories for a moment, as if seeking a way to describe the magnitude of the event. She spoke in a rare and quiet reflection.

"A volcano erupted in the year 1832, many years after Victor's death. It was such a tremendous explosion you could hear the sound of it as it traveled around the world several times." Marilyn turned to Abigail, who nodded in remembrance. "That was how Victor's death was among the Others."

The prosecutor paused respectfully for a moment, then continued. "And what did you do when you felt this, this mental shock wave?" the prosecutor asked.

"I normally traveled by whatever convenience was available; I rarely if ever traveled by foot. But that night I ran, knowing I could cover the distance quicker on my own."

Susan could feel the tension in the room growing once more as the prosecutor asked his next question.

"And what did you see when you arrived at the estate?"

"I saw a great fire in the night sky, and I knew the manor was burning, even from a distance. As I ran up the road, I could see a figure standing in the opened gate."

The prosecutor's voice was almost a whisper. "And who was the figure?"

"It was Ryan, and she was covered in blood. Not just covered," Marilyn corrected herself, "But drenched, as if she had bathed in a river of blood."

Susan flinched at the account, but Ryan did not. She stared woodenly forward as Marilyn continued.

"I asked her what had happened, and she said 'You know what I've done'. I said, 'It's not possible, you could not have killed Victor.'"

"And what did she say?" the prosecutor said.

Marilyn stared at Ryan. "She said that many things were impossible, and now she had done them all."

"And what was your reply?"

Marilyn seemed momentarily at a loss. "I was in shock, I could not comprehend that our leader was dead. I told Ryan she would have to take his place."

The prosecutor did not seem surprised at this seemingly contradictory revelation. "The law of succession," he said.

Marilyn nodded. "Of course. It was the one thing she could have done to at least mitigate an unforgivable act."

"And what was her reply to you?"

A strange look passed over Marilyn's face. "She told me I didn't understand what she had done. I told her, of course I understood what she had done. She had killed our King."

This, apparently, was unfamiliar territory to the prosecutor. He wrinkled his brow. "And what did Ryan say to you?"

Marilyn stared at Ryan, as if she could will the girl to explain the phrase that was now 200 years old. She hesitated, although she could not possibly forget words that had baffled her for two centuries.

"She said: 'No, I have done worse than that'."

The enigmatic statement hung in the air, and again, many eyes turned towards Ryan. But Ryan sat stiffly, her expression unreadable, her unblinking gaze forward looking at nothing.

The prosecuting attorney let the words linger a few moments longer, then he bowed to Marilyn. "Thank you, madam."

Marilyn stood as if to step down, but she was stopped by a clipped, British accent. "Not so quickly, your Honor. I have a few questions to ask the witness."

A ripple of surprise went through the courtroom and Abigail herself raised an eyebrow. She fingered her gavel. "Why certainly, counselor, it is your right."

Marilyn had obviously not expected this. She gazed at Edward with barely concealed contempt as she sat back down. She made a great show of settling in, then turned her icy gaze on him.

"By all means, counsel, ask your questions and be quick about it."

Edward gave a mocking show of confusion. "Oh, I'm sorry. I thought our Kind were never in a hurry."

The insult struck its intended mark and Marilyn shot him a venomous look. The mood in the courtroom subtly altered. Abigail herself looked with greater interest on Ryan's lawyer.

Edward stood and walked toward Marilyn. He paused about halfway there, as if mentally sorting things through. He glanced up at Marilyn.

"Now you," he paused thoughtfully, "You are one of the most powerful of our Kind."

Marilyn smiled a cool smile. "Yes."

Edward nodded his understanding. "And you, you once-,". He stopped, turning back to Ryan as if searching for a thought. "Ah yes," he said, as if remembering on his own. He turned back to Marilyn.

"Now you once Shared with Victor, didn't you?"

The blunt question brought gasps from many in the crowd. Abigail covered her mouth to hide a smile. The little man's theatrics were quite amusing. She glanced over at Marilyn, who was now infuriated.

"Yes," Marilyn said icily, "I once Shared with Victor."

Edward nodded, beginning his pacing once more. He appeared to still be sorting things out. "Now, this made you more powerful, correct?"

Marilyn nodded stiffly. "Yes, that's correct."

Edward glanced at Ryan who was watching him curiously. He turned his attention back to Marilyn. "Now, I don't imagine you Shared with Victor at all after Ryan became his companion..."

Marilyn stared at him in silent fury.

"Did you?" Edward prompted, turning to look sideways at her.

Marilyn shook her head. "No, I did not."

Edward nodded once more, as if digesting facts he already knew. He headed off in another direction. "So, if you Shared with Victor, which made you more powerful-." He stopped abruptly, turning to look at her fully. "Then that means you yourself usurped the hierarchy you have accused Ryan of violating."

Marilyn was livid and could not speak. The prosecuting attorney leaped to his feet.

"Objection, your Honor. The defendant has not been accused of violating the hierarchy. She is being tried for the murder of Victor Alexander."

"Oh really?" Edward asked before Abigail could rule, his insinuation obvious.

Abigail stopped her gavel halfway, again surprised at the skill of the defense attorney. She set the mallet down.

"Objection sustained, counsel. As enjoyable as this is, will you please stop baiting the witness?"

Marilyn turned her venomous look on Abigail as Edward nodded agreeably. "Of course, your Honor. My apologies." Edward started his slow walk, glancing over at Ryan.

"Now, Madame Fontesque-" he began over his shoulder. He stopped, as if trying to phrase a difficult thought. He shrugged, giving the impression there was no delicate way to say what he needed to say. He turned and looked squarely at Marilyn.

"You want my client, don't you?"

The uproar was immediate. The prosecutor leaped to his feet, shouting objections. Abigail's gavel came crashing down, at first drowned out by the noise. The continued rapping of the mallet was finally heard over the din, and the crowd settled.

"I object, your Honor!" the prosecutor said vehemently.

"On what grounds, counselor?" Abigail asked mildly.

The prosecutor, as dignified as he was, gave a brief impression of a fish thrashing about. "On the grounds of relevancy," he finished lamely.

Abigail shook her head. "I'm afraid this is highly relevant, counselor. It reflects on the credibility of the witness. Objection denied." She turned to Marilyn. "Please answer the question, dear," she said with just a trace too much enjoyment.

Marilyn turned back to Edward and her eyes fairly burned through him. He appeared oblivious to her anger. "Well, Madam?"

Marilyn would not look at Ryan. "Everyone in this room wants her," she said finally through gritted teeth.

Edward would not let her off so easily. "Including you?"

Marilyn's fury burned unabated. One could almost hear her teeth grind. "Including me."

Edward nodded. "And you wanted her, even when she was standing covered in her mentor's blood. In fact," he said, gazing out over the packed hall, "You wanted her more at that moment than you had ever wanted her before."

Marilyn was silent, and the silence was damning. Edward continued, his lilting English accent soft but easily heard in the vast hall.

"In fact, at that time, you offered to take Victor's place at her side, and in her grief and self-reproach, she refused you."

Marilyn glared down at Ryan. "She felt no grief or self-reproach."

Edward began walking away from her as if finished, but he paused to look over his shoulder.

"But you did offer."

Marilyn's silence again condemned her.

Abigail glanced over at Marilyn. She had expected as much, but had never been able to confirm what had transpired between Marilyn and the girl. She rapped once with her gavel.

"Although I'm quite certain we could continue for days without rest, I am just as certain Ryan's human companion cannot. We'll adjourn for a short while."

Ryan, Edward, and Susan were led to a room and cloistered. A Young One brought food for Susan. He glanced over at Ryan, his longing evident, but she lay on the couch staring up at the ceiling. Edward gave him a firm look of disapproval and he left, depressed he had not even been acknowledged.

Susan only picked at her food. She pushed away from the table and went and sat by Ryan's side. She put her hand on Ryan's forehead and was shocked at how hot she was.

Ryan smiled as she felt the cool hand. "Don't worry doctor. That's a fairly normal temperature for me." She turned her head to look at Edward.

"I wanted to thank you for your help thus far, Edward. I am sorry."

"Is there anything you would like to tell me at this point in time?"

Ryan turned her head and closed her eyes. "It will all come out sooner or later," she said. She lay there for a long while with Susan at her side. She finally spoke without opening her eyes. "Marilyn is at the door."

Seconds later, a light knock came and the door opened.

Marilyn stepped in, apparently having regained her composure during the break. She gazed at Edward coolly, but without anger. She glanced at Susan on the couch, raising an eyebrow at her proximity to Ryan. Susan stood, flustered, without really knowing why.

Ryan sat upright, rubbing her temple. "I wish this blasted headache would go away."

Marilyn motioned for Edward and Susan to proceed her through the doorway and Ryan stood to do the same. Marilyn stepped in front of her, however, blocking her exit. She stared down at the younger woman, grasping her hand in her own.

She raised the hand until the bandaged appendage was between them. She did not look at the hand, however, but maintained eye contact with Ryan.

"I hope your hand is better."

"My hand is fine," Ryan said evenly.

"Good," Marilyn said, her eyes drifting to Ryan's throat, "I don't want you to lose any more blood." Marilyn's tone was both casual and dangerous. "You'll need all of it when this is through."

Marilyn pushed away from Ryan, leaving her standing in the doorway. Ryan stared after the dark-haired woman as she disappeared down the hall.

The prosecuting attorney stood as the courtroom settled into a hush.

"I would like to call Rhiannon Alexander to the stand."

Ryan uncrossed her long legs and stood. Susan was reminded of the first time she had seen Ryan in the hospital ward, and was again struck by how physically impressive she could be. Ryan strode unhurried to the stand and then settled lithely into the chair.

The prosecutor approached. "Can you tell the court approximately when you were born?"

"I was born in the year of our Lord 1325."

The prosecutor paused. Even though this fact was known to him, having it spoken aloud was daunting. "And can you tell the court how old you were when you were Changed?"

"I was 19 seasons when Victor Changed me."

This brought murmurs to the crowd and Susan looked around. As near as she could tell, 19 was too young. The prosecutor glanced over at Ryan.

"Now, with the exception of your human companion, all of us have been through the difficulty of the transformation. Can you describe for us your Change?"

The prosecutor's attempt to find common ground with Ryan failed. She instantly paled at his mention of her Change, and she now looked at him with disdain.

"You cannot possibly imagine what my Change was like," she said, slowly enunciating every word.

The prosecutor was taken aback at her sudden intensity, and he changed tactics.

"Very well. Can you describe for us your life with Victor? Was he cruel to you?"

Ryan shook her head. "No, Victor gave me everything I could wish for."

The prosecutor seemed surprised at Ryan's willingness to speak kindly of her mentor. Surprised and suspicious.

"Everything you could wish for," he repeated, "And did he withhold anything?"

Ryan's answer was immediate. "His Memories."

The prosecutor seemed puzzled by her answer. "And when did you first begin seeing his Memories?"

Ryan was silent for a moment, knowing the impact her answer would have. "From the first time his blood touched my lips."

This brought much murmuring from the crowd. Abigail glanced down at the girl. She had long known of the abilities Ryan had acquired immediately, gifts which most would acquire over centuries, gifts that some would never acquire at all. Marilyn had also known, but few others.

The prosecutor could not believe what he was hearing, but he knew Ryan was not lying. He struggled to pursue this line of questioning.

"And these Memories he withheld, was it all of them, or-?"

Ryan finished the open-ended question. "It was only a few he withheld. As I grew older, I had greater and greater access to his mind, and it was only then I realized he was hiding something from me."

"What?" the prosecutor asked.

Ryan's silence was pronounced.

Abigail leaned over to her. "You will answer the question my dear."

Ryan's response was as stunning as it was abrupt. "I will not."

Marilyn moved toward Ryan but surprisingly, it was the prosecutor who spoke up to avert the situation. "I withdraw the question."

Marilyn glanced up at Abigail who, after a moment, nodded for her to withdraw.

The prosecutor stood thoughtfully for a moment, then changed tactics. "So how did you kill your mentor?"

The question sent a ripple through the crowd, but if it was meant to catch Ryan off guard, it failed to do so. She sat staring at the black man with her unblinking gaze, then began to recount the event in an entirely conversational tone.

"I bled myself until my body was nearly empty, and then I fed upon him until his heart stopped." Ryan appeared thoughtful. "It was the first time I had ever accomplished such a feat."

Susan was once more struck by Ryan's casual predatory nature, and the lack of reaction her words were met with. The prosecutor seemed to examine this statement from a purely analytical point of view.

"Surely that wasn't enough to destroy someone as powerful as Victor. It would have been no more than a momentary setback for him."

"You're quite right," Ryan said agreeably, "Which is why I cut him into pieces and ate him."

The reaction Susan was waiting for finally came. Disbelief and horror were on every face in the room, with the exception of Marilyn who was rather astounded at the ingenuity of it, and Abigail who was nearly startled into laughter. Even so, her head turned in astonishment.

"You cut him to pieces and ate him?" she repeated.

Ryan shrugged. "It was all I could think of at the time," she said as if in explanation.

"You cut him to pieces and ate him," the prosecutor repeated. He couldn't think of anything else to say.

"Yes," Ryan said simply, "I did."

The prosecutor walked back to his table and sat down heavily. He seemed unable to come to grips with what Ryan had just revealed. "I'm sorry," he said, shaking his head, "I have a hard time thinking of anything that would make such an act justifiable homicide."

Ryan's casual tone changed to one of steel. There was no sign of contrition or compromise in her voice. "That is because you have not seen what I have seen."

It was Abigail who would be the first to capitalize on Ryan's slip. "And what would that be, Ryan?" she asked smoothly.

Ryan's jaw tightened as she realized her mistake. She felt Abigail's sudden presence in her mind, and Marilyn's as well. Although they could not take her thoughts, they could certainly take her feelings, and that was what was betraying her right now.

The prosecutor, like all predators, sensed her sudden weakness. He stood and began circling for his attack.

"What did you see, Ryan? What was so horrible that would make you want to destroy Victor?"

Ryan closed her eyes, trying to shut out the presence of the Others, but even more, trying to shut out the flood of Memories coming back to her. The pain in her head was intense, and the pain in her heart more so.

The prosecutor changed tactics. "So you killed him, you killed him in a horrible manner." He began to speculate, re-living the crime. "And then, covered in blood, you go to Marilyn, and you confess."

Ryan closed her eyes even tighter, as if she could drown out his voice. The prosecutor was aware of her reaction and was encouraged to continue.

"But it's not a full confession. Marilyn accuses you of regicide, a tragic crime, but your reply is 'No, I have done worse than that'."

The prosecutor moved closer to Ryan, his insistence beginning to wear on her. "I have done worse than that," he repeated.

He moved even closer to Ryan, his words becoming seductive. "What could be worse than that, Ryan?" He leaned closer until his voice was hypnotic in her ear, his words wearing her down. "Victor was like a lover to you, he gave you everything.

"What could be worse than regicide, Ryan?" he whispered in her ear. "What could be worse than killing the man who gave you immortality, your lover, your mentor, your King?"

Ryan's head snapped upward and her unblinking gaze fixed upon the prosecutor. Her jaw was set, and when she finally spoke, her voice was steel.

"I will speak no more."

The prosecutor stood upright. He realized that no amount of persuasion or threat would make Ryan speak further. Abigail realized this as well, and softly rapped her gavel.

"The defendant may step down."

Ryan stepped down from the stand, brushing by Marilyn as she did so.

Marilyn gazed down at her coolly as she passed. Ryan stalked to her seat and sat down heavily, her barely contained fury evident. She stood up abruptly, startling those nearest her. Her words were scathing as she addressed Abigail.

"I weary of this charade, Abigail. So what now? You find me guilty? And what then?" she asked sarcastically. "Are you going to have me killed?"

Abigail shook her head, unperturbed at Ryan's temper. "You ever were the impatient one. No," she said, answering Ryan's question, "I told you many centuries ago I don't believe you can be killed."

"So what then?" Ryan demanded, "What is my punishment?"

Abigail smiled her enigmatic smile. "We felt perhaps an 'in-custody' situation would be appropriate."

Ryan nodded as if in understanding. "Oh, I see. And whose custody might that be? Yours, Abigail?"

Abigail shook her head regretfully. "No, I'm afraid not."

Ryan turned to Marilyn. "Yours?"

Marilyn smiled her cool smile, but she, too, shook her head. Ryan turned back to Abigail, her mounting frustration evident.

"Who's?"

Abigail glanced down at the paperwork in front of her and Marilyn also looked carefully away. After shuffling the paperwork, Abigail looked down at Ryan. "We feel you should be remanded to the custody of the only One who has any hope of controlling you." She said enigmatically, then paused, "But first we must call our final witness."

Ryan made an impatient gesture and sat down. A stabbing pain in her head made her reach for her temples. Susan looked over at her with concern. Ryan rubbed her temples vigorously, as if trying to leech the pain away. She dropped her hands in frustration, as if unable to comprehend what was wrong with her. Susan reached over and lightly grasped her arm in comfort.

Ryan glanced over to reassure Susan, but the words died on her lips as a strange look passed over her features. She turned away from Susan, staring ahead of her as if hearing some sound far off in the distance. Her hands again returned to her temples. The look on her face changed to one of concern, then disbelief. The color drained from her face as she slowly lowered her hands to the table in front of her, a look of dawning comprehension and shock on her fine features. She slowly shook her head.

Ryan took a deep breath and pushed her chair away from the table, seemingly exerting tremendous effort just to stand. She partially leaned on the table in front of her, then with another great effort stood fully upright, her eyes focused on the table in front of her. She steadied herself as all eyes focused on her.

And then she turned around.

At first, no one could grasp the look of stunned disbelief on Ryan's features, and indeed, it was Susan Ryerson who first turned to see what the young woman was looking at. The Others realized that Ryan was looking past them and they, too, turned to see what she was looking at.

At first they saw and felt nothing.

Then, they felt something extraordinary.

A tall, dark-haired man stepped from the shadows of the alcove into the light.

Ryan flinched as if physically struck and staggered against the edge of the table. Susan instinctively moved to help her, but her eyes did not leave the man as she slipped an arm about Ryan's waist.

The dark-haired man was easily the most beautiful human she had ever seen, rivaled perhaps only by Ryan herself. Tall and elegant, his broad shoulders tapered to a slender waist that was accentuated by the well-tailored suit he wore. His dark hair was immaculate, worn just above the collar, with the slightest touch of gray at the sides. He had fine features and piercing black eyes that were focused on no one but Ryan. His too-perfect mouth looked strangely familiar to Susan, but she did not have the time or wits about her to place it.

Susan knew who the man was, but turned to Ryan for confirmation. Ryan could not take her eyes from him, but silently spoke the name.

Victor.

The man's gaze moved briefly to the lips that wordlessly spoke his name, and there was the slightest trace of amusement in what could otherwise be described only as cold fury. Susan's one coherent thought was that once again, Ryan had given a rather watered-down description of their relationship. The eroticism and attraction between the two was unmistakable, as tangible as if they had been fully embracing. Victor's gaze flickered up until his eyes locked with Ryan's. He stepped forward.

The full force of his power became evident in the room and those who had known him in name only suddenly realized how little they knew. Victor moved with the preternatural grace of their Kind, and he moved with the dignity of a King.

Ryan could not move, could not speak, could only stand wordlessly watching her mentor approach. She was remotely aware of Marilyn slipping in behind her, but her attention was on Victor.

She stood upright as he approached, and did not resist when he took her hand and lifted it to his lips. He gently brushed a kiss across her skin.

"Hello my dear, I've missed you."

The greeting was sardonic and there was the slightest trace of amusement in his eyes. But the amusement did not hide the dangerous glint that resided there as well.

Ryan gazed at the hand he held in front of her. She felt Marilyn's presence behind her, felt the hundreds of eyes from the courtroom upon her, felt Abigail hungrily watching for her reaction. She knew she had been maneuvered into this situation, had been manipulated by forces wanting to see her humbled, wanting to see her lose control. Her jaw tightened imperceptibly as she straightened to her full height, gazing steadily into Victor's eyes. She had but a single card to play in a game she had seemingly already lost.

"Hello," she said with a slight but significant pause.

"Father."

Victor's mouth twitched, but beyond that, he showed little reaction. The amusement was more evident in his eyes now.

It took a moment for the implications of what Ryan said to sink into anyone else. It wasn't so much what she had said but the way she had said it, and Victor's reaction. The uncertainty in the room was palpable, as was the growing confusion.

Marilyn stepped forward, glancing at Ryan, then at Victor. Her voice showed the beginnings of a suspicion.

"What did she mean by that?"

Victor shrugged elegantly, as if this revelation were of no matter. "I assure you she does not mean it in a metaphorical sense." He turned his attention back to Ryan. "I see we are going to get right to the point. I imagine I should take the stand."

He released Ryan's hand and moved to the witness stand. Marilyn gazed after him, then turned to glance at Ryan with suspicion and disbelief. She stared at her a long moment, as if trying to comprehend what was happening.

Abigail herself was quite stunned by this turn of events. She had expected Victor's appearance, but the youngster had quite effectively blunted that impact with her own startling revelation. Abigail still was not certain if the child meant what she thought she meant.

Victor settled into the chair, his mannerisms highly reminiscent of the One who had so recently vacated the stand. He had the same cat-like grace Ryan demonstrated in her elegant sprawl, although Victor possessed more elegance and less sprawl than his unruly child.

The prosecutor stood uncertainly but Abigail would have no more of proper procedure.

"Just what exactly did she mean by that, Victor?"

Victor turned to gaze at Abigail, raising an eyebrow at her impropriety. He turned his gaze back to Ryan, his eyes caressing her.

"Rhiannon Alexander is my child in every way. I am responsible for her Change, and I am also her father."

The explosion in the courtroom was immediate. Abigail did not even attempt to regain control, so shocked was she herself. Edward turned to look at his client, stunned. Marilyn stood, her anger evident.

"That's impossible. None of us are capable of reproducing outside the Change."

Victor did not react to Marilyn's anger, indeed, did little more than shrug. The room quieted as his gaze returned to Ryan. "Many things are impossible," he said, softly echoing Ryan's earlier testimony, "And now I have done them all."

The room again exploded into exclamations of shock and disbelief. The only person who appeared curiously unmoved was Ryan herself as she sat gazing unblinkingly at her father.

Abigail rapped her gavel several times to regain control and the room quieted. She turned to Victor.

"And her mother," she paused, looking over at Ryan, "Her mother was human?"

Victor nodded. "Yes, Elena was human."

"So that was her name," Ryan said, softly sarcastic.

Both Abigail and Marilyn turned at Ryan's tone, and Marilyn's eyes narrowed. So this was the point of rift between the two.

Victor's tone hardened slightly. "Yes," he said, his own tone slightly sarcastic, "That was her name."

Victor's voice lowered, was unapologetic. "I told you that you were perfect in every way." He shook his head. "You were never human."

Ryan looked down at the table in front of her, her jaw clenching and unclenching as Victor continued.

"Your mother was spirited and intelligent and beautiful beyond belief, and I chose her out of thousands who were willing."

Ryan's head snapped upward. "But she was not willing," she said softly, evenly, staring him in the eye.

Victor did not deny this. "No," he said simply, "She was not willing."

Ryan's gaze did not waver, and her words, although horrendous, were entirely conversational in nature. "And so you kidnapped her, and then you raped her, and then you imprisoned her until she gave birth to me."

Ryan paused, the tension in her frame obvious. "And then you killed her."

Victor's fist came smashing down on the banister in front of him, splitting the railing and startling everyone. He spoke through clenched teeth. "My killing her was an act of mercy. She would have died anyway from the strain of giving birth to you."

Ryan did not hesitate. "But you knew that beforehand, didn't you?"

Victor sat back, the loss of control gone as suddenly as it appeared. He smoothed his suit, his lack of concern evident. "Yes," he said simply, "I did."

Ryan sat back, barely contained fury evident in every line of her body. Marilyn examined Ryan closely. Marilyn's initial anger had transitioned into fascination as she watched the scene unfold. She was quite impressed with the restraint Ryan was exhibiting. Under normal circumstances, Ryan would have already destroyed the room. Marilyn's eyes drifted to the split banister, then to Victor. No wonder.

Abigail was also fascinated by the unfolding drama. Although the explanation itself seemed impossible, it would account for everything: the girl's Change, her abilities, her power, her anatomy. She turned back to Victor, sensing there was more.

"And how did Ryan discover you were her father?"

Victor was suddenly vague. "I made," he paused, as if searching for the right words, "A miscalculation."

Ryan leaped to her feet, overturning the heavy oak table in front of her as if it were made of Styrofoam. Susan Ryerson nearly fell backward to get out of the way. Marilyn smiled. Now that was more like the girl.

"A miscalculation!" Ryan fairly shouted at him. "You should have told me! I never should have found out that way!"

Victor remained calm, unperturbed at her words and the violence that accompanied them. He gazed at her steadily. "No," he agreed, "You should not have found out that way."

Abigail was curious. "What way?" she asked.

Ryan turned to her, the fury spilling out in her words. "I have my mother's blood, too."

At first, the implications of her words did not sink in. It was Marilyn who first drew the correct conclusion.

"And her Memories," the dark-haired woman said in slow comprehension.

Ryan turned to her, her bitterness obvious. "And her Memories," she finished.

Abigail raised her hand to her chest at the full implication.

Victor's gaze did not waver. "I could not know that you would see her death."

Ryan turned to him. "I did more than see her death. I saw everything she saw, felt everything she felt, and lived every moment of her life right up until the moment you took it."

Ryan turned away, closing her eyes.

"And I saw it through her eyes, felt it through her mind," she stopped, almost unable to continue. "Just as if it were me."

An odd silence settled over the room and all eyes were upon Ryan. Ryan's gaze was distant for a moment, unfocused. Her eyes refocused and her gaze flickered to Abigail, to Marilyn, and to Susan. Susan had the impression that Ryan was trying to prepare her for something, but Susan could not fathom what it was.

Ryan took a deep breath and Susan was startled at the vivid picture that suddenly invaded her mind.

She saw the terror and pain of a young woman with golden hair, a woman who could only be Ryan's mother. She saw dark, shadowy pictures of Victor, methodically carrying out the abduction and the rape. She saw the golden-haired woman in the throes of a horrific childbirth, and finally she saw the beautiful, dark-haired man holding a bloody infant triumphantly up to the night sky.

And Susan felt things as well. She felt the woman's terror, her isolation, her hopelessness, and it was in stark contrast to the man's fierce joy at the birth of his unholy child. She watched as the light died in the young woman's eyes and began to burn fiercely in those of her golden-haired child.

The Others saw, too, perhaps even more vividly than did Susan. They all saw, and they all stared at the creature seated before them. Ryan was not like them, and yet was the ultimate expression of their Kind. Changed before she was ever born, she had never been human. She was the ultimate predator, born in death and carrying the echoes of its Memory through eternity.

Susan stared at the young woman before her. The story of Ryan's birth made the sins of Oedipus look minor. Not only was Ryan aware of her origins, she had been a part of them, re-living them from both her mother and father's perspective. She had killed her mother, both by her birth and through her father's eyes, and then she had killed her father in revenge. And the blood of both coursed hotly through her veins, bringing their thoughts, their dreams, and their Memories.

The silence was very loud until someone made the sound of clearing his throat. All eyes turned towards Edward.

"Your honor," he began, addressing Abigail, "I would like to move for a dismissal due to the fact that my client obviously did not commit the crime she is accused of," he said, nodding towards Victor.

Abigail glanced at Victor, then shook her head. "I'm afraid it's not that simple, Edward," she said, addressing him by name for the first time. "She did make the attempt."

Ryan returned to her seat, avoiding the table that was still upside down on the floor. She leaned back in her chair and crossed her arms, gazing coolly up at Victor. Marilyn moved to a position near her.

"So tell me, dear father, how did you survive the 'attempt'?"

Victor's gaze flickered to Marilyn, then back to his dark child. "Marilyn was instrumental in my recovery." He paused for a moment before continuing. "It seems you did not quite finish the job."

Ryan shrugged. "I was full."

Abigail again was nearly startled into laughter. Susan was appalled at Ryan's words but Victor did not seem at all angry. In fact, he seemed rather amused by the reply and the corner of his mouth twitched.

Susan glanced from father to daughter, just beginning to understand how complex their relationship was. Ryan had attempted to murder the man in front of her in a most horrific manner, and although Victor was angry about it, part of him seemed to view it as little more than an adolescent temper tantrum.

In the same way, Ryan, although obviously still infuriated with her father, seemed mildly chagrined at her actions, not willing to admit wrongdoing but perhaps embarrassed over what she had done.

Victor's tone was slightly chastising. "Did you really believe you had killed me? Surely you are now old enough yourself to realize you could not have succeeded."

Ryan paused for a long moment. "I had begun to suspect." Her eyes shifted to Marilyn and she changed the subject. "You must be very pleased with Marilyn." She now addressed the dark-haired woman directly. "So what did he promise you in return for your loyalty?"

Marilyn smiled her cool smile but it was Victor who replied.

"You."

Ryan was startled and Marilyn was pleased the answer had caught Ryan off-guard. Victor gestured casually in Abigail's direction. "Abigail helped as well."

Ryan did not miss the implication in that statement, either. Abigail had the grace to smooth her robes, only the slightest trace of her enigmatic smile about her lips. Ryan turned her attention back to Victor.

"Well," Ryan said, at a loss for words. She stared at Victor. "How unlike you," she finally finished.

Victor stood, now casually addressing the courtroom. "As is my prerogative, I hereby dissolve the Grand Council until which time it is needed again." He turned to Abigail. "Once Ryan has served the terms of her punishment, she will become my Second once more."

Abigail nodded as if this were expected. Victor continued. "When you are finished with your proceeding here, please join us."

Abigail nodded and Victor stepped down. He motioned to Marilyn who fell into step beside him. He approached Ryan, then stopped in front of her. Ryan stood. Edward also stood, and Victor took his measure for a moment.

"You have served my daughter well, Edward."

Edward bowed low. "I live to serve her, my lord." He bowed lower, "As I live to serve you."

Victor turned his attention to Ryan. He took her hand in his. "We must be leaving," he said, glancing at Susan. "Your companions must stay with us a short while longer, then they are free to do as they will."

CHAPTER 32

Susan was not allowed to observe their route of travel from the trial, nor was she exactly certain where the trial itself had been held, so she had little if any idea where they were. She rode in the limousine alone, her thoughts on the events of the last hours. So deeply immersed was she in these thoughts that she was surprised when the limousine came to a stop. The door opened and she stepped out, looking around in wonderment. She thought she would never find an estate to rival Ryan's, but now mentally revised her opinion. This house was exquisite, as were the gardens surrounding it.

Her first thought was for Jason and she was happy to find him in the bedroom she was led to. He bounced from the bed when he saw her and ran into her arms.

"Where's Ryan?" were the first words from his mouth.

She hugged him tightly. "She's here, munchkin. I think she's kind of busy right now."

"Oh," he said, relieved, "I was wondering where you guys went." He lowered his voice, eyeing the servant who stood in the doorway. "These people are kind of creepy."

Susan smiled tiredly. The servant remained expressionless, although Susan was certain she could hear. The woman offered her clothing and began to run a bath for her. Susan was soon luxuriating in the steaming water while Jason watched television. When finished, she pulled on the silk shirt and slacks she was given. She had the decadent thought that, although currently uneasy, she was getting used to being waited on.

It wasn't long before Jason tired and fell asleep on the bed. She pulled the top cover loose and tucked him in. She herself was tired, but didn't feel as if she could sleep. She went out onto the balcony and settled into a cushioned wicker settee. The night air was cool but the balcony was heated with outdoor lanterns and a servant brought her a wrap, which she draped across her legs. She was wondering about Ryan when she heard a knock at the door.

She started to get up but the servant stepped forward, politely shaking her head. She indicated that Susan was not to move and then she went to answer the door. Susan heard soft murmurs, and then Victor entered, crossing the room to the balcony. He pushed open the sliding screen door.

"May I join you?"

Susan started to stand but Victor shook his head. "No, please, sit down." The servant brought another wicker chair that Victor set across from Susan and then settled into, crossing one long leg over the other.

Susan stared at the man, again struck by his incredible beauty. It was perhaps only her past continued exposure to Ryan's magnetism that made Susan immune to Victor's charms.

Victor smiled and Susan revised her opinion. Well, perhaps not completely immune.

"I wanted to thank you for caring for my daughter. Ryan is an excellent judge of character. I'm certain her choice of you as a companion will prove as insightful as ever."

Susan shifted uncomfortably. She did not want to start liking this man.

Victor sensed her discomfort immediately. "You seem troubled, dear doctor," he said knowingly.

Susan did not quite know how to broach the subject. "Well, I'm certainly not passing judgment on you, but your relationship with Ryan does seem a little..."

She faded away, unwilling to finish the sentence. Victor had no qualms about finishing it for her.

"Incestuous?"

Susan nodded, trying to be as casual as he was. "Yes, I think that was the word I was looking for."

Victor removed a cigar from his inner pocket. He lit it expertly, taking a long pull on it then blowing the smoke away from Susan. He watched the wisps linger in the air for a moment, then spoke thoughtfully.

"You know, Dr. Ryerson, my birthday is closer to that of Christ's than it is to yours." He turned from the smoke to her. "All ties have blurred for me. Mother, father, brother, sister, they are all the same to me. Even gender has very little meaning for me, anymore. I would have the exact same relationship with Ryan were she my son."

This admission did not make Susan feel any better. Victor took another long pull on the cigar, then blew the smoke out, watching it curl upward in the light from the lanterns. He turned to Susan. "You must remember, Dr. Ryerson, that I am not human, nor is Ryan. Human taboos against incest serve a very real purpose, but they serve no purpose amongst our Kind. For me to blindly follow a cultural more which is inapplicable would be foolish." Victor watched the smoke curl upward. "Not to mention the fact it would have kept me from creating the greatest of our Kind to ever walk this earth."

Susan stared at him. "So is Ryan the greatest of your Kind?"

Victor shook his head. "Not yet. But she will be one day."

Susan had a sudden and strange insight. "This does not cause you concern."

It was not a question, but Victor answered it anyway. "Of course not, dear doctor."

Susan was beginning to understand things about Victor that even Ryan did not. He seemed aware of her sudden prescience and gazed at her through the smoke, contemplating.

Susan stared at him her suspicions growing. "You knew she would try to kill you."

Victor shrugged, the nonchalant gesture so reminiscent of Ryan that Susan for a moment had to remember who she was speaking to. "Of course. Ryan is the most efficient predator I have ever known." There was not the slightest bit of condemnation in the statement. The words were spoken casually and if anything, with a trace of pride. Victor took another long drag on the cigar, then watched the smoke curl upward. "I did not know, however, that she would be so creative in her attempt, nor did I know it would take me nearly two centuries to recover."

Victor cocked his head to one side as if listening to something far off in the distance. He changed the subject. "Your son seems to be sleeping soundly. If you yourself are not tired, you are free to move about the grounds. I would ask you not to leave because I have a gift for you."

Victor seemed restless, although Susan could not put her finger on exactly what gave that impression. Outwardly, he was as calm and elegant as ever. Susan put a voice to her suspicions.

"Where's Ryan?"

Victor was not the least bit fooled by the casualness of her inquisition. "She's with Marilyn," he said calmly.

Susan watched his expressionless face, choosing her words carefully. "That does not please you."

Victor chose his words just as carefully. "It does not displease me. It is something that must be done."

Victor stood abruptly, extending his hand for Susan's. Susan raised her arm and he grasped her hand, kissing it. He bowed. "Thank you for your time."

Susan watched the dark-haired man leave the room, noting that he and Ryan even stalked the same.

Ryan was stalking about the room, covering the full length of the suite. Marilyn watched the youngster's agitation from her vantagepoint on the sofa. She had always enjoyed watching the girl, and was especially enjoying it now. Ryan was attempting to conceal her anxiety by moving about the room, but her activity betrayed more than it concealed.

Abigail also watched the girl, albeit more surreptitiously than Marilyn. Her fingers were busy with the quilt she was knitting, but her eyes followed Victor's child about the room.

Ryan stopped to pick up a brass letter opener, absently fingering the object, and Abigail was reminded of a similar scene many centuries before. Ryan replaced the object and resumed her pacing. Abigail smiled. It was a similar scene, but Ryan was no longer a Young One. She was still intoxicatingly vulnerable, but now it was the vulnerability of a trapped wild animal.

Abigail glanced up at the doorway, cocking her head to one side. Victor would not come to rescue her from Marilyn this time.

Ryan moved to the fireplace, but she could not feel the heat from the flames because her own skin was so hot. She was startled by a cool hand on the back of her neck, brushing her hair away.

"Come and sit with me awhile," Marilyn whispered into her ear.

The words were half-invitation, half-command. Ryan turned and Marilyn was already re-seated on the sofa, as if she had never left. Ryan walked past Abigail and sat down stiffly on the sofa. Marilyn reached over and intertwined a strand of Ryan's hair around her finger.

"Do you remember," she began conversationally, "How the three of us sat like this years ago?"

Abigail smiled. She remembered.

Ryan frowned. She remembered as well.

Marilyn continued. "That was when you were but an infant, long before the Americas, long before you became so angry at Victor."

Ryan did not want to think back, but the Memories always kept the past so well in focus. She felt her anger at Victor momentarily flare.

Abigail was watching the girl shrewdly. "I remember, Marilyn, that this 'infant' nearly seduced you while you were attempting to seduce her."

Marilyn's eyes narrowed as she glanced at Abigail. "If I remember," she said icily, "You were the one who was entranced, unwilling and incapable of stopping me even though you were supposed to be 'baby-sitting'."

"Unwilling," Abigail corrected, carrying a stitch, "But not incapable."

Marilyn shrugged, as if it were no matter. She turned her attention back to Ryan, who was starting to relax against her will. Marilyn had always had this affect on her.

Marilyn moved closer to Ryan. The hand that caressed the hair now caressed the vein in her throat. Marilyn leaned closer, whispering in Ryan's ear.

"Do you know how long I've waited for this?"

Ryan shook her head barely able to keep her eyes open. She felt a languor steal over her entire body. The intoxicating whisper continued.

"I wanted you from the first moment I saw you, when you ran into the room, late for Victor's party, dressed like a stable boy."

Marilyn pulled several cushions onto her lap and then gently guided Ryan until she was half-supported by the pile of pillows. Ryan's body felt leaden and the coolness of the cushions felt good against her flushed skin. Marilyn again caressed the vein in her throat and this time Ryan closed her eyes, shuddering from the sensations.

Marilyn noted the response and smiled. She glanced at Abigail, who had stopped knitting and was now captivated by the scene. Marilyn leaned down and brushed her lips against the girl's throat, her eyes on Abigail. She spoke to Ryan. "How long has it been since you've Shared?"

Ryan at first did not understand the question. Even when she did, it was difficult to frame an answer because of her mind's muddled state.

"I've never Shared with anyone but Victor."

The answer so startled Marilyn that she momentarily drew back. Abigail herself was shocked at the reply. Although it seemed a perfectly logical answer, and indeed, the only answer the girl could have given, it seemed unfathomable that Ryan had not Shared in nearly two centuries.

"Oh my," was all Marilyn could say. She gazed down at the youngster who appeared to be in almost a drugged state, and then could not restrain herself any longer.

Ryan felt the sharp pain, both familiar and sweet. Its fire raced from her throat to her heart, and then to every extremity. She moaned and tried to twist out of Marilyn's grasp, but Marilyn was powerful and readjusted her grip. Ryan wanted nothing more than to give herself over to the sensation, but found that she could not. The languor was trying to steal into the deepest recesses of her mind, but a small part of her was watching dispassionately.

Marilyn was astounded by the power of the One she had just taken on. Warmth flooded every part of her body as the blood of Victor's dark child filled her veins. Wave after wave of pleasure began pounding through her body, coursing through her veins with every powerful beat of Ryan's heart.

Images flooded her mind, images so painfully bright and beautiful it made Marilyn feel things she had never felt before. She wanted to laugh and to cry and to let this powerful heart beat for her forever.

The rhythm did not slow, rather it seemed almost to pick up pace. Marilyn felt she could lose herself in this pulse. There was nothing beyond this rhythm. Just the pulse and the pause between the pulses.

The threat of the languor was even greater now for Ryan. She wanted nothing more than to lay her head down on Marilyn's lap, to just surrender to the dark-haired woman's embrace. She felt that even were she to give in to the lassitude now, Marilyn would be more than satisfied. She had felt the woman's astonishment at her power.

But it was not enough for Ryan, and although it took all of her strength, she reached up to stroke Marilyn's cheek.

Marilyn felt the touch, even in the throes of her passion. Her astonishment cut through her fevered feeding, and she realized one Need had been replaced by another. Her appetite had been sated and she was filled to bursting; now she desperately ached for release.

She realized what the girl was offering her.

She pulled away, gazing down at the demonic angel who had placed her in this position. Ryan gazed up at her, her movements still leaden but her eyes quite clear as she ran her thumb down the engorged vein in Marilyn's throat.

Ask me, came the voice inside Marilyn's head.

Marilyn wanted to moan in frustration, but not as much as she wanted the girl's teeth at her throat.

Do it.

Imperceptibly, Ryan shook her head. Ask me, came the voice.

Marilyn's frustration was immense. She wanted to tear the girl limb-from-limb. But not as much as she wanted to surrender.

"Please," she whispered through gritted teeth.

Ryan interlaced her fingers behind Marilyn's neck and pulled her downward, not gently. Her razor-sharp teeth bit into the soft skin and Marilyn arched upward but not away. Ryan held her firmly as the dark-haired woman's blood poured into her mouth.

Images began pouring into Ryan's mind and she began to see and experience Marilyn's life. Ryan felt suddenly as if she were Sharing with many strangers as well, and realized she was seeing every person Marilyn had ever Shared with. Not only was she seeing them through Marilyn's eyes, but she was feeling them as well, all distinctly yet all at the same time. Suddenly the images shifted violently and began to multiply, and Ryan was startled to realize she was now seeing and experiencing every person each of these people had Shared with. The visions began to branch out like some great tree spanning all of time, and Ryan's mind joined with thousands as they fed or were fed upon, as they killed or were killed.

The release was extraordinary for Marilyn. She saw and felt the visions as well, and although she was the carrier of such Memories, she herself had never seen them. She felt her own heart racing faster and faster, and it suddenly occurred to her the girl might kill her.

Instead of frightening her, the thought was exhilarating. She remembered what it was like to have this feeling, to be so completely out of control that not even death mattered. It was reckless, it was damning, it was euphoric, it was delirious.

It was ecstasy.

Ryan felt her own heart take over Marilyn's, pushing it faster and faster. She felt the woman above her move, but it was to pull her closer, not push her away. She suddenly understood the drive of their Kind, why it was so wondrous to kill another in passion. It was diabolical, it was wicked, it was pure self-gratification.

It was ecstasy.

Marilyn's heart stopped and Ryan hovered on the edge of pushing her into the blackness from which she might not return.

And then Ryan pulled away, pulling Marilyn away from the brink with her.

The dark-haired woman collapsed and within minutes was comatose. Ryan held her, somewhat bewildered over what had just occurred. She finally gently disentangled herself from Marilyn, and adjusted the other woman's position so she appeared comfortable on the sofa. Ryan adjusted the cushion under Marilyn's head, then without really knowing why, removed the coverlet from a nearby chair and draped it over the sleeping woman.

"She won't get cold, my dear. None of us do, remember?"

Ryan jerked upward startled. She had completely forgotten about Abigail, who was now sitting across the room in the shadows.

Abigail had moved to her current seating position for exactly that reason: she could see without being seen. She had also moved there because she had just witnessed one of the most extraordinarily erotic events of her life. She had watched many couplings over the years and voyeuristically enjoyed Sharing almost as much as the act itself. But she realized early on in this one that she was not going to be able to maintain her air of amused unconcern.

She had regained it now as she carried another stitch. "You really are Victor Alexander's child," she said meaningfully.

Ryan maintained her gaze, her cheeks betraying only the faintest hint of color. She glanced down at Marilyn, finding it difficult to think at that exact moment.

Abigail laid down her stitchery and stood, approaching Ryan. She stood in front of the girl, lifting a hand to her cheek. Abigail was surprised at the heat emanating from the young woman. Ryan grasped the hand and pulled it to her heart, and Abigail was again startled, but this time by her own reaction. She suppressed the flutter, still wearing her mask of unconcern.

Ryan was aware of none of this, so befuddled was she at that moment. Abigail gently removed her hand from Ryan's grasp, leaned forward to kiss her on the cheek, then made a stately exit from the room.

Ryan sat down heavily in the chair.

Victor was surprised and not surprised to see Abigail enter his room a short time later. He raised an eyebrow when he saw her luggage.

"Leaving so soon?" He leaned back in his chair. "Does this mean you don't want the gift I have offered you?"

"You know me too well for that, Victor. The truth of the matter is that I want to go back there right now and rip her to shreds."

"Or allow her to rip you to shreds," Victor replied dryly.

Abigail smiled her enigmatic smile, but did not disagree. "However," she continued, "I have always practiced considerably more self-restraint than Marilyn. Delayed gratification can be far more enjoyable than immediate self-fulfillment."

Victor was suddenly wary. "What are you saying?"

"I am saying, dear Victor, that you did not place any time constraints on this gift. I, therefore, am choosing to take it at some unspecified time in the future."

Victor's eyes narrowed. He was not happy at this turn of events. "You ever were the one to hold your cards the longest, Abigail."

"It makes playing them all the more enjoyable. But I do not hold them as close to my chest as do you, my Lord. I," she said with emphasis, "Do not have any children hidden away. But," she added as if an afterthought, "I will enjoy taking yours."

With that, the matriarch took her leave.

Victor was truly surprised several hours later when he heard familiar footsteps coming down the hallway. The knock on the door was a formality.

"Please come in."

Ryan opened the door, standing for a brief moment in the doorway. Victor was sitting across the room, dressed casually in a pair of slacks and a white cotton shirt unbuttoned at the collar. His tan throat contrasted sharply with the white shirt and his dark hair curled around the edges of the collar. He set his book on the adjacent nightstand, his eyes never leaving Ryan.

She looked a little tired, but other than that, as stunning as ever. Her hair was loose about her shoulders and she was dressed in the same casual manner he was. It was the first time the two had been alone together since his return.

Ryan moved a little further in the room, letting the door close behind her. "May I sit down?" she asked, both polite and formal.

Victor nodded. "Please do."

Ryan was at a loss what to say, so she allowed her eyes to drift around the room, taking in the tasteful, masculine decor. Her eyes finally settled upon Victor, who was still watching her.

"So," Victor asked, deliberately casual, "How was Marilyn?"

To Ryan's credit, her expression never wavered. "You knew."

Victor simply stared at her, asking for no elaboration.

Ryan continued. "You knew I was the more powerful."

Victor nodded, then said all he really needed to say. "Yes."

Ryan continued to gaze at him steadily. "Then why make me go through that?"

Victor did not apologize. "Because you did not know." He paused, then said, "Nor did Marilyn."

Ryan looked down, contemplating his words. Victor's next words were sardonic. "Besides, my dear, you wanted to Share with her."

Ryan's eyes flickered upward to his and she had the grace to appear embarrassed at the revelation. But with the embarrassment was a glint of the ever-present mischief he remembered so well.

Victor sighed. "You will still have to deal with Abigail at some point in time in the future."

Ryan's brow furrowed slightly. Abigail was quite a different story from Marilyn. In some ways, Ryan felt she might be the far more dangerous of the two.

Ryan changed the subject slightly, trying to sound as casual as her father. "Speaking of Marilyn, did you Share with her in my absence?"

Victor saw through the casualness. "Yes," he said, "I did."

There was no break in Ryan's composure. "And did she satisfy you?"

Victor could not conceal his smile. He saw the telltale signs of Ryan's rather formidable temper forming, so he answered truthfully.

"Marilyn ceased to satisfy me the day you were born."

Ryan's composure did not waver, but Victor knew she was secretly pleased. Her countenance darkened, however, and Victor knew she was thinking of her birth.

Ryan stood and walked to the window. She looked out into the darkness, her hand intertwining itself in the tassel to the shades. She untangled the hand, then tangled it again. She began her question slowly, her voice filled with rare hesitation.

"Did you care nothing for her?"

Victor looked down at his hands, knowing whom she was speaking of. "Your mother?"

Ryan nodded, still looking into the darkness. "Yes, my mother."

Victor shook his head, knowing he could not lie to her. "No, not at the time."

Ryan took a deep breath, but before the pain could spread, Victor continued.

"I could not allow myself to care for her, or you would not be here."

Ryan swallowed hard, a distinctly human gesture which held no purpose for her whatsoever. Victor continued.

"But I see much of her in you, and I think that I have grown to love her over the years."

Ryan held her breath for an endless moment, another distinctly human gesture. She waited to see if the pain would spread as it always did, but Victor's concession seemed to keep it at bay. His words did not make the pain cease; they were not as much as she had hoped for. But they were a point of departure.

She turned away from the window, glancing at the door. Victor also turned his attention to his next approaching visitor.

Both identified the footsteps and Marilyn did not bother with the formality of knocking. She strolled into the room, looking all the world like someone who had just achieved her heart's desire. Two servants with her baggage were in tow.

The servants were left in the hallway as Marilyn closed the door. Victor gazed at her. "I trust you are satisfied that our bargain is fulfilled."

Marilyn let her eyes rest on Ryan. "Oh yes, dear," she said to Victor, "Completely satisfied."

Victor raised an eyebrow at the innuendo. It seemed no matter how powerful Ryan had become, Marilyn's sensual teasing of the girl would continue unabated. It appeared from the color in Ryan's cheeks that the suggestive comments would continue to hit their mark, as well.

Victor's eyes narrowed slightly. Marilyn was in incredibly high spirits, contrary to his expectations. He had thought she might be somewhat subdued after her contact with Ryan. But she acted for all the world like a cat that had just gorged on cream. He had a sudden flicker of suspicion.

Marilyn rested her hand on Victor's shoulder, and her eyes rested on Ryan. "I'm not certain which was more enjoyable, my Lord. Finally taking her, or taking her with your blessing."

Victor glanced up at the dark-haired woman. "I would hardly call it my blessing, Marilyn. I had my reasons."

"Oh," Marilyn said significantly, "Oh, that's right. I quite forgot. You were trying to communicate something to me, I believe."

Victor's suspicions were growing. It seemed even Ryan was catching on to what the dark-haired woman was implying. "What are you saying, Marilyn?"

Marilyn dropped her pretense, savoring her words as she spoke them. "What I'm saying, little one, is that you cannot teach me something I already know." She dropped her hand from Victor's shoulder. "It appears in this instance, my Lord, that I had you both."

Before either could reply, Marilyn stepped toward the door. "I shall be returning to France immediately. I do hope you will come to see me, very soon." She let one last glance linger on Ryan, then on Victor. "I could get used to having you two around."

With that, she was gone, leaving both Ryan and Victor in silence.

"Well," Victor said dryly, breaking the silence at long last, "See what you will have to deal with one day?"

Ryan was not quite as dry as Victor. "She is quite manipulative, isn't she?"

Victor nodded. "And she's not nearly as bad as Abigail."

Ryan nodded, unconsciously mirroring her father's gestures. "Yes, I know. That's what I'm afraid of." She turned to Victor. "Now that I have fulfilled at least some of the obligations you have set before me, is there anyone else you've promised me to? Anyone else I must settle with?"

Victor gazed at his golden-haired child a moment, his dark eyes gleaming. "Only me."

Ryan turned to him, her anger immediately evident in her posture. But Victor's expression was not one of condemnation, nor was there any anger in his words. In fact, he was casually examining his fingernails. "And I believe you still feel you have a score to settle with me."

Ryan's anger cooled slightly, but she was skeptical. "What exactly did you have in mind?"

Victor was silent for a moment, still preoccupied with examining his fingernails. He finally folded his hands onto his lap. He gazed up at her. "I thought perhaps a duel would be appropriate."

"A duel?" Ryan repeated, cocking her head to one side. "What kind of duel?"

Victor shrugged. "The kind you used to engage in all the time. It hardly took more than an evil look for you to throw down your gauntlet."

Ryan was still suspicious. "And what would be won or lost in this duel? I have already proven I cannot kill you."

Victor shrugged. "That does not mean you cannot beat me. If you win, I will give you back your freedom."

"And if I lose?"

Victor paused before replying. "Then you will take your rightful place among the Others."

Ryan's head jerked upward. "I have no desire to live among the Others."

"I know," Victor said, "But you have obligations. I did not create you for purely selfish reasons. You have responsibilities you have thus far avoided. It is time for you to grow up."

Ryan's jaw set. "Very well then. A duel. And when will this battle take place?"

There was a glint in Victor's eyes. "We can begin now."

CHAPTER 33

Ryan stood in the clearing, hefting the sword. The cool night air felt good on her skin and the dim light from the waning moon was perfect. It was just enough illumination for her to clearly see Victor, who was standing at the other edge of the trees hefting the weight of his own sword. They were the only two figures within miles.

Ryan swung the sword expertly, leaping up onto a nearby boulder. She could barely contain the shiver of excitement that ran up her spine, an ancient and predatory reflex. The hilt of the weapon felt good in her hand.

Victor approached, still swinging his own sword as Ryan leaped down and landed lightly on her feet. He raised the hilt of his sword to her in salute.

"To first blood," he said mockingly.

Ryan did not miss the multiple meanings in the sentence. She raised her own sword in salute. "To first blood," she agreed.

Like lightning, Ryan thrust forward, faster than any human eye could see. But Victor was there, parrying the attack effortlessly. He countered and sparks flew from the swords.

Ryan stepped back, nodding approvingly. "Not bad. I see your skills haven't rusted. Perhaps you have something new to teach me?"

Victor smiled, his eyes gleaming. "There is still much I can teach you."

On the last word, he thrust forward, even faster than Ryan's initial attack. Ryan parried but the attack was a feint and she was forced to step back to counter his second strike.

"Hmmm," she said, swinging her sword as if just loosening up. "Very nice."

On the last word she again thrust forward, striking with incredible force. Victor blocked the blow and Ryan lunged sideways, jabbing forward. Victor parried. Ryan began to deliver a flurry of blows and Victor parried them almost before they were initiated. So rapid were the exchanges and so graceful were the participants, the battle appeared to be almost a dance.

Offense and defense changed rapidly; the aggressor could only hold such a position until the other altered tactics, at which times the roles would shift dramatically. One moment Ryan would appear to be winning the fight in splendid fashion; the next moment she would be diving to avoid decapitation.

The battle was as much a mental one as a physical one. So great were both their reflexes that ground was only gained by correct anticipation. So evenly matched were the two opponents that ground was only lost by an incorrect guess.

Victor was enjoying himself immensely. He was stronger than Ryan but, by the gods, she was fast. Her fighting style was so similar to his own he could almost predict her strategy. But she would occasionally switch up, utilizing new tactics, and only his own preternatural reflexes would save him. She was merciless, never relenting and capitalizing on the slightest mistake.

As far as Ryan could see, however, Victor wasn't making any. His style was deadly precise, as it had always been. Any passion Victor felt was harnessed and expressed in his lethal swordsmanship. No matter what combination of tactics she placed together, he seemed to defend against them effortlessly, transitioning into an attack which often left her stumbling backwards to regroup.

On one of the rare occasions when Ryan appeared to be winning their very physical chess game, she took the opportunity to flee. It didn't seem that either was making any headway in the flatlands so she decided to change the battleground. A thick cover of trees might give her the advantage. She headed for the forest, glancing over her shoulder as the first light of day peaked over the far hills.

Susan opened her eyes. She turned her head, surprised to see the amount of light streaming through the closed blinds. The sun was obviously already high in the sky. She turned to look at Jason who was lying in the bed next to her. He was still sound asleep. She wondered if he had slept at all when they had been apart.

Susan's thoughts turned to Ryan and she gently disentangled herself from her sleeping son. As she sat upright, she saw a new set of clothing laid out. She quietly dressed, then peered out the doorway. She squared her shoulders and moved into the hallway.

She walked through the great mansion. It seemed empty of people, but did not feel so. She had fleeting impressions of movement, of shadowy figures seen only out of the corner of her eye. She suddenly knew what Jason meant by "creepy." Susan wondered why Ryan had human servants, but Victor's were of their Kind.

She did not find Ryan, but found the next best thing. Edward was seated on the verandah sipping a glass of champagne. He seemed troubled, although his face bore his usual impassive expression.

Susan glanced around the courtyard. "Where are Ryan and her father?"

He was silent for a long moment, gazing off in the distance. He appeared to be listening to something Susan could not hear. He took another sip of champagne, then broke his silence. "Ryan and her father are fighting."

Susan sat down heavily, trying to quell her upset feelings. "I did not think either of them were the type to continuously argue."

Edward shook his head. "No," he said, "You don't understand. They are actually, physically, engaged in battle."

Susan turned to look at him. "What do you mean?"

"I mean," Edward said with emphasis, "They are engaged in a duel."

Susan let out a small gasp. "A duel? With what? And for how long?"

Edward's gaze was distant again. "I believe they're using swords," he said his accent pronounced, "And the battle has lasted almost ten hours now."

Susan was shocked. "How long will it last?"

Edward shrugged his shoulders, resigned. "If I know those two, it could go on for days."

Ryan was hiding behind the tree that under normal circumstances would provide both cover and concealment. With Victor, however, it provided only cover because she could not hide from him.

Ryan was incorrect. It would not provide cover, either. The sword came whistling through the air and took out a huge chunk of wood as bark went flying everywhere. It was nearly enough to topple the tree, and aided by a good push from Ryan, it did so. The tree went crashing down in Victor's direction, splintering wood everywhere as it fell to the ground with a tremendous thud.

But Victor was no longer there, and only his mocking laughter drifting through the forest gave any indication that he had been.

Ryan frowned. Their cat-and-mouse game continually shifted, with each taking turns in the roles. In the last hours, however, she seemed to be spending far more time as the mouse. Her senses strained the forest in front of her as she began to move forward.

She could feel him in front of her because his presence was immense. But she could not accurately pinpoint his location because he was clouding her mind.

From the very onset of their battle, Ryan had been amazed by Victor's prowess; her respect for his abilities had been vigorously renewed. Victor had always possessed a combination of pure strength and exquisite skill that made him a formidable adversary. But now it seemed it was coupled with a mental power that made him unconquerable. Ryan did not know if Victor had recently acquired this power or if she had just been unaware of it before.

Ryan chastised herself as she silently crept through the forest. Victor had taught her better than that. No enemy was unconquerable.

She ducked as the sword came slicing out of nowhere. Victor materialized behind her and it was only her own extrasensory abilities that kept her from being decapitated. Her anger flared and she struck out at him, launching a flurry of blows that he defended against, forcing her to step back. His defense was effective, but Ryan was glad to see it was not effortless.

Victor paused, stepping back out of reach of his angry child. He lowered his sword, his words casual.

"Not bad. I'm glad to see you listened to at least a few of the things I taught you."

Ryan was suddenly defensive. "I listened to everything you taught me." She turned his challenge back to him. "And was I such a poor student?"

Victor shook his head, his eyes gleaming. "No, not at all."

Ryan raised her sword as if to renew the battle, then lowered it as a thought drifted across her mental peripheral vision. Victor was aware of her brief deliberation and struck before the thought could formulate.

Ryan's sword came up as if with a mind of its own. The incoming blade was deflected upward and Ryan was already countering downward. But Victor effortlessly stepped out of harm's way and the sword tip dug into the soft, wet earth instead.

The musing again drifted across Ryan's mind, unformed and obscure. There was something about Victor's abilities, something very akin to hers, something very different from the Others...

Ryan stood upright, the sword held loosely in her hand. "You're not like the Others."

Victor held his own sword loosely, casually examining it in the fading light. Ryan marched towards him, holding her sword in front of her. The tip of the sword wavered near his heart.

"You're hiding something else."

Victor gazed down at her. He shrugged casually, arrogantly. "There are many things you do not know."

The sword tip thrust into his clothing, threatening to tear the fabric. "You are more like me than the Others."

Victor glanced down at the sword poking him in the chest. "I would suggest," he said mildly, "That you remove that."

Ryan did not move the sword and Victor's weapon flashed upward. Even though Ryan knew what he would do, she still could not counter his phenomenal speed. Sparks flew and her sword nearly flew from her grasp as he smashed the weapon from its threatening position. He brought his own weapon to bear and now it was Ryan who found herself with a sword tip at her throat.

The tip of the sword wavered, caressing the air in front of Ryan's face. Victor's attention was focused on the end of the weapon, and on the throat that lay just beyond it.

"No," he said, distracted by the blood he could see pounding in her carotid artery, "I am not like the Others."

The sword wavered, this time actually touching Ryan's skin. She shivered as the cold steel grazed her throat, but the shiver was not from fear.

Victor gazed at the tip of the sword, now pressed against his child's throat. His words were entirely conversational, although it was apparent his attention was elsewhere. "And you, you are not even half human."

Ryan stared at him down the long length of the sword. "What are you saying?"

The sword again wavered, this time tracing the outline of her cheekbone, then her jaw.

"I think it's quite obvious what I'm saying."

Ryan's eyes narrowed. "Then you were not fully human, either."

Victor shrugged, as if it was no matter, and it was in this moment Ryan took the opportunity to strike. Her sword came flashing upward as she simultaneously stepped to the right, turning her head. The move was similar to Victor's but just different enough and so skillfully executed that it was successful.

Or nearly so.

A fine, red line appeared on Ryan's cheek as blood began to seep from the wound. Ryan's hand slowly found its way to her cheekbone, her fingers touching the cut and coming away crimson. She gazed at the blood on her fingers, then at her father.

"First blood," Victor said, his tone casual but the look in his eyes not.

Ryan raised her sword but Victor grabbed the weapon by its blade, oblivious to its sharp edges. He yanked it from her grasp, ignoring the wounds it inflicted upon him to do so. He raised the tip of his sword to her throat, this time moving closer.

Ryan felt the tip press against her throat and felt the blood on her cheek begin to slowly make its way downward.

"I," she said evenly, "Will not yield to you."

Victor smiled, remembering a defiant little peasant boy nearly seven centuries earlier. "You already have," was his reply.

With one quick flick of his wrist, the sword sliced into Ryan's neck. The pain from the cut made Ryan gasp but it was not pain that buckled her knees when Victor moved behind her. She felt arms embrace and imprison her, felt his mouth cover the blood pulsing from her neck.

Victor himself was nearly overcome with emotion from the moment her blood touched his lips. He knew his dark child had become strong, but until that moment when her blood began to mix with his, he had truly not known the extent of her power.

He staggered backward, barely aware of his surroundings and unwilling to break their long overdue embrace for even a moment. He found the rock and settled upon it, drawing her lithe frame close to him. Her blood continued to pour into him, seemingly endless, and he did not feel it when she drew his wrist to her lips, letting razor-sharp teeth whisper over his skin.

Their union became total. Ryan's powerful heart fell into synchrony with his. She saw his death through his eyes, felt the pain of the blood-red haze he had spent so many months in. She walked with him and as him through a shadowy netherland, coming to a stop at the edge of a great chasm. She stood on the edge of a brink and looked into a blackness so complete that no light could escape nor exist within it. She turned from the brink to look back at the only thing possessing the power to pull him away from death, and was shocked to find she was looking at herself.

Victor, in turn, saw the death of Ryan's mother through Ryan's eyes, and then through Elena's eyes. To suddenly feel Elena's helplessness and terror was like the shock of ice-cold water. Never having experienced the Memories of a human, he suddenly understood the impact of Elena's death upon Ryan. The realization that the woman was her real mother had created a mind-numbing horror in Ryan, one which self-preservation had replaced by fury.

Ryan and Victor both saw the monstrous acts of the other in perfect clarity with perfect understanding, forcing them into a strange and powerful empathy. To Share in such inviolate union was to become the Other; to continue to hate under those circumstances was to hate one's self.

It would be many hours before either would pull away from the other. And then it would be with the understanding that they would never truly be separate again.

CHAPTER 34

Susan walked downstairs, wondering if she would see Ryan or Victor today. She saw Edward standing in the doorway of the balcony, looking out onto the patio below. She moved to his side and her musings regarding the two were answered immediately. Ryan and Victor sat at the table underneath the umbrella, looking less like mortal enemies and more like two lovers enjoying a late morning repast. They were talking and laughing, and Ryan appeared more relaxed and animated than Susan had ever seen her.

Edward seemed to almost read her thoughts. "You find their relationship very disturbing, don't you?"

Susan sighed, trying not to be judgmental. "Perhaps I'm just being too clinical."

Edward glanced over at her. "What do you mean by that?"

Susan gazed at the two through the window. "Do you know, physiologically speaking, what an orgasm is?"

Edward, despite his patrician appearance, was not at all shocked by the question. "My expertise is in law, dear doctor. No, in physiological terms, I don't know what an orgasm is."

Susan turned to look at him, pausing only for a moment.

"It's a blood rush."

Edward gazed at her with his unblinking eyes, then turned his attention back to the two on the patio.

Susan gazed down at the them. Ryan and Victor were not touching but there was an unbearable intimacy about the them. Their ease of conversation and coordination of movement bespoke the extraordinary depth of their relationship.

"Why," Susan began, addressing Edward again, "Is Ryan so reluctant to take her place amongst your Kind?"

Evidently this was not a simple question for Edward to answer. It was several moments before he could frame a reply, and even then he chose his words carefully.

"I would not presume to speak for Ryan, but I believe her reasons are as complex as she is. I know Ryan does not think much of our Kind because they are so manipulated by their own passions. I think that, in a way, she fears the loss of control she sees within them, knowing that it lies within herself as well. I also think that the burden of their desire is very great on her. Ryan is extraordinarily sensitive, and it exhausts her to be the object of such unbridled lust."

Susan was astounded at his level of insight, as well as the empathy and compassion he displayed for Ryan. When she spoke, she spoke softly.

"Why does it not affect Victor this way?"

Edward's reply was soft as well, his British accent pronounced. "Victor's personality is much different than Ryan's. Having never met Ryan's mother, I am guessing that in some ways Ryan is very much like her."

Edward settled into silence, but evidently he was still contemplating Susan Ryerson's question. It wasn't long before he began again.

"Ryan's relationship with her father is also infinitely complex. I think that at times she rebels against him, and at the same time, lives to serve him. I don't think that anyone, with the possible exception of Victor, knew how deeply Ryan mourned him. And I don't think that anyone except for Victor knew how extraordinarily happy Ryan was to see him alive. Ryan will do whatever Victor asks her to."

Susan gazed down at the two on the patio. "So Ryan will take her position within the hierarchy?"

Edward turned to her with a keen expression. "I think that Ryan will remake that position."

Susan's brow furrowed. "And will Victor approve of this?"

Edward turned away from her, placing his hands on the railing in front of him. "If I know anything of Victor, he's counting on it."

Edward was silent for a moment, then changed the subject. "Speaking of your earlier 'blood rush,' dear doctor, have you thought at all about Victor's offer?"

Susan nodded. She had thought about little else the last few days. "I was somewhat caught off-guard by the whole thing." She shrugged, thinking aloud. "But there are other considerations. What about Jason? Ryan's father was quite blunt about the dangers of the Change. He said he could appoint someone who could increase my chances of survival, but I risk dying horribly. What would happen to Jason?"

Edward glanced at Susan knowingly. Ryan would care for the boy under any circumstances, and the young woman standing before him knew that.

The two fell into contemplative silence, watching the golden-haired youngster and her dark-haired father. The silence was just beginning to weigh heavily when Susan again spoke. She began hesitantly, but her words grew stronger as she continued.

"You know, some African cultures divide people into three categories: the living, sasha, and zamani. When a person dies, they become sasha, the recently dead, or more colorfully, the 'living dead.' When all those who knew this person are they themselves dead, the person becomes zamani, or the truly dead."

Susan turned to Edward. "Do you know what's so strange about your Kind?"

Edward turned to look at her, but did not speak.

"Popular myths call you the living dead. But according to these African terms, you're not the living dead, but still the living." She turned back to gaze at the light reflecting off the window in front of her. "But all of history is sasha to someone like Ryan. All of history is the living dead."

Susan fell silent and Edward bowed. "I will leave you to your thoughts, Dr. Ryerson."

Susan nodded back and Edward departed. Susan felt a sense of disquiet as she gazed down at Ryan and her father, an unease that had begun stirring long ago when Ryan first told her of the Others. No indication had ever been given that they would be interested in human affairs.

No indication had been given that they were not.

She had always been concerned about Victor, at least until Ryan had told her he was dead. Then her thoughts had turned to Marilyn, or perhaps

Abigail...

Susan's thoughts trailed off as she gazed at the pair seated on the verandah, then coalesced into a single, frightening thought.

Now she was not so certain she had been concerned about the right one. Ryan had seemed so distant from the human race, so uninterested in either humanity or her own Kind. But now that she had connected with both, it was possible her attention could become more focused.

Susan stared down at the two on the terrace. She felt a slight chill as Ryan cocked her head to one side, a contemplative look on her face. With an enigmatic expression that did nothing to soothe Susan Ryerson's fears, Ryan gazed directly upward into the other woman's eyes....

And she smiled.